David Morton was born into a farming family in a small Norfolk village. He read English at Cambridge, and since then has spent much of his career working in advertising. He has travelled widely and, to research *The Hyena Run*, he journeyed alone into the war-torn border areas of Mozambique, Zimbabwe and South Africa. He currently lives and works in Singapore.

The Hyena Run

David Morton

HEADLINE

Copyright © 1987 by David Morton

First published in Great Britain in 1987
by Judy Piatkus (Publishers) Ltd,
of 5 Windmill Street, London W1

First published in paperback in 1988
by HEADLINE BOOK PUBLISHING PLC

ISBN 0 7472 3163 X

Printed and bound in Great Britain by
Collins, Glasgow

HEADLINE BOOK PUBLISHING PLC
Headline House
79 Great Titchfield Street
London W1P 7FN

For Ann, Nancy and Joe –
who suffered

The Hyena
'This carnivore, found in Africa south of the 14th parallel feeds on sick or defenceless animals'

Collins Encyclopaedia of Animals

'Witches are supposed secretly to keep familiar beasts of the night or of stealth, such as hyenas . . .'

Michael Bourdillon, *The Shona Peoples*

Note

Post-independence Zimbabwe is divided on tribal grounds. The majority tribe, the Shona, occupy the central and eastern thirds of the country, while the western third, Matabeleland, is the home of the Matabele. Other tribes, small in number and influence, are concentrated in the marginal lands close to the national borders. They include the Shangaan. The acronyms ZANU and ZANLA refer to the predominantly Shona ruling party led by Prime Minister Robert Mugabe. ZAPU, the main opposition party, is led by Joshua Nkomo, and is almost entirely Matabele in composition. ZIPRA is its outlawed military wing.

Acknowledgements

Many people have helped me in my researches for this book, some of them unwittingly. For reasons that they will appreciate, I do not propose to mention by name the numerous kind friends who helped me during my travels in Zimbabwe and South Africa, some at considerable risk to their personal safety. To those people I can merely express my most sincere and heartfelt gratitude. However, I can mention those who helped me in the U.K. They include Simon Reynolds, Dr. Barry Munslow, John Bacon, Sally Hine, Alan and Kerry Taylor, Karen Crane, Hal Hamilton and Richard Down of Sports Action Ltd, and Ken Miller, who drew the map. But most of all I want to thank Anne Butterfield. Without her encouragement, support and active participation, this book would never have been written.

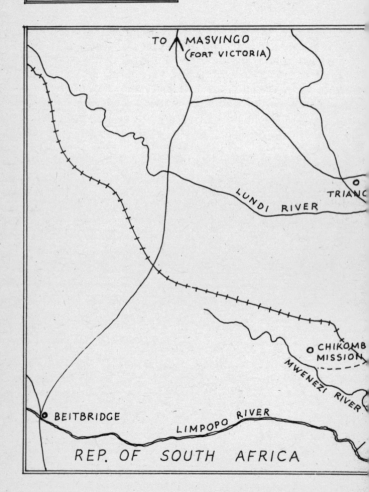

ZIMBABWE —
THE LOWVELDT

TO MASVINGO
(FORT VICTORIA)

LUNDI RIVER

TRIANG

CHIKOMB
MISSION

MWENEZI RIVER

BEITBRIDGE

LIMPOPO RIVER

REP. OF SOUTH AFRICA

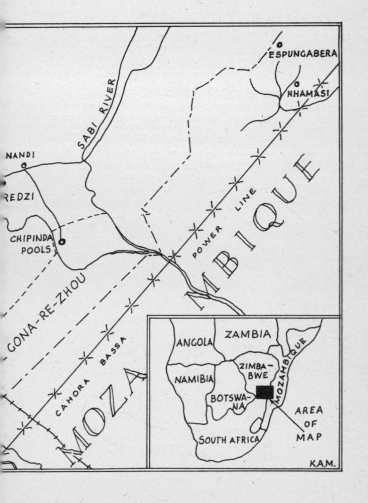

ESPUNGABERA

NHAMASI

SABI RIVER

NANDI

REDZI

CHIPINDA
POOLS

GONA-RE-ZHOU

POWER LINE

CAHORA BASSA

MOZA

MBIQUE

ZAMBIA

ANGOLA

NAMIBIA

ZIMBA-
BWE

BOTSWA-
NA

MOZAMBIQUE

SOUTH AFRICA

AREA
OF
MAP

K.A.M.

The Hyena Run

Part One

The Lowveld

It was raining that last day, the first rain since February, a fine African rain that varnished the mopani leaves and crusted the dust. Guti, Ellie called it. In London she'd have called it drizzle. Her use of the Rhodesian vernacular irritated Joe obscurely; that and the cramp he felt in his right thigh, and the smearing of the wipers on the windscreen. 'Any time now,' he said, 'we shall hit a cow. I can't see.'

'I'll take over. You're tired.'

'I'm O.K.'

'You're sure?'

'I'm sure.'

The tar had run out south of the Tanganda turnoff, where the European farms had ended, and the road was ridged like corrugated iron. The hired Datsun Pulsar squawked and rattled. In the back seat Cassie slept, the vibrations rippling the soft skin of her cheeks. Six years old. Ben, a year younger, fiddled with a piece of string, winding it in and out of his fingers, practising the reef knots and running bowlines that Ellie's mother had taught him. They were taking the loop road, down between the mountains of the Eastern Border and the Sabi River, through the tribal lands and across to Chiredzi. There was another route, shorter but less picturesque. Perhaps they should have taken that.

Joe braked suddenly to avoid a scotch-cart loaded with firewood that materialised in front of them. The driver, wrapped in a blue and white checked blanket, gazed at the car without curiosity. 'Look, Ben,' said Ellie, 'there's a cart being pulled by three donkeys.'

1

'Where?'

'Back there.'

'I didn't see it.'

'You should look.'

'I did.'

'I sometimes think,' Ellie said to Joe, 'that we shall get home and the children won't have seen anything at all.'

They'd been on the road too long, that was the trouble; a night here, two nights there. The children had enjoyed the train most, the twenty-four hours they'd spent crawling up the single track through Botswana. There they'd been able to race up and down the corridors, swing on the bunks. And across the border there had been soldiers to stare at: squat black men in camouflage with bands of machine-gun bullets strung across their chests, and armoured troop carriers at the rail crossings. But the car was tough on them, and now, with camping gear taking up half the back seat, they were crushed on top of each other, hot and irritable.

It was primarily Ellie's trip, her homecoming after ten years in London. Years in which a war had been fought, and Rhodesia, the old white Rhodesia she had known as a girl, and had rejected as a student, had disappeared to be replaced by a new state with a new name and a man her mother still regarded as the anti-Christ installed as Prime Minister. Joe had come with her out of curiosity and love. The children had come because a month is too long to be parted.

They'd seen the sights – the Falls, Kariba, the Zimbabwe Ruins – and they'd met Ellie's friends from long ago, the radicals from the University, the thinkers and doers, now settled into their middle-aged occupations. They'd met the children, and swum in the swimming pools, and eaten steaks and drunk beer, and discussed taxation and land reform and the problems in Matabeleland, and how they used to go dancing with the black whores at the old Fed Hotel. They'd visited Ellie's old home in Fern Valley and picked fruit from the orange trees her father had planted the year she had left.

It was Penny, Ellie's ex-roommate, now the wife of a Harare priest, who had suggested the camping trip and offered the equipment. And it was Ellie, giggling from too much wine on the stoep of the rectory, who had accepted.

2

'We can't leave Africa without spending at least one night in the bush,' she had told Joe. She'd bought borewors in Mutare, dark brown sausages that reminded him of dog turds, and strips of biltong to chew in the car. They were going to build camp fires on the banks of the Lundi River, and watch the animals come to drink, and the sun setting.

'What do I do,' Joe said suddenly, 'if I meet a hippopotamus?'

Ellie giggled. 'Raise your hat and say "Good afternoon."'

'No, seriously.'

'I don't know. Run like hell, probably.'

Joe glanced at his wife. The light tan she'd picked up suited her, and the sun had brought out freckles and flecked her hair with gold. She was a tall woman, long-limbed, with a firm body that had survived the birth of the kids. Not conventionally beautiful, but all right. Distinctive.

The smile still played about her lips. 'Anyway,' she said, 'I've had a lot of experience with hippopotami.'

'When?'

'Living with you all these years.'

'You hear that?' Joe inclined his head in Ben's direction.

'What?'

'Your Mum thinks I'm a hippopotamus.'

'She's right.'

'What hippopotamus? Where's the hippopotamus?' Cassie was awake now.

'It's Daddy,' Ben explained. 'Mum thinks he's a hippopotamus.'

'So do I.'

'So do I.'

Joe growled in mock anger. 'You wait till I stop this car.' Through the rear mirror he could see the children's blond heads bobbing up and down as they laughed.

Later the sun broke through, slicing the mist into small segments that became white high-flying clouds. An August Sunday. As they crossed the flat bridge over the Sabi they saw women washing bright clothes in the river, spreading them to dry on the already warm rocks, and groups of boys bathing naked in the deeper pools. In the kraals, men clustered round the open-sided cooking huts, being served with their midday meal. A laughing woman in vivid red put down her wheelbarrow to wave. At Rupangwana Store people lounged in their Sunday best, enjoying the sunshine, drinking African beer out of cartons. In the mealie fields the dead stalks of last year's harvest littered the bare red soil.

They stopped to eat lunch under a baobab tree, spreading out the food the hotel had provided on the warm bonnet of the car, sharing the cheese rolls and oranges with the small ragged children who materialised from nowhere. Ben and Cassie regarded them with awe, as they would alien beings from another planet.

'Daddy,' Cassie asked, 'why are they so poor?'

'Because we're so rich.'

'But we're not rich.'

'Yes we are.'

Cassie was silent, digesting the information with her cheese roll.

'But we're not very rich,' she said finally. She had a way of reaching conclusions that stopped a conversation dead.

'How much longer, Mum?' Ben asked when they were back in the car.

'An hour, two at the most. Then we can find a nice spot and put our tents up.'

'Like Wales?'

'No, not exactly like Wales.' In Wales it had rained for the entire weekend and the car had sunk gently up to its axles in mud. 'You'll be able to watch all the animals coming to drink – elephants, impala. Maybe if we're lucky we'll see some sable. You mustn't paddle in the river though.'

'Bilharzia,' chorused the children. The lesson had been rammed home.

'And crocodiles. There are big crocodiles in the Lundi.'

'Do they eat people?' Ben asked anxiously.

'Yes.'

'I don't like it, Mum.'

'You'll be perfectly safe.'

Glancing in the mirror, Joe noticed that the boy had begun to suck his thumb. He was thinking about the crocodiles. He was a nervous child, despite his occasional bravado, small for his age. Joe said, 'If one comes I'll grab it by the tail and swing it round and throw it up the nearest tree.'

The children were laughing once more. Ellie reached across and brushed back a strand of Joe's hair, kissing him on the neck. The car veered. 'Hey, control yourself,' he said. For a moment their eyes met.

With the sun came the dust, billowing in soft red clouds behind them, coating the rear window, clinging to faces and clothes. A dark brown army truck, headlights blazing, passed them at speed filled with soldiers and rifles, heading God knew where. The round pole and mud huts with their thorn fences were left behind and the bush began, bare and dry. Baboons sat like old men at the side of the road. When they saw a sign reading 'Gona-re-Zhou National Park' they turned left.

Then there was no more traffic and no more people, just the silent bush and a pair of eagles circling in a thermal. When the children complained of thirst they stopped to drink orange squash from the flask but didn't linger. Fifty kilometres of bad dirt road and the inevitable chaos of setting up camp still lay ahead.

It was after they crossed the concrete bridge over the waterless Mahande River that they saw the men. The road curved slightly beside some low boulders, becoming narrower. At the bend in the road were six men, eight at the most, in what seemed to be camouflage fatigues. Some of them were wearing forage caps. They were holding automatic rifles with curved magazines. One of the men stepped into the road and held up his hand.

'Roadblock,' said Joe, slowing so that the dust they were trailing overtook the car. 'Get the passports, honey, and the driving licence.' He was not unduly worried. There had been many roadblocks since they had left Harare. They had become familiar, part of the local scene.

Ellie fumbled in her bag, the compact green canvas one she had bought in Selfridges to hold the detritus of the journey, and then glanced up again. 'Joe,' she said uncertainly, 'I don't like the look of those men.'

'They're army, that's all. The others were police.'

The children woke, complaining. 'Where are we, Mummy?'

'It's OK. We're nearly there. It's just a roadblock.'

'Oh.'

Cassie settled down to sleep again, but Ben remained awake. He liked seeing the soldiers. He liked their guns.

There *was* something wrong, Joe realised as he drew up alongside the men. Their leader, the man who had held up his hand, was short, bearded and very thin. His uniform was ripped, his face absurdly whitened with caked dust, like theatrical makeup. The other soldiers, some little more than boys, were dressed in civilian clothes and ragged bits of camouflage gear. One of them wore a tee shirt with the words FANTA written on it. They looked frightened, their eyes constantly scanning the bush and the road. Joe wound down the window and Ellie leaned across him.

'Masikatii,' she said, giving the midday greeting in Shona, 'maswera here? Did you spend the day well?'

The man did not reply but made a quick movement with his gun, indicating that Joe should get out of the car. Joe switched off the engine, took the documents from Ellie, and stepped into the road. 'Passports,' he began to say, 'holiday. We're on holiday . . .'

'Joe!' He had half-turned at Ellie's shout when the butt of the man's gun hit him above the left ear and he fell heavily. The gun descended again, and he heard the sharp crack of his collar bone breaking.

'Joe! You bastards, leave him alone!' Ellie's voice was shrill with shock. She was being dragged from the car now, together with the children. Joe clutched his shoulder and stared into the muzzle of the man's gun. There was a ringing in his ears like the noise of a far-off telephone. The pain came at him in waves.

'Stand!' The man's voice was accented, surprisingly boyish.

Joe rolled on to his front, the pain jerking gasps from his lungs, the remains of his lunch swelling up from his stomach. Slowly he got to his feet. 'Please,' he said, 'please, we're . . .'

It was Ellie's turn to scream. One of the soldiers had gripped her by the neck while another pulled at her rings, the wedding ring and the thin platinum ring with the solitaire diamond. 'For God's sake,' Joe heard himself shouting, 'give it to them! Give it to them! You want money? We've got money. Dollars!'

But Ellie struggled, fighting for her rings. She fell and was kicked once, twice. Joe noticed that Ben, standing upright against the car, was peeing himself, the urine running down his bare leg and gathering in a pool in his sandal. 'Daddy,' the boy said quietly. 'Daddee.' Cassie was crying noiselessly.

Joe fumbled in the pocket of his shorts. 'Here,' he said, 'money. Take it. Let us go, please.'

The boot of the car was open now, and camping equipment and food and suitcases were on the road, one of the men ripping at the soft canvas of the cases with a knife. The bag with the kids' toys, the Roald Dahl books, Cassie's Barbie Dolls. Underwear. A box of Tampax skidding away under the car. 'You bastard!' Ellie's voice rose in pain as her attacker, his foot on her wrist, wrenched the rings from her knuckles.

'Take the money!' Joe screamed. 'TAKE THE MONEY!'

His wallet fell to the ground, spilling credit cards and traveller's cheques. A hand scooped it up, and another hand was at his wrist, wrenching it back, his muscles grating the broken bone. It was his watch they wanted, the Cartier watch that Ellie had given him on their tenth anniversary, engraved with their twin initials. As it was ripped from him, the metal strap dug deep into the flesh of his hand.

The men, silent till now, began to shout, gesturing at the road and at each other. They were in a hurry, gathering food and clothes into bundles using sheets and towels. In a moment, Joe was thinking, they'll be gone, and this will all be over, a memory.

But there was the muzzle of a gun in his back, and Ellie was being jerked to her feet. 'Walk,' the bearded man was shouting. 'Walk!'

The children were already in the bush, half-running to keep up with the man who was gripping their wrists. They were not crying now, concentrating on keeping their feet. Ellie stumbled after them, then Joe, the gun still jammed in his back.

They were on a narrow path, no more than a game track, which led to a low kopje just visible above the mopani trees. Joe glanced back, but the road – and the car – were gone. Ahead of them doves scattered like shrapnel.

They were climbing now, skirting huge tumbled boulders, panting with the effort. Up ahead, one of the children,

Cassie, cried out. Joe could see the red blood from a gash on her leg. 'Please,' he said, 'the children. Let me have the children.' But the men made no sign of having heard or understood. I could have stopped this, I *should* have stopped this, Joe was thinking. He shouted: 'Cassie!'

She turned, her eyes misted with terror, and was immediately jerked forward again. 'I'm coming, kids!' Joe yelled, and broke into a run, stumbling against rocks. 'Cassie!' Ben!'

And then he stopped.

Slowly, infinitely slowly it seemed, the bearded man raised his gun. Joe looked at the man's face in those last moments. It was not dust, he decided, that whitened the man's cheeks but some kind of skin complaint, a rash. The whites of his eyes were tinged with yellow.

The gun, when it sounded, was not loud. Pop pop pop. Three dull smacks. He felt, strangely, as though somebody had hit him from behind. There was no pain, just a warm sticky dampness under his shirt.

'Daddee!' he heard the children screaming. 'Daddeeee . . .'

There was something wrong with his left leg. He decided to sit down for a while.

Part Two
Harare

Footsteps.

Clip clip clip. Shuffle.

Stop.

Silence.

No, not silence. Not exactly silence. From somewhere far away the soft hum of traffic, and chirp of small birds.

An itch on his nose.

A tiny pinprick of sensation, broadening like ink spreading on blotting paper.

Bloody itch.

He wrinkled his nostrils. Sniffed. He felt vaguely cold, and his body felt heavy, so very heavy.

He opened his eyes.

'Good morning.'

He examined the face that hovered above him. Soft brown eyes, a narrow nose with a precise tip, skin the colour of milky coffee. He decided that it was probably the most beautiful face he had ever seen. 'Have you lost your manners?' the face said, and smiled.

Joe cleared his throat, swallowed. The inside of his mouth felt rough and dry and tasted of stale vomit. 'Good morning,' he said.

'That's better. You've had such a long sleep, I began to wonder whether you'd ever wake up. How do you feel?'

'Thirsty. There's an itch on my nose.'

'What do you want first, a scratch or a drink?'

'Both.'

A tinkle of laughter, high-pitched, like one of those little bells Victorian women used to summon the maid. 'I can see you're going to be quite a handful, Mr . . . er . . . You do have a name, don't you?'

'Joe,' he said. 'Joe Lejeune.'

'OK, Mr. Joe Lejeune. First the scratch, then the drink.'

He slept again, a calm, quiet sleep like a baby, and when he awoke he was alone. Pale sunlight squeezed between the slats of a Venetian blind and laced across his face. There was a slight smell of disinfectant. From where he lay he could see only part of the room, the ceiling, a section of white wall, the angle of a door, a clock. It was two-fifteen in the afternoon.

He tried to shift himself to see more but there was something gripping his neck and the effort produced a stab of pain that brought water to his eyes. His thirst had returned, as bad as ever, and he ran his tongue around the inside of his mouth and smacked his lips.

He tried to pull his thoughts together but they refused to respond. There were questions he should ask, statements he should make, but what were they? His brain felt leaden and there was a pulsing ache between his eyes. He was aware only of a sense of loss, of loneliness, vague and unfocussed. He began to cry.

He was still crying when the woman returned. There was the clip clip of her footsteps, and the soft thump of a door. If she noticed his tears she did not comment on them. She was doing something near the bed, adjusting a drip. Joe could see the slight staining of sweat beneath the arms of her white uniform.

'Comfortable?' Her voice was brisk.

'I'd like to sit up.'

'That's not possible. Any pain?'

'No.'

'Good.'

She bent over him briefly, and Joe realised that she was not beautiful, not at all, but tired-looking with dark hollows around her eyes. She jammed a thermometer into his mouth and left the room. He heard her shouting to somebody. She was gone a long time.

When she returned and removed the thermometer Joe noticed a badge on her left breast. It read I.V. Rodrigues, SRN. 'Where am I?' he said.

'In hospital in Harare. They brought you here by helicopter. An army patrol found you.'

'Can I see my wife and children?'

Sister Rodrigues paused. 'You have a wife and children, here in Harare?'.

'I don't know.'

'You must know if you have a wife and children.'

'They were with me when . . .'

The nurse made a clicking noise with her tongue. 'Nobody told me anything about dependants,' she said.

Panic. A blind, red panic like a curtain, like a heavy red cloth thrown over his face. The path, the trees, the rocks. Cassie's face. Ellie in her pink shirt. The children's voices. 'Dadeee!' 'Dadeeee!'

'I want to see them,' he shouted. 'I want to see them NOW!'

He tried to get up but couldn't move. They'd weighted down his body but he struggled. There was a sudden searing pain in his right hand which made him gasp.

'Be still!'

It was the voice of the schoolroom, hard and sharp. Joe obeyed instinctively, becoming conscious of a cold wet feeling where his hand was.

'Now look what you've done. You've pulled your drip out. If you can't keep still you'll do yourself serious harm.'

Then Sister Rodrigues smiled and her face was transformed. 'We'll see what we can find out about your family, Mr. Lejeune,' she said. 'Don't worry.'

Sometimes he slept. Sometimes he was awake. The distinction between the two states was not particularly clear to him. From time to time Sister Rodrigues or another younger black nurse came in to check the drip or to take his blood pressure or his temperature. The hands of the clock jerked round. The strips of sunlight moved away from his bed until he could no longer see them.

He thought, mostly, of nothing. Sometimes about the children, about Cassie's reading and how she would cope with Class Three when she returned to school in September. Once he thought about his wedding day: the quiet ceremony in the

11

Hampstead Register Office and the feeling of total joy that had possessed him that day. He remembered the way everyone had laughed when the Registrar read out Ellie's preposterous names: Ellen Mary Victoria Jane Cordelia Sackville-Smith. Jane after her grandmother, Victoria after her aunt, Cordelia because her mother had seen a film of King Lear during her pregnancy. And he remembered that first night in the sloping hotel room in Winchester when the wardrobe door had creaked open suddenly when they were making love.

Oh Ellie, my love, my love.

Clip clip. This time Sister Rodrigues was not alone. 'This is Mr. Harrington,' she said. 'The surgeon.'

The examination was brief and painful. It was only then that Joe realised that his left leg was encased in plaster and was suspended from a pulley rigged up above the bed and the upper part of his body wrapped in bandages.

Sister Rodrigues replaced the dressings deftly. The surgeon washed his hands. He was a large, barrel-chested man in his forties, more like a farmer than a surgeon. 'I understand you're worried about your family,' he said. 'Well, I'm afraid I don't have any positive news for you. The Army as usual didn't tell me anything, except that you were being case-~~vacced here.~~ God knows why they didn't take you to Masvingo or Triangle which is right on the doorstep. The helicopter crew probably fancied a night in town.' The surgeon dried his hands and crossed over to the bed. 'However, at the sixth attempt I managed to get through to the police at Chiredzi who have been liaising with the army battalion who found you. Apparently they do know about your wife and kids, and are doing their best to find them. They've found your passport, by the way. I didn't realise you were an American.'

'I've lived in England for thirteen years.'

'You're losing your accent, you know that?'

Joe managed a smile.

'And your wife – she's an American, too?'

'English. She spent twelve years in Rhodesia when she was a girl. In Umtali.'

'Been revisiting old haunts, hey?'

12

'Yes.'

'My wife's an Umtali girl, too. Mutare, I should say. I'll never get used to these bloody name changes! Beautiful little town.'

'We went there.'

Joe closed his eyes, suddenly too tired to talk. When he reopened them the surgeon was still there. He was talking to Sister Rodrigues about urine. Joe said, 'They will find them, won't they – Ellie, Cassie and Ben?'

'The army have got excellent trackers. Ex-guerillas many of them. It depends how much of a start the bandits have got, and who they are, and where they're going. During the war many people, even quite young children, were kidnapped and marched hundreds of miles through the bush, and were released, sometimes months later, totally unharmed.

'But some weren't?'

The surgeon was silent for a while. 'No, some weren't.'

'What are the chances?'

'Fifty-fifty.'

'Fifty-fifty.' Joe repeated the words slowly, trying to grasp their meaning. Fifty-fifty. Fifty-fifty. A fifty percent chance. Toss a coin. Heads they're alive. Tails . . .

The surgeon spoke again to Sister Rodrigues, this time so softly Joe could not make out the words. He took a slip of paper from his top pocket and wrote something on it. When he turned back to Joe he said, 'I must tell you that the police want to interview you. I'll have to let them in at some stage. Certainly before Friday.'

'Friday?'

'We shall have to take you back to the theatre on Friday, I'm afraid. There are a few more repairs I need to do.'

'What repairs?'

'This and that.'

Joe closed his eyes. Dear God, there was more of it. More pain, more bad dreams. 'Please,' he said. 'Just tell me.'

'Everything?'

'Yes.'

The surgeon drew a deep breath and glanced at his watch. 'OK, we'll start with ballistics. First, high velocity bullets.

13

The gun that guy used on you, did it have a curved magazine, like a banana?'

'Yes.'

'Kalashnikov, AK 47. Russian designed, probably made in China. Standard terrorist weapon during the war. There are thousands of them around still, in arms caches. They fire large bullets, hundred and twenty grains with steel cores, and they fire them fast – muzzle velocity is a little under two thousand miles an hour. So what happens when one of these bullets hits you? Or in your case, when three of them hit you?'

'They go straight through and out the other side?'

The surgeon smiled. 'I wish it was that simple. Did you do any physics at school?'

'Some.'

'Remember the definition of kinetic energy? Mass times velocity, etcetera. Basically, the bigger the bullet and the faster it goes, the more energy it transmits to whatever it hits – which in your case was your left leg, the left side of your abdomen and your shoulder blade. What this energy does is to blow a hole thirty or forty times the circumference of the bullet. In the process bones splinter, veins and arteries rupture, and all sorts of nasty things happen. Luckily for you that guy hadn't got his catch on automatic and he couldn't aim too well, or we wouldn't be here talking to each other.'

Joe was silent for a while, digesting the information. Thirty or forty times the circumference of the bullet. A hole as big as a fist. Bigger, maybe. He tried to picture a hole as big as a fist in his leg, but failed. 'So it's bad, is it?'

'Well, your left leg's pretty chewed up. The bullet cut the main femoral artery, damaged the vein in passing, and smashed the femur. I've done a graft on the artery using a piece of vein from your right leg, but I'm going to have to do some more work on the bone on Friday. I'll probably have to pin it. I've also had to cut away some of the muscle where it was damaged, so you'll be left with a little bit of a hole. The artery, of course, was where you lost all that blood. But don't worry, you'll walk again, no problem, though you may end up with one leg a little shorter than the other.'

'And the rest of me?'

'Just a flesh wound in your abdomen, luckily. Half an inch

14

to the right and it would have gone straight through your peritoneal cavity, in other words your guts, and you'd have been a dead man. As it is you'll have a little scar when I close the wound. Your shoulder area, though, is a bit more problematical. They're difficult things, shoulders. There'd obviously been some sort of blow in the area before the shots were fired.'

'He hit me with the gun.'

'Which accounts for the simple fracture of the clavicle. The bullet, of course, hit you in almost exactly the same place, glanced off the broken bone and then proceeded to whizz about like it was in a pinball machine. It hit your scapula, got deflected again, and came out through your upper arm. There's a fair bit of muscle damage as a consequence. I think you may have some trouble with your shoulder movement in the future, but maybe not. That could depend on how conscientious you are about your physiotherapy.'

There was a tap on the door, a black face at the glass panel. The surgeon glanced over his shoulder and nodded. 'I've got to go,' he said. 'But just think on this: you could be in a lot worse shape, one hell of a lot worse. I'll fix you up on Friday, then it's rest, physio, learning to walk again. Then home you go.'

The pain was returning, a deep dull bone-grinding pain. 'I don't have a home,' Joe said, through the pain.

'You must have friends, somewhere you can stay while you convalesce?'

It was difficult to think. 'Yes,' he said.

'Good.' The surgeon paused at the open door. 'I'll send my secretary up and you can give her the details. Of course, nobody knows you're here, do they?'

'No,' said Joe, gasping now with the pain. 'I guess they don't.'

That night he saw the dead bodies of Ellie and the children. They were lying side by side, naked, on the bare earth. There were holes the size of a fist where their faces should have been.

At ten o'clock he started screaming. He screamed for twenty minutes. He ripped the drip from his arm, and with his free hand pulled the dressing from his side and smashed the

15

water jug on his bedside unit. When the duty doctor arrived with the night sister he fought with them. They were joined by two more men who held him down while the doctor injected something into his arm. There was blood on the floor, and saline solution from the drip bag, and broken glass. He remembered the doctor's frightened eyes and the sound of a bell ringing before he took the slow slide into oblivion.

'Joe!'

Daylight. Sun striping his face.

'Come on, Joe, wake up!'

Sister Rodrigues' voice. 'He'll be feeling a bit confused. We had to give him quite a large dose of chlorpromazine.'

'Fuck off,' said Joe. 'Why don't you all fuck off.' Sleep, that was all he wanted. Sleep, sleep, sleep.

'Mr. Lejeune!'

'Go screw yourself.'

'Mr Lejeune, please!'

Bitch. Bloody bitch. With her prim walk and that bloody squawking voice!

'Perhaps we should come back later,' a man's voice said.

'No, he needs to wake up now. Mr. Lejeune, open your eyes. There are friends of yours here to see you.'

'They're dead. I saw them. They had no faces. Their faces were gone.'

'Mr. Lejeune, will you open your eyes.'

'Can't you understand, they're dead!' Joe was crying now, huge sobs convulsing his body.

'Joe, this is Penny.'

'They're dead.'

'You stayed with us, with Ellie and the children, remember? Come on, open your eyes.'

Penny. Penny and David. A large white house with a green lawn. A redbrick church. Bottles of wine. The kids dancing naked in the garden sprinkler . . .

Joe opened his eyes. 'Penny,' he said. 'Oh God, Penny, what am I going to do?'

She leant forward and put an arm round his head. Her breast grazed his cheek, soft through the material of her shirt. Fresh sobs rose from within him.

'They're not dead,' she said gently. 'You mustn't think that.'

'I saw them. They were lying there. They had no faces.'

'You were dreaming, that's all. Just dreaming.'

'We'd have come earlier, but we had no idea you were here.' It was David speaking. Joe remembered his voice, the slightly hesitant quality, the way the words seemed to jam in his throat and then spill out with a rush. 'It's the most terrible, terrible thing to have happened.'

'They'll come back, Joe. You mustn't give up hope. Not ever. I know they'll come back.'

Joe looked up into Penny's face, at the perfect white oval framed by bushy black hair, and then to where David stood by the foot of the bed, a thin, awkward man, looking doubly awkward in his priest's collar. 'Why didn't you tell us this might happen?' he said.

'We didn't know.'

'You live here. You *should* know! You should have stopped us going.'

'Ellie wanted to go,' said Penny softly.

'But you suggested it.'

'You're not being fair.'

'Why the hell should I be fair? You tell me. Why should I? We could have stayed in Harare. We could have . . .' Joe began to cough, fighting to breath, his shoulder pushing agonisingly against the bandages. Penny took her arm away and stood up.

Sister Rodrigues said, 'Calm yourself, please, Mr. Lejeune.'

Slowly the coughing subsided. Joe looked at Penny. Suddenly he felt completely certain that this pair, this so-called religious pair, these so-called friends, had deliberately and callously sent Ellie and the children to their deaths. 'You killed them,' he said.

Penny was shaking now, close to tears. 'I don't know how you can say that,' she said. 'That's the cruellest thing anybody has ever said to me.'

Joe closed his eyes. 'Go away,' he said quietly. 'Just go away from me.'

'I think we should go, Penny. He's very distressed, and you're getting upset.'

'Christ, will you go!'

Penny sniffed. Her eyes were wet. 'We'll be in in a day or so's time when you're feeling better,' she said.

'I don't want to see you again – ever.'

'You don't mean that.'

'Wanna bet?'

David said, 'Look, is there anything you want? Anybody we can telephone? Ellie's mother?'

'No. Oh shit!' The sobs were back, twisting his body, fighting the morphine. Oh shit. Oh Ellie Ellie. The touch of her hand, the sound of her laughter, the silly voice she put on at bedtime when she was reading to the kids. 'Stay with me,' he said. 'Please stay with me. I didn't mean what I said. You must believe me. Say you believe me.'

'I do,' said Penny softly, still sniffing. And she put out her hand and stroked his hair, and they wept together, the two of them.

It was mid-afternoon and time for his X-ray before David and Penny went away.

The fat man in the shiny synthetic suit was sweating heavily. Sister Rodrigues said, 'Ten minutes, no longer. Do you understand me?'

'These nurses,' said the fat man as she went out. 'They terrify me.' He sat down heavily on the red plastic chair beside the bed, and produced a card. It had a coat of arms, the words 'Zimbabwe Police Force', a blurred black and white photograph and the name 'Welcome Mtisi, Inspector'. It was grubby. The Inspector replaced the card in an inside pocket and took out a white handkerchief. He wiped the moisture from his forehead. He had a strong, sour smell. 'I would like to ask you a few questions,' he said. 'Establish the groundwork, if you follow me?'

His precise, pedantic English reminded Joe of a bad thirties film. His pink and white spotted necktie didn't. The Inspector replaced his handkerchief and took four folded sheets of paper and a notebook from one of his side pockets. He unfolded the papers and flattened them on his knee, then he held them up for Joe to inspect.

They were photocopies of the immigration forms that Joe

and Ellie had filled in at Plumtree. He could see Ellie's signature on two of them, her bad writing made worse by the swaying of the train. 'I take it these are the forms you filled in when you entered Zimbabwe?' said the Inspector.

'Yes.'

'And the particulars on them are correct? You are a graphic designer by profession?'

'Yes. I run my own company in London.'

The Inspector wrote in his notebook. Glancing down, Joe could read: 'The particulars on the Immigration form are correct.' The Inspector's tongue followed the movement of the pen. He looked up. 'And you confirm that you were visiting Zimbabwe for vacation purposes?'

'Yes.'

'Visiting friends?'

'Yes.'

He wrote slowly, 'Visiting friends. Vacation purposes.' He was like a joke policeman, Joe decided. Like something out of Gilbert and Sullivan. Any minute now he'd stand up and sing 'When constabulary duty must be done, must be done'.

Joe hummed a few bars. Inspector Mtisi's head jerked upwards. There was something in his look that stopped Joe dead. It was a look that spoke of the padded cell, the underground interrogation room. The Inspector said, 'I'm surprised that you can sing when your wife and children are in such a predicament.'

'I'm sorry. I think it must be the medicine they've given me.'

'Ah, the medicine.' The answer seemed to satisfy the Inspector.

Joe said, 'I want my family back.'

'I am in hourly contact with my colleagues in the Lowveld. The case is progressing well.' The Inspector returned to his notebook.

'And that's all you've got to tell me, is it?'

'In essence, yes.'

'In essence? What do you mean by "in essence"? Have they picked up any tracks? Have they identified who the bandits are?' Joe spoke with mounting urgency. Perhaps the fat policeman was keeping something from him, deliberately concealing the truth. And he'd been lying back humming Gilbert and Sullivan, for Christ's sake!

The Inspector sighed deeply, took out his handkerchief and wiped again at his forehead. 'This case has been given the highest priority,' he said. 'The highest priority.'

'You've got nowhere.'

'It is early yet.'

Joe tried to rise, but the pain slammed him back. 'Four days. You've had four days.'

'I'm sorry.'

'Sorry!'

'You must be patient.'

'Look, I want to see the consul. The American Consul. The British Consul. Any fucking consul.'

'There is no need to employ obscene language, Mr. Lejeune.' The Inspector spoke slowly.

'So I can't see the consul?'

'Both the American and the British consuls have already been informed. No doubt you will hear from them in due course.'

'When? Next year?'

'They are being kept fully acquainted with developments.'

'Well the next time you acquaint them with developments, tell them I want to see them.'

'As you wish.'

'I do wish.'

Inspector Mtisi wrote the word 'Consul' in his notebook, underlining it with unnecessary vigour. 'Mr. Lejeune,' he said sharply, 'you must now answer my questions. Your information could be vital to the successful outcome of this investigation. Please co-operate.'

Joe felt suddenly tired and hopeless. He needed Ellie, her touch, the smell of her. Not this farce. Not this sweating fat man. And the consul, what could he do? Make some kind of limp protest? Apply 'diplomatic pressure'? Probably not even that. It was not the first such kidnapping, and it wouldn't be the last. It would merit a footnote, no more, to be added to the weekly report to Washington or London. 'OK,' he said quietly. 'Ask me the questions. I'll co-operate.'

The Inspector sighed deeply and turned to a new page in his

notebook.' 'Why were you going to the Gona-re-Zhou?'

'Ellie did some field work there when she was at university. She'd always said how beautiful it was.'

'Your wife was at university here in Zimbabwe?'

'Yes.'

'I'd understood she was British.'

'She is. She came out here with her parents when she was eleven.'

'And subsequently returned to England?'

'After twelve years. She couldn't take the regime.'

'The white racist regime of Ian Smith?'

'That's the one.'

The Inspector looked up. 'She is therefore a friend of Zimbabwe?'

'You could say that.'

'Then it is doubly unfortunate that this tragedy has happened.'

There was a long pause while the Inspector wrote 'Friend of Zimbabwe' in his notebook. Then he said, 'I want you to answer this question carefully, please. Did anybody in Zimbabwe have a grudge against her? Or against you?'

Joe shook his head. 'Ellie did say that the Rhodesian Special Branch had a file on her, but that was years ago.'

'She was active in the liberation movement?'

'No, just a student with a tendency to shout her mouth off.'

'And subsequently?'

'She went on shouting her mouth off – but that was back in England.'

Ellie. Dear Ellie. She was always so *committed*: Chilean refugees, Amnesty International, CND, lead pollution . . . Joe remembered the endless marches down Whitehall, the rallies in Trafalgar Square, carrying heavy badly-painted banners, the children in pushchairs. It always seemed to be raining. And the arguments, late into the night, usually in the kitchen, when he'd take the contradictory point of view just to be bloody-minded. 'No,' he said. 'I don't think she's got any enemies here.'

The Inspector wrote: 'No Enemies.' He said, 'You will appreciate that I am trying to establish a motive.'

'Try robbery. They stole everything we had.'

'Naturally that is our conclusion, too. But other avenues have to be explored.'

'Of course.'

A dribble of sweat was running down the Inspector's cheek. He used his hand this time to wipe it away. 'I'd like you to describe the men who robbed you.'

'They were black.'

'And all black men look alike?'

'I didn't say that.'

'It is a common opinion among white people.'

'Not this white person. The guy who shot me was short – five five, five six. He had a beard and some kind of skin complaint. The others were young, wearing bits of camouflage dress. One of them had a yellow tee shirt with FANTA written on it.'

'How many men were there?'

'Six, eight . . . I didn't count.'

'You'd recognise them if you saw them again?'

Joe was conscious that the Inspector was watching him closely. 'The bearded guy, yes. The others, possibly. They carried AK rifles.'

'You know about weapons?' the Inspector asked sharply.

'Only what I've been told. The surgeon, Mr. Harrington, told me. Curved magazines, like bananas.'

'You've discussed details of the incident with Mr. Harrington?'

'Yes.'

'And with anybody else?'

'Some friends who came to visit.'

'Names?'

'David and Penny Sweetman.'

'Address?'

Joe felt his irritation rising again. 'Why does it matter who I discussed it with?'

'Address please.'

'I asked you a question.'

'Mr. Lejeune, you promised to co-operate.'

'I merely want to know why it matters.'

'State security could be involved.'

'State security! A load of half-starved bandits a threat to state security? In that case, you must have a very insecure state.'

22

Inspector Mtisi's eyes narrowed. He put down his pen. 'Mr. Lejeune, I must warn you that you could be committing an offence under the Law and Order (Maintenance) Act.'

'The what?' Joe found himself laughing but stopped. It hurt.

'It is illegal to provide assistance in any form to enemies of the State.'

'And by not giving you my friends' address I'm rendering assistance to the enemies of the State? It's in the telephone directory, for God's sake!'

'You have also made a slanderous attack on the democratically elected government of Zimbabwe.'

'Well,' said Joe slowly, 'now I know.'

'You could find yourself in real hot water, Mr. Lejeune.'

'What you're saying is, you'll haul me out of bed and throw me into prison. Is that the way it works in the democratically elected government of Zimbabwe?' Joe's amusement was turning rapidly to anger.

'I have taken down everything you've said, word for word,' said the Inspector.

Joe glanced down at the notebook. The last thing the Inspector had written was 'Yellow tee shirt with FANTA'.

'Like fuck you have,' he said.

The Inspector ignored the remark. He shifted slightly to conceal the book with the bulk of his arm. 'Now, please, the address.'

'St. Anthony's Rectory, Milton Park.'

'Ah, a priest.'

'What are you going to do now? Go round there and arrest him?'

'Mr. Lejeune, you are in an emotional state. It is the medicine.'

'It's the Zimbabwe police force.'

The Inspector suddenly smacked his thigh with great force. The noise was like a gunshot. 'Answer my questions!' he shouted. 'You're wasting my time! Apart from the rifles, was there anything to identify the equipment the men were carrying? Was there anything made in South Africa, for instance?'

'No.'

'You're certain?'

'They didn't have any equipment.'

'Ammunition?'

'I didn't see any.'

'They must have had ammunition.'

'I didn't see any, I told you!' Joe was shouting now, his body rigid with tension. 'Nor did I see any Outspan oranges or bottles of South African wine. And I certainly didn't spot a single Cape Apple!'

The door flew open and Sister Rodrigues advanced into the room, holding a pair of surgical scissors at a dangerous angle. 'Get out!' she snapped, her face pink. 'This is an intensive care unit. How dare you cause a disturbance!'

Inspector Mtisi stood up hurriedly, dropping his notebook. He was sweating worse than ever. He grunted loudly when he bent down to pick up the book. 'I'm finished,' he said.

He walked slowly towards the door. At the washbasin he stopped, put out a hand to steady himself. 'Mr. Lejeune,' he said, 'before I go I have to inform you of a top-level decision at the direct behest of Comrade Zvarevashe, Minister of State in the Prime Minister's Office Responsible for State Security. The decision is this: At no time should you talk to representatives of the national or international media about the incident, without official permission. It is felt that to do so could directly prejudice the outcome of our investigations. Is that clearly understood?'

'Crystal clear.' Joe's voice was heavy with irony. He took strength from the menacing figure of Sister Rodrigues.

'We will ourselves in due course issue a press statement about what has taken place. This decision is taken entirely in your own interests.'

'Go,' said Sister Rodrigues.

'We will keep you informed of all developments.'

'Did you hear me!'

As the door swung behind him, Joe could hear the Inspector talking rapidly in Shona to somebody outside.

'They're pigs,' said Sister Rodrigues.

'The police?'

'The C.I.O. The Central Intelligence Organisation. They were pigs under Smith, they're pigs now. They've put a policeman on the door, would you believe it?'

24

'They're probably worried I'll escape.' Joe managed a quick smile.

'You're not going anywhere,' said Sister Rodrigues. 'Except to the theatre tomorrow morning.'

Nothing.

Nothing.

One week. Seven days. One hundred and sixty-eight hours. NOTHING.

David had been in touch with the priest in Chiredzi. There were roadblocks, he'd said. A lot of troops. They were trying their best. They'd brought him some photographs and a cutting from Tuesday's *Herald* which spoke of South African involvement in the attack but gave no details.

On the Friday he'd been with Ellie. He'd lain there with her in a strange, warm, weightless world somewhere between sleeping and waking while John Harrington had hammered steel spikes into his thigh bone. And when he awoke he was in a different room, in a different bed, and his mind was filled with the pain of parting.

Two days after the operation Sister Rodrigues unwrapped his hand and removed the drip and he was able to eat a bowl of Pronutria and milk without difficulty. That same afternoon a short white woman with an oversized bust told him to get out of bed. Supported by the physiotherapist on one side and Sister Rodrigues on the other, he walked to the far side of the room where the lavatory was. Afterwards, back in bed, he lay exhausted, gasping for breath like a runner at the end of a marathon.

A man came from the British High Commission. He was younger than Joe and wore a lightweight white suit and a green tie. He introduced himself as Mr. Chadwick, not mentioning his Christian name. The young black girl who accompanied him wrote things down in shorthand on a notepad. Mr. Chadwick told Joe that the British Government had expressed grave concern at the kidnapping, but they were satisfied that the Zimbabwe Government was doing everything in its power to track down the kidnappers and rescue his wife and children. In the circumstances there was little more he could do. After enquiring about the state of Joe's finances and offering to contact Ellie's mother in England, he left. Nobody showed up from the American Embassy.

That evening, when John Harrington came to examine him, Joe told the surgeon that he wanted to die. Without pausing in his examination, the surgeon said, 'Sister Rodrigues, what do you say to people who tell you they want to die?'

'I say OK, in that case I'll go home and let them get on with it.'

'And do you?'

The Sister smiled. 'Not often. I need the money.'

Joe found himself laughing but it hurt, and when they'd gone and the door was closed he stopped laughing and groped for the photographs that Penny and David had brought him.

They'd been taken on the same afternoon three weeks earlier. There'd been quite a party, old friends from Ellie's university days gathered for lunch on the stoep of the rectory. And in the middle of it all, Ellie.

Ellie talking, waving her hands as she made some impassioned political point. Ellie laughing, her head thrown back in the cushioned wicker chair. Ellie drinking, her face seen through a forest of wine bottles.

And there were the kids, Ben and Cassie, waiting expectantly for the ice cream that Penny was scooping out into cones or playing with the Sweetman's four-year-old daughter Becky, dancing in the rainbow spray of the garden sprinkler.

And there was the one he liked best, the one taken in the late afternoon when all the wine had been drunk, and the food eaten, and the shadows had grown long: the one with Ben, exhausted and happy, curled up sleeping, and Ellie, quiet for once, looking down at the little figure on her lap with such tenderness and love.

'Wait for me,' he said out loud to the woman in the photograph. 'Please wait for me.'

Four days later there was a press conference. Comrade Samuel Zvarevashe, Minister of State in the Prime Minister's Office Responsible for Security, an impeccably dressed man in his early forties with a broad nose and small, deep-set eyes, posed for photographs next to Joe's bed, switching on various expressions of concern as the cameras clicked.

Foreign journalists stood around eyeing the scene with undisguised cynicism. The local pressmen wrote furiously, obviously accustomed to taking dictation from the Minister, who read out a list of 'South African inspired atrocities' from a buff folder and parried all questions on the progress of the search.

Inspector Mtisi, who was stage managing the event, had promised Joe 'a little chat' with the Minister when the press had departed, but Zvarevashe was running late and there was not time. When Joe protested, the Inspector mentioned Joe's visitor's visa. It had only three weeks left to run, he said, and its renewal was 'entirely at the Minister's discretion'.

The dreams returned, and this time they didn't leave him. During his waking hours they receded until they became a jumble of fractured sounds and images, like a television set glimpsed through the open doorway of a distant room. But at night they occupied him entirely.

Sometimes they were soft, comfortable, coherent. For instance, Sunday morning in the flat, the kitchen table strewn with plates and toast crumbs, the Sunday paper divided between them, Ellie exclaiming 'Christ!' every few seconds, indignant at some article she was reading, the kids building Lego spacecraft on the floor.

At other times the dreams broke and scattered and cut into him like crushed glass. A single scream. The drip of red blood on to a bare white foot. The point of a gun, pressing and pressing into his spine. Ellie's voice saying, 'I don't like the look of those men, Joe.'

And then they would become indistinct, blurred like a bad video, the faces, the voices scratched and distorted. They melted and re-formed into new dreams. The kids, thin and ill and silent, stumbling through the bush, drinking from stinking pools. Bilharzia worms burrowing beneath their skin into their warm red veins and multiplying until there were no veins any more, and no flesh, just a stinking palpitating mass of worms.

And the rape. That dream came, too, with Ellie white and

bloody, her legs spread as the men queued to couple with her, the kids watching with dull eyes.

And Cassie, maybe Cassie . . .

Sometimes Mtisi was there. Sometimes the policeman from outside the door in his buff uniform. Sometimes John Harrington.

And when Penny came to see him, she was part of the dream. And Sister Rodrigues. And the oranges in the dish. The photographs in the wallet. The bedside jug of water. The white, silent room.

The familiar touch of cool fingertips. Joe opened his eyes to see Sister Rodrigues. He hadn't heard her come in. It was a Wednesday evening three weeks after the shooting. He felt dull with fatigue from too much physiotherapy, and too long talking with the new man from the British High Commission who'd brought him no news and discussed repatriation.

Sister Rodrigues put a finger to her lips. 'I've brought a friend to meet you,' she said. 'This is Larry Wakeman.'

A tall black man in an ill-fitting ward orderly's coat approached the bed and stretched out a hand. 'Good to see you again,' he said.

Joe met the man's eyes. The accent puzzled him: American, mid-West, Chicago or thereabouts.

The man said, 'I was at that press conference with Zvarevashe.'

Then Joe remembered. He'd stood at the back of the room and asked several questions about what exactly the army had found that proved South African involvement in the attack. The Minister had given no direct answers and there had been some antagonism between the two. 'I'm not supposed to talk to journalists,' Joe said.

'I kind of guessed that.' Larry Wakeman perched himself on the side of the bed, selected one of the apples Penny had brought, and bit into it. 'Don't worry. Your own private police force has gone off to get a free meal in the staff canteen, courtesy of the good Sister here.'

'You've got information?' Joe was aware of a sweet smell coming from the man. Some kind of aftershave or body lotion.

'No.'

'Then what do you want?'

'That's a pretty broad question.'

'For God's sake.' Joe closed his eyes.

'He can help,' Sister Rodrigues said. 'He's got contacts.'

'What contacts?' Joe made no attempt to hide the weariness he felt.

'Just contacts.' The American laughed softly. 'It's pretty damned difficult to hide a white woman and two kids in this country without word getting out.'

'So when word gets out, you come and tell me.' The man's over-familiarity was beginning to irritate Joe intensely.

'He just wants you to tell him exactly what happened.' There was anxiety in Sister Rodrigues's voice.

'So he can get an exclusive?'

Larry Wakeman laughed again. 'The story's cold, man. You think anyone would be interested?'

'Please, Joe,' said Sister Rodrigues. 'He can help you.'

'I'm tired.' He looked up at the nurse, at her tight, strained face. It had not been easy setting up this meeting, he suddenly realised, and felt a surge of affection for her. 'I'm sorry,' he said.

'So tell me,' Larry Wakeman said.

The story was well-rehearsed by now. Too well-rehearsed. Stale. As he spoke, it felt like he was describing something he'd read or seen on a news report. The journalist asked a couple of questions: about the weapons, and the direction the men had taken after the attack. He finished his apple and selected and polished another one.

There was a brief silence. Larry Wakeman adjusted his position on the bed. 'OK,' he said, 'I'm clear on that. Now let me tell you what I think. I think this has all the signs of being a ZIPRA attack.'

'ZIPRA?'

'The military wing of ZAPU, old man Nkomo's crew. Matabeles. Of course, Nkomo denies any personal involvement, but it's pretty certain that groups of them are being trained down in the Transvaal and are being sent back over the border. They've been hitting white farmers, villages, even the occasional tourist. "Destabilisation" is what *Time* magazine calls it, keeping Mugabe on the hop, though there's two sides to that. The Gona-re-Zhou's a bit outside their usual orbit, but not that far outside. My guess is that if your family are still alive they've been taken to Matabeleland, probably somewhere out in the far west beyond Kezi. I'd also guess there's been at least one ransom demand that Zvarevashe doesn't want to talk about.'

'Money?'

'Release of political prisoners, maybe other concessions. It's the usual pattern in these kind of cases.'

'So they're at Kezi?'

'Maybe. Maybe not.'

Joe's tiredness had gone now. He repeated the name to himself. Kezi. Kezi. He must get a map and pinpoint the place. Then, when he was out of plaster and fit, he could hire a car, perhaps find a gun from somewhere, learn how to use it. . .

Larry Wakeman seemed to have read his thoughts. 'You're not thinking of a one man rescue mission?' he said. 'Because if you are, forget it. Even if they're alive, and there's no guarantee of that, and even if I'm right about Kezi, you'd get nowhere. Correction: you'd get yourself into a small cell in Chikurubi Prison, or dead. The army will pick you up as soon as you show your nose down there. They don't like strange white men with guns.'

'I've go nothing to lose.'

'Except your fingernails, very slowly – that's your friend Mtisi's speciality, by the way, and other little physical discomforts. No, leave it to me for a while. I may come up with something.' The journalist paused. 'There's also something else you should be aware of. It's my guess that right now Comrade Robert Mugabe and Comrade Samson Zvarevashe ain't trying too hard to find your family.'

'But they've had roadblocks, trackers . . .'

'And what have they come up with? A little evidence – the nature of which, for security reasons they conveniently can't disclose – that this attack was masterminded by the South Africans. And where does that evidence point? Straight at Joshua Nkomo. It gives Mugabe an internationally justifiable excuse to move one of his less pleasant army units – probably the Fifth Brigade, who've been trained in modern genocide techniques in Korea – back into Matabeleland to shoot the shit out of the poor bastards down there. Then he can claim bloody chaos and declare a one-party state with himself as unopposed leader. End of story.'

'So they won't find them, is that what you're saying?' Joe spoke quietly.

Larry Wakeman shrugged. 'They may, who knows? I hope they do. But if they don't, everybody will understand why they've had to do what they've had to do.'

'Bastards, BASTARDS!' Joe's shout hit the silent hospital with the force of a mortar shell. 'Fucking bastards!'

'Hey, man.' The journalist rapped the plaster on Joe's leg sharply. 'I've got contacts, I told you.'

'And what do I do, for Christ's sake?'

'Stay here. Get better.'

'I'm going to find them,' Joe said. He was sweating, shaking violently. 'You'd better tell them that. I'm going to find them! Fuck those bastards.'

'Yeah. Fuck 'em.'

'Move it. Come on, you lazy bastard. Move it!'

Contacts. He couldn't wait for contacts. Bastard leg, bastard bastard leg! Six times he went to the window when Larry Wakeman and Sister Rodrigues had gone, and six times back again, wrenching at the metal frame he'd been given, forcing himself forward, legs parted because of the plaster and pins, a splay-legged old man's shuffle. 'Bastard legs!' he shouted at his reflection in the window, at the thin white face with its unfamiliar beard, at the green gown, the white plaster, the silver and plastic frame. On the seventh turn he fell awkwardly, tangling with the metal struts of the frame. His cry of agony brought the young policeman running in from the corridor outside. Bastard legs.

At the weekend Penny and David brought him letters. One from Ellie's mother, almost illegible because of the tremour of Parkinsonism. The other from the guys in the Studio, written on the buff stationery he'd designed himself when he and Mac had first formed McConnell Lejeune Associates five years previously and set up shop in the old market offices overlooking Covent Garden Plaza. The letters were like something written in code, irrelevant, unintelligible, signals from another planet. With the letters was a newspaper cutting, three days old, from the leader column of the *Zimbabwe Herald*. It was headed 'Comment', subheaded 'S.A. Bandits'. It read:

"Last week's revelation by the Minister of State (Security) Cde Samuel Zvarevashe of the kidnapping of a British tourist and her two children, and the shooting of her husband (an American who has become a naturalised Briton), has once again highlighted the pernicious determination by the racist regime in Pretoria to destroy our country by striking at its economic base: in this case, tourism.

Evidence found at the kidnap site provides proof positive to confirm the common knowledge that dissidents are recruited, trained, indoctrinated, equipped and deployed into Zimbabwe by South Africa for the purposes of destabilisation, as is being done to Angola and Mozambique.

The stark fact is that Zimbabwe and South Africa (by proxy, through its agents) are engaged in a direct state of military confrontation, not only in Matabeleland, but increasingly throughout the whole southern half of the country. There is no doubt that it is vitally important to maintain the presence of maximum military force in that region. There is equally no doubt that the world beyond our borders should be told the real truth behind this latest cowardly attack on innocent visitors to our beautiful country."

David said, 'We thought you might be interested.'

'They're giving it top priority,' Penny said.

Joe snorted and turned his head away.

They watched him for a while in silence, then David said, 'We had a visitor yesterday – a journalist. Larry Wakeman. He said he wanted to help you. He asked for all sorts of background information on you and Ellie.'

'You talked to him?'

'No. I told him we'd been forbidden to talk to the press. He was very persistent but I think he got the message eventually.'

'I don't know what's so wrong with talking to the press,' Penny said.

David said, 'They probably feel they need to take precautions. It's no more sinister than that.'

'Precautions against what? The truth?'

David grinned wryly. 'Since when have they been interested in the truth?'

Joe said, 'He's been to see me.'

'Larry Wakeman?'

'He says he can help me. He says he's got contacts.'

'Contacts with whom?'

'I don't know. People in Matabeleland.'

David snorted with laughter. 'Oh, he's got contacts all right, but I don't think they're in Matabeleland. That guy's practically a member of the Government.'

Joe glanced up in surprise. 'That's not the impression I got.'

David spread his hands. 'Maybe he's changed his mind, but there was a big feature on him in the *Herald* about a year ago. Apparently he spent the last two years of the war living in the bush with ZANLA, Mugabe's guerrillas. He was the only Western journalist who did. If I remember right, he flew to Tanzania then walked down through the bush until he made contact with them. Obviously, what he wrote must have pleased the Comrades or he wouldn't have got out of there alive, and they sure as hell wouldn't have spent a whole page singing his praises in the newspapers. He works for one of the international news agencies. I forget which. His office is at Williamson House, corner of Baker and Angwa. Mugabe's probably asked him to keep an eye on you.'

Penny sighed deeply. 'David, for goodness' sake, why on earth would they bother to do that?' To Joe she said, 'He sees a conspiracy under every bush.'

David shrugged. 'OK then, maybe he's just looking for a story.'

'It's gone cold,' Joe said.

David laughed again. 'He told you that? Don't you believe it.'

It was so slow. When he pushed himself too hard his whole body seemed to lock itself into a single knot of pain. Twice the physiotherapist ordered days of complete bedrest. John

Harrington came in and told him he would delay the healing process if he pushed it too far. Joe ignored his advice. There was no word from Larry Wakeman, and Sister Rodrigues seemed embarrassed when Joe mentioned him. Maybe news of his visit had got out. The following Sunday Joe noticed that the policeman had gone from the door, and the next day, early, they wheeled him down for X-ray. In the afternoon Penny arrived in the church Renault 4 to take him back to the Vicarage.

Down Mazoe Avenue and left into North Avenue, bougainvillaeas and hibiscus bright in the hedges. Groups of black housemaids in pink nylon housecoats sitting splay-legged on the grass beneath the broad shade of the jacaranda trees, chatting, laughing. Aged white couples taking bags of groceries out of cars. Orange Rixi taxis, Mazda pickups and Datsun saloons. A truckload of troops heading west, bristling guns. Then left again into Prince Edward Street, past the broad green expanse of the Alexandra Sports Club, dotted with white youths in striped rugby shirts, the goalposts pointing two fingers skywards at those who said that colonial Africa was dead. Joe felt drunk with the light, the colour, the noise.

Penny was an erratic driver, fumbling for a paper tissue in her bag, narrowly missing wandering African cyclists at road junctions. Gesticulating, pointing out little items of interest and referring them back to Joe, cursing the gears when they failed to engage. She swung the car left into Harvey Brown Avenue and left again into Repton Square with such force that a shower of unidentifiable objects fell from the parcel shelf and clattered about on the floor.

St. Antony's Vicarage was tucked away beneath the msasa trees at the far end of the square, a white two-storied house behind galvanised gates and an hibiscus hedge. It stood edge-on to the road, facing the square red-brick church. Penny roared the car up to the gates and stopped dead in a shower of dust and fallen leaves. She stuck her head out of the window. 'Oliver!' she bellowed. To Joe she said, 'I can perfectly well open the gates myself, but he gets upset if I do.'

A thin, hook-nosed man in an oversized blue shirt and

34

floppy fawn trousers emerged from the garden, smiling broadly and clapping his hands in greeting. He unwound the chain from the gate and opened it. Penny re-started the car and accelerated it up to the back door of the house. Oliver shambled after them.

Penny got out of the car. 'Oliver,' she said, 'this is Mr. Joe. You had your day off when he came last time.'

'Kwaziwai. Makadini?' said Oliver, snaking an arm through the window to grasp Joe's hand.

'That means "Hello, how are you?",' said Penny. 'You should reply "Tiripo makadiniwo".'

Joe tried to get his mouth round the twisted vowels and consonants, but failed. Instead he said, 'Good afternoon.'

'Oliver will help you out of the car,' Penny said. 'I've made up a bed in the study so you won't have to take on the stairs. There's a toilet right next door to it.'

Later, on the stoep, Joe chose the chair that Ellie had sat in when they had been to the Vicarage those few weeks before, an upright wicker chair with low arms, rather than the more comfortable steel-framed lounger that Penny had prepared for him. Oliver fetched a carved footstool from the house for him to rest his leg on. David came across from the church and Becky appeared from somewhere in the garden. Oliver made the tea and put it on the table. It was a bright blue, fresh afternoon, like an afternoon in England in the early summer.

The unvarying rhythm of Vicarage life took over. He had breakfast in his room each morning, and then, slowly and painfully, he got himself dressed in the outsize tracksuit that Penny had found for him. She was away most mornings, teaching at the girls' school. Becky was at her nursery class. David was in and out from the church. They lunched on the stoep at noon, and dined there each evening. Oliver came and went, clipping the grass with shears, watering the plants in the big African grain pots, hanging out washing, shaking dusters. Twice a day Joe set out with his frame to make a slow circuit of Repton Square. He was stopped frequently by old white women who in some mysterious way seemed to know not only his name but the most intimate details of his injuries.

As time passed, individual days began to lose their shape and coherence and blend themselves into a single continuous span. There were moments of euphoria, usually at night, when the certainty that Ellie and the children were still alive and waiting for him possessed him entirely. But increasingly his hours in the wicker chair on the stoep were spent not reading, not thinking even, but in a sort of numb torpor that a visiting old lady once mistook for prayer. Penny took him to the hospital once a week for his examination, and out of deference to his hosts he went to church on Sundays. Gradually David gave up trying to talk to him about politics or parish matters, and Penny was able to make him laugh less and less, and then not at all.

A man from the High Commission called in twice during the month. There was no progress to report, he said. On the second occasion he brought Joe's passport, visaed until the end of March. Joe got the impression that the kidnapping had slipped someway down the order of priority and, in the absence of further developments that was where it was likely to remain. Larry Wakeman's 'contacts', and the information they were supposed to provide, slipped from his mind entirely.

October came in hard and dry and hot. The grass browned and shrivelled on the lawn despite Oliver's efforts with the sprinkler. At dinner the talk was of drought and the disastrous consequences if the rains failed for a third year.

On the fourteenth they removed the plaster from his leg, hacking through it with shears, twisting the steel spikes from his bone with a brace. His leg swelled until it looked like the leg of the Michelin man. Where the bullets had entered and exited there were purple pits. His skin was flaked and scaly like a reptile. The physiotherapist prescribed a programme of exercises that ran to two sides of a sheet of A4 recycled paper, and told him not to put his foot on the floor. He was fitted with a pair of grey elbow crutches. When Penny drove him home, the Avenues glowed with the purple of the jacarandas. That evening she mentioned airfares and flight times to London.

It was like being released from prison, the freedom he felt with the plaster gone. Within a week he could swing himself along on his crutches at considerable speed and made expeditions along the Avenues and to the Montague Shopping Mall. Sometimes he ate lunch at Guido's in the Mall, a T-bone steak or peri-peri chicken. He'd have two, sometimes three Castle lagers with his meal. He struck up an acquaintance with a red-faced man with a long greying beard who told him that he was a survivor. 'We're all survivors,' he would say, sweeping an arm to include the whole room. 'All of us. Even the Afs.' The mural of Old Venice with gondolas was flaking where the chair backs rubbed against it. The fans turned overhead, creating small draughts that lifted the paper napkins on the tables.

On Mondays and Thursdays he walked to the hospital where he submitted placidly to the physiotherapist's pummelling fingers. The stiffness was beginning to leave his shoulder, though the strength had still not returned. The swelling in his leg began slowly to subside. On Tuesday November the fifteenth a call was received in St. Antony's Vicarage. It was from Inspector Welcome Mtisi at Harare Central Police Station. Penny answered it, and when Joe returned from the bakery on Prince Edward Street where he was buying bread, she took him into town in the car.

He stood still for a while after Penny had left. It was early afternoon. Heat bounced from the pavement, hurting his face and eyes. Across the road at Inez Terrace Bus Station market women sat patiently behind piles of tomatoes and oranges, suckling small brown babies or crochetting circular table cloths in cream-coloured wool.

He felt an acute and growing reluctance to enter the vast modern biscuit-coloured building behind him. He wished he'd answered the call from Mtisi himself. Maybe he could have gleaned something from his tone of voice, caught him off-guard and got the answer to a direct question – something, anything, that would have prepared him for what was to come. He'd grown used to his own helplessness and ignorance, he realised. He felt comfortable with it. Perhaps even now he should walk away, buy a ticket, take a taxi to the airport. At least it would leave his dreams intact, the good dreams and the bad. It was not just the scars on his body that were beginning to heal. He felt vulnerable, panicky, curiously short of breath. A dull ache was developing in his leg. The curved supports of his crutches felt like manacles on his arms.

'May I be of assistance, sah? Do you require assistance to mount the steps?' A young policeman stood beside him, boots gleaming, teeth white.

'I'm sorry?'

'The steps are steep, sah.'

'No, thank you. I can manage.'

A grey Nissan truck came down Inez Terrace at speed and swung down the ramp behind the police station. Two black faces were visible through the steel mesh at the back, and four hands. Joe followed the vehicle with his eyes. The young policeman backed off and stood at a respectable distance. Joe smiled at him. The smile was immediately returned. 'I've got to do these things myself,' Joe said.

'Ah,' said the policeman. 'Rehabilitation.'

'You're dead right.' As he pulled himself up the twin flight of steps to the glass door at the top, Joe tried to square the politeness and civility of the young policeman with what he knew of the man he was going to meet. He failed.

The office was small and white-painted with a narrow window containing thick glass toughened with wire netting. There was a wooden desk of old-fashioned design on which stood an elaborate double pen holder and a telephone. Two grey filing cabinets stood against one wall. On the other were hung twin portraits of President Canaan Banana and Robert Mugabe. The room had a sour smell.

Inspector Mtisi dismissed the escorting officer with a wave of his hand and advanced towards Joe. 'Mr. Lejeune,' he said, 'so good of you to come. You appear to be making a very satisfactory recovery. Come, take a seat.' Before Joe had time to react, he had taken his arm and guided him to a plastic-padded metal chair. 'I'll put your crutches in the corner,' he said. Joe parted with them reluctantly. He felt that surrendering the crutches in some way cut off his means of escape.

The Inspector went to one of the filing cabinets and unlocked it, took out a buff folder which he spread on the desk. 'Mr. Lejeune,' he said, 'I am glad to report that we have made great progress since we last met. Our Security Forces have not been idle – indeed, far from it. They have pursued the bandits responsible for the attack on your family with great vigour and persistence. As the saying goes, If at first you don't succeed, try, try and try again. Well, Mr. Lejeune, they have tried, and they have tried again, and they have succeeded.'

'You've found them?'

The Inspector paused. 'We have traced and eliminated the bandits responsible.'

'Eliminated?' Joe felt a growing sense of unreality, as though he was taking part in a film or a play.

The Inspector smiled. 'Unfortunately, they attempted to resist arrest. In consequence our forces had no alternative but to open fire. We did, however, succeed in capturing one of the gang alive. He is wounded but in no danger. He has made a full and frank confession.' He produced a number of sheets of typescript, stapled together. 'I have it here,' he said. 'Unfortunately the statement was made in Sindebele, which, as you know, is the language commonly spoken in Matabeleland, and we have not yet had time to arrange for a translation to be made. However, I will paraphrase its contents. Naturally, certain sections of it I cannot reveal to you for security reasons.'

'Listen,' said Joe harshly, 'before we get to that, will you please tell me what has happened to Ellie and the kids?'

The Inspector's eyes met his, and held them. 'Mr. Lejeune,' he said quietly, 'I think you should wait until I have been through the statement. It is quite possible that it will answer many of the questions you will naturally be anxious to ask me.'

Joe shrugged. 'Do I have any alternative?'

The Inspector glanced again at the statement and cleared his throat. 'The name of the captured bandit is Kephas Ndhlovu,' he said, 'and what he says is this: he was trained in South Africa at a place called Letaba, and entered Zimbabwe in April 1983. In the company of a number of companions he then embarked on a series of outrages against people and property in Southern Matabeleland, including bus robbery, the rape, mutilation and killing of five women and children in the Dibilishaba Communal Lands, and the murder of a white farmer in the Kezi district.

'Because of security operations by the Zimbabwe Army

and Police, the gang were forced to leave their home area and travel east. On the eighth of August they were south of Chiredzi near the Nandi-Chipinda Pools road. They were short of food and money. Their leader, a man named Lucas Ncube, suggested that they stop and rob a car driven by a European. They waited until one was sighted and then stopped it. They stole everything they could carry, then took the four Europeans, a man, a woman and two children, into the bush. There Lucas Ncube shot the white man. He was left near the road . . .'

The Inspector stopped. 'Mr. Lejeune,' he said, 'I think you must prepare yourself for what follows. So that there can be no doubts, I will translate the bandit's words directly for you.'

'Please,' said Joe quietly. He was conscious of the blood pounding in his head.

'Very well. This is what the bandit Ndhlovu says. "After two days one of the children became sick. We had an ukwejisa – that is a meeting – to decide what to do. Some of us urged that the woman and children should be set free. Others, including Lucas Ncube, disagreed. When the ukwejisa was concluded, Lucas Ncube and a man called Twoboy Khumalo took the woman and children into the bush. Shots were heard. When the two men returned, they were alone."'

Joe gripped the arm of the chair as though the black plastic and metal might explode and hurl him forward into space. The pounding in his head was like the firing of heavy guns. 'Where are they?' he said.

'I'm afraid we didn't recover the bodies.'

'Why not?'

When we went to the place where the bandit Ndhlovu told us that the shooting had occurred, the bodies were no longer there.'

'What do you mean, not there?'

The Inspector breathed heavily. 'You must understand, Mr. Lejeune, it is a long time since August, Hyenas, jackals . . .'

Joe bent forward and put his head into his hands. She would have known. Ellie would have known what was coming. He could see them, the three of them, stumbling forward over the rocks, through the thorns. He could see them turn, the children puzzled, holding Ellie's hands. And Ellie so quiet, so calm. Thinking of the children. Putting her arms round them. And then, in those last moments, looking up at the men with the guns . . .

'Hyenas,' he said.

The Inspector said, 'The Prime Minister and Comrade Zvarevashe have asked me to give you their sincere condolences. To which, of course, I add my own.'

'No,' said Joe. 'Not hyenas.'

They'd seen hyenas at Kariba one night when they were staying with Phil Dyer early in the holiday. There were a pair of them on the garbage dump among the rusting tin cans and broken bottles. They'd been pulling at something. When they'd looked up, straight into the car headlights, he'd seen their black-edged jaws and the shining of their eyes. Their jaws could mark steel, he'd read somewhere. Oh Lord. Oh sweet Lord. For the first time in his life he wished he had the comfort of prayer.

Minutes passed. They might have been hours. Outside in the corridor there were footsteps, the jingle of keys. Then the Inspector said, 'I'm afraid I have one last painful duty for you to perform, Mr. Lejeune. We are anxious to bring the bandit Ndhlovu to justice with the minimum of delay. In order to facilitate this, and to prevent any possibility that there might be a miscarriage of justice, I must ask you to confirm the identity of the bandits we have killed and captured as the men who were responsible for the attack upon you and your family.'

'I don't understand.'

Inspector Mtisi hesitated. When he spoke it was slowly, simply, as though addressing a child. 'I have some photographs here. I want you to look at them, and then sign a statement we have prepared for you which says that you recognise the men you see.'

Joe realised that the policeman had taken a number of large black and white photographs from the file and was pushing them towards him across the desk. The Inspector said, 'They are not the most pleasant of snaps, I am afraid.'

Not knowing what he was doing, or why, Joe took the pictures. The first one was a number of black men laid side by side on what looked like concrete. Their arms were spread above their heads. One of the men was wearing a FANTA tee shirt, the others, tattered bits of civilian clothing. Their bellies were swollen tight over the waistbands of their trousers. There were many bullet holes. Their clothes and arms and faces looked as if they had been sprayed with blood.

He stared at the pictures for a long time, still not under-standing. The Inspector said, 'The other snaps are close-ups. You will find them more explicit.'

Joe shuffled through them. The faces of the dead men seemed strangely artificial, like wax heads. Their eyes were closed, faces expressionless. When he had finished looking at them he said, 'Who are these men?'

'Mr. Lejeune, these are the men who attacked and robbed you. Please look at them again. Take your time.' The Inspector reached across and spread the pictures like playing cards along the edge of the desk.

After a while Joe said, 'They were wearing camouflage gear, the men who stopped us. Some of them were wearing camouflage gear.'

'So you said at our previous interview.'

'That's why we stopped. We thought they were the army. None of these men are wearing camouflage gear.'

Then, something else caught his eye. He picked up the picture of the man in the FANTA tee shirt. It had been a yellow tee shirt. This was white. And the bearded man, the leader, the one with the skin complaint, where was he? There was a man with a beard, sure, but he was too young, and his beard was too long, and his skin was as smooth as a baby's. 'These are not the men,' he said quietly.

The Inspector stiffened with irritation. 'Nonsense, Mr. Lejeune. Please sign this statement.' He placed a typewritten sheet of paper in front of Joe. It read, 'I, Joseph Lejeune, hereby confirm that the photographs I have been shown are those of the men who took part in the assault on myself and my family on the Nandi-Chipinda Pools road on August 8th 1983.'

'But they're the wrong men. Why should I sign a paper which says they're the right men when they're not?'

'Mr. Lejeune, you must understand that those men had

been dead for some time before the photographs were taken. Certain changes take place in bodies after death, particularly in the hot sun. Gases . . . Appearance can change considerably.'

'And what about the camouflage gear, where's that gone to? And the tee shirt?'

'What about the tee shirt?'

'It was yellow. The man in the picture's wearing a white one.'

The Inspector hesitated, something close to uncertainty in his eyes. He picked up the picture that Joe had indicated and examined it carefully. 'I'm sorry, Mr. Lejeune, the tee shirt is yellow. Light yellow. The quality of the photography . . .'

'Is perfectly adequate. In my job I deal with black and white photographs every day. That guy is wearing a white shirt. Not yellow, white. Show me the picture again.'

'That is not necessary.' The Inspector slipped the photograph back into the file and gathered up the others. 'The photographer himself will vouch for the colour of that shirt.'

'Where is he? I want to see him.'

'Unfortunately he is not in Harare.'

'How convenient.'

The Inspector sighed. 'Come now, Mr. Lejeune, you are beginning to behave in a ridiculous manner.'

'It's not me being ridiculous.'

There was a sudden silence. The Inspector seemed uncomfortable. Once or twice he darted a look at the door as if he was expecting somebody. He was beginning to sweat, Joe noticed.

'Come on, tell me', Joe pressed him. 'Why aren't they wearing camouflage?'

Once more the Inspector sighed. 'They are not wearing camouflage because it is illegal, Mr. Lejeune. The wearing of camouflage by unauthorised persons is forbidden by act of Parliament. When they were apprehended, those men were wearing the clothes you saw them in. I am not denying that they may have worn camouflage during their attack on you, but they were not wearing it when they were apprehended. Now will you please sign the paper?'

Joe felt suddenly calm, alert. Mtisi wanted him to sign. It

was important to him, vitally important. Zvarevashe, maybe even Mugabe, was waiting on the signature. Joe was now convinced that there was something wrong. If these weren't the men, if the pictures were fake, if the bandit's 'confession' was just a pack of lies, then . . . 'Nothing on this earth will induce me to sign that paper,' he said. 'I refuse to take part in this fraud.'

'Mr' Lejeune,' the Inspector said sharply, 'there has been no fraud, as you put it. We merely wish to secure a speedy conviction.'

'OK then, where's this so-called bandit? What's his name – Novoludo? Why can't I see him?'

'Ndhlovu. One moment.' The Inspector picked up the telephone and dialled a two-digit number, said something quickly in Shona and replaced the receiver. 'If you will be patient,' he said.

He got up and straightened the already straight picture of President Banana on the wall. 'Mr. Lejeune, you seem to have adopted an obstructive and unhelpful attitude to our enquiries from the beginning. We, for our part, have done our best to treat this behaviour of yours with sympathy and understanding. We appreciate how you feel. Many of us have lost loved ones in the war, and sometimes it is difficult to come to terms with this loss. There is a tendency to look for some-body to blame. We have done our very best to resolve your case successfully. We are modestly proud of our efforts. The terror gang responsible will terrorise innocent people no longer.

'Unfortunately, we did not reach your wife and children in time to save them. They are dead. You must accept that they are dead, Mr. Lejeune, however difficult that may be, and not try to blame us. Instead you must help us to bring the surviv-ing bandit to the justice he so richly deserves with the mini-mum of delay. Then I strongly suggest you return to England and attempt to rebuild your life.' He stopped, wiped his brow with a handkerchief. 'In any case,' he went on, 'what reason could we have for trying to deceive you?'

'You tell me.'

'The answer is none. We have eliminated a band of very dangerous dissidents, trained in South Africa and sent into

44

this country to commit acts of terror such as that which they perpetrated upon you. We have nothing to hide.'

'You're lying.'

'Mr. Lejeune, we are not lying.'

'OK then, show me the bodies. If they are dead I want to take them home with me. To England. I want to establish how they died and when.'

'As I have already explained, hyenas . . .'

'Hyenas! Fuck the hyenas! Did they eat their clothes, their shoes?'

'Hyenas will eat anything.'

'Even non-existent bodies?'

A police siren wailed. The Inspector went to the window and looked out. 'We seem to be getting nowhere,' he said. 'I suggest that when you are slightly calmer you take another look at the photographs. You will see then that there has been no mistake.'

Footsteps. A knock at the door. 'In!' said the Inspector.

Two uniformed policemen entered. Handcuffed between them was a youth in his early twenties. He wore a ragged blue shirt torn at the shoulder and a pair of grey trousers, one of the legs of which had been torn away to reveal a blood-soaked bandage beneath. He wore no shoes. His face was puffed and swollen. One eye was closed. There were what looked like splashes of dried blood on his shirt. The policemen drew themselves to attention.

'This is the bandit Ndhlovu,' Inspector Mtisi said. And then he suddenly shouted at the man in what Joe took to be Sindebele.

The man looked up, and then looked at Joe. For an instant their eyes met. There was no spark of recognition.

The Inspector shouted again. Ndhlovu mumbled something in reply.

Mtisi turned to Joe. 'He confirms that you are the white man that Lucas Ncube shot on the Chipinda Pools road.'

'Bullshit,' said Joe. 'I've never seen this man in my life before, and he's never seen me.' He got up from the chair and faced the captive. 'Go on, tell him. You've never seen me before. Tell him the truth.'

'He doesn't speak English,' said Mtisi.

Suddenly Ndhlovu said, 'A little bit English.'

'OK,' said Joe. 'Now you tell him. Have you seen me

before? Go on, man. Maybe you can save yourself. Tell him, just tell him.'

For a moment Joe thought the man was going to speak but then he looked at Mtisi and at the two policemen on either side of him. When he turned back to Joe his swollen face was expressionless.

'He doesn't understand,' said Mtisi.

'Like fuck he doesn't understand!' Joe hopped towards Ndhlovu. 'Tell him!' he screamed. 'Tell him!'

But Mtisi had made a quick movement with his head and the handcuffed man was hustled from the room. The door slammed shut.

Joe turned to Mtisi but lost his balance. The Inspector grabbed him. His movements were quick for such a large man, his grip tight. He led Joe back to the chair.

'There is your proof, Mr. Lejeune. Now, would you like to see the photographs again before you sign the statement? I have also a second statement here confirming your identification of the bandit Ndhlovu. Both require your signature.'

'No!' shouted Joe. 'No, no, no!'

'In that case, I shall reluctantly have to recommend to the relevant authorities that your visitor's visa, which I understand has been extended until March, should be terminated forthwith.'

Joe sat still, panting slightly, then he grabbed the papers and signed.

'Thank you Mr. Lejeune. Your co-operation is greatly appreciated.'

Mtisi went to the corner and returned with the crutches. 'Mr. Lejeune,' he said, 'if I might say so, I think you should seek psychiatric help. We have excellent psychiatrists in this country.'

'Go fuck yourself,' said Joe.

Williamson House. He remembered the name because when David had mentioned it, it had made him think of Danny Williamson in the Studio. The taxi driver knew the place. Joe gave the guy a five dollar bill and didn't wait for the change. Larry Wakeman would listen. There was a good story in it, a damned good story. All the stuff about Wakeman being a member of the Mugabe government was so much crap. It had to be. David was full of crap like that.

'Ellie,' he said to himself over and over again as he took the lift to the second floor of the steel and glass building. 'Ellie. Ellie. Ellie.'

He found the journalist alone. He was wearing a white short-sleeved shirt piped with red, and red jeans of the same tone. He was in a small glassed-off area to one side of the main office, operating the telex machine. Tape hung in bunches from hooks. There was a poster on the glass reading 'Keep in Tune with Radio Mozambique'. An expensive reel-to-reel recorder was playing David Bowie. Wakeman said, 'Hey man, sit down. I just got to finish punching up this story.'

When he came out he shook Joe's hand. 'Sorry I didn't catch up with you,' he said, 'but nothing gave. Anyway, I gather they've got the bastards.'

'You know about it?'

'I make it my business to know these things. You've been to see Mtisi, I guess. I'm sorry about your wife and family.'

'They're not dead,' Joe said.

The journalist looked at him in surprise. 'I don't follow.'

'They've got the wrong men. Ellie and the kids aren't dead because those men didn't kill them.' Joe stopped suddenly. Maybe it was the air conditioning, but he felt cold, very cold. He began to shake violently.

Larry noticed. 'I got some Scotch here,' he said. 'You want some?'

Joe nodded numbly. Larry fished out a half bottle of Johnny Walker and two glasses from the desk and poured a couple of measures. Joe took the glass and drained it, gasping as the alcohol burned its way down into his stomach. 'They've got a confession,' Larry said. 'They've issued it to the press.'

'Lies.'

'That's not the impression I get. This man Ndhlovu . . .'

'I've never seen him before. They showed me pictures – I never saw any of those men before. And the clothes were wrong.'

'Wrong?'

'There was a tee shirt, a FANTA tee shirt. The one in the

47

picture was white. The one I remember was yellow. And the dead men were wearing civilian clothes, not camouflage.'

'Camouflage?' Larry seemed puzzled. 'You mean the guys that attacked you were wearing camouflage? You didn't tell me that.'

'I didn't think it was important at the time.'

Still looking puzzled, Larry went towards the window. Before he reached it, he turned. 'Any identifying features? Shoulder tabs, that kind of thing?'

'No.'

'And on their heads?'

'Forage caps. Bush hats. Some of them were bare-headed.'

The telex began to chatter in the glass-walled room. Larry went to the machine, ripped off the sheet, scanned it briefly and then placed it in a wire tray labelled 'Central Africa'. He walked slowly back to the desk and sat down. 'OK,' he said. 'I think I've got the picture. Let me tell you what I know. Lucas Ncube and Twoboy Khumalo, the two guys Ndhlovu named, were active ZIPRA fighters during the war, associated closely with Masuku, one of Nkomo's commanders. When Mugabe started moving in on ZIPRA in 1982 and arrested Masuku, Ncube and Khumalo fled to Botswana and holed up at Dukwe refugee camp. From there it's more than likely that the two of them went down to South Africa for training and came back into Zimbabwe in April. So I'm afraid that particular story holds up. Ndhlovu I'd never heard of. Or if I have, the name didn't register. But that doesn't mean he wasn't part of the group.

'The C.I.O. have got a pretty good intelligence network down there, so it's entirely probable that the Army were told that Ncube and Khumalo were back in Matabeleland, and were moving in on them. So where do they go? East. It's the only place they *can* go. According to my information Khumalo has a Shangaan mother, and it's Shangaan tribal territory down there, which makes it even more likely. They probably established themselves in Sengwe or Matibi, and from there made the attack on your family back in August.'

'But they didn't,' said Joe.

Larry drained his Scotch. 'I think they did, Joe.'

The phone rang. Larry picked it up. He said something sharply in Shona and put the receiver down. 'That's my wife Eva,' he said. 'We're speaking Shona this week – when we're speaking at all.'

Joe said, 'You're going to do something about it?'

'About Eva?'

Joe felt his anger rising. 'About the lies they're telling.'

Larry took a deep breath. 'Listen, Joe,' he said quietly, 'I think you've got to accept that at the time of the attack you were confused, frightened. Lots of black faces . . .'

'Bullshit!'

'The story holds up, Joe, Ncube and Khumalo . . .'

'And the tee shirt?'

'There's hundreds of those tee shirts around, thousands. White, yellow, green, blue, black . . . Maybe the guy had a whole set. Your wife and family are dead, man, and those guys killed them. You've got to accept that.'

'No!' Joe smashed his fist down on to the desk. 'I won't! Not till I see their bodies.'

'Then you're going to have a long wait.' The journalist ran his fingers through his hair. 'Listen to me,' he said. 'Even if you're right, even if those guys didn't do it, the chances that your wife and kids are alive are remote. I mean, where do you hide a white woman and two white kids for three months without word getting out? It'd be suicide.'

'You told me – near Kezi.'

'Forget Kezi. I checked it out. My contacts . . .'

'They're at Kezi, I know they are.'

Larry stood up. 'Jesus Christ, man,' he said, 'will you see reason? Look, I can think of one other theory. Just one. Assuming this is some kind of devious plot by Zvarevashe – which it isn't – there's only one possible motive for it: that you were attacked by a group of guys from a regular army unit. It would account for the fact that they were wearing camouflage. If the Fifth Brigade were down in the Lowveld I would have said it was a real possibility – but they're not. It's Fourth Brigade territory, and it's just not their style. In any case, if it was the Army, your family are dead for sure. And believe me, you'll get nowhere in this country trying to pin anything on the Army.'

'But you'll help me?' Joe felt the shaking, stilled by the Scotch, return.

'I don't follow?'

'You'll write this up. Get it printed in whatever papers you work for. You'll say there's been a set-up, that they've shot and tortured a whole lot of innocent guys. That Ellie and Cassie and Ben are probably still alive out there somewhere.'

'I'm sorry,' said Larry. 'I can't do that.'

'Why not?'

'Because you're wrong. And even if you were right, nobody would want to know.'

Joe got to his feet. He gripped the edge of the desk to stop his shaking. 'You're just a Mugabe stooge,' he said. 'Like the rest of them. Worse than the rest because you pretend not to be. Just a fucking Mugabe stooge! I've heard about you. I know what you're like.'

The telex machine chattered again. 'Look,' said the journalist, 'I'm kind of busy.'

Joe picked up his crutches and went to the door. 'I'm going to Kezi,' he said. 'I'm going to find them.' He went out and punched at the lift button.

'You're off your head!' Larry shouted. 'You hear me? Go home! Go back to England!'

The lift doors opened, and then closed again.

The police patrol picked Joe up at three minutes past midnight, wandering in the middle of Rotten Row, dodging traffic. He'd lost one of his crutches, and his clothes were stained with vomit and blood from a cut near his ear. When the police tried to get him into the car he fought with them. They took him to Beatrice Road Police Station and put him in a cell. He told the police he was going to Kezi, and he called them lying black bastards. One of the policeman hit him hard in the stomach. At two a.m. David arrived and took him back to the Vicarage. The police decided not to press charges. The Duty Sergeant's son was in David's confirmation class.

He stayed in bed until mid-afternoon. When Becky called him for lunch he ignored her. Once he heard the telephone ring. Apart from a slight headache, and some pain when he breathed deeply, he felt fine. Never better. He was thinking, planning. He'd found a couple of maps behind David's desk, and spread out the sheet covering the southern half of the country on the bed. He was concentrating on the Kezi area.

He hadn't realised how close Kezi was to Bulawayo, just south of the Matopos Hills. It was a one-horse town, he guessed, like so many they'd passed through on their travels: a church, a bank, a filling station, a couple of African stores, not much else. Probably not even a hotel. He'd avoid Kezi if possible, unless his search took him there. The Matopos, that would be where they would be. There was a cave marked, Silozwane, with a cross denoting a place of special historical interest. There'd be other caves no doubt. There were a lot of mines south of Kezi: the Antelope, Sun Yat Sen, Legion, Blanket. Where there were mines there'd be mineshafts, abandoned buildings. He'd take it slowly, systematically, square mile by square mile. He'd find someone, a guide, a tracker, who spoke Sindebele. He'd wire Mac for money and buy a car – no, better, a Land-Rover. And camping equipment. And a gun. That one was more difficult. He'd find some farmer, maybe, willing to part with one for a consideration, no questions asked. He'd cross that bridge when he came to it.

But first he had to get fit. That was the priority. It would take him two weeks. No, more. Four, probably. He'd do exercises. Press-ups. Fuck the pain. Swimming was good. He cursed the Vicarage for not having a pool, but there'd be one nearby. He'd ask Penny, she'd know. Some neighbour. Somebody who came to church.

He rolled up the map and swung himself out of bed. His remaining crutch was resting against the table, but he ignored it. He was due at the hospital on Friday. The physiotherapist had said last time that all being well he'd be allowed to walk on the injured leg then. Well, all was well. He knew it without being told. He'd surprise the bitch, anticipate the event.

He put the foot on to the ground. A stab of pain transfixed his body and made him shout out loud, but he persisted and, clutching the top of the bookcase, walked one step, two. 'Penny!' he bellowed. 'Penny, I'm walking Penny!'

She didn't come. He walked a few steps more, still clutching the bookcase, and then two more steps to the bed.

The pain was bad but not that bad. Not like the pain when he was shot. Bearable. He lay on the bed panting, gasping for breath, laughing. 'I can walk,' he said. 'I can walk walk walk.'

Still laughing, he pulled on a pair of shorts and a tee shirt and walked slowly towards the door.

They were discussing him. Joe could sense it the moment he stepped out on to the stoep. Penny and David were sitting at the table, lunch things still not cleared away. They stopped talking when they saw him and turned to stare. 'I can walk,' he said to Penny. 'I can walk with both feet.'

'But it's too early.'

'I couldn't wait till Friday. It's easy. It doesn't hurt.' Penny's face, he noticed was blotched, puffy, as though she'd been crying. David looked thin and strained.

'You missed lunch,' Penny said.

'I wasn't hungry.'

Becky was playing on the lawn with her rabbit. The animal, affected by the heat, sat panting, unwilling to move. Oliver was clipping strands of new grown grass from the rockery near the church wall. 'Sit down,' David said.

Joe took the offered chair. Penny said, 'There's cheese and some ham.' She pushed plates towards him.

Joe ignored the food. He looked around. On the flamboyant tree behind the church the first flame-coloured blooms were opening. White and red butterflies jerked across the lawn. The tabby cat from next door was sitting in one of the flowerpots, watching the rabbit. 'Come on, Flopsy,' Becky said, poking the rabbit on its haunches. The animal hopped once and stopped. It continued panting.

Joe said to David, 'I want to ask you about Kezi.'

David didn't reply. He exchanged glances with Penny. His neck, Joe saw, was red where his clerical collar had been chafing. Penny looked at Joe. 'Larry Wakeman rang,' she said. 'He was worried about you.'

'You told him I was OK?'

'I told him you were asleep.'

She averted her eyes, embarrassed, uncomfortable. Suddenly David said, 'Sometimes it's very difficult for people to come to terms with bereavement. It's too final, too absolute. Sometimes it's easier to believe that the loved one is still alive.' He spoke stiffly, as if aware of the sound of his own voice. 'It's a recognised part of the grieving process. It happens particularly when death has been sudden from an accident, or a sudden unexpected illness like a heart attack. During the war it was common, very common. I saw it in the parents of young men killed in the bush. In young wives . . .'

Penny said gently, 'What David is trying to say is that we understand the way you feel. We want to help you to come to terms with what's happened. We want to come to terms with it ourselves.'

Joe poured himself a glass of orange juice and drank some of it. He flexed the muscles in his wounded thigh. 'You know somebody with a swimming pool?' he said. 'I want to do swimming, a lot of swimming.'

Penny leaned forward and put her hand on his. 'Please, Joe, listen to what we're saying. It's important.'

'That Indian diplomat you were telling me about. He must have a pool.'

'If you had faith,' David said, 'any kind of faith, it would help. It would help immeasurably.'

Penny said, 'Larry Wakeman has seen Mtisi. He's met the bandit for himself, seen the photographs you were shown. There's no conspiracy, no fraud, nothing. The man was tortured, he said, but he didn't seem to think there was anything unusual in that. It all checks out. Wakeman's very worried about you. He seems to think you'll do something stupid, get yourself killed or arrested.'

'We're worried about you too,' said David. 'Desperately worried.'

There was a long silence. A motorcycle buzzed past the hedge. Oliver's shears went clip clip clip at the grass.

Penny said, 'If only they'd found them. It would have been distressing, but at least you would have known.'

'Known what?' said Joe.

He didn't want to think about what Penny was saying. He wanted to think about swimming pools, long blue swimming pools with lines of corks bobbing. He was swimming a slow breaststroke, the only stroke he found really comfortable, pushing the water before him in low curls. He'd start with ten lengths maybe, and the work up to fifty, a hundred. The physiotherapist had recommended swimming. It exercises the whole body, takes the weight off the injured limb. It would give him time to think, too, work things out. He must get better maps and books, read up everything he could find. Maybe even start to learn Sindebele . . .

'Joe, we're talking to you!' David's voice brought him back with a start.

'Mtisi gave you no indication of where exactly it happened?' Penny asked.

'They're not dead.'

David swallowed. 'I know it might be hard to accept,' he said, 'with them still being missing, but they're dead, Joe.'

He didn't want to hear all that shit. He drained his orange juice and slapped the glass on to the table. 'You think what you like,' he said. 'You wanna believe that guy, you go ahead. He doesn't know the truth when it hits him between the eyes. I was there. I know what I saw. I don't have to face up to anything, because I know.'

Penny lit a cigarette with shaking hands, once more close to tears.

And then, suddenly, Joe's anger left him. 'Penny,' he said, 'what do you want me to do – fly home to England and forget about Ellie and Cassie and Ben, when I *know* they've got the wrong men? When I *know* they're still alive?'

'But you don't know,' said David.

'Oh, yes I do. I know because I choose to know.'

'That's ridiculous.'

Joe spun to face the priest. 'What was it you said?' he demanded. 'If I had faith? If I only had faith. Well, I've *got* faith. I've got faith that they're alive. That's my faith.'

David flushed a bright pink and avoided looking at Joe. 'I had thought of holding some sort of memorial service, getting all Ellie's friends together.'

'David, for Christ's sake!' Penny flared.

He flushed again, stammered. 'It just seemed to me. . .'

Penny turned to Joe. 'The Petersens have a pool,' she said. 'They live up in Colenbrander Road. I'm sure they'll let you use it.'

The report was in the *Herald* next morning. The headline

read, 'Kidnap Gang Smashed', and there was a picture of Samuel Zvarevashe. Joe didn't bother to read it. Penny fixed up for him to use the Petersens' pool as she had promised, and he went over at ten. It was oval-shaped and the water was green and tasted bad, but it was better than nothing. He remembered the Petersens from church. They were an old couple. He had white hair and a big belly. She was small, with skin as creased and brown as a walnut. They said how sorry they were about his wife and children, but at least justice had been done.

Joe swam four lengths that first day. On the fourth length he thought he was going to drown. He was conscious of nothing while he swam, except for the pain in his body and the way his lungs burned for oxygen. He drank a Castle with the old man afterwards at the mosaic and thatch poolside bar. Petersen told him he'd made his money in chrome during UDI. Mugabe didn't like him, but he couldn't afford to kick him out. He hadn't gapped it down to South Africa at Independence like the others, and didn't intend to now.

Later, David gave Joe a lift into town. They made the journey in silence. Joe guessed that somehow, obscurely, the priest felt humiliated by what had happened on the stoep the day before. They went to Barclays on First Street, and Joe went to the mezzanine floor to Cables, Drafts and Transfers where he arranged for £2,000 sterling to be transferred from his account in London. With the money he intended to buy training shoes, a tracksuit, a set of weights if he could find them, and a bicycle, and put the rest towards the Land-Rover. He'd write to Mac and get him to ask Morgan to make more funds available. The clerk said the money would take five days to come through, maybe longer.

On the way home David had to call in to see a sick woman in Highlands. While he was there, Joe went into the second-hand bookshop in Newlands Shopping Centre and bought a paperback edition of the *Royal Canadian Air Force Physical Fitness Book* for 50 cents. He determined to work through it, cover to cover. He was walking easier now. His leg still hurt where he pressured it, but the muscles already felt firmer. Outside on the pavement, waiting for David to return, Joe exercised his left arm, revolving it like a windmill. A group of small black boys watched him, astonished.

That day, and for several days afterwards, people called at the Vicarage to express sympathy: old friends of Ellie's, neighbours, people from church. Joe accepted their condolences in silence, and waited until they went away. Most didn't stay long.

By Friday he was swimming twelve lengths of the Petersen's pool. Mrs. Petersen had taken to laying out a towel for him each day, and the old man ordered chemicals to clean up the water. At the hospital, the physiotherapist expressed her sympathy at his bereavement, and anger at his disobeying her orders. She told him that swimming was good exercise. He told her he'd consider taking it up.

'Front lying, hands under the shoulders, palms flat on the floor. Touch the chin to floor in front of hands – touch forehead to floor behind hands before returning to up position.'

It hurt. It hurt a lot and it wasn't getting any better.

'Stationary run. Lift feet approximately four inches off floor. After every seventy-five steps do ten half knee bends. Repeat sequence.'

Some days it was his shoulder that hurt, today it was his legs. There was a numbness in his foot that worried him. Each step sent a shudder of pain up his body and into his neck.

'Feet together. Hands on hips, knees bent to form an angle of a hundred and ten degrees. Do not bend knees past a right angle.'

Sunday morning. He could hear the singing from the church. 'Lift up your heart, lift up your voice. Rejoice again, I say, rejoice.' The wooden boards of the stoep creaked and bent where his feet hit them. Thirty-four, thirty-five, thirty-six. It had taken him twenty-two days to reach level three in the book. It should have taken him eight. He had the achievement level of a sixty-year-old. His own father could do better. Old Petersen with his belly and varicose veins could do better. A one-legged, brain-damaged cripple could do better. Forty-eight, forty-nine, fifty. Exercises shouldn't hurt, the book said. Fuck the book.

'Straighten to an upright position, raising heels off floor.

56

Return to starting position each time. Keep feet in contact with floor.'

It was December 11th, and he was failing. Failing! Penny had said before she went to church, 'Ease up. Take it easy. Sunday's a day of rest, in case you hadn't heard.' Well, he hadn't heard. Fifty-five, fifty-six, fifty-seven.

He'd got nowhere. Twenty days in and he was still here on this dusty, creaking, god-forsaken stoep. He hadn't the strength to take on a two-year-old child, and he'd got nowhere about finding out about Kezi. All the books on Matabeleland seemed to date from the 1890s. There was plenty about Lobengula and Rhodes, nothing about Matabeleland now, just guidebook stuff which was worse than useless. He couldn't even find a Sindebele dictionary when he went to look for one.

Sixty-two, sixty-three, sixty-four. If he just pushed harder there'd be a breakthrough, some kind of breakthrough. There had to be. He needed it. He ached for it. He sweated for it.

Sixty-nine, seventy, seventy-one. The money hadn't come either. He'd written to Mac and Mac had told him it wouldn't be ready till after Christmas. Christ! Did it take so long to put five grand into a bank account? So much for all that sympathy. So much for 'We'll do anything to help.' Fuck him. Fuck Morgan. Fuck the lot of them.

No money. No strength. No information. He had his bike of course, a light blue Armstrong he'd picked up from a small ad in the *Sunday Mail* for $300. That was good. That was a beginning. He'd been round town and out to the suburbs, and on Thursday he'd gone all the way to Lake MacIlwaine. He'd make another long trip soon. The Mazoe Dam maybe, or Goromonzi, somewhere like that.

But he shouldn't be here at all. Not now. Not after three weeks. He should be somewhere south of Bulawayo, making friends with the missionaries, investigating caves. He was weak, pathetic, repulsive. A grown man given to weeping in his room.

Sometimes he understood why. At night, when the tree crickets were chirruping outside his window, he knew that it was not weakness or lack of money that stopped him but fear.

He was not frightened for himself. He no longer feared

pain or humiliation but knowledge. It was the same fear he had felt once before, that day at the police station when he had gone to see Mtisi. Only in ignorance could he protect his dreams, his delicate, carefully-nurtured dreams, vulnerable as slender-stalked flowers. The truth, whatever it was, would smash them, beat them to the ground. He didn't need the truth. He couldn't risk it. Without the dreams he was alone and life could not continue. Perhaps he should go home.

But it was the dreams themselves that stopped him. It was Ellie, Ben, Cassie, the substance of his dreams. In the good dreams they were waiting for him, always waiting, infinitely patient. They depended on him, they trusted him. To leave them would be to betray them, and he couldn't contemplate such a betrayal.

And even the bad dreams spoke to him, the dreams of bleached bones, of ants nesting in rotten flesh, of rape and pain and terror. Those were the dreams that urged him on, that pursued him to knowledge, that fed his fear. He had to find them. He had to know.

Once more the circle would close, and the sweat would rise on his body, and the tears would come.

Seventy-three, seventy-four, seventy-five. He slumped to the floor, his chest heaving, sweat drenching his tee shirt. People were coming out of church now, in small family groups, clustering at the door, picking up teacups from the trestle table, David standing amongst them in his green cope, hands clasped. One or two, old women mostly, waved at Joe with small, restrained waves. He spotted the Petersens. They were talking about him, sympathising with David and Penny. What a tragedy, what a burden. Wouldn't he be better off back in England, starting life over again.

Shit. Shit shit shit.

His language was getting worse, the obscenities of impotence. He must go, he must get out of here.

Penny was coming across the lawn hand in hand with Becky, the little girl demure in her white church dress. Joe had begun to hate the closeness of this tight family, the way they drew into themselves. Penny could sympathise but she couldn't understand. He was an outcast. He needed the company of other outcasts.

'Breakfast,' said Penny, smiling as she reached him. 'Bacon and eggs.'

Joe knew he could no longer play happy families.

He found the Rondavel by chance. He'd asked old man Petersen if he knew anybody who rented rooms, and he'd sent Joe to see his grand-daughter who lived in a communal house in Marlborough. She wasn't there when Joe arrived, but there was a guy with long hair who was carving an electric guitar from a slice of hardwood. He told Joe about the Rondavel. He thought there might be a space. He said, 'Ask for Christina. Tell her Jeff sent you.'

It was off Widdecombe Road, in the south of the city on the way to the airport, a couple of circular thatched huts joined by a sprawl of flat-roofed rooms and corridors. There was a high fence, a large flamboyant tree, and behind the rainwater tank a candelabrum tree, its cactus branches like so many gnarled hands. A sign on the gate said 'Beware of the Dog', but there was no dog, just geese. Three of them. They squawked and hissed when Joe came.

The girl called Christina was making earrings in the first of the huts. It was surprisingly tall, a cool building, with a concrete floor. Parts of a bicycle lay in one corner, and an old Remington typewriter. Some children's books were arranged on a board held up by bricks. She was twisting earrings from fuse wire, lacing red and white and black Swazi beads. There was a large round table made from what looked like an old cable drum. She was twenty-five, maybe more, with dark hair cut like a brush. She was wearing loose white shorts and a red singlet. The nipples on her compact breasts were prominent.

Joe watched her through the open doorway. She was aware of him watching but didn't look up. She twisted at the wire with pointed pliers. Still not looking up she said, 'You want a room?'

'How did you know?'

'Jeff rang. You're a friend of Marianne's.'

'I know her grandfather.'

'Old man Petersen?'

Joe nodded. Only then did the girl raise her eyes to his. They were smallish and dark, set in a sharp-featured face. She was not beautiful, but looking at her he felt a twinge of desire for her breasts, her smooth brown thighs. He thought of making love with her slowly, taking care over each movement. There would be a quiet climax, a sigh, a shiver. He checked the thought, embarrassed and guilty.

She said, 'He's a pig, old man Petersen, a crook. Why should I have anything to do with you?'

'I just use his swimming pool,' Joe said. 'Exercise.'

She turned to her jewellery again. 'So?'

'I hardly know him. I need to exercise my leg.'

Christina glanced at his leg. The hole where the bullet had been and the incision the surgeon had made were vivid against the pale skin. She said, 'You're the guy who got shot, the kidnap guy. I've seen your picture.'

'In the paper?'

'Uhuh.' The girl threaded some more beads. The earrings were bad, clumsy. The wire was too soft. After a while she said, 'What are you doing here?'

'What Jeff told you, looking for a room.'

'You're staying for a while?'

'A while.'

'You got any money?'

'Some. Enough.'

The girl paused, considering. 'You should go to a hotel,' she said.

'I don't like hotels.'

'Me neither.'

Joe smiled. 'At least we've got that in common.'

'And nothing else?'

'I didn't say that. I don't know. Perhaps we've got a lot in common.'

Joe went over to the table and picked up one of the earrings. 'You sell any of these?' he said.

'Some. Wanna buy a pair?'

'I don't thing they'd suit me.' The girl didn't laugh. 'About this room,' he said.

'Hundred a month.'

'I can have it?'

The girl smiled suddenly. 'Sure. Why not?'

*　　　*　　　*

The room was small and bare. There was a bed made from unplaned wood, a thin mattress, a mirror, and on the wall, surprisingly, an ornate carved crucifix in gilt metal. It reminded Joe of a room in a monastery he'd once visited in Spain. A hundred a month. He paid and moved in next day while Penny and David were out. He didn't leave a forwarding address.

The room suited his mood. He bought a mat for his exercises from a market woman and spread it on the floor. In one of the outbuildings he found a pair of mounted kudu horns which he hung on the wall as coathangers. He got to know the twisted metal Christ on the crucifix by touching it with his fingertips. On the back was stamped the word VERONA. He bought a bottle of local gin and a couple of glasses.

The house snake he also got to know, and the little girl. The house snake, a small wormlike creature, lived in a clump of grass in a clay pot on the stoep. The little girl was Christina's daughter, three years of age, sharp-boned like her mother but fair-haired. Her father, Joe found out later, was a Dane, a hitchhiker who'd called in one day and stayed around for a while. The girl's name was Tansy. That first morning she came in and watched while he was doing his exercises. She said nothing. She watched him for a while and then began to imitate him: running on the spot, touching her toes. She wore a tiny pair of blue knickers and nothing else. The snake's name, she explained when they paused, was Snake. They'd called him that because it seemed appropriate.

'What does appropriate mean?' Joe asked.

'I don't know.' She laughed and skipped outside into the sunshine.

That night he met Lookout.

He hadn't know there was anybody else, Christina hadn't said. Then he heard Bob Marley from the end hut, and smelt dope.

Rasta locks, straw mats, Xhosa blankets on a bed. A couple of hunting spears in the corner and an imported Hitachi stereo system. 'Hey,' said Lookout.

There was a pile of marijuana the size of a small mountain on a low table. Lookout was shovelling it into plastic bags with a brass scoop. He was perhaps twenty, perhaps thirty, perhaps older. Bob Marley sang, 'No woman no cry'. Lookout was smoking a joint the size of a policeman's truncheon. He handed it to Joe. 'Hey,' he said again. There was a picture of Haile Selassie nailed to the wall, and another picture torn out of a magazine: Trenchtown Jamaica. The dope hit Joe's skull like a hammer.

'Hey,' said Lookout, laughing. He held up a bag. 'You wanna buy? Ten dollars.'

'I live here,' said Joe.

Lookout started laughing. He laughed like it was the best joke he'd ever heard. 'I thought you was the honky come for the mbanje,' he said.

'Mbanje?'

Lookout pointed at the table. 'Mbanje. Dagga. Marijuana. You're not from here?.

'London.'

'Hey! Brixton. Front Line. You been down the Front Line? You been down Railton?'

Joe nodded. He remembered the Sunday afternoon three years ago – or was it four? – when he and Ellie had slipped the police cordon and walked down Railton Road. The stink of smoke. The broken glass. The burned out cars. Firemen were hosing down the smoking shell of a pub. People were watching – black people, white people – strained faces in upstairs windows. He remembered the people. Then the mbanje blurred his vision, cutting out the people, leaving only the red of the fire engines in his brain. He sat down heavily on the bed.

Lookout said, 'You know Finsbury Park?'

Joe shook his head to clear it. 'Yes. Finsbury Park.'

'I lived there. I was studying at the North London Poly. You know the North London Poly?'

'Not well.'

'Law. I studied law. I'm a lawyer. But I say, Fuck the law!' Lookout began to laugh again, his locks bouncing like the tassels on a parasol. 'Fuck the law. Law makers. Law breakers. That's the law.' He pointed at Haile Selassie. For some reason the sepia picture reminded Joe of a stuffed eagle.

'He looks like a stuffed eagle,' Joe said.

'Hey,' said Lookout, and stopped laughing.

The honkies came for their mbanje, three of them, young guys of eighteen or nineteen. They drove their pickup truck into the yard making the geese squawk. They asked where the mbanje had come from.

'Mozambique,' Lookout said.

They sat and smoked a joint. They giggled a lot and said 'Hi' to Joe. He was thinking about red fire engines. They put dollars on the table.

When they had gone, Lookout said, 'Here is a fact of life that may concern you. Take a fifty kilo bag of mealie meal and cross the border into Mozambique and you can return with fifty kilos of mbanje. It's the only thing that grows there. Mbanje and bullets, hey?'

Sometime around midnight Christina came in. Joe, who had been sleeping, woke with a start. She was wearing a long white loose-fitting dress and no shoes. With the light behind her she looked like she had no clothes on. 'You seen the lightning?' she said.

'What lightning?'

'Come,' she said. She took his hand and led him outside. Above the city, to the north, lightning flickered between heavy clouds. It was like no lightning Joe had ever seen. Christina said, 'I call it tabernacle lightning. It's where God lives.'

Afterwards she brought guava juice and they sat and drank it. When Lookout had finished drinking he put down the glass and lay on the mat. 'Hey,' he said, and was silent.

They were all silent for a long time. Outside the gates there was an insistent yelping, and then a series of low howls. Joe felt the hair on the nape of his neck prickle. Christina noticed his tension. 'Jackals,' she said. 'They come in to scavenge at the dustbins. I think they want to get at the geese.'

The howling continued for a while and then faded. A car passed. Joe said, 'I didn't know you got jackals in towns.'

Lookout, whom Joe had thought was asleep, said, 'We get all kinds of things in town. You wouldn't believe the things we get in town.'

'Worse than jackals,' Christina said.

'Like what?'

'Like old man Petersen, 'people like him. Like that guy

who keeps the store in Widdecombe Road. He's English. He's got a Great Dane he's trained to attack black people, then he complains when the kids throw stones at it. He told me it costs twenty-seven dollars a week to feed that brute. Twenty-seven dollars a week! When there are people starving in this country.'

'Hey,' said Lookout. 'You got a point there. A political point.'

They lapsed into silence once again. The worst effects of the mbanje had worn off, and Joe felt pleasantly light-headed and comfortable. For short periods of time he was almost happy. He felt the urge to touch Christina's hair, and reached out to place his fingers lightly on her springy scalp. For a moment she gave no indication that she had noticed, then she said, 'You want to talk about it?'

'About what?'

'About why you're so unhappy.'

Lookout sat up. 'Hey,' he said. 'There's unhappiness in my house. I don't allow unhappiness.'

Christina said, 'He's the kidnap guy. You remember, the English family – where was it? Chipinga?'

'Chiredzi,' said Joe.

'He got shot,' Christina said.

'I recall something of that kind,' Lookout said. 'Hey, what's it like being shot?'

'Not very nice,' said Joe.

'Ask a stupid question.' Lookout lay down on the floor again.

Then the misery, held back by the mbanje, suddenly took control. Joe could feel it physically swelling like the tide. It started at his legs and rushed upward, occupying his body and then the whole of his brain. He groped in the back pocket of his shorts for the photographs, bent and tattered now. He handed them to Christina. 'Ellie,' he said. 'Ben and Cassie. They're still alive. You've got to believe me. Everybody says they're dead, but they're alive.'

'I believe you,' said Christina quietly. She was looking intently at the photographs. To Lookout she said, 'You want to see the photographs?'

He stretched out a hand and took them, glancing at them

briefly. 'Yeah,' he said, 'they're alive all right.'

'He's psychic,' Christina said. 'His grandfather was a n'anga.'

'A n'anga?'

'A medicine man, a healer. If Lookout says they're alive, they're alive.'

'You better believe it,' said Lookout, and handed back the pictures. Joe suddenly began to cry.

'Hey,' said Lookout.

'Let him cry,' said Christina.

She came and sat on the bed next to Joe and put her arm round him. She had a soft, sweet smell.

'Shhh,' said Christina. 'Don't make a sound. There's no need to talk.'

Joe flinched slightly as the cool trickle of oil hit his back, then the girl's warm hands were there, smoothing at the oil, working it in to his shoulders and neck. 'Jojoba oil,' she said. 'Relax. You're too stiff, too tight.'

They were naked under the flamboyant tree, he and Christina, on a blanket on the goose-clipped grass. Tansy, naked also, was playing with a bucket of water, floating sticks, scattering leaves, singing. It was mid-afternoon, and the air was heavy with the rain that would not fall.

He'd shared Christina's bed that night, not making love but lying close, comforted by her touch until late morning. Sometime during the night they had been joined by Tansy, and it had been the little girl's movements, not the sun, that had awakened them. When they were awake, Tansy had traced his wounds with her fingers, puzzled, while Christina fetched orange juice and thick brown bread and honey. Then they had eaten together and sat in silence while the sun climbed the sky.

Christina poured more oil, concentrating on Joe's injured shoulder. As she bent for the bottle, Joe felt the soft brush of a nipple against his skin. 'You're beautiful,' he said, meaning it.

'So are you.'

Her hands felt like magic hands, charming the pain from the joint. Where the scar tissue was purple and sensitive to the

65

touch she used a single finger, sometimes two, working the oil along the line of the wound, circling the pits where the bullets had been. Thunder rumbled comfortably somewhere far away. The house snake rustled in its pot.

'Better?' she said at last.

Joe rolled over and looked up into her face. 'Oh yes,' he said.

Christina smiled. 'We don't allow unhappiness in this house. That's what Lookout says.'

'Where is he?'

'Gone. He left early. He'll be back.'

Joe groaned. 'I must do my exercises,' he said.

'Not today. Rest today. You're too tight. All I could feel was tightness.'

'I'm not fit. I've got to get fit.' Joe tried to rise, but a soft hand held him down.

'Rest,' the girl said. 'Relax.'

Joe lay back.

Tansy called across: 'I've made a boat. It's got a leaf for a sail.' She held up a piece of dripping greenery.

'That's good,' said Christina. The little girl returned to the bucket.

For a while Joe watched a column of black ants moving around the base of the flamboyant treet. A plane circled low overhead, dipping down towards the airport. Clouds were building in the north, stretched and fat and violet. Small flies buzzed and crawled. Christina was right, he thought. He was too tight, too tense. Maybe that was why he wasn't getting anywhere with the exercises. But there was so little time.

She was reading his thoughts. 'What are you going to do?' she said.

'I'm going south to find them.'

'That's good. They'll be expecting you.'

'When the money comes.'

Christina lay down beside him. 'Why do you need money?' she said.

'To buy a Land-Rover. To buy a gun.'

Joe felt the girl's body stiffen. 'A gun?'

'You know where I can get one?'

'Lookout might know.'

66

'I'll ask him.'

'He knows most things.'

'A nice guy,' Joe said. He wondered if they were lovers, or had been in the past, felt a twinge of jealousy.

After a pause Christina said, 'Don't get a gun. Take food, Mealie meal, not a gun.'

Joe shook his head.

The girl, who had turned on to one elbow, lay back and closed her eyes. 'Always guns,' she said.

Lookout didn't return that night, nor for three nights after. Joe spent the time exercising in his room and riding his bicycle. The rain came, invariably at night, the clouds building steadily during the heavy, hazy afternoons. There was talk of the drought breaking, and on his rides out of town Joe saw lines of people planting maize seeds in the wet, red earth. Giant green snails were crushed by passing cars.

He realised, with a shock, that Christmas was coming. The shops in First Street and Gordon Avenue were bright with decorations. On the 13th a call came from Barclays telling him that the money from Mac had arrived. He collected it and opened an account at the same branch. Seven and a half thousand dollars. He began to look at Land-Rovers in the used vehicle yards in Manica Road and Stanley Avenue, learning the intricacies of four wheel drive and freewheel hubs but not buying. He was waiting for Lookout.

Lookout returned, finally, on the Saturday night. Joe had finished his six-minute stationary run and was relaxing, arms loose, sweating lightly, when he heard music and noticed a light across the yard. The evening storm was beginning, fat rain drops splattering on to the thatch. The rain wetted his head as he crossed the strip of grass to the open doorway.

To his disappointment, Lookout was not alone. He was sitting on the bed, and on the floor was a plump black girl with braided hair twisted into intricate patterns on her head. They were eating something out of brown paper bags. Cartons of Chibuku beer stood open on the table.

'Hey,' said Lookout, catching sight of Joe. To the girl he said, 'This is Mr. Joe Lejeune, neighbour and friend. Joe, this is the lovely Rose.'

The girl smiled coyly and lowered her eyes. She wore a

67

tight, pink and white-striped dress. She was barefoot, a pair of white high-heeled shoes on the mat beside her.

'I want to talk,' Joe said.

'Go ahead.'

Joe looked at Rose.

'Hey,' said Lookout. 'Private matters.' He nodded towards the door.

Without a sound the girl got up, put on her shoes and went out. They watched her cross to the stoep and stand there. Lookout laughed. 'A Shona woman. That's what every man needs, a Shona woman.'

Joe tried to smile but failed. 'I need a gun,' he said.

The laughter left Lookout's face. 'Hey,' he said. 'A gun.' Outside, the tempo of the rain increased suddenly, flailing at the roof, squirting from the blocked gutter on the stoep.

'Chrissie told me you could get me one.'

Lookout swigged some Chibuku, put down the carton. 'That's a serious thing you're asking. A serious thing.' He crossed to the Hitachi and flipped over the record. More Bob Marley. 'A serious thing,' he said again, before the music began.

'I'm serious,' Joe said. He could feel himself becoming agitated.

Lookout sat down again. 'I called you my friend,' he said, 'but I don't know who you are. You could be anybody – some government guy.'

'You know who I am.'

'I know who I think you are.'

'My picture's been all over the papers, Chrissie recognised me.'

Lookout's eyes narrowed. Joe got the sudden impression that he was enjoying himself and felt his tension turning to anger. 'Just answer me,' he said. 'Can you get me one or not?'

'What for do you want this gun?'

'I'm going to look for my wife and children.'

'Playing soldiers, hey?'

'No, not playing soldiers. Jesus Christ!'

Lookout held up his hands. 'OK, OK, don't shoot. I'm only the piano player.' He waited a second or two then said, 'So when you've got this gun, which I may or may not be able to get for you, you're going off with it into the bush?'

'Yes.'

'So what happens if they catch you? Hey, this guy's got a gun. Where's the licence? What are you doing with this gun, murungu? What do you tell them, Lookout got it for you? Do I need that sort of trouble?'

'Please,' said Joe. 'I need one.'

'How much do you need one?'

Joe drew a deep breath. 'How much do you want?' he said.

Lookout suddenly began to laugh, slapping at his thigh. 'Hey, you really need it, don't you?' he said. 'You're a dangerous man, Mr. Joe Lejeune. A dangerous man.' He stopped laughing. 'Five hundred for me. Another three hundred for the gun. US dollars, not Zimbabwe.'

'I don't have any US dollars.'

'What you got, Sterling?'

'Just Zimbabwe dollars.'

Lookout shook his head. 'That's bad,' he said.

Joe was beginning to get the drift. 'How bad?'

'Two hundred dollars bad.'

'OK. Seven hundred for you. Four hundred for the gun. Half now, half when I get the gun.'

'Half now,' Lookout said.

A woman answered the door. She was fat and had a scarf tied back over her hair. She led them through into a tiny living-room. The rain drummed steadily on the bare asbestos roof. They were somewhere east of the city, off the Mutare road in a cul-de-sac of tight-packed identical breeze-block houses. Passing the bedroom Joe noticed five, maybe six, children sleeping together on a double mattress on the floor.

There were three men in the living-room seated round a formica-topped table. A fourth man sat on a mattress against one of the walls. A single bulb glowed with a dim yellow light. They greeted Lookout formally, clapping their hands. The man on the mattress was old and very thin. He muttered something and smiled. He had no teeth. The other men were younger, in their thirties.

The woman brought two chairs and Lookout and Joe sat down. Lookout began to talk in Shona, directing his remarks at the smallest of the three men at the table. The small man had a moustache. Two of the fingers on his right hand were missing. Lookout talked for a long time, occasionally indicating Joe, then finished and rested his arms on the table.

There was a lengthy silence, broken only by the sound of the rain and the mutterings of the old man. Eventually the small man spoke in English to Joe. He said: 'I have heard your request and agree to it.'

There was another silence. The three men were looking at Joe. He was obviously expected to reply but for some reason he could think of nothing to say. In the end he said, 'Thank you.'

'Five hundred dollars,' the small man said.

'Five hundred?'

'That is the price.'

'I need ammunition.'

'It includes ammunition.'

'What sort of gun?' Joe said.

'What sort you want? FN? UZI? LDP?'

'Something small. Powerful.'

'A pistol?'

'No, not a pistol.'

The small man said something to the man on his left and nodded. The second man had scars on his cheeks like tribal markings, but they were too irregular. Knife wounds. The small man turned back to Joe. 'OK,' he said. 'An LDP.'

'I don't know the LDP.' Joe didn't know any guns at all, but this wasn't the time to say so.

'Zimbabwe gun. Small. Three kilos. Fire with one hand or two. Semi-automatic.'

'A submachine gun?'

'Semi-automatic.'

'And ammunition?'

'Nine milimetre. Five hundred rounds.'

Joe nodded and counted out two hundred and fifty dollars on to the table. 'The rest when I get the gun,' he said.

The small man took the money. 'Tuesday,' he said. 'I get it Tuesday.'

'I'll come here?'

The small man shook his head and consulted with his

companions. Then he said, 'Cecil Square. Twelve o'clock. Sit on one of the seats. We'll find you.'

They stood up, shook hands. The woman, who had been listening from the doorway, came in to show them out.

'Hey,' said Lookout when they were back in Chrissie's car. 'Three fifty you owe me.'

'When I've got the gun,' Joe said.

Lookout laughed loudly. 'Just testing,' he said. 'Just testing.'

The rain slashed at the windscreen.

Perhaps he was being paranoid. He asked Chrissie. 'Am I being paranoid?'

'Yes,' she said, and smiled.

But the car was there, if not tailing them, taking an identical route into town.

Joe glanced back. There were two men in the car, black men, youngish. It was hard to see with the reflection of the sunshine on the windscreen. It was a white Datsun, its left wing crushed slightly from some minor collision.

Chrissie had seen it first, noticing it parked up the road when she'd gone to get bread, and now it was following them into town. It was only chance that Joe was going in with her at all. She was taking Tansy to the Monday morning clinic and he was going to Manica Road to take a second look at a Land-Rover. If he'd been on his bike as he usually was he could have taken a short cut, followed some path or back alley, lost the men.

The Datsun stayed behind them, turning right at Forbes Avenue, up Fifth Street, into Samora Machel. It was only when they turned up the ramp to the second floor of the Parkade carpark that he noticed it was gone.

'Be careful,' Chrissie said, when they got out. 'Don't talk to any strange men.' She laughed and kissed him lightly on the cheek.

Joe took the lift down and through the Arcade into Union Avenue. He checked the street for the white car but there was no sign of it, nor did there seem to be anybody following on foot. Maybe Chrissie was right, maybe it was just coincidence, but he remained watchful, checking at intersections, examining passing cars.

At Ace Motors in Manica Road East, Joe wrote a cheque for $4,000 and bought a grey 1975 Mark 2 long wheelbase Land-Rover. It had fitted freewheel hubs, mud winches and protective mesh. He fixed up the insurance and later that afternoon drove it back to the Rondavel.

On the Tuesday morning, to be on the safe side, Joe took the bike down to Cecil Square, chaining it to the railings and slipping in through the gate near the Publicity Bureau. The trees and grass were an intense green after the rains. Flower petals lay scattered beneath the bushes like red, blue and white confetti.

The gardens were crowded with secretaries eating lunch out of plastic boxes, women resting after a morning's Christmas shopping, businessmen strolling, carrying briefcases, black children running and shouting, the inevitable loungers and scroungers. Joe saw, to his irritation that all the benches were occupied. He'd have to sit on the grass. He wondered why the men had chosen Cecil Square to meet him, and at midday. There were so many people. Too many people.

He found a dryish spot under a jacaranda tree, spread out the nylon bag he was carrying and sat down. It was quarter to twelve, he'd checked the time at the Publicity Bureau. He must get a new watch to replace the stolen one, he reflected. Something cheap. A digital from one of the stalls in Kenneth Kaunda Avenue. Doves hopped about on the grass.

He hadn't been followed, he was pretty sure of that. He'd taken the long route into town, past the golf course, just to be certain, stopping from time to time. He was inclined, on second thoughts, to dismiss the incident with the white Datsun. He must guard against paranoia. It would slow him down. He clicked his fingers and hummed tunelessly, feeling a growing excitement, exhilaration almost. He had the Land-Rover and any minute now he'd have the gun. Then there'd be nothing to stop him, nothing! Of course, the gun was a problem. What was it – an LDP? He'd never seen one before, let alone fired one. He wished he'd asked the man for an instruction book.

He'd take the gun back to the Rondavel and strip it down, get to know every moving part, oil it, learn to fit the magazine and so on. Then tomorrow, on the road south, he'd find a likely spot in the bush and fire off as many rounds as he needed at a tree or a rock just to get the feel of it.

Minutes passed. The clock on the Cathedral struck twelve. He glanced round. A youth was approaching, dressed in ragged jeans and a shirt open to the waist. He was carrying a plastic carrier bag. Joe stiffened.

'Carvings, sir?' The youth held out a soapstone rhinoceros. 'Rhinoceros. Elephant. Very nice carvings.'

Christ, it was all he needed, some bastard hanging around trying to sell him things! 'Go away.'

'Very nice carvings, sir.'

'Piss off.'

'Giraffe.'

Joe made to get to his feet. The youth backed off. 'Did you hear me?' Joe said.

'Sorry, sir,' said the youth. 'Very sorry.'

And then Joe spotted them. Two men, no, three. They'd been there all the time. Must have been. One of them sat on a bench reading the *Herald*. Another near the Third Street entrance. A third lounging by the path. The man with the newspaper was one of the men in the white Datsun. Joe was sure, pretty sure.

It was a set up. A bloody set up. His eyes circled the park. The youth with the carvings was making towards the Stanley Avenue gate. One of the men, the man by the path, walked casually across the grass to intercept him. They were talking. The youth was opening his carrier bag, showing the man his carvings. They glanced back in Joe's direction.

He must get out. Now.

There was no one, as far as he could see, guarding the Second Street Gate, the one by the Publicity Bureau. It was sixty yards, seventy at the most from where he sat. He groped in his pocket for the key to his bike chain, found it, got up and began to walk with studied casualness towards the gate.

Without looking round he became aware that the man with the *Herald* had left his bench, and that the other man, the man near the Third Street Gate, was also moving. They were coming at him diagonally, in a pincer, cutting his retreat.

He began to run, smashing into people, shoppers, a woman

73

in a striped uniform. His leg hurt, and his shoulder, the scar tissue stretching agonisingly over the surface of his wounds.

He made the gate, the street. A tourist bus had just parked. Japanese men in safari suits blocked his way. He hit them at a run, slamming into cameras and maps and shoulder bags, wrenching at the chain on his bike, forcing the key into the lock. He swung himself into the saddle and out towards the Gordon Avenue intersection.

There was a squeal of brakes from an orange taxi, the driver shouting from the window. And behind him, pulling out from the curb, he was sure, almost sure, was the white Datsun.

He took the corner at forty-five degrees, using his foot to slide himself round. Ahead of him was a stretch of tarmac flanked by delivery trucks, a series of concrete bollards and the raised brick surface of the First Street shopping mall. At the pavement café shoppers and young white kids sucked cokes and ate burgers beneath twee thatched sunshades. They shouted as he slid through between tables and outstretched legs out into First Street.

That would stop them. That would stop the bastards. Try driving their bloody Datsun through that lot.

He looked back to check and then suddenly up ahead of him was a silver and turquoise Christmas tree slung with lights. He tried to brake but the bike bucked like an out-of-control horse, and he was slewing across the ground into the raised white concrete flowerbed in which the tree stood . . .

It was like being shot all over again, the feeling of disassociation and terror. There were people surrounding him, running across from the shops and the café. He was aware, somewhere, of women's voices singing 'Ding Dong Merrily on High.' Somebody was shouting something into his ear, pulling at his arm. It was his injured arm and the pain made him scream. An old fat white man was bending, pressing at his body. 'Where does it hurt?' he was saying. Someone else, a woman, was saying, 'Don't move him.'

And then, unexpectedly, there was Penny's face. 'It's OK, I know him. Joe, are you OK?'

She put an arm round him and helped him to his feet. 'Penny,' he said.

'This is a pedestrian area,' somebody else said. 'It's disgraceful. He should be reported.'

'The men,' Joe said. 'Where are the men?'

'What men?'

'A white Datsun.' Joe looked round wildly.

'I can't see any men.' Penny said. 'Where have you been, Joe? We've been worried about you. Where are you living? Are you hurt?'

He shook his head. 'My bike,' he said. 'The men. I've got to go.'

A policeman materialised, pushing his way through the crowd. A woman was hanging on his arm, saying, 'He came straight through the café on that bike and hit the Christmas tree. Somebody could have been seriously hurt. There are children . . .'

The policeman, a middle-aged black man with an unhappy face, shook himself free. 'Are you hurt, sir?'

'No.'

'You realise it is an offence, riding a bicycle in a pedestrian area?'

A small black boy picked up Joe's bike and wheeled it back to him. Joe took it without acknowledgement. For a moment he considered making a break for it, down Gordon Avenue into Angwa Street. He said to the policeman. 'I've got to go.'

'When I've finished, sir.'

Penny was talking now. She was saying to the policeman, 'I know him, constable. He's been ill. I'm the wife of the Vicar of St. Anthony's. I'll see to him.' Joe noticed that she had Becky with her, holding hands, looking solemn.

The policeman hesitated. He glanced round at the crowd which was growing by the second. He looked worried. Old habits of deference to Europeans died hard. To Penny he said, 'He should see a doctor, maybe.'

'Yes,' said Penny. 'I think he should.' She took Joe's arm.

The policeman said, 'Don't do it again, sir.'

'He won't,' said Penny.

Penny gave a boy twenty cents to look after the bicycle and took Joe into Barbours, past Santa's Grotto and up in the lift to the Terrace Restaurant. The white families who were lunching stopped talking to stare at him. He realised that his

75

tee shirt was ripped and his knees were bleeding. They went to a table overlooking First Street.

'Have you eaten?' Penny said.

'No.'

'Ham salad?'

Joe didn't reply.

Penny ordered three ham salads. 'I want an ice cream, Mummy,' Becky said.

'Later.'

'Oh, Mummy!'

'We've been worried, Joe. We thought you might have gone to Matabeleland on some stupid rescue mission. Then Mrs. McArthur said she saw you in Manica Road yesterday. Where are you living? Why didn't you leave us an address? I've got letters for you, from Ellie's mother and a couple of others from England. And Mr. Prentice from the High Commission has been trying to contact you.'

Joe wasn't listening. He must go, he was thinking. Leave Harare tonight. He'd collect the Land-Rover from the Rondavel and just go. Fuck the gun. He could get another. There must be hundreds around. Or maybe he didn't need a gun. Maybe Chrissie was right. Maybe he should take mealie meal . . .

Penny was still talking. 'It was just luck that we happened to be in town today. I've done most of the shopping already. You're really sure you're not hurt?'

'Mummy,' Becky said, 'I don't like ham.'

Penny ignored her. 'Who are these men?' she said.

'Just men.'

'You're in trouble?'

'No.' Joe was looking round, searching for some way, any way, to escape. The balcony was too high.

Penny was quiet for a while, then she said, 'These men. They do exist, don't they?'

'Of course they exist.'

'I'm sorry. I shouldn't have said that.' She laughed nervously and put her hand on Joe's. 'Listen, come to us for Christmas. We've got David's mother coming and one of my schoolfriends from South Africa: Janey. Ellie knew her. It'll be quite a nice little party. I've already got your present, by

76

the way. Come and share Christmas with us.'

The waiter came with the salads. Becky said, 'I don't want this meat.'

'Eat it, darling, please.'

'No.'

'No ice cream in that case. Then I think,' Penny said to Joe, 'that after Christmas we ought to sit down and sort out what you're going to do.'

Joe looked round the restaurant. 'The toilet?' he said.

'Back there, near the door.'

He got up and threaded his way between the tables. Near the door he glanced back. Penny was cutting up Becky's ham, urging the little girl to eat. He slipped out and into the lift. 'Ground floor,' he said to the attendant.

He didn't return to the Rondavel until dusk because he knew the men would be waiting for him. Instead he took the road west out of town towards Murewa, stopping at a store to buy coke and bread which he ate under a msasa tree. Then he circled round towards Goromonzi and back on to the Mutare road.

There was a small track behind the Rondavel which led to an overgrown orchard of mango and citrus trees. The Africans used the track to collect fruit and to shit at the base of the tree trunks. Concealing his bike, and stepping gingerly in the half-light, Joe worked his way through to the chain-link fence behind the garage.

The Rondavel was in darkness. By now there should have been a light burning in the yard. Perhaps Chrissie had forgotten to switch it on. He stopped for a moment or two, listening. A dog was barking some way away, and there was the sound of traffic from the Widdecombe Road, but otherwise silence. No voices. No music. If Lookout was there he'd have heard music. A gnarled mango tree, its branches already heavy with green fruit, straddled the fence and overhung the garage. It was not difficult to climb, and seconds later Joe was dropping lightly down onto the carpet of bougainvillaea which sprawled across the garage roof. From his perch he could see the road lit by the streetlamps, and part of the yard. There were no cars.

He laughed softly to himself. He was being stupidly overcautious. He could have ridden straight up to the front gate. And even if the men were waiting for him, what could they say? What could they do? All he'd done was sit in a park in downtown Harare. There was no law against sitting in a park. Still laughing, he swung himself over the edge and down.

And then he stopped.

The gates were open. They were never left open because of the geese. Chrissie had told him again and again. And where were the geese? They should be squawking, hissing, rushing towards him, necks stretched.

He glanced through the garage door. The car was there so Chrissie must be home. 'Chrissie!' he called softly. 'Chrissie, are you there?'

Silence.

Cautiously he walked round, past the rainwater tank and into the yard.

The Land-Rover was gone.

Lookout. It must be Lookout. He must have taken it. Gone to see some of his friends in one of the Townships. Christ! He'd left the keys hanging on a nail near his bed. Stupid. Bloody stupid. He should have taken them with him.

Furious, Joe crossed the grass and stepped up onto the darkened stoep. His feet clattered into something. He bent down and picked up a piece of broken pot – the house snake's pot – and there, just visible a few feet away, was the snake itself, squashed and bloody. He recoiled from it in horror. 'Chrissie! For Christ's sake, where are you?'

The door to her hut was open. He went in, groping for the light switch. The light didn't come on. The soles of his sandals crunched on something which felt like broken glass. Then he hit the table. It was upturned, half-blocking the entrance. He staggered back, clutching his knee.

He could see now, his eyes adjusting to the gloom. He was treading on earrings, wire and beads. And the glass from the broken lightbulb. Tansy's books, the typewriter and the wicker chair had been thrown into a corner. There was something wet, sticky glistening on the wall near the window. He could smell the scent of jojoba oil. In the kitchen behind he could see pots and plates, lentils and rice, pulled from the cupboards littering the floor.

'Chrissie!'

He stumbled out onto the stoep and into the girl's bedroom. This time the light worked. 'Chrissie!'

At first he thought she wasn't there but then he saw her behind the overturned bed, half-hidden by the cupboard door. She was sitting very still, Tansy on her lap, surrounded by piles of crumpled clothes. 'Chrissie, for Christ's sake, are you OK?'

She looked up slowly. There was a red welt, the beginnings of a bruise, on one of her cheeks. 'You bastard,' she said. 'You bloody bastard.'

Tansy, silent until that moment, suddenly began to cry with a high-pitched wail.

Joe watched the mother and child hopelessly. He put his hand on the bed as if to right it, but Chrissie said, 'Take your hands off that.'

'I was only . . .'

'Go away.'

Joe felt tight, breathless, panicky. He glanced quickly round the room as if expecting physical assault from some unexpected angle. 'What happened?'

'You can see.'

Tansy continued to wail. Chrissie did nothing to comfort her.

'Who was it? The police?'

'Fuck off, won't you!'

'They were after me,' Joe said.

'After *you*!'

The girl's rage terrified him. He backed away. 'Lookout?' he said.

'They've got him.'

'Oh God.'

Joe glanced through the window. In the yellow light from the streetlamps he could see the door to Lookout's hut hanging open, and the mess inside. 'Why?' he said.

'You know why. They found the gun.'

'What gun?'

'We were OK till you came. We were happy. Why couldn't you have left us alone?'

He was entreating now, pleading. 'But, Chrissie, I went to

town to get the gun. Those men, the men in the white Datsun . . .'

'They were here. They were looking for the gun. They found it, and the mbanje. You bastard, you didn't have to bring them here.'

'But Chrissie . . .'

'I could kill you,' the girl said slowly. 'If I had a gun or a knife, I could kill you.'

He found a hotel, he wasn't sure where. One of the Avenues. The man at reception wanted cash in advance. Joe wrote the name John Edwards in the book and invented an address in Mutare. It was a twin-bedded room with plastic furniture, on the second floor. He locked the door and took the bottle of gin from his bag. The toothmug was cracked and coated with a film of soap, but he didn't notice the taste.

He didn't know how long he stayed in the room but it was a long time. He drank, didn't sleep much, and became abusive when the woman came in to clean in the mornings. On the third day the manager came, knocking on the door, asking if he was O.K. Joe gave him a fifty dollar bill and he went away. He had food sent up once a day, and more bottles of gin. Late at night he shouted a lot and there were complaints from other guests.

And always the men were there: early in the morning, late at night, sheltering under the jacarandas when the rain fell. At times there were several of them, once a small crowd. The white Datsun appeared and disappeared regularly. Sometimes he heard the men talking into a radio.

They didn't both him much. He watched them less out of apprehension than curiosity. It was like a spectator sport or theatre. Yes, more like theatre: the comings and goings, the worried glances up at his window. Often, when he'd poured himself a drink, he'd raise his glass and toast the men below. 'Bottoms up,' he'd say.

He could outlast them, he knew that. He had patience, money, time. They'd get bored, restless, more pressing duties would arise. Then, when their backs were turned, he'd be gone where they'd never find him.

The loss of the Land-Rover annoyed him, of course,

increasingly so as the days passed. It was the only thing they'd taken, the only thing he needed. If he had the Land-Rover he'd be out of this shit-heap of a city for good, travelling south, windows open to the warm wind. Jesus Christ, it annoyed him. Bastards! Once he opened the window and yelled out to the man below: 'Give me back my fucking Land-Rover!' But the man turned away, pretending not to hear.

But what the fuck? He could get another. Or maybe a motorbike, a trail bike. He could hitch a lift if he had to, or ride the African buses. He could make his face black. That was a thought. There was some chemical that changed the skin pigment. He'd read a book about it a long time ago, when he was at High School. Some guy who changed into a black man and went down to Mississippi, or was it Alabama?

He tried to remember what the chemical was called, but gave up. The gin was making him forget things, or was it old age? He'd been neglecting the exercises. He must start them again.

And Ellie. He was forgetting her, too. And the kids. Sometimes he repeated their names to himself to fix them in his memory. Ellie. Cassie. Ben. He spread the photographs, crumpled and torn, on the bed and looked at Ellie's face. He tried to remember what it tasted like, what it felt like, to kiss her. He imagined making love with her but failed. It was too insubstantial, like making love with a ghost. And when he got an erection, just once, just that one time in the bathroom, it was Chrissie he thought about and not Ellie at all.

One day it was Christmas. It had to be, Joe knew, because of the drunken Africans shouting in the night and slamming car doors. And because the next day they sent him up pale slices of turkey swimming in thin gravy, and a dark brown lump of cake in a pudding dish.

He put the radio on while he ate and a man sang, 'When Santa got stuck up the chimney'. He washed down the meal with gin, and later was sick in the bathroom. A boil had come up on his neck and his wounds were troubling him. 'Happy Christmas!' he shouted to the men across the road. 'Happy fucking Christmas!'

Two days later he went out.

He hadn't planned it. It wasn't part of his strategy to go out, not while the men were there, and they were there, waiting in the Datsun. It was mid-evening and he'd been drinking a bit – brandy, just to make a change. He just felt like going out somewhere. Anywhere. Not the great escape, oh no, that could wait. When the man on reception held up a bill, Joe shook his head. 'I'll be back,' he said, and winked. He'd had a bath, combed his hair and put on the only pair of slacks he possessed. It felt like he was celebrating his hundredth birthday.

There was a taxi outside, just one, the driver waiting with the interior light on, but Joe ignored it. The walk would do him good. Across the road the men in the white Datsun were staring at him so hard they made him laugh. Deliberately, and with a smile still on his face, he crossed to the car and banged twice on the bonnet. The men jumped as if they'd been shot. They were both wearing white shirts and had expensive gold watches that glinted in the light from the hotel.

'Wake up!' he shouted to them. 'Wake up, you dozy bastards!' Then he blew them a kiss and walked off down Selous Avenue.

It was a hot night, humid, boiling up for rain. There were some stars in the west above the trees of the Public Gardens. He searched vaguely for the Southern Cross but couldn't see it. He began to whistle. He didn't check to see if the Datsun was following, but at the Park Lane junction he noticed it, a hundred yards back, moving slowly, its lights jolting as its wheels hit the storm drains at the side of the road.

The Monomatapa Hotel loomed ahead, its lit windows curving into the night sky. There were kids on the terrace drinking, young white kids, shouting, swilling pint glasses of beer under striped umbrellas. There'd been too many black faces recently, Joe thought, too many flat black faces. The white girls looked beautiful in the golden light, big tits squashed into skimpy print dresses. 'OK, you honky bastard,' he said to himself, 'it's your tribe.' And pausing to wave at the Datsun, now parked self-consciously amongst the Mercedes and country pickups, he ducked down and into the Wine Barrel bar.

He drank Black Label in pint glasses, squashed against the

bar by the pressure of warm white flesh. He ordered the pints in pairs to save time, sweating despite the air conditioning, the freezing beer shocking his guts. A girl with long dark hair was crouched in a corner by a microphone, singing 'Let me take you by the hand and lead you through the streets of London'. She looked a little like Joan Baez, and when she stopped singing and announced another song Joe realised that she was Australian. 'OK, Sport!' he called to her, between the clutter of blond heads. They laughed at that, the Rhodies. Someone slapped him on the back. The waiter, the only black face in the room, squeezed between the drinkers, carrying trays, pocketing change.

The man next to Joe, big-boned and red-fisted, was clutching a glass and talking to his companion. 'They flagged me down so I stopped. They said, "Give this woman a lift into Bulawayo". There was a fat old ambuya with a piccanin. I said, "I'm not a taxi service, there's a bus behind." They said, "This is a time of reconciliation." That's great, hey? Reconciliation. Norma said, "Give her a lift, for Christ's sake." I said, "You must be joking. Duck!" and I slammed the door and put my foot down. "No munts in my car," I said, "not now, not ever."'

'Jesus,' said his friend. 'You mad bastard! They could have revved you.'

'So what's new?'

'Yeah, but with Norma there.'

'Are you going to Scarboro Fair?' sang the Australian girl who looked like Joan Baez. Joe caught the barman's eye and ordered another two pints of Black Label.

After he knocked the guy's beer from his hand he had to go. A big circle opened up on the floor, and a girl stood there mopping at her dress. Where the beer wetted it the material clung to her legs, showing their outline. She had fat thighs.

'Hey, you,' said the red-fisted man. 'Say sorry to the lady.'

The girl with the guitar stopped playing. People turned to look. Joe clutched at the bar for support and muttered something.

'That's not an apology,' the man said.

'Sorry,' said Joe.

'That's better,' the man said. 'When you've paid for my

83

beer you can go home.' Joe tried to leave, but the red fist was gripping his arm. 'Ninety cents.'

Joe found a dollar. The fist took it. 'Now go,' the fist said.

The people watched him go – not the way he had come in but up the steps into the hotel lobby. Americans with suitcases stood around, and a clutch of fat Africans in suits. The doorman ran to open the door and he was out, into Park Lane. Before he left the hotel he heard the Australian girl begin to sing again.

The rain revived him, giving him strength. It must have been raining hard while he was inside, the gutters were awash. Now it was a thin drizzle. The black streets shone in the red and yellow light. Cars sluiced past.

He began to walk, sometimes holding on to the blue lamp-posts for support. His thin shoes let in the wet and it felt like he was paddling at the seaside.

He walked a long way, in which direction he didn't know. If the white Datsun was around it didn't bother him. He sang a little. Parsley, sage, rosemary and thyme. There was a sour taste in his mouth. He drenched his palate with saliva and spat into the road. He was thinking about the man with the red fists. He was thinking what he should have said to him. He'd felt scared, that's what worried him. Frightened of a big white Rhodie who wouldn't allow munts into his car. Christ, what a wimp he was, what a fucking wimp. OK, never again; not ever again would he allow it to happen. He should have said, he should have said . . .

He needed a piss, that was the problem. His bladder ached. Anywhere would do. He found a hedge, clutched at the foliage with one hand and groped at his zip with the other. There were thorns in the hedge and he recoiled with the pain. The stream of urine hit his shoe, wetting it still more, warming it. There was a notice near the hedge and a wrecked car. The notice read 'Queen of Sheba, 101 Rotten Row', and underneath it there were smaller notices, faded with the rain, quoting prices for firewood and scrap copper. There was an overgrown garden and beyond it, half hidden by foliage and lit with a dim light, a low building with a dark corrugated roof and a wide stoep. The door was open and a fat woman stood silhouetted against the light. There was a vague sound of music.

He tried to remember something that David had told him.
Oh yes, he'd quoted the phone book: 'Japanese Swedish
Lifeguard Massage Parlour. Prop. Miss Kubie.' He remembered. Miss Kubie. She was the Queen of Sheba. Massage,
like Chrissie. Oh God, like Chrissie. He leant against the
rusted car. Jesus, what had he done to Chrissie to make her
hate him? He thought of her hard little breasts and big
nipples. 'You're tight. You're too tight,' she'd said. He
grabbed onto the rusted metal of the car to stop his grief and
loneliness. The Queen of Sheba stood, not moving, in her
lighted doorway.

After some time he felt better. The rain had stopped. There
were more stars above the city and a white moon. Do you
wanna dance, under the moonlight? He was going to dance.
He had to dance.

He tried a few steps, stumbled, almost fell. He walked on a
while. There was a big neon sign in the sky, high up above the
trees: Queens. He remembered the Queens. He could dance
at the Queens. Oh, yes. Dance, dance, dance.

Hot Sounds, another sign said. Dandaro Lounge. Have a
Pepsi Day. Razzles Cocktail Bar. Gilberts Gin. He traced
the music to a doorway in Pioneer Street. Reggae music. He
could see the lights flashing. Youths stood around watching
him, and a girl, a single girl.

Stone steps, the sound getting louder. Four men in bright
shirts, one with a shaved head, forcing him to squeeze past.
Two men on the desk shouting at him. Two dollars. A purple
stamp on his wrist.

Silver and black. Ultra-violet strobe. Red plastic.

A drink. He needed a drink. In the bar a man was shaking
his hand. 'Good evening, sir. Pleased to meet you, sir.' He
winced as the man's little finger dug into the palm of his hand.
'What brings you to the Queen's, sir?' the man was saying,
holding the handshake. Joe wrenched his hand away. 'Hey,'
said the man.

Lion lager. Plastic glass. Dance, he'd come to dance. He
moved out towards the music.

It was hard to dance, so hard. His legs hurt. They were so
young, the black girls who turned away from him. Do you
want to dance, under the moonlight? They were laughing,

some of them. Laughing. Shit! Was he so funny? Was he so fucking funny, wanting to dance? They were no more than schoolgirls – fourteen, fifteen, sixteen – but dressed to kill, teeth glowing violet in the light. Oh shit, he couldn't dance. What are you bastards laughing at, hey? My white face, is that so funny? Is that so very funny?

Another drink. The man in the bar was saying, 'I'd like to interest you in a business deal, sir.'

'Fuck off,' Joe shouted, and lurched across to a red stool, spilling beer, holding on, just holding on.

Christ, he felt sick. Ill. He was dying. The knowledge came at him in waves. The bullet, the one in his guts, it was still there. He could feel it. That bastard surgeon had lied to him. It was there, eating away at him from the inside. He put his head in his hands, his brain exploding with the music.

When he looked up he saw them. They were near the door, talking to the shaven-headed man, looking in his direction. The two bastards from the Datsun, their white shirts turned purple. Checking up. Keeping an eye on him. All right, you bastards. All right, you smug bastards with your gold watches, this is where it ends, this is where it all ends.

He stood up suddenly, his plastic glass clattering to the floor, the beer wetting his trousers. He struggled through the dancers, shoving them from his path, screaming at the men above the sound of the music.

They were gone. He pushed past the shaven-headed man and down the stairs. 'Come here, you motherfuckers,' he was shouting. 'Come here, you fucking bastards!'

He fell the last few steps, sliding agonisingly through the door and across the pavement. Then he was up and running. The men were at the corner, moving towards the car, but there were people blocking his path. So many people.

A fat girl grabbed his arm. 'Hey, lovey,' she said, putting her face up in a show of devotion. 'Hey, lovey. Lovey, lovey.' He pushed her hard. She fell back against the wall, her head making a dull thump as it hit the concrete.

It was too late. Too late. He heard the car start up.

Then he saw the other men. There were four of them, young guys, shirts open to the waist, medallions glinting, moving in towards him. 'Mabunu,' they said, spitting the words. 'Mabunu. Come here, Mabunu.'

One of them took something from his pocket. There was a click, 'Hey, Mabunu,' they said, still moving in. 'The money. Give us the money.'

Terror smacked at him, sobering him. He glanced round. There was space between the parked cars. Just enough space. Down Pioneer, across Manica . . .

They were coming for him too fast. His leg! Fuck his leg. Oh Jesus. 'Mabunu!' they were shouting. 'Mabunu!'

They caught up with him against the wire fence of Apollo Car Sales, pressing him against it, bouncing him off, their hands at his shirt, ripping at his pockets.

He managed to twist away, ducking. There was a sharp pain in his arm. Blood. He stood still. The knife man circled him, coming in again . . .

And then the truck came.

It came from nowhere, straight at him across the pavement, horn blaring, lights on full. Joe was aware of a thin white man jumping from the truck, something metal in his hand. A tyre lever it looked like.

He hit the knife man on the arm. Once. Twice. There was a crack. The other men scattered, running.

'Get in,' the white man was shouting. 'Get in, you stupid bastard!'

Joe wrenched at the handle, falling in face downwards. Then, tyres squealing, doors flailing, they were away into Rotten Row, travelling north at speed.

'I've been cleaning up the truck,' the man said. 'You threw up all over it.'

Joe winced at the daylight and tried to speak, but his voice wouldn't work properly. It felt as if there was something disgusting glued to the inside of his throat.

'How's your arm?'

Joe looked down. There was a broad slice of sticking plaster on his right forearm. 'Hurts,' he managed to say.

Everything hurt. His body, his head, his legs, his arm. It was difficult to distinguish between hurts. He was lying on a narrow bed, naked except for a sheet. A chill breeze blew through an open window.

'It'll mend,' the man said. 'It's deep but it'll mend.'

'Could I have a drink of water.'

The man smiled. 'Just water? You're sure you want just water?'

'Just water.'

'I'll get it.'

He was in a small bare room, with polished floorboards. On one wall a series of carved wooden spoons with circular bowls ranged downwards in size like flying ducks. There was a hard-backed chair, a small wardrobe. On the wardrobe was pinned a picture of Sydney Harbour Bridge. It was a page from a calendar dated May 1975.

The man came back with the water. He was thin and a little under average height, with hollow cheeks, straight fair hair, a close-cropped beard. He was wearing a khaki bush shirt, shorts, and sandals made from what looked like bits of car tyre. He was in his late twenties, Joe thought. Possibly older.

Feeling better, Joe handed back the glass. 'Thanks.'

'Don't mention it.' The man held out his hand. 'Ross Tobin.'

'Joe Lejeune.'

They shook hands self-consciously. Despite the economy of his movements there was something awkward about Ross Tobin, a schoolboy gaucheness that Joe guessed might appeal to the maternal instinct in women. Somehow it didn't match with his memory of the man who'd wielded the tyre lever the night before.

'I think they were going to kill me,' Joe said.

Ross shook his head. 'No, they just wanted the money. If you'd gven them the money they'd have let you go.'

'I don't think so.'

'I know the way those guys work.'

'They called me mabunu.'

'That means white bastard. Boer.'

'Thank you, anyway.'

There was an awkward silence, then Ross said, 'I've got things to do.' He left the room as silently as he had entered it.

Soon after, Joe heard the sounds of hammering on metal. Easing himself to his feet with difficulty, he went to the window. The house was in a clearing ringed with tall trees, gums and msasas, some way out of town it looked like. Littering the foreground and extending up to the house itself were the shells of many cars and trucks. The hammering was coming from one of them, a Mazda pickup jacked up onto bricks and missing its wheels. Ross's legs were visible underneath the vehicle. Lying in the grass nearby was a large dog, a setter, enjoying the warmth of the sunshine. The morning was blue and fresh after the rains of the night before.

A floorboard creaked behind him. Joe turned, suddenly conscious of his nakedness, clutching at the sheet from the bed. A young black girl in a cotton dress stood in the doorway. She was holding shorts and a shirt.

'Mr. Tobin said give you these.' She proffered the garments uncertainly.

'These are not my clothes,' said Joe. 'Where are my clothes?'

'I wash them.'

The girl put the things on the bed.

'Thank you.'

She smiled quickly and left. Outside the banging continued.

When he was dressed in the too-tight shorts and shirt, the girl brought him bread and jam and tea, which he ate in the living-room. The house was large, old for Africa, with white-painted walls. The polished floorboards were loose under the nails that secured them. There was a three-piece suite with stained gold-coloured upholstery, and a cheap table and chairs. A collection of walking sticks and African axes stood in a tall pot. Above the stone fireplace was a painting of a bull elephant, trunk raised, ears spread in menace. There was a zebra skin on the floor, dirty and curled at the edges. And books. A few books.

When he had finished eating Joe went to the low bookcase and looked at them. Roberts' *Birds of South Africa*; *Trees, Flowers and Grasses of Rhodesia*; *Birds of the Lowveld*. A Shona dictionary, volumes of memoirs of the early pioneers, some copies of *Time* magazine. Ellie always used to say you could tell a man by his books. A large mottled green and black bound book caught Joe's eye. On the spine was the single word *Contact*.

He pulled it out and flicked it open. It was full of pictures of the Rhodesian war. Helmeted pilots in Vampire jets. White men in camouflage, clutching rifles and leaping from helicopters. Ian Smith smiling at disabled soldiers in wheelchairs. And, sickeningly, pictures of mutilations: women with their lips cut off, a dead village headmen splashed with blood. 'Mao-inspired terrorism at work in Rhodesia', a caption read. He was about to return the book to the shelf when a section at the back caught his eye: 'Rhodesian Honours and Awards'. On page 207 a name had been underlined. '29th October 1976. 2Lt. R. S. Tobin. Silver Cross of Rhodesia. For Conspicuous Gallantry.'

'I didn't realise I still had that book.'

Joe turned guiltily. Ross had entered in total silence, instinctively avoiding each creaking floorboard. There was grease on his shirt and flecks of dry grass in his hair.

'I'm sorry. I shouldn't have . . .'

Ross smiled. 'No, I'm glad you found it. I'll get Winnie to burn it. It's not the kind of book the Comrades approve of.' He took the book and dropped it into a metal waste bin. 'It's a load of shit, anyway. Half the pictures are faked.'

'I saw your name.'

'It was a long time ago.'

'You saw a lot of fighting?'

'A bit. A little bit.' He sat down at the table and felt the teapot. 'Winnie!' he shouted. 'Tikupi!'

The black girl came in with a cup.

'You met Winnie?'

Joe nodded.

'Winnie, this is Mr. Lejeune. How's his clothes?'

'Not dry, Mr. Tobin.'

'She's a good girl,' Ross said, when the girl had gone out. 'A good worker.' He poured himself a cup of tea.

Joe wondered about the man and the medal. There were only a handful awarded, he'd noticed. It had to be special. He wanted to ask about it, but there was something about Ross's reaction to the subject that stopped him. Instead he said, 'You live here alone?'

Ross nodded, 'Yes.'

'The cars?'

'I buy them and do them up, make a buck or two. Nothing too strenuous. And you?'

Joe hesitated. 'I'm staying here for a while. I'm from London.'

He could feel the man's eyes on him, examining him, coming to conclusions. It was a disconcerting feeling. Ross said, 'You're the guy whose wife and kids got taken in that ambush.'

Jesus Christ, was there no one who didn't know? 'You remember?' Joe said.

'When I heard your name and saw those bullet holes in your body. A neat job. Who stitched you up, old man Harrington?'

'You know him?'

'Oh, yes. He's good. Where are you staying?'

'The Courtenay, Selous Avenue.'

'A hotel?'

'I was staying at a place out near Widdecombe Road but . . .'

'There's a bed here if you want it.'

Joe shook his head quickly. 'No, I . . .' He stopped.

'Please yourself.'

There was a note of regret in Ross's voice. Might he be lonely, this man with oily hands? The red setter padded into the room and slumped near Ross's chair. He fondled its ears and the hair near its collar.

'Nice dog,' Joe said.

'Yes.'

'What's its name?'

'Chaka.'

Joe clicked his fingers. 'Here Chaka!' The dog looked up but didn't move.

'If you were an Af,' said Ross, 'he'd have your hand off. He's a good boy.'

The dog wagged its tail.

'You've got a lot of books about the bush,' Joe said. 'Birds.'

'A few. I don't read too much.'

'You spend a lot of time in the bush?'

'Some.'

'Tracking?'

'When I need to. Mostly I just walk. Get away from it all.'

'You take a gun?'

91

'Sometimes, sometimes not. It depends.'

'On what?'

'Where I'm going. What I'm doing.'

Joe hesitated, then asked the question that had formed in his mind when he first saw the books: the only question he wanted to ask, and the question he feared most. 'Can you sell me a gun?'

There was a long silence. Ross stroked the dog again, then said slowly, 'You want to buy a gun?'

'If you've got one to sell.'

'Why?' His voice was suddenly hard.

'My own reasons.'

'If I sell you a gun, I want to know why.'

Joe stood up suddenly. The shaking, the terror, was returning. 'I've got to go,' he said.

'Your clothes aren't dry.'

'I'll wear then wet.'

He made for the door but Ross's command stopped him. 'Come back. Sit down.' There was a note almost of brutality in his voice.

'I don't mind wet clothes,' Joe said quickly.

'I said sit down.'

Joe did as he was told, seating himself stiffly on the chair next to Ross. 'OK,' said the fair-haired man. 'Now tell me why you want a gun.'

Joe told him everything, at first reluctantly and then with increasing vehemence; about the kidnapping itself and his days in hospital, about Mtisi and Zvarevashe and the lies he had been told. About the Rondavel, and Chrissie and Look-out and Cecil Square and the hotel and the white Datsun. And about Kezi. When he had finished he sat back in the chair, still shaking, exhausted.

Ross said nothing. He poured Joe a cup of tea and pushed it across to him. The tea was lukewarm, strong and bitter-tasting. Joe drank a little and put the cup down.

After a while Ross stood up. 'I've got to think,' he said. Moments later the banging resumed in the garden.

When Winnie came in to clear away the breakfast things, Joe remained where he was, not moving or attempting to meet the girl's eyes. For a time the banging continued and then stopped. He heard running water from the bathroom and, shortly afterwards, the sound of an engine. A buff-coloured Nissan truck swung out of the gate, between the gum trees, and was gone.

Before the dust had settled Joe knew that he had to leave. He had no alternative. It was his own fault, his own stupid fault. He could have rested up here, stayed a few days, maybe learned a few things that would have been useful. This guy was an expert, a real expert. The first expert he'd met. He should have said he was a tourist or something, some dumb stupid tourist who'd got himself into trouble in a strange city. It was just plausible. He could have invented something about the bullet wounds – a hunting accident, anything. Instead he'd sat there and given his real name and then asked a total stranger to sell him a gun, and not only that, he'd told him why. He must be mad. He must want his head tested.

But then, maybe it would have been all pointless anyway. What was that guy doing there last night? Had it just been coincidence? Did he just happen to be driving along Manica Road at that exact moment? Maybe he'd been watching him all along. Less suspicious, a white man.

Christ! He'd be in town in half an hour or less, reporting back to the police, the C.I.O. or whoever was paying him. Joe was on his feet in an instant, making for the kitchen.

Winnie was cutting up vegetables. She looked up at him apprehensively.

'My clothes.'

'Wet.'

'I don't care if they're wet. Where are they?'

She shook her head slowly, as if not understanding.

Joe wrenched open the back door. His clothes were there, spread on a thorn bush, damp but no longer dripping. He ripped them from the bush and went into the bedroom at a run. It took him seconds to change, a minute longer to find his shoes which were slung beneath the wardrobe. They stank of vomit as he put them on, making his gorge rise.

In the garden there were buckets of oil, gearboxes half-hidden by rank grass. Black and white crows pecked and flapped in the trees above. He ran at first, following the track between the gums which formed a small wood, a plantation.

Brilliant yellow-breasted birds flittered between the branches. It was a long way to the road, and hot despite the shade. Dust coated his shoes, and his shirt, already wet, became wetter, stained and sticking to his back. His body ached, and his arm throbbed where the knife wound was. After a while he was forced to slow to a walk.

It was a mile, maybe two, to the road, and when he reached it it was scarcely even a road, just a rough dirt track hardly wider than the track to the house. He paused, gasping for breath. The sun glistened on the tightly curled leaves of tobacco in the field bordering the road. Beyond the field more gum trees closed off the horizon.

Instinctively he turned left, keeping close to the trees, ready to jump for cover if Ross should return, or the white Datsun. For half an hour he walked, meeting nobody. Then a woman passed with a bag of mealie meal on her head, and soon afterwards an old African on a bicycle. He stopped when Joe called to him, smiling broadly, and pointed in the direction of Harare. It was twenty miles, he said.

Joe had been walking the wrong way.

When the man had gone, he sat down on the stiff grass at the roadside, put his head in his hands and wept.

He stayed there for a long time at the side of the road, not moving, not even thinking. Then he stood up and walked slowly back to the house.

He was sitting under a thorn bush on the ripped out seat of a Ford Zephyr when Ross returned. It was almost dark, and the headlights of the Nissan caught him, blinding him, forcing him to shield his eyes with his hands. Ross slid the truck to a halt and leapt out. He was carrying a brown nylon bag which he dropped at Joe's feet. 'Your stuff,' he said. 'I collected it from the hotel. You are Mr. Edwards from Mutare, I presume?'

'Listen,' said Joe. 'I said . . .'

'I know what you said. Come and have a beer. I've got your bike in the back, by the way.'

As they walked towards the house, Ross said, 'I met a mate of mine in the police. He says if I bring the papers and a note of authorisation from you, he can get your Land-Rover released. Apparently they took it by mistake. They've been trying to contact you.'

'You told the police where I was?'

'Why not?'

Joe stopped. 'You bastard!' he said.

'Hey, hold on,' Ross said. 'I've got an old mate in the police, that's all. I just thought I'd see if he could do something about the Land-Rover.'

'I was right about you, dead right. It was no accident you turned up when you did last night. Who's paying you, hey? Zvarevashe? The C.I.O.?'

Ross laughed. 'I wish they were. I could use the cash.'

'You're watching me, aren't you? They sent you to watch me.' Joe's eyes fell on the dark shape of the Nissan. The keys were still in the ignition, he was sure.

Ross read his thoughts. 'I've got them here,' he said, and patted his pocket. 'You can have them if you want.'

'I do want.'

'OK,' said Ross mildly. He took the keys from his pocket and dropped them in Joe's hand. 'Now where are you going to go?'

'Wouldn't you like to know?'

'Not much.'

Ross turned back towards the house. At the door he stopped and turned again. 'Something you ought to know about me before you go. I was a Selous Scout. Counter-insurgency. The apple of Ian Smith's eye. And as far as the Comrades were concerned, that makes me slightly lower than a heap of shit.'

'You're lying.'

'Why should I lie? I can prove it if you want.'

Joe was silent. Then he said, 'Last night in Manica Road . . .?'

'A certain young lady in Cranborne Park. Recently divorced. Kept her knickers on so I came home early.'

'Just coincidence then?'

'Just coincidence.'

'Oh, Jesus.' Joe put his forehead in his hands.

Moments later he felt an arm round his shoulders. 'Come and get your beer,' Ross said.

They cleared a space on the stoep, shifting bits of car bodywork, radiators, door panels, and set up a couple of chairs. Frogs were calling from the marshy vlei behind the house. Winnie paused to say goodbye on her way home. She was carrying her shoes and various bits of food in a cardboard box on her head.

They drank the beer from the bottles, feet up on the rails, Chaka slumped nearby. Ross was different after his trip to town, Joe sensed. He was more relaxed, expansive almost. 'This friend of yours in the police, did he say why they were following me?' Joe asked.

'No.'

'But surely . . .'

'I don't think they *were* following you.'

'I know what I saw.'

'Sure you do. You saw what you wanted to see.'

Ross's tone began to irritate him. 'You're wrong,' Joe snapped. 'Those bastards . . .'

Ross sucked at his beer. 'You were in the wrong place at the wrong time, that's all. They'd been after that guy Zinyemba . . .'

'Zinyemba?'

'Lookout Zinyemba. He had half a ton of dagga in cardboard boxes under his bed. They knew about him. They'd been watching him. They probably thought you were involved.'

'But afterwards, at the hotel. They followed me to the Queens. They were there last night.'

'I've been thinking about that,' Ross said slowly. 'And do you know what I think? I think there are more white Datsuns in Zimbabwe than any other make of car.'

'Which is why they chose it.'

'I don't think so.'

Joe was silent for a moment, staring out into the gathering night. After a while he said, 'I wish I could believe you.'

'Try.'

'And if I don't?'

'Then you don't.'

Joe got up and went down the steps onto the grass. The sky was bell-clear, mussel-shell blue, pierced with stars. From somewhere a long way away came the pulse of a drum. He glanced back at the man on the stoep who had bent towards the dog and was talking in gentle undertones. Perhaps Ross was right. There were a hell of a lot of white Datsuns. There were Datsuns wherever you looked. Everywhere.

If so, what did that make him? A nutcase? A victim of delusions? Maybe his belief that Ellie and the children were still alive was also a delusion. Perhaps he was going gently mad without realising it. Joe Lejeune, a suitable case for treatment. Poor old Joe. Perhaps that was what Penny was thinking, what Mac was thinking back home in London . . .

Christ, no! That was no way to carry on, no way at all. He remembered the bandit Ndhlovu, the terror in the man's eyes. He'd wanted to tell the truth. He'd opened his mouth to tell the truth, despite the torture, despite the men holding him. Tomorrow he'd get the Land-Rover and just go. He owed it to that man, and to Ellie, and to himself. He swigged a couple of mouthfuls of beer and turned back towards the stoep. 'I'm going,' he said. 'Tomorrow.'

'Where?'

'Down south, Kezi. You said you'd think about a gun.'

Ross put down his empty bottle. 'You finished your beer? Want another?'

'A gun.'

'I'll get us another beer.' Ross went into the house. The light came on in the kitchen. There was the sound of the fridge door opening and closing. Ross returned, handed Joe a bottle and sat down. 'You're going to get yourself killed,' he said.

'That's my business.'

'If I give you a gun, it's my business too.'

'I'm prepared to pay.'

'That's not the point.' Ross shifted round to face Joe. 'Listen,' he said, 'You know nothing. Nothing! You don't know the language, you don't know the people, you don't know the bush. I'll bet you've never even picked up a gun outside the shooting range at a funfair.'

'I can learn.'

'By that time you'll be dead.'

'Perhaps it's how I choose to die.'

'You're talking shit.'

A large bird flew overhead on silent wings like a white ghost. Chaka looked up and whimpered. Ross said, 'The

Shona believe that if an owl sits on the roof of a house it predicts death.'

'It's not sitting on the roof.'

'Lucky for us, hey?' Ross laughed, and slapped his knee.

They drank in silence for a while. The owl circled again, quartering the yard before gliding off in the direction of the gum trees. The night air was heavy with the vibrations of frogs and tree crickets. Suddenly Ross said, 'I'd better come with you, I guess.'

'I'm sorry?' said Joe, not understanding.

'I said I'd better come with you and look for your wife. You're stupid but you're a nice guy, and I don't like to see guys getting themselves killed.'

'You mean that?'

'Sure I mean it. I wouldn't have said it if I didn't mean it.'

'But why? You don't know me. You don't know Ellie.'

Ross smiled. 'Lets just say I miss the mopani flies and the stale water. Hey, I got some steaks in town. You hungry?'

Joe didn't question Ross further on why he'd agreed to come, half afraid that he might change his mind. Instead, as they ate the steaks and drank more beer, he surrendered himself to quiet elation like a kid anticipating a party. He showed Ross the pictures of Ellie and the children, talked about their life in London, the flat, about his work in Covent Garden. He talked about Ellie a lot – her toughness, her instinct for survival – and of course the kids. As he talked, it was as if they were slowly returning to life, their flat images on the photographs taking on flesh and blood and bone. Ross listened to him quietly, smiling sometimes, asking the occasional question, seeming to share his mood. Then, when the beer was gone and the glow of the embers in the braai was dying, they went into the house.

Ross fetched a notebook and pen from a drawer, and a calendar from the kitchen. They sat at the table. A single mosquito droned around the room like a radio controlled model. Ross snapped open the notebook, bent the spine back and laid it flat on the table. He clicked out the point of the pen. 'OK,' he said. 'Let's quit pissing about and get on with it. First, there's something I've got to say to you, and I want you to listen carefully. It's quite possible we'll find nothing. In fact, more than possible: probable. It's a long time since it all took place. But if we do find something it could be dangerous, very dangerous. I've got no desire to be killed, or to end up in some filthy prison cell, so I want to make one thing clear. We do this *my* way. What I say goes. If I call the whole thing off at any point, it's off. Do you understand?'

Joe nodded, mesmerised by the change in the man. There was a tension, an urgency, a suppressed excitement. His voice was clipped, taut, in startling contrast to the lazy drawl of moments before.

Satisfied, Ross continued. 'You accept my orders at all times without question. Make suggestions by all means, but do nothing unless I say so. That way we'll stay alive and stay friends. If you've got any objections, tell me now, before we start, and we'll both save ourselves a lot of time and energy.'

'I've no objections.'

'Good.' Ross picked up the calendar and studied it. 'It's the twenty-seventh today. We'll give ourselves four day's planning and equipping which takes us to the thirty-first. Then we'll have a piss-up to see in the New Year and get going on the first.'

'Nineteen eighty-four,' said Joe. 'I've read the book.'

It was a weak joke, but Ross made no sign of having heard it. He was already scribbling in the notebook. He finished writing and sat back in the chair. 'OK, vehicle and equipment. We've got two choices: my Nissan or your Land-Rover. I've promised the Nissan to a guy in Greendale, and quite honestly I need the cash. So, if we can, we'll take your Land-Rover. I'll pick it up tomorrow. What is it?'

'1975 Mark 2A. Long wheelbase.'

'Safari body?'

'Yes.'

'Equipment?'

'Electric mud winch. Protective mesh. Freewheel hubs.'

'Forget the freewheel hubs. Mileage?'

'70,000.'

'What kind of nick?'

'It seems OK.'

'That's not good enough. I'll check it over when we get it back here. I broke a Mark 2 a couple of months ago so I've probably got most of the spares we'll need. The rest we'll have to buy, beg, borrow or steal. How are you for cash?'

'I've got about five thousand, plus a thousand in US dollars in traveller's cheques. I can wire for more.'

'No need. Keep the US dollars whatever you do. Then tomorrow, when we go into town, get yourself five hundred in cash and make an arrangement to be able to withdraw the rest from the bank in Chiredzi.'

'Chiredzi?'

'We'll base up at Chiredzi.'

'But I thought Kezi . . .'

'Where'd you get this thing about Kezi?'

'From a journalist. He reckons the dissidents would have . . .'

'Who says we're looking for dissidents?'

'But I . . .'

Ross put down his pen. 'Listen,' he said. 'Forget what you've been told. Forget any theories you've got, any ideas. They'll only waste our time. Those guys who robbed you could have been anybody, anybody at all. There's only one place to start, and that's where it happened, Chiredzi. Then we'll take it from there. Anyway, who is this journalist?'

'A guy called Larry Wakeman.'

Ross seemed to stiffen.

'You know him?' Joe said.

'Who doesn't?' Ross turned back to his notebook. 'OK, so that's the vehicle taken care of. Now, equipment. The winch you've got. I can supply spares, shovels, sandmats, radiator mesh, an extra spare wheel, toolkit. We'll take my twelve volt welder, and petrol cans: four five gallon jerries, plus the front and rear tanks will give us a range of 400 miles bush driving which should be enough.'

'What about water?' Joe asked.

'We'll come to that. Next, supplies and expendables. Dry rations, tins and biltong we can pick up at the Chiredzi supermarket as and when we need it. I've got some plastic boxes. We'll need a cooker and gas cylinders. The cooker I've got. We'll get spare cylinders in town tomorrow. Now, water. We can't depend on the rains because they look like they,ll never come. There'll be water in the main rivers, the Sabi,

Lundi, Nuanetsi, and that's about it. It's going to be very hot – forty-two, forty-four centigrade. In that kind of heat it's twelve pints of water a day minimum for each man, and that's just drinking. We'll take four five-gallon cans – twenty gallons. If we're going to be away from civilisation for a long time, we can add some more. OK?'

'OK.' Joe felt bemused by the speed with which the list was growing. He glanced at the watch on Ross's wrist. It was already past midnight. Chaka scratched himself and adjusted his position beneath the table. The mosquito continued to drone.

Ross checked the list and appeared satisfied. 'Right, personal clothing and equipment. What have you got in the way of bush clothing? Not a lot by the look of your bag.' He ripped a sheet of paper from the notebook and fetched a second pen, handing it to Joe. 'Write these down,' he said, 'and you can get them in town tomorrow. Two khaki or green bush shirts, one long-sleeved. One pair shorts, same colour. A pair of green or khaki veldschoen. I'll show you the sort. I think they're what you call desert boots in England. Two khaki or green bush hats, in case you lose one. Also you'll need a pair of overalls, again khaki or green – might have a spare pair somewhere. A watch is essential – I notice you don't have one – and a leather cover for it to stop reflection.

'Sleeping bags I can supply, and plastic ground sheets, and water bottles though we'll need more. I can probably borrow some. I've got some packs which should do us, and webbing. Anything else? Oh, yes. Spoons, forks, mess tins, those I've got. You'll also need a good folding knife. Get the best you can find. I've got a skinning knife which I'll take, and a panga.'

'What's a panga?'

'A slashing knife. You must have seen them – long, with a curved blade. A sort of machete. And we'll need a saw. The elephants down there have a nasty habit of dropping fully grown trees across the road.'

'What about tents?'

'No tents. If it rains we get wet. Oh, add matches and a tin opener to your list. And a compass.'

Joe wrote down 'matches, tin opener, compass'.

'Right,' said Ross. 'Medical supplies. I want to take a J-Pack or its equivalent.'

'A J-Pack?'

'They were issued to platoon commanders during the war: drip bags, tubes, that sort of thing. Also field dressings, gauze, bandages, morphine or sosogon, antibiotics. I'm trying to think of a medic who might swing the lot for us . . . anyway, we'll get them somehow. You do understand, of course, that if anybody gets seriously hurt there'll be no helicopter to casevac us out? We'll be on our own.'

'I understand,' Joe said quietly.

'So let's stay out of trouble. OK, what else? Oh, yes. This lot you can add to your list, Aspirin – no, codeine is better. Elastoplast, a big tin. Penicillin ointment if you can get it. Insect repellant. Salt tablets. Snake bite kit. Water purifying tablets, and anti-malaria tablets. Have you been taking any?'

'I stopped.'

'Well, start again. I've got some Daraprim somewhere. We'll take one each tonight before we go to bed. Today's Tuesday. I'll make it your responsibility to see that we take our Daraprim each Tuesday. Get a bottle of a hundred when you're in the pharmacy. And I think that's medical taken care of.'

Ross shifted on his chair, stretched and yawned. He smiled suddenly at Joe. 'Don't look so worried,' he said. 'We're nearly through. We probably shan't need half this junk, but if we don't take it, you can bet your life we will.' He glanced down again. 'What's left? Compasses we've got down – that's wrist compasses. Maps, of course, one in fifty thousand. I've got some, I don't know how many. Any others we'll get from the Surveyor General's Office in Samora Machel. Also a lantern and torches. And, we'd better take one of those metal things – I can't remember what they're called, Dead men I think – to connect the winch rope to if there's no handy tree. I've got one in the yard somewhere.'

He stopped and flicked back over the list. 'That's the lot, I think. Anything else occur to you?'

'Camouflage gear?'

'No way. When we get stopped by the police or the Army, which we shall, they're going to start asking unpleasant questions if we're sitting there looking like the bloody Green Berets. That's something else we need to sort out by the way:

an official reason for going down there.'

'Do we need a reason?'

'We need a reason.'

'Tourists?'

'Not at this time of the year. Anyway, we'll be going places where no tourist ever goes. No, I think you'd better become a rich American trophy hunter – after elephant, probably. I've got a safari operator's licence which has lapsed. You can become my client. I'll go to the Parks and Wildlife and get the licence renewed, and I'll get you a permit. I think it's two hundred bucks. Trophy fees are extra, but since there isn't going to be a trophy they won't apply. I'll fix it, I've got good contacts there.'

Joe grinned. 'I don't see myself as the Hemingway type.'

'Who?'

The Snows of Kilimanjaro.'

Ross looked blank.

'Forget it,' said Joe.

Ross closed the notebook. 'One other thing,' he said. 'I want to take Enos.'

'Who's he?'

'An African I worked with at the end of the war in a two-man reconnaissance unit. He's about the best tracker I know of, and he's bloody handy if things get rough. Also, he's black which means he can go where we can't: chat up the women, go to the beer drinks, ask questions. Object?'

'No.'

'Obviously I haven't had time to get hold of him, so I don't know if he's willing. But if he is, he'll probably want paying.'

'How much?'

'Depends how long we'll be gone. Two hundred bucks, maybe a bit more.'

'That's OK by me,' said Joe. 'I hope he'll come.'

Ross laughed, 'I think he will. He never could resist a bit of fun. It'll also mean we're three, so if anyone gets hurt there'll be two men to carry him.'

'When can you see him?'

'We'll go round and see if we can find him tomorrow, after we've been into town. Tired?'

Joe nodded.

'OK. Let's go to bed. Chaka! Come on, boy. I'm just out to check the gates. See you in the morning.' He paused at the door. 'Daraprim,' he said.

Joe looked sheepish.

'I'll get them,' Ross said.

Later, in his narrow bed, Joe lay for a long time, his eyes open. Things were moving fast, too fast. He felt like he was in an out-of-control car with a mad driver heading God knows where. To oblivion, maybe. Sandmats, water bottles, drip bags . . . You must accept my orders at all times . . .

Why was he doing it, this guy? Stale water and mopani flies? What kind of reason was that for putting your life on the line? Joe had known him barely twenty-four hours, yet already they were hatching plots about big white hunters and game permits, about trackers and beer drinks.

Was it money? Was that the reason? He hadn't mentioned money except for the African. No, not money. Unless someone else was already paying him . . . If so, who? The South Africans? Maybe that was it. Maybe they were paying him to . . .

Always conspiracies! They tired him, defeated him, bored him. He should trust the guy. He should just go along with him, swim with the tide and hope the tide took him to Ellie. Stale water and mopani flies. It was as good a reason as any. Time would tell.

Next morning Ross worked on the Nissan, preparing it for the guy in Greendale, while Joe broke down the lists of the night before into manageable sections and sorted out the Land-Rover papers. Later they drove into town.

Ross lived in lush country. Red earth. Olive green tobacco fields. Broad silken-tasseled stands of maize. Citrus trees marching like well-drilled soldiers across the folds in the land, dividing at outcrops of red rock. The track to the house joined another track, broader and better graded, which in turn joined the Chinhoyi road south of Nyabira. They passed a white farmer in a Land Cruiser to whom Ross lifted an arm in greeting. Coming into town they skirted the white blocks of the University.

The place was surprisingly crowded, full of white matrons

with small children and blacks with string bags, and it took Joe longer to find the things he needed than he'd anticipated. Once or twice as he crossed roads he found himself looking at the cars. Ross was right. There were a hell of a lot of white Datsuns. Every other bloody car, it seemed. The realisation made him smile. At the bank he was surprised to find that he had nearly seven thousand dollars in his account. The financial arrangements were made swiftly and with a minimum of fuss. In Baker Avenue he saw Chrissie and Tansy, but they were on the other side of the street and didn't acknowledge him when he waved. He wondered about Lookout and what would happen to him. The sun was hot and the weight of the bags hurt his shoulder. He was thankful not to meet Penny.

Ross met him at twelve at the corner of Samora Machel and Second Street. He was driving the Land-Rover. The police had handed it over, he said, no fuss. After that he'd gone to the Parks and Wildlife in North Avenue, and the permit shouldn't be any problem. He'd got somewhere on the J-Pack front, too. There was a young Yugoslav medic who owed him a favour. Joe noticed that a book on Cecil Rhodes which he'd left in the Land-Rover was missing, and later discovered that some of the tools had gone from the locker under the passenger seat. Ross said he was lucky the wheels were still there. There were an extra three hundred miles on the clock, and an empty tank.

They filled up with Blend at the Caltex garage in Manica, and headed south into Prince Edward Dam Road. A platoon of red-bereted military police were manning a roadblock, but waved them past. Africans wobbled on either side of them on bicycles and crowded buses. Small white clouds flecked the ground with shadow. On the bus stops were posters advertising Premier No. 1 Roller Meal. Ross told Joe that Chitungwiza, where they were headed, had a population approaching a million. It was the Soweto of Harare.

They passed a People's Market selling onions, tomatoes, oranges and cabbages, and swung up into a maze of unpaved streets lined with identical breeze-block and asbestos houses. Mealies crammed the tiny front gardens and laced the narrow strips between the plots. Here and there bougainvillaea straddled a wire fence, splashing its colour untidily, like paint spilt from a pot. Children playing football in the dust paused to stare. The smaller ones waved.

After a while they turned into a road slightly broader and longer than the rest, and pulled up outside a house. It had a small stoep tacked onto the front, but otherwise it was indistinguishable from the others. Two young children of six or so were playing in the road outside, and when they saw Ross they ran up shouting loudly, laughing, quivering with joy as he handed them a packet of sweets each which he produced from his pocket. They immediately sat down in the dust to eat them.

A thin woman with a tired face came from the rear of the house, clapping her hands in greeting. Ross introduced Joe in English and then spoke to the woman in Shona. She pointed to where a pile of sand spilled from a garden and into the street a few houses down. Ross thanked her. As they drove slowly down the bumpy road the children ran alongside them, laughing and shouting.

Ross got out and went into the house the woman had indicated. He emerged soon after with a short, thickset man of about thirty. He had a small moustache, and was wearing blue dungarees splashed with pink plaster. 'This is Enos,' Ross said.

Enos wiped his hands on his dungerees and shook hands with Joe. 'Pleased to meet you,' he said. The children stood watching respectfully, chewing sweets, awed by the presence of their father.

Ross and Enos talked for a long time in Shona. Joe heard his own name being mentioned once or twice, and the words 'Chiredzi' and 'Land-Rover'. Enos nodded frequently, smiled once briefly. Then he shook hands with Ross, reached into the cab and shook hands again with Joe, turned and went back into the house. Ross started the Land-Rover. 'He'll come,' he said. 'He said not to bother about the money, but he doesn't mean it.'

'Nice guy,' Joe said.

'He is. Just so long as you're on his side.'

Ross leaned from the cab and said something in Shona to the two children, who burst into loud laughter. 'OK,' he said. 'Let's go.'

106

There were problems with the Land-Rover. Not big problems, but problems. One of the rear springs needed replacing, and there were oil leaks from the shock absorbers. The rear tank had been cracked and imperfectly welded and needed work, but at least the gearbox and the steering were OK.

They worked on the vehicle until dark, and for most of the following day. In addition to making good the repairs, Ross fitted temperature and oil-pressure gauges, an eight-bladed fan, and replaced the clutch slave cylinder seals, plugs, points and fan belt. Joe cleaned the air filter and changed the engine oil. Later he helped Ross to dart weld protective plates behind the rear axle to prevent further damage to the tank in deep gullies. When they had finished Ross went into the house and emerged with a Sharp cassette tape player which he fixed beneath the parcel shelf.

They talked while they worked, mostly of the kidnap and its aftermath. Joe tried to describe the men, their dress, the weapons, but his memory of the incident was fading, coalescing into a series of still frames like snapshots, each distinct in itself but seemingly unrelated. He realised he was no longer able clearly to recall the place where it had happened except in the most general terms. 'Mopani trees,' he said. 'And rocks.'

Ross grunted, obviously unimpressed, and asked him in which direction the men had gone. Joe didn't know. 'Keep thinking,' Ross told him. Once Joe asked Ross about the war, what it had been like, but he became silent and refused to be drawn. Joe didn't ask again.

On the Thursday afternoon, while they were cutting and welding the protective plates for the rear tank, Joe mentioned guns, and how they'd forgotten to include them on the list. This time Ross didn't avoid the question. 'We'll take three,' he said. 'They're all licensed, legal and above board. We'll take my 375, and an old Lee Enfield which used to be my father's. Also a silenced .22 for small game. That'll do us for now. If things look like getting rough, we'll have to make other arrangements.'

'What other arrangements?'

'Other arrangements.'

'They had AKs,' Joe said.

'So you told me.'

Ross pulled on his goggles and started to weld. The conversation was obviously closed.

That evening, after they had finished work, Ross took Joe to a low range of outbuildings behind a mango tree in the rear garden. 'This was the kia,' he said. 'The old servants' quarters. Winnie wanted to come and live here when I took her on, but I said no. Before you know where you are, they'll bring their uncles and their cousins and their sisters and their aunts, and you'll end up supporting the lot of them. I just use it for storage.'

At the entrance of one of the rooms was a heavy wooden door secured with a padlock. Ross opened it. It was filled with bush gear, a lot of it ex-army stuff by the look of it. Tents and sleeping bags, boxes of mess tins, waterproof capes in drab green, bundles of webbing, lanterns, a small mountain of backpacks. Hanging from a hook was what appeared to be a parachute. Joe whistled.

'Waste not, want not,' said Ross, and grinned. 'You'll find most of what we need in here, including the overalls I promised you. I've got things to pick up in town tomorrow: the permit, the medical stuff, a few Land-Rover spares and so on. The room next to this is empty. I'll give you the key. While I'm gone I want you to take the list and sort out the stuff we need, checking it off. That'll give us Saturday to get hold of anything we've forgotten, and to load up.'

'I'll start now,' said Joe.

'Tomorrow,' said Ross. 'Come and have a beer.'

He was gone early the next morning, soon after Joe was up. It had rained in the night and the drops on the grass sparkled in the bright sunshine. On Ross's advice Joe had started his exercises again, and before he dressed he did thirty minutes of Level 4. He was surprised at how strong he'd become. Only the press-ups bothered him, the strain on his injured shoulder producing the occasional agonising spasm of pain. The knife cut on his forearm was healing quickly, and he had removed the plaster.

After Winnie had brought him breakfast, he went to the kia and started to work through the list. A tiny gekko, clamped to the wall by its suckered feet, watched him, apparently unafraid.

Ross was right. There were most of the things they needed in the store room even with extra equipment for Enos, and the line of ticks on the list grew satisfactorily, as did the piles of gear in the empty room. He sang as he worked, cheerful, glad to be concentrating on the task in hand. At noon he went indoors and ate a sandwich and drank a glass of lemonade. He tried to talk to Winnie but gave up. Her English was limited, and her thick accent difficult to understand.

It was mid-afternoon when he heard the phone ring in the house, and saw Winnie coming across to fetch him. It would be Ross, he guessed, checking up on something. The phone was in the hall on a rickety table, a carved stool next to it. Joe sat down and picked up the receiver.

The voice on the other end was not Ross's but Larry Wakeman's. There was no preamble. 'I want to talk. Come into town, to the office.'

'How the hell did you know I was here?' said Joe, astonished.

'It's a small town.'

'You've got information about Ellie?' For a moment there was a blaze of hope.

'No.'

'Then what?'

'This evening. Around six. I'll be in the office.'

Joe became irritated. 'I'm busy, and I've got no way of getting into town. Can't you tell me on the phone?'

There was a slight pause then Larry said: 'OK, listen. I want to warn you about that guy Tobin. He's not there, is he?'

'Ross? No.'

'Good. Now I don't know what you're getting into with that guy, but my advice is: don't.'

'I didn't ask your advice.' Joe's irritation was increasing.

'He's bad news, Joe, very bad news and I'm not kidding. He's a killer.'

'This country's full of killers.'

'Not his sort. He was a Selous Scout.'

'He told me.'

'He told you?' Larry sounded surprised. 'OK, well, I'll tell you again. There aren't many Selous Scouts left in Zimbabwe. You know why? Because when Mugabe took over he kicked them out. Most of them are down in Namibia working

109

for the Boers. Some are in Mozambique with the MNR. You heard of Koevoet? The torture and killings going on in Ovamboland? That's where the Selous Scouts are.'

'I'm not interested.'

'Well, get interested in this. In 1976 my wife Eva was in Mozambique at a refugee camp. Nyadzonya, just across the border from Inyanga. It was August the ninth and they were having a celebration. They were all gathered together singing songs, listening to speeches. Men, women and children. Then a column of armoured vehicles with Mozambican Army markings drove through the gates. They thought it was the Mozambicans come to join the fun, and rushed forward to greet them. There were Selous Scouts in those vehicles, with twenty-milimetre canon and heavy machine guns. They opened fire and a thousand people were slaughtered, not just shot but blown to bits. The people who crawled underneath the vehicles for cover were shot with pistols. The Selousies burned the hospital with the patients inside it.

'Eva managed to escape into the Nyadzonya River which ran behind the camp. The water was full of people, most of whom couldn't swim. Fortunately, Eva knew how to. She managed to grab hold of a small boy of about four or five who was drowning and got his head up above the water. Then the Selous Scouts came down to the river and started shooting at the people in the water. The river was full of blood; people being shot, people drowning. Eva dived down under the water trying to escape. She still had hold of the little boy but he struggled and she had to come up for air. One of the Selousies saw her and started shooting at her. A bullet hit the little boy in the head and went through Eva's arm. She was covered with bits of the boy's brain. She let go and dived down again.

'She stayed under water for a long time. There were a lot of reeds at the side of the river and she managed to get to them and hide herself in them. The Selousies came along the banks shooting at people in the reeds, but they didn't spot Eva. Then they went away. She stayed in the river all day and all night, and came out the following morning. There were dead and dying people everywhere. They had to bulldoze pits to bury the people in. Children. Old men. Your friend Ross

Tobin was on that raid, commanding one of the Ferret Scout Cars.'

'I've heard enough.'

'There's more, a lot more.'

'I said I've heard enough! Why the hell are you telling me all this?'

'Isn't it obvious?'

'No,' snapped Joe. 'It isn't.'

'Go home. Come back for the trial, but go home. That guy's evil, man. Evil.'

Joe tried to control his anger, tried to stay calm, but failed. 'I don't give a shit what he did in the war!' he shouted. 'Mugabe's men were doing things just as bad. It's over. It's all over. As far as I'm concerned he's a nice guy who's going to help me find Ellie.'

'She's dead, Joe.'

'Go to hell!' He slammed the phone back onto its rest. 'Bastard,' he said to himself. And, more loudly, spitting out the words: 'Bastard! Bastard!'

In the kitchen Winnie looked up at him fearfully.

Ross returned soon after five. He'd got the hunting permit, a box of medical supplies, and a gasket set and replacement water pump for the Land-Rover. All had gone well, he said. The Yugoslav medic who'd got them the J-Pack had invited them to a New Year's party at Avondale on Saturday night. It sounded like it might be a good piss up.

Joe decided not to tell Ross about Larry Wakeman's phone call. But he thought about it. That night in bed, and sometimes later, when they were in the bush, he thought about it.

Until the time came when he understood.

They went into town again the following morning and got the last of the things from the list: the penicillin ointment, a pair of veldschoens that actually fitted. Joe went to the record bar at the back of the OK Bazaar and bought some tapes. The Rolling Stones, which Ross said he liked, and a collection of Thomas Mapfumo songs. Ross had to go to the police station to check up on one of the gun licences, but was not gone long. They were back at the house by noon.

The afternoon they spent loading, backing the Land-Rover up to the kia. It took a long time, Ross insisting that things were stowed meticulously, their exact positions noted down on a piece of paper. When they had finished they had a couple of beers on the stoep and then a bath each. 'Make the most of it,' Ross said, as Joe ran the taps. 'Water rationing starts tomorrow. Then they'll shoot if you use a drop too much.'

Joe assumed he was joking.

The party was not a great success. The braai failed to light and the beer ran out. Joe found himself pinned into a corner by a fat English medical research assistant who asked too many questions. The Yugoslav doctor sang songs in his native language and a white Rhodie girl became hysterical and had to be taken home. It rained heavily.

They left soon after midnight and drove back, dodging drunken Africans. Chaka, prowling the garden, rushed to the gates to greet them. They were asleep by one o'clock.

Part Three

The Lowveld

They'd wanted to be on the road by six-thirty but it was gone seven before they left. Winnie had come in specially, and Ross spent a long time going over the instructions he'd written out for her about feeding and exercising Chaka. Joe gave her ten dollars which Ross said was too much. At the last possible moment Ross went into his bedroom and came out carrying the three rifles securely strapped into canvas gun cases, which he stowed in the back of the Land-Rover. Chaka, chained to a running line, leapt and barked as they drove out between the gum trees.

The city, full by this time on a weekday, was deserted as they crossed it and turned down towards Chitungwiza. Girls dressed in their Sunday clothes and youths in clean shirts were walking along Prince Edward Dam Road. In the Township, people were hoeing their mealie patches and gossiping in gateways.

Enos was waiting for them when they reached his house, and came out, smiling, carrying a nylon bag. As they left, Joe saw two small faces pressed against the glass of the front window. 'I can't believe it,' he said, as they joined the Beatrice Road, heading south. 'I just can't believe we're really going.'

Ross winked and said nothing.

For a long time they drove in silence, Joe at the wheel, getting the feel of the Land-Rover. The road ran straight and smooth, undulating slightly through lush green Highveld ranching country. Friesian cattle and windpumps. Farm houses set far back along private tracks behind the msasa trees. In the farm compounds the huts drowned in stands of tall mealies, the labourers resting, talking, enjoying the morning. Crocodiles of children headed along the side of the road, dressed for church.

After Chivhu the road began to dip and the land became poorer, drier. Clouds of butterflies, white and the occasional vivid orange, drifted across the road like snow. Despite the weight of gear on board, the Land-Rover ran smoothly, the miles slipping effortlessly away behind them. After a while Ross talked to Enos in Shona, making gestures with his hands and laughing softly. Then they put on a cassette and Mick Jagger sang, 'She's a Honky Tonk Woman'. Stamping his feet on the metal floor, Ross sang along, and whooping, Joe joined him.

At Masvingo, empty, dusty, and noticeably hotter than Harare, they parked the Land-Rover and went to the Paradise Restaurant where they ate hamburgers and drank cokes. They sat around for a while afterwards, relaxing, digesting. Enos filled a pipe and smoked it. When they returned to the Land-Rover there was a large hand print in the dust on the rear door where somebody had tried the lock.

Beyond Masvingo the road began a sharp descent, winding down between strange purple bulbous hills. The Munakas, Ross thought they were called. The occasional Mercedes or Peugeot passed them at speed, heading north from the border at Beitbridge, jammed with white families and luggage. For a while they followed an African pickup. The men and women in the back waved and smiled.

With every kilometre the drought strengthened its grip. The rivers which snaked through culverts beneath the road became trickles then dried altogether. Bare red earth replaced the tall waving grass on the verges, and the mealies in the fields were stunted and dying. Thin donkeys cropped at isolated patches of green.

The heat became intense, splashing the road with mirages. Only the forward movement of the Land-Rover, forcing air into the cab, made driving tolerable. South of the Tokwe River, Joe pulled into a layby and Ross took over.

At the wheel Ross became more talkative. 'Bloody terrible,' he said, indicating the bush. 'By now this should be green, all

114

of it.' There'd been no rain, he said, for three or four years in some places.

Enos nodded slowly in agreement, a man of few words. It was bad, he agreed.

Ross began to talk about Chiredzi. He'd been in contact with some people he knew there, a farmer and his wife. They'd base up there for the time being.

'I thought we'd be in the bush,' Joe said.

'There's time enough for that. Time enough.' Thomas Mapfumo was playing on the Sharp. Ross reached down and ejected the cassette. 'Listen,' he said, 'we need to consider how we're going to play things down there. It's a small community. Everybody knows everybody else's business. The moment we arrive the entire white population will know we're there and will want to know why. I think maybe we should tell the truth. We'll say you're not happy with the Army's version of what happened, and you've come to look for the truth. We may get some information that way.'

'But the hunting business?' Joe said, puzzled.

'That's strictly for the Army and the African authorities.'

'You think that's wise?'

'I know these people. I was based down there during the war at Buffalo Range. I spent holidays down there as a kid. They're not fools. The moment we start driving round asking questions, they'll smell a rat.'

'If you say so.'

'I do say so.' Ross shot Joe a sharp glance.

'OK,' said Joe mildly.

Ross changed gear and moved out to overtake a green bus. Acrid diesel smoke from its exhaust filled the cab and made their eyes water. 'Stinking bloody things,' he said.

They drove in silence for a while. Then Joe said, 'These people we'll be staying with?'

'Harry and Betty Barton. They farm just to the north of Chiredzi. I was at school with their son Robin. We were friends right through.'

'He lives down here too?'

Ross was quiet for a moment. 'He's dead,' he said finally.

'I'm sorry.'

Ross shrugged. 'It happens. He was killed during the war.'

'A soldier?'

'A Reservist. He was in the process of taking over the farm. Old man Barton was going to retire and go down to Natal to live. After Robin was killed, the old man decided to stay on.'

'There were no other children?'

'There's one grandchild. He must be eight now, I guess.'

'Robin's kid?'

Ross nodded. 'I think old Harry's trying to hang on until the boy's old enough to run things himself.'

'What about the boy's mother?'

'Connie? She was killed, too, at the same time. There was an ambush. They'd been to see friends, got stopped on the road. Usual kind of thing.'

'The boy wasn't with them?'

'Oh, yes, he was there, but for some reason he wasn't touched. Maybe they didn't see him, I don't know. He was only two at the time.'

'Poor kid,' said Joe quietly, imagining the bloody bodies and the terrified child.

'We slotted the bastards who did it a week later. Not that it matters now, anyway.'

They left the Beitbridge road at Ngundu, snaking up towards low jagged hills like ruined castle ramparts. The bush became greener and thicker. There'd been some rain. Pole and thatch huts began to appear, clinging to the slopes like brown toadstools. Cattle and goats grazed at the roadside. Herd boys clutching their bark whips watched blank-faced as the Land-Rover passed. One of them was holding a plastic bottle.

Herd boys.

Suddenly Joe said, 'He had a plastic bottle.'

'Who did?'

'When I was shot, there was a herd boy.' It had returned now as if a window had opened in his mind. Cows . . . The smell of them. They'd had big square bells round their necks. Jostling, dribbling spittle from their wet mouths. There had been so many of them. So much pain. His leg. He remembered the blood pumping out. Splash, splash, onto his white foot. And the boy, thin-faced, with terror in his eyes. He'd backed off, two scrawny dogs at his side. 'Please fetch my wife,' he'd said to the boy. 'Please. Please.' Red blood. Red trees. The boy running. The horizon swelling and twisting. Sticks. Individual branches writhing like snakes. The bare red earth smacking at his face . . .

'You didn't tell me about this.' Ross's voice was terse.

'I didn't remember.'

'Jesus.' Ross shook his head. 'What else have you bloody forgotten?'

'You see things.' It was Enos speaking now, slowly and quietly. 'When you're herding cattle you see things. You remember.'

Joe felt a sudden burst of excitement. 'You mean, if we can find this boy . . .?'

'If,' said Ross.

'He had two dogs, very thin. He was ten or eleven. I'd recognise him. I know I'd recognise him. He must have come from some village nearby.'

Ross changed down to overtake a large truck loaded with sugar cane. When they were past he said something in Shona to Enos who nodded and replied briefly. Ross turned back to Joe. 'It was near the Mahande River you were shot, wasn't it?'

'Yes.'

'It's a European ranch, the Flying Star. One of the biggest in the district. I know the bloke who owns the place, Jack Hammond. There are no villages near there.'

'But there was a boy.'

Enos said, 'When there is no rain you walk many miles with your cattle. You break down fences.'

'You mean he could have had his cattle on there illegally?'

'It's possible.'

Joe spun to face Ross. 'This guy Jack Hammond, he'd know, wouldn't he? He'd know, if they were running cattle on his land illegally, which villages they came from?'

'Yes, he'd know.'

'Then we can find him. We can find the little bastard! He'd have seen them. He'd have seen where they went!'

'Maybe.' Ross fell silent again. He seemed strangely subdued, Joe thought, almost irritated by the new development. Maybe it was a deliberate ploy not to raise his hopes too high. Yes, that had to be it.

But it was a start, a real start. And they hadn't even got there yet.

Beyond the hills the huts ceased and the bush crowded in again. Butterflies, more than Joe had ever seen before, streamed across the road from left to right in vast white clouds, smearing the windscreen, fluttering dead and dying into the cab. Yellow hornbills swooped from tree to tree.

Then, without warning, the cane fields began, head-high walls of vivid green. There was more traffic now, European families in cars. Then houses, neat, identical houses with solar panels on the roofs, and the smoke and stink of a cane mill. 'Triangle,' said Ross. 'The original company town.'

The transformation was acute, almost comic. Smooth verges trimmed to a bowling green finish. Company policemen in pith helmets. And everywhere the Triangle symbol: on the storage sheds, on the main gates of the office complex, on the signposts, at each section turning. It was a South African company, Ross explained, with thousands of acres of cane under irrigation. They got the water by canal from Lake Kyle more than a hundred kilometres to the north. 'Mugabe leaves them alone,' he said. 'He can't afford to do anything else. They've got company shops, company schools, a company hospital. Even a company church.'

'It gives me the creeps,' said Joe. 'I don't know why. It's unreal.'

'It's bloody profitable. Bloody well run. Twenty-five years ago all this was virgin bush. Tell me one black government that could set up something like this and run it.'

Joe shrugged. 'Maybe the Nigerians?'

Ross snorted.

They were through Triangle now, and into the bush again. Baobabs, their trunks like grossly swollen human legs, stood sentinel in the mopani scrub. A single track railway line ran alongside the road for a while. They passed an experimental sugar station to their right. Then Buffalo Range: the ranch offices, a store, a butchery, and to the left signs for Buffalo Range airport.

Ross turned to Enos. 'Remember the airfield?'

Enos laughed.

Ross said to Joe, 'We were stuck up there on that airfield

for months in '76. Christ, I got sick of that place. Chiredzi Fort they called it. More Like Chiredzi prison. We had a few good times though, hey, Enos? Shangaan women. He's partial to Shangaan women is our Enos.'

Enos guffawed, said something in Shona. It was Ross's turn to laugh.

They passed the turnoff to Chiredzi soon after, pressing ahead now at speed along the smooth, empty road. The bush reasserted itself, game fences strung like ribbons at the roadside. 'Buffalo Range Ranch to the north, Fair Range to the south,' Ross explained. 'They're game ranches, like the Flying Star. Mostly they run impala but some cattle. They rent out the hunting, and cull for meat. I'd guess they've been having a hard time with this drought.'

They drove over Chiredzi River Bridge, a flat span above the dark waters that twisted between rocks and reeds. Then a railway crossing. They swung north onto a broad, well-graded dirt road. Ten minutes later a sign half-buried in the scrub proclaimed: Chungwe ranch. H. Barton.

A narrow, deeply rutted track led through dense bush, thorns scraping at the bodywork. And then, a few kilometres on, the bush fell back and they found themselves in wide irrigated cotton fields. Huts began to appear, crude pole and thatch structures, at first in ones and twos, then in small groups. Old men sat in doorways, raising their hands in greeting. Cooking fires spiralled blue smoke into the early evening sky. A strikingly beautiful young woman paused to watch them, leaning on her hoe in a mealie patch. Ahead of them were cotton sheds, a partially-dismantled tractor, and a spreading marula tree. Beyond the marula was the house, low-roofed, white-walled, squatting among immense flowering shrubs.

Ross pulled the Land-Rover to a halt beneath the tree and switched off the engine. There was the barking of dogs. 'Chungwe,' he said. 'This is it. Notice anything unusual?'

Joe said, 'It's all unusual.'

'There's no security fence. Never has been, not even during the worst of the war. Even after Robin and Connie were killed and people were urging Harry to put one up, he refused. He's a stubborn old bastard.'

A slight, fair-haired boy in tee shirt and shorts emerged from the house. He was almost dwarfed by a huge Rhodesian ridgeback dog which rushed to the garden gate, barking, followed by a tiny, skidding terrier. The three men got out, glad to stretch their legs. 'Hi, Danny,' said Ross. 'I don't expect you remember me.'

The boy shouted at the dogs to quieten them, and opened the gate. The animals raced across, wagging their tails, leaping, hysterical with joy.

The boy considered Ross for a moment. 'I've seen your picture,' he said. 'With Dad. Fishing.'

'Inyanga,' Ross said. 'I'd like to see that picture sometime. How's your Gran and Grandad?'

'OK, I guess.'

'Ross!'

Harry Barton came down the path to greet them. He was a tall man, well over six foot, red-faced, white-haired, a big belly tucked into a pair of khaki trousers. He was in his early seventies, Joe estimated as Harry grabbed Ross's hand and shook it vigorously.

'How you doing then, Harry?'

'Pretty good. Mustn't complain.'

'And Betty?'

'She's well too. A bit of back trouble, but you've got to expect it at our age.'

Ross indicated Joe. 'Harry, this is Joe Lejeune.'

Joe winced at the grip from Harry's immense fist. 'Foreign name, is it?' the old farmer said.

'French. My father's family were French-Canadian.'

'Thought so. You're welcome anyway. Come on in, young man. And you, Ross.' He turned to the boy. 'Danny, take Ross's man round to the compound. Tell Emmanuel to see to him.'

The house was cool and dark, the curtains drawn against the glare and the heat outside. A table was laid for a meal, plates bottom upwards. 'Come through and have a drink,' Harry said. 'Lemonade?'

He led them into a large, high living-room, timber-ceilinged. There was a chintz-covered lounge suite, a beaten copper frieze of buffalo over the fireplace. On the walls hung

120

two leopardskins and the stuffed and mounted head of a wildebeeste. Wide, heavily-curtained windows looked over a railed stoep. Beyond, sloping downwards to a river valley, were citrus trees, and beyond the citrus the bush. 'Agnes!' Harry shouted, and left the room. 'Agnes! Lemonade!'

'They're Seventh Day Adventists,' Ross said when he was gone. 'They don't drink alcohol. A lot of the farmers round here are the same.'

Harry returned moments later. 'Sit down,' he said. 'Betty's resting. She'll be out in a while.'

A thin black girl in a blue housecoat brought lemonade and glasses on a tray. Harry said something to her in a language that Joe hadn't heard before. She looked frightened and went out. 'She's new in the house,' said Harry. 'She's learning.'

'Harry's one of the few white people who can speak Shangaan,' Ross said.

'There's five of us,' Harry said. 'Six counting Danny. He speaks it better than I do. He could speak Shangaan before he could speak English. He'll probably be the last. It's a dying language.' He poured the lemonade and addressed Ross. 'Good journey?'

Ross nodded.

'Your mother all right, is she?'

'Fine. Never been better.'

'I meant to go and see her when I was down South last year. Didn't have the time.'

'Shame.'

Harry drained his glass at a gulp. 'So why have you come to see me? I wasn't clear from your call. Can't hear the phone properly these days anyway. Betty says I'm getting deaf. I think it's the phones. They're not as loud as they used to be since this lot took over.'

'You haven't changed, have you?' said Ross, and smiled.

'Not me.' Harry chuckled.

Joe noticed a wedding photograph on a low table beside the old man's chair. Danny's parents, he guessed. It must have hurt the old man badly, his son's death. But at least he had the boy. He doted on the boy, that was clear.

Ross said, 'You remember back in August, the kidnap and shooting on the Chipinda Pools road?'

121

Harry nodded. 'Bad business.'

'Well, Joe's the guy who got shot. It was his wife and kids who were taken.'

The old man shifted in his chair to look at Joe. 'It's hard, isn't it?'

'Yes,' said Joe.

'I know how you feel. My son and daughter-in-law were killed at the end of the war.'

'Ross told me.'

Harry paused, remembering. 'Lejeune . . . I recall the name now. Foreign. It said in the *Herald* they caught someone.'

'They've got the wrong man,' said Joe quietly. 'They tortured him to make him confess.'

'I can believe that. I remember saying to Betty: They'll try and pin it on South Africa. And sure enough. . . . Yes, I remember it well. For a couple of weeks afterwards the place was crawling. They must have had five hundred men down there. It was on Jack Hammond's place, the Flying Star. They broke down the fences, shot up the game, came here once wanting to know if we'd seen any dissidents. I said the only dissidents we got round here are the bloody Army. They didn't like that, you know. The officer got quite shirty. After that they went away. We haven't seen them since, apart from the usual mob. And I tell you this – if they ever met any real dissidents they'd run like hell in the opposite direction.'

Joe became aware that Danny had slipped into the room and had sat down on a hard chair at the back. He was holding a bow and arrow, listening intently to what was being said. 'There's some lemonade, Danny,' the old man said, noticing him.

The boy came forward on silent sandalled feet and poured himself a glass. He returned to his seat.

Ross said, 'We've come down here to try and find out what happened.'

'Well I hope you succeed. It's been a long time.' Harry looked at Joe. 'I'll tell you something, Mr. Lejeune . . .'

'Joe.'

'Joe. I'll tell you this: if anybody'll find out what happened, it'll be Ross here. You've heard about his war record?'

'Yes,' said Joe. An image of the Nyadzonya river running red with blood came into his mind, but he dismissed it. 'I heard.'

'Silver Cross of Rhodesia. Not many of those ever got awarded.'

Ross looked embarrassed. 'That's not the sort of thing you're supposed to talk about these days, Harry,' he said.

'I'll talk about what I choose to talk about.'

'I'm sure you will.' Ross laughed. 'Any theories?'

'About the kidnapping? Not really. I don't think it was local boys. It's not their style. How many men were involved?'

'About eight,' Joe said.

'Doesn't sound like local boys. They work in twos and threes. They've got guns some of them, of course. There've been one or two firefights. But what motive would they have? They don't need to rob cars. They can make all the money they need poaching game. They make a fortune, a bloody fortune! They set twenty, thirty snares a night sometimes, down by the river there. They'll take anything: leopard, rhino, sable, impala. They even catch bloody cattle! And what do the police do? Nothing. They can't even prepare a docket properly. And if they get them to court they get let off, or fined some piddling sum, and they're out doing it again the following night. Go and see Jack Hammond. He might have some ideas. He keeps his eyes and ears open.'

'Tomorrow.' Ross shot Joe a swift glance then said, 'Incidentally, Harry, is Jack getting any problems with illegal grazing?'

'Who isn't. It's bad all over. Very bad down there on the park borders.'

'You know who's doing it?'

'I know who's doing it up here. Down there, no. Jack would, probably. You can't blame them, in a way. Before this last rain the tribal lands were like a desert. They fed their cattle on leaves for a time, but even those began to run out. There's been incredible mortality. Some of the people are in a bad way, too. A friend of mine told me they're living on reeds down there west of the Nuanetsi. They make some kind of porridge from them. But what can you do? I've lost half my cattle, and God knows how many head of game. Then they drive their herds in and take what little grazing there is.'

The old man fell quiet, pondering his problems, then he looked up and said, 'I expect you'll want to wash. Danny, take them along and show them their room, will you?'

Betty Barton came in for supper. She was a large woman, white-haired like her husband. They said grace and ate cold chicken, salad and potatoes. The meal was conducted in a silence broken only by the various requests for butter or bread or lemonade from the diners. It was a family custom, Joe came to realise, to take meals in silence. Afterwards, in the living-room they drew back the curtains, and as the huge red sun sank into the bush, Harry read from a large black bible. Proverbs 5: 'For the lips of strange women drop as honeycomb, and her mouth is smoother than oil: But her end is as bitter as wormwood, sharp as a two-edged sword . . .'

When the reading was over, Betty Barton asked Joe about Ellie and the children, and he told her. She was a gentle woman, soft-spoken, sympathetic. Joe suspected that all her married life she had been overshadowed by her forceful husband. She talked for a while about how Robin and Connie's deaths had changed her, and about the day it had happened. How, when they were late, Harry had taken his FN and gone to look for them, and how he had found Danny pulling at his mother's dress and saying: 'Wake up, Mummy. Wake up, Mummy.' She cried a little, and blew her nose. Joe noticed that Danny, who had listened in silence to his grandmother's words, showed no emotion. Perhaps this story too had grown stale with retelling.

Joe asked the boy about his bow and arrow. 'It's Shangaan,' he said. 'A hunting bow.' He gave it to Joe who held it, admiring its lightness and the tapered smoothness of the wood. The arrows were flighted with speckled guinea fowl feathers. 'I shot a mamba with it one time,' the boy said. 'In the marula tree. I got it through the head, first shot. I've got a picture.' He rushed from the room and returned with a colour photograph. He was standing beneath the tree, the long brown snake impaled on the arrow he held.

'He was so proud,' Betty said.

'Do you get many mambas?' Joe asked the boy.

'Quite a few in the mealie fields.'

Joe felt relieved that Ross had remembered to include a snake bite kit on the list.

Harry, who had been silent since supper, began to talk about the Shangaan. 'They were Ndwandwe people originally,' he said, 'from Zululand. Their own chief, Zwide, was overthrown by Chaka, and about a hundred and fifty years ago the warriors of the tribe were forced to flee north. There were three groups of them. One lot, led by Nxaba, and later by his grandson Mzilikazi, settled around Bulawayo and became the Matebele. The second group crossed the Limpopo and drove right up through the middle of Mashonaland, looting and plundering and killing, and eventually ended up in Tanzania. The third lot, led by a man called Manukosi Shotshangana, occupied Southern Mozambique, and the Lowveld here, and parts of the northern Transvaal. The warriors intermarried with the Hlengwe tribe, whose area this was, and created the Shangaan kingdom. The Amatshangana, the people of Shotshangana. The language is a mixture of Hlengwe and Zulu. There's no other language like it.'

'And they used bows and arrows like this?' said Joe.

'Yes. Bows and arrows and dogs. They were great hunters and cattle herders. I was one of the first white ranchers in the area, and when I came here in 1945 these were all Shangaan hunting grounds. They lived along the rivers, but travelled huge distances after game. When they made a kill they'd stop, make camp, dry the meat. If it was an elephant, the ivory would go to the chief, and the meat would be shared out. Now, of course, it's all changed. They're a minority tribe, and the Government don't like minority tribes. The children are forced to speak Shona at school. They don't wear traditional dress any more. The men spend most of their time poaching, using dogs and snares, and selling the meat and hides and ivory for cash. It's a tragedy. A tragedy . . .'

The old man's voice trailed off, and he lapsed into silence.

After a while Betty cleared her throat. 'It's late,' she said.

The house was dark by nine o'clock.

They shared a room down a long white corridor at the rear of the house. Joe slept heavily, fatigued with the journey and the heat. When he woke, Ross's bed was empty and there were voices and the sound of tractor engines outside. He looked at his new watch. It was shortly after six a.m. He groaned, swung himself out of bed and went to the bathroom where he sluiced his face with water.

In the dining-room, Ross was eating breakfast alone. The family had finished, and their places were already cleared. He looked up from the paw-paw he was spooning, and grinned. 'What kept you?'

'It's six,' said Joe, incredulous. 'Six o'clock.'

'Lowveld time. You'll get used to it. Get the work done before the heat. Old Harry was outside with the boys an hour ago.'

Agnes came in with a jug of milk for the Granola, and left silently. Betty's voice could be heard in the distance, talking a mixture of Shangaan and English. There was a clatter of plates. The ridgeback padded in and flopped down on the linoleum-tiled floor. Joe said, 'You think we'll get somewhere with the herd boy?'

'God knows. I've already rung Jack Hammond. He's got to go to the dip this morning, but he'll see us around noon. I explained what we were doing, and he said he'd try to help. He's got some white rhinos, by the way. They captured them in the Gona-re-Zhou and he's got them in a boma, feeding them until the drought breaks. I thought this morning we should go down the road and try to find the place you were shot. There might be something there, something the army missed. And it might just jog your memory.'

'You think there might still be tracks?'

'No way. Not after six months. We can have a look round, though. We may get some idea of the direction they took from the lie of the land. Don't be too hopeful, that's all.'

Joe munched at his Granola then said, 'What I can't understand is why, down here, everybody believes me when I say Ellie and the children are still alive, yet nobody believed me in Harare. Everybody there thought I was mad, stupid.'

'I think they believe they *could* be alive,' said Ross slowly. 'And that's good enough for them. They're gamblers or they wouldn't be down here at all. And they saw the way the Army carried on.'

'What do you think?'

Ross dug at his paw-paw. 'Let's say this. If it was a horse, I don't think I'd put my money on it.'

'But sometimes the outsider wins,' Joe said.

'Sometimes.'

When they left the house the heat was already building. The thermometer on the outside wall read eighty-eight degrees. Enos was waiting for them, sprawled on the bonnet of the Land-Rover in the shade of the tree. He was smoking his pipe. When he saw them he jumped smartly down. There was a smug expression on his face. 'I know what he's been up to,' Ross said. 'Dirty bastard.' He spoke to Enos in Shona and slapped him on the back. The black man laughed.

Harry was in the yard working on the engine of the tractor, Danny holding spanners for him. When he heard the Land-Rover start up he turned and waved. Lines of men and women wearing wide straw hats were hoeing in the fields. The scene reminded Joe of pictures he had seen of slaves on Southern plantations before the American Civil War. 'It's like *Gone with the Wind*,' he said to Ross.

Ross grunted but said nothing. Perhaps he didn't get the analogy.

At the tar they turned left, and then, a few hundred metres later, right. 'Remember the sign?' Ross said. It read 'Gona-re-Zhou National Park'.

'Yes,' said Joe quietly. 'I remember.'

He'd wondered how he'd feel when he saw the sign again, the white, corrugated road, the blank green bush. During those long days in hospital, and later at the Vicarage he'd thought about the road sometimes, and it had frightened him. It occurred to him that maybe that was why he'd wanted to go to Kezi. Maybe it was just to avoid travelling this road again. But Ross had been right: this was the only place to start looking. Deep inside himself he'd known that all along and yet all he'd done was talk about Kezi. Kezi Kezi Kezi. Some place a hundred, two hundred, God knows how many hundred miles away on the other side of the country. When Larry Wakeman had flung the name at him he'd leapt on it and clung to it, like a terrier clinging to a rat. What the fuck had Kezi got to do with anything? Little by little he was beginning to understand. He waited for the fear to begin.

To his surprise it didn't, at least at first. He felt strangely detached from the landscape and the memories. It was as though the robbery, the shooting, had happened to a different person. Somebody he knew well, with whom he shared the most intimate of secrets. but who, in some mysterious way, was a complete stranger. He found himself able to recall the most insignificant of details. A wrecked truck at the side of the road. Ellie talking about crocodiles in the Lundi, and how terrified Ben had been. The kids complaining of thirst and the stop to drink orange squash. Eagles. Maybe the same eagles that were circling overhead even now. They'd passed a bus, he remembered, a yellow bus with 'Chiredzi' on the signboard, and there was a crossroads somewhere. He said to Ross, 'There was a crossroads.'

'That's the entrance to the Flying Star, Jack Hammond's place. It's a way up here yet.'

They drove steadily for fifteen or twenty minutes, passing no other vehicles. The bush on either side of the road was as empty as it had been that day back in August, but a little greener. There were more insects, too. Butterflies and large black dragon fly-like creatures. And cicadas. They were louder than he remembered them. Glossy blue long-tailed starlings flew in twos and threes between the taller trees.

They came to the Flying Star crossroads, and beyond it the flat bridge over the Nyamasikana River. The bush was thinning. Once, between the stems of the trees, they saw a small herd of impala. The stag, ears quivering, watched them as they passed. Not far now. Joe felt a tightness in his stomach, a breathlessness which took him by surprise, and which he tried to control.

'Mahande River,' said Ross, slowing, the concrete slabs of the bridge surface suddenly smooth after the jolting of the dirt. 'Say when.'

Joe fought the panic that was coming in at him now, hard and fast. There was a bend, he remembered. They'd turned a bend. He could see the bend up ahead, the road twisting suddenly to the left. He said to Ross, 'Slow down. Take it slowly.'

When they came to the place he half-expected the men to be there, with their guns and their tattered camouflage fatigues.

But there was nothing. Just the empty bush and the wide verge, green now instead of brown. 'OK,' he said. Ross drove off the road and killed the engine.

They sat for a while, not moving, cicadas rasping like electric drills. The heat flowed in through the open windows, pumping sweat from their bodies. Joe was conscious of the pounding of his heart, a desire to grab the wheel from Ross and drive just anywhere, somewhere far away from this place. He began to shake.

'You all right?' Ross said.

'Yes. Fine.'

'You don't look it.'

'I said I'm OK.' His voice sounded unnaturally loud. He opened the door.

His feet kicked up small puffs of white dust as he stepped into the road. The heat burned through the soles of his shoes. He said, 'It was here. Somewhere here. It's hard to say exactly where.' The car. He forced himself to think about the car. He wondered what had happened to it, where it had gone. They'd taken it for tests, fingerprints maybe. Then they must have returned it to Hertz. No doubt they'd charged his Amex Card for the whole time it was gone. It had been a white Datsun! The irony of it suddenly struck him and he smiled to himself.

'What's the joke?' Ross asked.

'It was a white Datsun.'

'What was?'

'The car we were driving when we were stopped.'

Ross raised an eyebrow. 'Well, now,' he said. 'What a coincidence.'

They laughed together, the tension broken.

The roadside was scored with the tracks of heavy Army vehicles. There'd been at least one tank involved by the look of it. Enos, who was examining the ground closely, tutted with disbelief, He picked up a cigarette packet. Kingsgate. 'Yours?' he asked.

Joe shook his head. Enos threw the packet down and continued his search. A huge black bird took off from the bush nearby, and then another. They flapped slowly away, booming loudly. 'Ground hornbills,' Ross said. 'Ugly bastards.'

For half an hour they watched as Enos worked his way inch by inch along the sparse grass of the verge. He found a small piece of yellow paper which Joe thought could have come from one of the car hire leaflets he'd picked up in Harare before he and Ellie had left, and a scrap of rag, white material blackened with oil, which Ross said maybe had been used for cleaning a gun. That was all. When Enos at last straightened up and joined them he said, 'They've done a good job, those boys.'

'You expected to find more?' Joe asked.

'Oh, yes. They had good boys working on this job.'

Joe glanced up anxiously, but Ross didn't seem worried. 'They've got good trackers,' he said. 'Very good trackers, ex-terrs. I didn't think to find too much. Let's look for this path you told me about.'

The bush was thinner than Joe had remembered it, low scrubby mopani, hardly head-height. Tiny yellow and green flowers nestled at the base of the shiny butterfly-shaped leaves already closing against the heat. Here and there were the bleached white shells of giant snails. Enos began to cast in a deep semicircle, starting at the four-stranded game fence and working outwards. As Joe and Ross followed him, the ground began to rise, almost imperceptibly at first, then more steeply. The rocks began, and just visible between the gnarled mopani trunks was the low kopje. They picked up a path then, close by, a second, both leading towards the kopje. 'Which one?' Ross asked.

Joe didn't know. They both looked familiar. Ahead of them, from the summit of the kopje, a baboon called: 'Wah-hoo!' The baboon family could just be seen, scuttling over the rocks, led by a large male. 'Try the left,' Joe said.

Enos led, zig-zagging, covering a yard or so of bush on either side of the track as he climbed. The rocks began to close in. There was a thorn bush with inch-long white thorns, a large boulder specked with yellow lichen.

Lichen.

Joe remembered the feel of the lichen, its scaly touch, like a reptile, like the face of the man with the gun. And Cassie. The blood on her leg. Her thin, high voice calling him. 'Daddeee! Daddeee!'

130

'It's here,' he said quietly.

Ross and Enos, who had moved ahead, stopped, turned, and walked slowly back down towards him.

He told Ross that it was the heat. But it was the place itself, the rocks, the lichen, the trees, which seemed to suck the energy from his body. Inexplicably, his leg began to hurt, where the wound was, and his shoulder. Sweat trickled into his eyes, blinding him. He sat down beneath the thorn bush and covered his face.

When he looked up again he saw that Ross was examining something he'd picked up beneath an overhang of rock. There was a flash of sunlight on metal. Ross called Enos to him and they discussed the find. They spoke in Shona, very quietly.

After a while Ross came over to where Joe sat and squatted down beside him. He was holding a brass cartridge case. 'I think we've got something here,' he said.

The case was about one and a half inches long, narrowing towards the tip. Joe wiped the sweat from his eyes and took it, rolling it between his fingers. It was surprisingly shiny and new-looking. There were some letters and numbers stamped on the head. He read them out. '22. RPR. 80. What's it mean?'

'It means the other end of this little bastard probably ended up inside Joe Lejeune. It's short-cased 7.62mm rifle ammunition. AK 47 ammunition. It was made in Romania – see, RPR, Romanian People's Republic – at State factory number 22. And 80 is the year it was made. 1980.'

Joe examined it again, repelled yet fascinated by the tiny cylinder of metal. He handed it back. 'I'm surprised the army didn't find it,' he said.

'It was under the rock over there. If we can find out who's been using 1980 Romanian 7.62 ammunition we might well be on our way to finding out who actually fired the gun.'

'You can find that out?'

'Possibly. There's a guy I know in Harare, I'll call him tonight. He might be able to fill us in. The interesting thing is, it's new ammunition, made since the end of the war, so it hasn't come from some arms cache somewhere. How you feeling?'

'Better,' said Joe.

'It takes a while to acclimatise. Just take things easy.'

Joe nodded and got to his feet. There was hope now, real hope. It energised him. He wondered vaguely who it was that Ross knew in Harare who could supply the information they needed. His mate in the police, maybe? He seemed to have connections everywhere, this guy, based on wartime allegiances, Joe supposed, a sort of subversive old boy's network. It obviously worked with considerable efficiency. He decided to push a little. 'Can't there be tests done on it?'

'What sort of tests?'

'I don't know: finger prints, ballistics, something like that.'

'Too long ago. Anyway, even if we could find somebody to do it, what would it tell us? The headstamp's enough. Let's keep looking.'

They searched for an hour, moving slowly up the kopje, but they found nothing more. There'd been three shots, there must have been three cartridges. So where were the other two? Had the bandit himself picked them up? Or the army? More likely the army. It struck Joe that maybe this was the 'evidence' that Zvarevashe had referred to at the Press Conference in the hospital. Yet why should Romanian ammunition have anything to do with South Africa? And if it did have, why didn't Zvarevashe say so when challenged? He mentioned his thoughts to Ross who dismissed them. 'They probably had their own reasons,' he said. 'Or maybe they're waiting for the trial. Maybe they think it'll make more impact at the trial. Who knows.'

The top of the kopje was a natural amphitheatre of rock into which a number of paths wound. The sandy soil between the loose scree was scattered with baboon droppings. Smears of white ash marked the sites of long-extinguished fires. On the flat undersurface of an overhanging rock were the faded outlines of bushman drawings, kudu and rhinoceros. Enos dropped to his haunches and examined a patch of soft dust beneath the rock. 'Herd boys were here,' he said. 'Before the rains. They had dogs.'

Joe followed Ross to where Enos was pointing. Just visible beneath the crisp prints of baboons were some indistinct older markings of human and dogs footprints. 'How many boys?' Ross asked.

'Two, maybe three.' Enos picked up a couple of small quartzite pebbles. 'They had catapults.' He mimed the action of firing one.

'I only saw one boy,' Joe said.

'That doesn't mean there weren't others, Ross said. 'Anyway, with a sign this old it's impossible to say when it was made. There have been boys here since. More likely than not.'

'So what does it tell us?'

'Not much. The boy you saw could have been here when he heard the shots. If so, he probably got scared and hid, and then came out later and found you. But that's just guesswork. As I said, it's all too long ago.'

'Do you think the men brought Ellie and the kids up here?'

'I don't know. Any sign of anything else, Enos?'

Enos shook his head and stood up. 'Too many baboon,' he said.

'Stinking bobbejaans,' Ross said. He took off his bush hat and wiped his forehead with his hand. 'It's getting too bloody hot up here.'

'You said you might be able to tell something from the lie of the land.'

Ross spread his hands. 'Take a look.'

On all sides of the kopje the bush stretched out, sparse, flat, featureless. In the distance was a range of blue hills which seemed to be floating in the heat haze. Game trails crisscrossed between the mopanis. 'They might have gone to the hills,' Joe said.

'And they might not. There's three hundred and sixty degrees worth of direction out there. Take your pick.'

Something moved in the bush to the west, the dark bulk of a buffalo. It disappeared into a gully. If the boy had been hiding up here, Joe realised, he would have been able to see the bandits clearly, Ellie's pink tee shirt, the kids' golden hair. He'd have watched to make sure they had gone before he would have dared to come down. 'They see things, herd boys,' Enos had said. And this boy had good reason to look.

'If we can find that boy,' Joe said, 'he'll have seen them. He must have done.'

'*If* he was up here.'

Joe turned to gaze out again over the bush, but Ross

133

checked him. 'There's nothing more,' he said.

Together they walked back towards the road.

The Flying Star was a big place, seventy thousand acres, Ross reckoned, maybe a hundred, stretching from the Chiredzi River almost to the Sabi. Only the old Nuanetsi Ranch had been bigger, and that was broken up now. As the narrow track wound westwards from the Chipinda road, kilometre after kilometre, Joe wondered that so much of the surface of Africa could be owned by one man.

Eventually the level mopani woodland gave way to open grassland dotted here and there with windpumps and low circular concrete water tanks. Emaciated cattle bearing the Flying Star brand on their flanks stood motionless in pools of dense shadow beneath flat-topped acacias. Only the butter-flies moved. The midday heat gripped the land, seeming to wring the life from it.

Then, quite suddenly, the road forked and began to climb up between tumbled basalt boulders. The blue waters of a dam appeared, and a stand of tall nyala berry trees. Beneath them were what looked like the buildings of a small African town. Small black children playing in the dirt at the side of the road waved as they passed.

A thin, intense-looking white man in khaki bush gear was waiting for them in the shade of one of the largest of the trees. He was in his late fifties, Joe guessed, his face prematurely lined beneath a deep tan. Ross drew the Land-Rover to a halt beside him.

They got out and Ross shook hands. 'Tobin,' the man said. 'It's been a long time.' He turned to Joe. 'And this is your friend.'

'Joe Lejeune,' Ross said. 'Jack Hammond.'

'You must be aching for a beer,' Hammond said.

Joe noticed that he had made no acknowledgement of Enos's presence. The black man seemed unworried by the fact and sauntered off in the direction of a low building where men in overalls were lounging, some of them gnawing at green mealies. It was a store by the look of it. Rows of tins and bottles could just be glimpsed through the open doorway. Behind and to the left of the store were machine shops, equipment sheds and a small sawmill. Various items of heavy machinery stood around. Beneath another of the trees a boy with bare feet was washing a large Mercedes. Chickens scratched and fluffed.

Ross and Joe followed Jack along a path hung with red and purple bougainvillea. At the end was a stout welded steel gate and a heavy mesh security fence laced with barbed wire. As Jack opened the gate a pair of golden retrievers raced up, barking and wiggling their bodies. There were smooth green lawns, flowerbeds, the blue of a swimming pool. The house, a large, low, white-walled building, was partly shaded by a spreading acacia tree hung with weaver bird nests. A stoep, which ran round three sides of it, was heavily screened with wire mesh. 'Grenade screens,' Ross said. 'Better safe than sorry, hey, Jack?'

Jack shrugged.

A door on the stoep led directly into the sitting-room. A huge pair of elephant tusks, mounted in silver and hung above the stone fireplace, dominated the room. There were muzzle-loading rifles on the wall, and a small library of books on Africa. In one corner of the room was a bar in varnished wood with stools topped with zebra skin. Jack went behind the bar and opened a fridge. He produced three bottles of Castle, and glasses. 'Cheers,' he said as they drank.

He put down his glass and rang a small silver handbell. A middle-aged black woman wearing a fawn overall came in. Jack said a few staccato words in Shangaan to her and she left. 'Lunch will be ready in a while,' he said. 'Meantime, relax.' He looked keenly at Joe. 'So you're the guy all the fuss was about?'

'I guess so.'

'I remember that day well. It was a Sunday. I'd been into Fort Vic to visit relatives. When I came back there was a roadblock up at Nandi Junction, troops everywhere. They wouldn't tell me what was going on. The boys told me when I got back here. They casevacced you out pretty quick?'

Joe nodded.

'You're OK now?'

'I get some pain. Not too bad.'

'Somebody up there must be watching over you, that's all I

135

can say. Remember much about it?'

'Some things. Not much.'

'It was a police patrol found you, not the Army like they keep claiming for some reason. Our local boys. They found the car, stuff lying all over the place, realised there must be something wrong. Joshua was with them, his brother works for me. They'd picked him up for something – stealing batteries. He tracked you. The police called the Army and they brought in an Alouette and casevacced you out. Another half-hour and you'd have been dead. They thought you were dead when they found you.'

'*I* thought I was dead,' said Joe.

Jack Hammond smiled and poured out the remainder of his beer. Ross, Joe noticed, had fallen silent, and was fiddling with the silver bell. Outside, a purple loerie clucked like a chicken. Joe said, 'Joshua, this guy Joshua, do you think he could have seen anything?'

'He could have.'

'Where can we find him?'

'Beitbridge Prison. They weren't just any batteries he was stealing: they were Army batteries.'

Ross laughed suddenly, loudly. 'Army batteries. Stupid bastard! Got another beer, Jack?' There was a tension in his voice that puzzled Joe.

Jack uncapped three more Castles, and handed one to Ross. To Joe he said, 'So you think they've made a cock-up, got the wrong blokes?'

'I know they have. They showed me pictures. Dead men. They were nothing like the gang who stopped us. It's not a cock-up, it's deliberate.'

'And you've come to find out the truth.'

'Yes.'

'Good luck to you. I didn't realise there was a woman and children involved until I read it in the paper. There's been no communication from them?'

'No.'

'If they were being held for some reason there should have been. A ransom demand.'

'Nobody's told me anything. They just said they were dead. Shot. Eaten by hyenas.'

Jack Hammond was silent for a moment, sipping his beer. 'Let me say this,' he said, 'I'm willing to bet it wasn't local boys.'

'So Harry Barton said.'

'I'm also willing to bet that if they're alive they're not being held round here. I'd have got to know about it somehow if they were. The army blokes I talked to seemed convinced it was ZIPRA dissidents.'

'Do you think so?' Joe asked.

'It's possible. It's a bit off their usual track, but it's possible. It's pretty wild bush down there in the park. Given a water supply they could hide up for weeks without anybody knowing – except maybe Chenjerai.'

'Who's Chenjerai?' said Ross, suddenly interested.

'He runs the anti-poaching unit.'

'Based at Chipinda?'

'He comes and goes. He catches more poachers than the police and army put together. He's an ex-ZANLA terrorist, one of Mugabe's lot.'

'So you think he might know something?' Joe said.

'Maybe, if he was around. Sometimes he's up in Wankie or Mana but when he's here he has men out in the field pretty well permanently in patrols of two or three. There are twenty, thirty men in all. They've got a Puma they ride around in. Call up Jamie McAllister tonight on the radio. He's the Warden at Chipinda. He'll tell you where they are.'

'But surely if they'd seen anything they'd have told the Army,' Joe said.

'They might, and they might not. There's not a lot of love lost between the Army and the game department. This is Zimbabwe, don't forget. If the right arm knows what the left arm is doing at any given time, you can put it down to luck or coincidence.'

A gong sounded suddenly, almost comically, somewhere close at hand. 'Grub up,' Jack said. 'Bring your glasses.'

They followed him down a short passage hung with hunting spears into a dim, shuttered dining-room. Silver and china glowed on an exquisite rosewood dining table. An immense ham rested on a stand. Joe and Ross sat down while Jack picked up the carvers. 'Ham suit you?' he said. 'It's our own,

137

baked to my mother's recipe. She's a Yorkshirewoman. I get the black treacle sent from England.'

He carved slices a quarter of an inch thick and spread them on plates. A young black girl came in with vegetables, potatoes and round gemsquash like green steaming cannon-balls. She served them silently and left. 'So you've been down the road this morning,' Jack said, when they were eating.

Joe nodded, his mouth full.

'Any luck? The Army worked over that area pretty hard. Too damn hard.'

Joe swallowed. 'A cartridge case.'

Ross, who had not yet started to eat, produced the case from the pocket of his bush shirt and gave it to Jack.

He examined it, peering at the headstamp. 'AK,' he said. 'Recent.'

'Romanian,' Ross said.

'Where'd you find it?'

'On the kopje.'

'Which kopje was that?'

'Just past the Mahande River.'

Jack handed back the case. 'Malevula. It's supposed to be an old Hlengwe burial place, but I have my doubts. And that was where you got shot, was it?' he said to Joe.

'Yes.'

'I thought they found you nearer the road.'

'I must have crawled somehow, I don't know.'

'Lucky you did. What do you make of it, Ross? Who'd be using that kind of ammo?'

'I don't know. I'll try and find out tonight.'

'I can't say we've seen anything like it round here. It's mostly stuff from the war.'

They chewed for a while then Jack said, 'I gather you want to know about illegal grazing?'

'There was a herd boy,' Joe said. 'When I was shot. He found me. I asked him for help but he ran away. He must have seen what happened. If we can find him maybe he can tell us something.'

Jack nodded. 'Well, I can tell you where he came from. That's the easy part. There are half a dozen villages on the south bank of the Lundi, near the Chiredzi River confluence:

Hahlani, Machuwete, Makosiya, Chitsange, Chambuta and one other I forget the name of. He'll have come from one of those. They drive their cattle across the new Lundi bridge before dawn. We've tried to stop them, but it's impossible. The District Administrator in Chiredzi seems to think I ought to be grateful for their presence on my land.'

'We didn't see any sign of them today,' Ross said.

'That's because we've had some rain. They've got a bit of grazing closer to home. If it doesn't rain they'll be back in a couple of weeks. But you won't get anything out of them, I'm warning you.'

'We can try,' Joe said.

'You can try. The Army tried. After the kidnapping they went in there and scared the shit out of those poor bastards. Whether they got anywhere I don't know, but they weren't too gentle. Not that it's anything new as far as those particular Shangaan are concerned. They've had it in the neck from everybody. From us ranchers who came along in the forties and fenced in what they regarded as their traditional hunting grounds. From the Game Department who set up the Gona-re-Zhou in the sixties. Then early in the war they were hit hard by ZANLA groups coming up from Mozambique, and the Security Forces who came down looking for them. They had their huts burned and were shoved into Protected Villages, which as far as I'm concerned were about on a par with the concentration camps I saw in Burma in 1944. And then, when it was all over and they were allowed to go home and rebuild their kraals, they found themselves out on a limb as a minority tribe with bugger all say in the running of their own affairs, constantly harrassed by police and game people trying to control the poaching. So they're not too co-operative. In their shoes, I don't think I would be.'

'You must have contacts,' Ross said.

'Yes, I've got contacts, if you can call them that. There's a Headman called Elias at Chitsange. If he's sober he may help. Try taking a bottle of gin. And of course there's John, the brother of Joshua who I was telling you about. He comes from Hahlani. He's down at the dip today. It might be a good idea if you took him with you. He could interpret if nothing else. But whatever you do, and I'm saying this particularly to you,

139

Ross, go easy on them. Explain the situation. Say you're nothing to do with the Army or the game department. Observe all the formalities. If you do that, maybe you'll be lucky and they'll talk. But I'll be very surprised.'

Ross didn't seem too concerned. 'It's a long shot anyway,' he said. 'Even if we find the boy, there is no guarantee he'll be able to tell us anything useful.'

'It's worth a try,' said Joe quickly.

When the meal was over, and they'd drunk tea in the sitting-room, they picked up Enos from the store and went to see the rhinos. Jack led the way in a battered open-topped American jeep, two scrawny ranch hands clinging to the roll bars as the vehicle dipped and bucked along a series of interlacing tracks, spewing clouds of dust high into the super-heated air.

Ross, who kept the Land-Rover at a distance to avoid the worst of the dust, talked a bit about Jack as they drove. 'He's an awkward sod,' he said. 'Too bloody awkward. He arrived here with a few quid in 1945 and built this place up from scratch. He stayed put right through the war. There's nothing between here and the Mozambique border except bush, which meant that the Flying Star was the first stop for every gook that walked across. He survived half a dozen full-scale attacks. Once about a dozen of them cut the security fence and got right up to the house. Jack and his boy fought them off with FNs and killed a couple of them. His wife couldn't take the life and gapped it down to South Africa. Harry told me this morning she hasn't come back and Jack's bitter about that. His son's in the States somewhere, in college. His daughter's living with the mother. I came out here two or three times during the war, that's when I got to know him. He hasn't changed. He makes most of his money out of rich Americans who come over here on hunting trips. He knows this area better than any man alive, I guess, with the possible exception of Harry.'

Joe glanced across at Ross who seemed more relaxed now they were on the move again, away from the house. But there was something bothering him, something not quite right. It had to do with Jack, Joe sensed. Some incident from the war, maybe. 'You don't like him too much?' he probed.

'Jack? Oh, he's OK. I like him right enough. He can be stupid at times. He caused us problems during the war.'

'What kind of problems?'

'Failing to report terrorist presence on his land. He seemed more concerned with preserving his property than winning the bloody war. One time we got wind that his boys were supplying food to the insurgents. When we came to pick them up he waved an FN at us and told us to piss off. We had to stick him inside for a while.'

'Inside?'

'Prison.'

Up ahead the jeep was slowing, the dust plume thinning, contracting. They swung into a broad clearing among tall mopanis. A stockade of stout logs bound together with steel cables was set up at the rear of the clearing. There were racks of what looked like hay or alfalfa, and a water cart, Jack put the jeep beneath a tree, Ross slid in beside him. Joe noticed that there were ladders set up against the stockade walls. It gave it the appearance of a Western fort in a cowboy movie.

They climbed the ladders and looked down into the pens. There were fourteen rhinos in all, some with calves. They were painfully thin, the corrugations of their ribs clearly visible through their thick skin. They seemed placid, almost tame, allowing Jack to pat their heads and pull at their horns. Only in the end pen was there protest, a big bull rhino with a bloody mess where his horn should have been, charging the stockade wall repeatedly.

'He lost it in the capture,' Jack said. 'We had a bit of a fight, him and me and the other blokes involved. We darted him, but for some reason the tranquilliser didn't work too well. We chased him for what, three, four kilometres and he still wasn't giving in. It took thirty men with ropes to bring him down in the end. Then the poor old bastard smashed his horn when we were getting him into the truck.'

'It must hurt him,' Joe said, wincing as the huge beast ground his wound into the rough mopani logs.

'It makes him angry. And when he gets angry a rhino charges, which hurts him again, which makes him angry again. It's a vicious circle. Maybe we can release him in a month or so if the rains come, and the others. They're about

141

all there are left down here, these lot. We think we missed four in the capture, and we know for certain that two of those are already dead.'

A light wind was blowing up from the south, rustling the mopanis. In the pen the demented rhino grunted and thumped. Ross, Joe noticed, was glancing at his watch. Enos squatted beneath a tree chatting to the two ranch hands. Eagles circled on a thermal. Suddenly, and without being conscious of having formulated the thought in his mind before he spoke, Joe said, 'They were very young.'

'Who were?' Jack asked.

'The men who stopped us. The leader was older, the one with the beard, and there was one other older one but the others were just boys – sixteen, seventeen. Very young, and thin.'

'Starving?' Jack glanced up from the rhinos, obviously keenly interested.

'I guess so. They were much thinner than anyone I've seen round here.'

'And they stole food from you?'

'Yes, and money, and jewellery.'

Jack fell silent, thinking. Ross watched him closely. There was real dislike between the two men, Joe was certain. When Ross spoke, his voice was sharp, almost angry. 'You didn't tell me this.'

Joe shrugged. 'I just remembered.'

'You didn't tell anybody else? Mtisi? The police?'

'No.'

'It might have made a difference.'

'I told you, I only just remembered.' It was Joe's turn to become irritated. 'What language were they speaking?' Jack asked.

'The man with the beard spoke English. The others, I don't know.'

'Any accent?'

'It's pointless asking him that,' Ross said. 'Completely pointless.'

'Please,' said Jack quietly. 'Allow me the courtesy of deciding what is and what is not pointless.'

For an instant Joe thought an argument was going to flare,

but the moment passed and Jack resumed his questioning. 'Anything else you remember?'

'Only that they were wearing bits and pieces of camouflage gear. And one of them, one of the young boys, had a tee shirt with FANTA written on it.'

'And guns? Did they all have guns?'

'Most of them. AKs.'

Jack pondered for a short while, and then turned slowly to Ross. 'I don't know what you're going to find out from that cartridge,' he said, 'but as far as I'm concerned, everything Joe's said to me points in one direction: Mozambique.'

'Bullshit.'

Jack spread his hands. 'Well, for what it's worth, that's my opinion. There've been cross-border raids, a lot of them, mostly Mozambique Government Militia looking for food. They're starving down there, I mean really starving – dying. They come across, shoot buffalo, cattle, anything they can find. There've been firefights. There was a big clash down near Mablauta a few months ago. The Army and the game department were involved. Apparently the raiders dropped their rifles and ran. Nothing's been said officially, of course. It wouldn't look too good if it got out, Zimbabwe shooting at her closest ally. But it happens, believe me.'

Joe suppressed his excitement with difficulty. 'So you think that one of these bands of militia could have taken Ellie and the children into Mozambique?'

'It's possible.'

'But unlikely,' said Ross. 'Listen, we've got to go. I've got a phone call to make.'

'Just a minute,' said Joe suddenly angry. 'You can't just dismiss what Jack says.'

'He can do what he likes,' said Jack. 'He usually does.'

They climbed down the ladders and walked back to where the vehicles were parked. The rhino in the end pen continued to charge. Cicadas strummed. Jack suddenly pointed upwards to where a large bird circled on outstretched wings. 'A bateleur,' he said. 'It just shat. That's how they mark a kill, by shitting on it from a great height.'

Joe wondered for a moment whether there was some hidden meaning in the remark, but decided there wasn't. It was just an eagle shitting. All the same, it seemed strangely appropriate. 'Look, Jack, these Militia,' he queried. 'Would they travel that far from the border?'

'If they were desperate enough.'

'And they're desperate?'

'Oh yes, they're desperate.'

Ross cut in. 'It's an interesting theory, Jack, but theories aren't going to get us anywhere. We'll check out this cartridge case and take things from there.' He spoke softly, as if aware that he'd pushed things too far.

'Suit yourself. You still want to find this herd boy?'

'If we can.'

'Ring me then. Tell me when you're going. I'll have John waiting for you at the crossroads. And don't forget the gin.'

'We won't.'

Enos left the tree and came towards them. The three of them got into the Land-Rover. Jack held up a hand. 'You know the way out?'

'We can find it.'

'OK, then. Listen, I'll keep my eyes and ears open. You never know, something might turn up.'

'Thanks,' said Joe.

The rancher seemed relieved to see them go.

Joe waited until they hit the Chipinda road before he mentioned Mozambique. 'I don't understand why they couldn't have been taken across the border,' he began.

'I didn't say they couldn't have.'

'But it's not likely?'

'No, it isn't. Look, I'm sure Jack's right. I'm sure groups of Mozambique Militia do come across, though I hadn't heard of it happening before. But what earthly reason would they have for capturing a white woman and two children? What purpose would it serve?'

Joe thought for a moment. 'Perhaps it was a mistake. Perhaps they didn't intend to capture them.'

Ross snorted. 'You don't kidnap people by mistake. And if you do, you get rid of them pretty damned quick.'

'They tried to get rid of me.'

'Well, if Jack's right, maybe they got rid of your wife and children, too.'

'Maybe.'

Joe stopped, suddenly aware of what he'd said. It was such a strange phrase, to get rid of. You got rid of garbage. You got rid of fleas from the cat. You got rid of a clapped out car. Could you also get rid of a family, of ten years of life, of three human beings more familiar in many ways than yourself? Could you get rid of all that love? Well, maybe you could. Three shots is all it would take. Three squeezes on the trigger. And he'd admitted it. For the first time he'd allowed himself to admit it.

He glanced at his two companions. Their faces were expressionless. They were right. It was facts that mattered, not theories. Not Jack Hammond's damned theories. And they had a fact, a genuine, solid, three-dimensional fact: the slim brass cylinder in Ross's top pocket.

Ross made his phone call from Harry's office, a small room built onto the rear of the house. He was a long time gone. While he waited, Joe went onto the lawn with Danny and they set up a target and fired arrows at it. Joe's shots were wild and high. Several times the boy had to crawl into the shrubs to retrieve the speckle-feathered shafts. The two dogs watched, lolling in the afternoon sunshine, tongues hanging wetly.

It was past six before Ross emerged, slipping silently round the edges of the house, surprising them by his presence. Joe and the boy had stopped shooting sometime before and were squatting in the shade talking about hunting dassies – rock rabbits – and how good they were to eat.

Ross dropped to his haunches beside them. Danny looked up at him, uncertain, wondering whether he should go. Ross told him to stay put and patted him on the head. There was admiration in the boy's eyes, hero-worship almost. Joe guessed the old man had been telling him stories of the war. Ross said, 'These phones.'

'You got through?' Joe said.

'Eventually. At the sixth go.'

'And?'

It's Romanian as I thought. AK ammo. Apparently, back in December 1982 the Army ambushed a group of ZIPRA bandits near Mwenezi – Nuanetsi as it used to be called – which is only about 100 kilometres west of here. They killed five of them and captured two. They also recovered a large quantity of arms, including a number of brand new AK 47s, and considerable amounts of Romanian 7.62 ammunition with the same headstamp as the case we found. The poor bastards they captured apparently admitted that they'd been provided with this hardware by the South Africans, and subsequently this has been confirmed. Since then, cases with this particular headstamp have been turning up all over Matabeleland. They think it comes from Angola originally, probably captured by South African forces from Communist armouries. End of story.'

'So it's ZIPRA?'

'It looks like it unless some of that ammo has got into other hands, but that's not too likely. I also got confirmation, by the way, that the Army found those other two cartridge cases, and that they were both identical to ours. Obviously that was the evidence your friend Zvarevashe was referring to at the press conference. He probably didn't produce it because he didn't want to alert the South Africans that they were on to this particular batch.'

Joe was silent for a while, digesting the information. It checked out, all of it: Ndhlovu's story, what Larry Wakeman knew of Ncube and Khumalo, and now the ammunition. Maybe this was it, the end of the road. He should call it a day, go back to Harare and see David about the memorial service.

He thought back, trying to recall the pictures that Mtisi had shown him, the way Ndhlovu had looked at him. Could he have been so wrong? He'd been confused, desperate. The brain plays strange tricks. He'd been wrong about the white Datsun. The men at the Queens. So many mistakes. So many . . .

Boys! The sudden vision he'd had of his attackers that morning when he'd been at the rhino pens returned with the force of a gut-punch. They'd been boys. Not grown men like Ndhlovu. Not like these seven bloated corpses on the concrete floor. It was impossible to mistake an emaciated adolescent, even one swollen in death, for a grown man. And Ndhlovu was in his early twenties at least. Whatever else checked out, that didn't. 'Ndhlovu was too old,' he said.

Ross looked puzzled. 'I don't follow.'

'The bandit Mtisi showed me at the police station. And those bodies in the photographs. They were just boys who stopped us. I told you this morning.'

For some time Ross made no reply. He seemed ill at ease. He took the cartridge case from his pocket and set it up on end in a bare patch of soil. It gleamed in the lengthening rays of the sun. When he spoke there was an edge to his voice. 'Listen Joe, I don't give a stuff about what you may or may not imperfectly remember about a group of anonymous black men who pumped this and two other 7.62 mm slugs into you way back in August. The fact is, we know who we're dealing with. Not locals. Not the Army. Certainly not Mozambican Militia. This is a ZIPRA attack, and I suggest you accept that fact.'

Joe stared at the case. 'And if I don't?'

'Then there's not much more I can say.'

Joe looked up slowly. 'I still say they've got the wrong men.'

'Jesus!' Ross got to his feet and strode a few paces towards the house. Danny, perhaps thinking the conversation was at an end, followed him. He held out his bow. 'Hey, Ross, you want a shot?'

'No!'

The boy fell back, hurt by the violence of Ross's response. The ridgeback raised its head from its paws and growled quietly. 'I was only asking,' the boy said.

Ross paused. Looked at the child. His face softened. He patted Danny's tight hair. 'Maybe later, hey?'

'OK.' Satisfied, the boy padded off on silent feet, the dogs following.

'Look, Ross,' Joe began, 'I'm sure you're right when you say it was ZIPRA, but why couldn't it have been another gang? Maybe the Army made a mistake. Maybe they deliberately faked the evidence. They must have been under a lot of pressure. There are other ZIPRA gangs, surely? Mtisi seemed to imply . . .'

'Mtisi?' Ross laughed softly. 'So what are you trying to say to me?'

'I'm saying we should find this herd boy and get the truth out of him.'

147

'And if we don't find him?'

'Somebody must have seen them somewhere.'

Ross shook his head slowly. 'You're a pig-headed bastard, you know that?' He paused, glanced around, almost as if he was expecting his remarks to be overheard. 'What the fuck?' he said finally. 'I'm in no hurry to get back to Harare. Let's give it a go.'

They went into Chiredzi early next day to fill up with fuel and buy gin, and at Ross's suggestion, a number of twenty-five kilo sacks of mealie meal. It was a spacious town, white bungalows set far back in bougainvillaea-hung gardens. The wide neat-curbed shopping street, lined with banks, agricultural engineers and clothes shops, was already filling with cars and dusty country pickups when they arrived soon after eight. White women greeted one another and chatted in patches of shade cast by the concrete awnings of the stores. Black shop staff carried purchases to cars, pushed loaded trolleys.

At the Mobil Station at the bottom of the street they put 135 litres of Blend into the various tanks and cans in the Land-Rover, and topped up on oil and water. While they were filling, the blue-coated pump attendant scraped the accumulation of dead insects from the windscreen. Joe counted out 121 dollars and 50 cents into the man's hand.

Outside the Chiredzi Supermarket a white Land-Rover was parked. They drew into a space beside it and went in.

They were buying mealie meal, eight sacks, and directing an African to take it out for them when a tall sandy-haired man in his forties approached. He was wearing the khaki and green uniform of a Game Warden. 'Ross Tobin and Joe Lejeune,' he said. 'I'm right?'

'Right,' said Joe, astonished.

The man grinned. 'There's no such thing as a secret in the Lowveld. Actually, Jack Hammond told me about you this morning when I called in to see the rhinos. I'm Jamie McAllister, warden at Chipinda.'

They shook hands. 'I gather you wanted to see me about Chenjerai,' the man said.

'Not here,' said Ross, indicating the black faces that were turned towards them.

148

Jamie nodded his understanding. 'Listen,' he said, 'I want to get through here. No doubt you do. I'll meet you up at the Planters and we'll have a coffee or a beer or whatever. We can talk there. You know the Planters Inn on Marula drive? In an hour?'

'An hour,' said Ross.

The man was late, and they'd finished their coffee by the time he turned up. They were sitting beneath flamboyant trees at a metal table. Insects danced over the murky waters of a swimming pool. The hotel was deserted, decaying slightly. They'd had to shout to get the coffee, and when it came it was lukewarm and tasted of sour milk. Ross said, 'Try a beer. It's safer.'

Jamie laughed. 'I think I'll pass. I can't spare too long, anyway, there's a lot to do. It's my monthly trip into town. I've got to get chicken feed and fuel yet. And I've lost Emmy, my wife. Last seen in Bata trying on every shoe in the shop.' A red-coated waiter materialised and hovered near the table, Jamie waved him away. 'Always around when they're not needed,' he said.

He waited until the man had gone. 'Jack told me your story. All I can say is how sorry I am. Emmy was really upset at the time, and for days afterwards. How are you feeling?'

'OK now,' Joe said.

'That's good, that's really good to hear. If we can help in any way . . . I gather you found a cartridge case up on Malevula Kopje.'

'7.62,' Ross said. 'Almost certainly ZIPRA.'

Jamie raised an eyebrow. 'That surprises me,' he said. 'Down in the south of the Park, maybe. But up here . . .'

'There's always a first time,' Ross said.

'I guess so. Of course we get bands coming through the whole time. ZIPRA, Mozambican Militia, MNR, poachers. But with only twelve scouts to patrol two and a half million square kilometres, maintaining any kind of effective ground coverage is a farce. A total bloody farce.'

'The MNR?' Joe asked.

'The Mozambique National Resistance, Renamo. They're the South African backed bandits causing mayhem across the border. You've heard of them, surely? As far as I can make

149

out, they're being trained in the Transvaal. They sometimes take a short cut through the Gona-re-Zhou.'

'Don't the Army stop them?'

Jamie laughed. 'The Army are terrified of meeting anybody carrying so much as a pop gun. They stay safely in their camps, coming out when the coast is clear to scare the shit out of the locals, and to bother innocent people using the Park. That's about the strength of it. The buggers are out and about today on the Chipinda road. I hope you've got a good story if they stop you.'

'A hunting permit,' Ross said.

'I'll make you out a Park Visitor's permit, that should help. Not that they can read too well, most of them. Get some cigarettes while you're here. They're useful. So you want to talk to Chenjerai?'

'Maybe he saw something,' Joe said.

Jamie hesitated. 'He'd probably have told me if he had. When did it happen? August?'

'The seventh.'

'I'm not sure he was around. I'll have to check. But, anyway, you're in luck. He's down there at the moment. He came in from Hwange two days ago.'

'That's Wankie in English,' Ross said.

Jamie guffawed. 'I always though it was an unfortunate name.' He looked at his watch. 'You're coming down to check out Matibi, Jack tells me.'

'Yes.'

'Listen, I've got a guest hut that's going begging. You're welcome to base up there and eat with us. You'll be right on the spot – an hour at the most and you'll be in the villages. And you'll be able to catch Chenjerai when he comes out of the bush, which is about the only way you will catch him.'

'Sounds good,' said Ross.

Jamie got to his feet. 'We'll expect you later today, then. We'll be back about four, four-thirty. There's no fuel down there, by the way, so bring plenty.'

They reached Chipinda Pools at six, lurching down the deeply-rutted track to the complex of low white buildings on the banks of the Lundi River. The Shangaan Jack had promised them had been waiting at the crossroads and was perched in the back on the sacks of mealie meal. He was a close-faced man, hook-nosed, who had failed to return Joe's greeting. There'd been no sign of the Army.

The Warden's house was perched on a low rise overlooking the river. He was already opening the gate in the security fence as they pulled up. A ridgeback, bigger even than Harry's, bounded up to greet them. 'Down, Josh!' Jamie shouted. The dog obeyed instantly. 'He's called Josh after Joshua Nkomo,' the Warden explained, 'because when he was a puppy he was fat and crafty. He's not so fat now, but he's still crafty. The African Scouts are terrified of him.' Joe saw that the Shangaan, who had got out of the back of the Land-Rover, was staying well clear of the huge dog. 'And who's this? Jamie asked, indicating Enos.

'Enos. He's working with us.'

'Manheru Enosi,' Jamie said to the black man, clapping his hands in greeting. 'Maswera here?'

'Taswera maswerao,' Enos replied, returning the greeting, delighted at being acknowledged. As a black man in the Lowveld, Joe reflected, one had to be grateful for small mercies. Sometimes it seemed to him as if the news of Ian Smith's downfall hadn't reached this far south.

'And John,' Jamie said. 'John and I are old acquaintances.'

The Shangaan looked anything but pleased to see the Warden.

Enos and John went off to the compound, a complex of brick huts just visible behind a stand of riverine acacias. When they were gone, Jamie said, 'I think Jack Hammond might have found you somebody more reliable than that guy. We've had him for poaching two or three times. The Scouts won't take it too kindly when they realise who he is.'

'He comes from one of the villages,' Joe said.

'I don't care where he comes from. Just keep an eye on him, that's all.'

Emmy McAllister, a small, dark, darting woman with something of the action of a disturbed beetle, greeted Joe and Ross at the house, plumped cushions on the chairs which lined the low stoep and dashed kitchenwards to get beer. She had a pronounced South African accent and a new, tightly permed hairstyle, the result no doubt of the day's expedition to Chiredzi. The whiff of suburbia that she exuded seemed uncomfortably at odds with the wilderness that surrounded them.

Jamie motioned them to a chair. As they sat, a loud splash and a cackle came from the river beyond the fence. 'Croc,' said Jamie. 'There's a big old bastard lives on the other bank. We call him Adolf. He's having a go at the ducks.'

Joe thought about Ben and his worries about crocodiles. He mentioned it to the Warden.

Jamie smiled. 'You'd have been safe enough,' he said. 'Just as long as you didn't go paddling. They take the odd piccanin, and sometimes a woman fetching water, but mostly they just stick to fish and ducks.'

'What's that?' asked Emmy, returning with the beer.

'Crocs. I was saying you're safe enough if you stick to dry land.'

'That's what you told Mum.' There was a disapproving look on Emmy's face.

Jamie threw back his head and guffawed. 'Her Mum came up from Joburg to stay the June before last. We walked down to the Chiviriga Falls. I'd told her the crocs were safe, but then, would you believe it, a little bastard, only half the size of that one over there had a go at her. Straight out of the water, jaws open. It wasn't a serious attack, but it did the trick. She went home a week early.'

'I can't see what's funny about that,' said Emmy primly as Joe and Ross joined in the laughter. But then she, too, started to laugh.

'Welcome to Chipinda,' said Jamie. 'You don't have to be mad to live here, but it helps.'

A purple loerie cackled from a thorn tree as if in agreement.

When the sun had dipped beneath the rim of the bush Emmy cooked steaks and heated sadza on the braai. They drank more beer. Mosquitoes whined and bit. They were a strange pair, Jamie and Emmy, perhaps really a little mad, Joe thought, competing for attention the one with the other like a couple of children. Emmy still seemed genuinely distressed by the kidnapping. Perhaps it reminded her of her own vulnerability. Living at Chipinda must feel like living in a house on the edge of the world.

When Emmy allowed him to, Jamie talked about the Gona-re-Zhou. It was long and narrow, he said, forty to fifty kilometres wide, butting up to the die-straight Mozambican border. Chipinda Pools was the administrative centre for the northern half of the park, Mabalauta for the south. Three great rivers flowed through it, draining the Lowveld: the Nuanetsi, which joined the Limpopo near Pafuri, and the Lundi and Sabi Rivers which combined near the park border, snaking through Mozambique to the Indian Ocean south of Beira. Between the rivers lay vast stretches of waterless sandveld, mopani country, dotted with shallow seasonal pans to which the game moved during the summer rains, returning to the rivers when the pans dried.

It was wild country and dangerous, some of it still not fully explored. From time to time the Game Scouts or Chenjerai's men would come across the skeletons of Mozambicans who'd crossed the border illegally and died of thirst out there in the trackless mopani. There were few visitors, and those mostly locals from Chiredzi or Triangle who, because of lack of fuel and water, stayed at Chipinda or close by on the banks of the Lundi.

But above all, Jamie told them, it was elephant country, home of the biggest tuskers south of the Zambezi. The biggest of them all, called Dhlulamithi, a Shangaan word meaning taller than the trees, and whose left tusk was so long it scraped the ground as he walked, had been shot in 1967 by a visiting South African Brigadier. His successor, a forty-year-old bull called Kabakwe, whose ivory promised to be even bigger, still roamed the scrub west of the Lundi. They'd constructed giant radio collars from industrial webbing and fibreglass to track his wanderings.

'Jamie's an elephant man,' Emmy said, butting in when the opportunity arose. 'Always was, always will be. Thinks like one. Eats like one. The older he gets, the more he looks like one.'

'There you are,' said Jamie. 'That's what fifteen years of married life does to you.'

Joe realised they were still deeply in love, this strange, isolated pair.

Once started on the subject of elephants, Jamie was not easy to stop. The herds in the Gona-re-Zhou had a reputation for viciousness, he said, a quite justified reputation. The older ones, most of them, were carrying lead from poachers, or hunters, or the days of tsetse control. But above all from the war. The herds were led by dominant cow elephants of great age and cunning. In other places, at Wankie or at Mana Pools a single cow would charge when threatened. In the Gona-re-Zhou the entire herd, even the youngsters, would go for you. And they weren't just trying to scare. They were out to kill.

The McAllisters talked long and hard into the night. Jamie switched eventually from elephant to hippo. He discussed culling, the capture of the rhinos, sable antelope, the great central plateau of Nyamatongwe where a lost city was supposed once to have stood. Emmy in her turn talked about London, a visit she'd made there as a schoolgirl in 1959, and about Princess Diana and Prince William. She displayed an encyclopaedic knowledge of the British royal family, and a profound admiration for both the Queen and Mrs. Thatcher, whom, Joe suspected, she thought of as one and the same person.

It was past one before Joe and Ross gratefully closed the door of the guest hut, checked the mosquito screens and fell into their beds.

Joe woke once in the night, sweating, the mosquito bites on his legs and arms itching intolerably. It was a cough that had woken him, a single dry cough that seemed to come from immediately outside the window. He felt the hairs on the nape of his neck begin to prickle. Then a dog began to bark and he heard Jamie's voice telling the animal to be quiet.

'Leopard,' murmured Ross, only half-waking. 'Outside the fence. Go to sleep.'

By six-thirty they were eating the substantial breakfast that Emmy insisted on providing for them of eggs from her own fowls and bacon from Chiredzi. While they ate Jamie brought maps and checked out their route. An old habit from the war, he told Joe. There was an illegal settlement across the river not marked on the map, he said. It might be worth a visit. He wished them luck. Emmy said she'd do coq-au-vin for them that night, and had they any preference for starters? Joe and

Ross said they hadn't. She gave them chilled orange squash in a vacuum flask for when they got thirsty, and a packet of sandwiches with enough for Enos and John.

That morning John joined Ross and Joe in the cab, Enos taking his place on the mealie sacks in the back. As they lurched out of Chipinda Pools Joe tried to question the Shangaan about what his brother had seen the day they'd found him, and about the villages they were going to visit. John replied only in monosyllables. If he knew anything, it was obvious he wasn't saying. He seemed unhappy about the expedition, and a little afraid of Ross. As the heat increased, he began to sweat heavily.

The Lundi Bridge was new, a flat, single-tracked concrete structure. Beyond the river the settlements began; crude huts, many just rough assemblages of poles and thatch, scattered amongst the acacias and sausage trees. They swung north-west following the course of the Lundi, the rutted track no more than a wide path between small fields of stunted mealies. Tiny lumpy clouds flecked the dusty blue of the immense sky.

Joe looked at the map. 'This should be Chitsange,' he said, and glanced at John for confirmation.

There was no response.

'Is this Chitsange?' Ross spoke sharply to the man.

'Yes.'

'Where does the Headman Elias live?'

John shrugged.

'You don't know?'

John shrugged again.

'Christ!' hissed Ross between his teeth.

Some women were crossing the track, coming from the river with galvanised water cans balanced on their heads. One or two of them had shiny-headed babies strapped to their backs. They stopped to stare. Ross brought the Land-Rover to a sudden halt. 'OK,' he said. 'If you don't know, they will. Go and ask them.'

John got out reluctantly and went over to the women. They didn't seem to recognise him.

'I thought he was supposed to come from round here,' Joe said.

'Don't be fooled,' Ross said. 'They're probably his sisters.'

John was a long time talking to the women. Several times he pointed at the Land-Rover, and at the bush, then he walked slowly back, got into the cab and closed the door. 'They say the Headman is very sick,' he said.

'I don't believe you.'

John's face was expressionless. 'Very very sick.'

'Perhaps he really is sick,' Joe suggested.

'Bollocks.'

Ross opened the door and called to the women. They approached sheepishly. 'OK,' he said to John. 'Now ask them to tell us where the headman lives.' There was real menace in his voice.

John looked for a moment as though he was going to wrench open the door and run off into the bush. Instead he said something quickly in Shangaan to the women. The oldest of the group, a fat woman in a blue flowered dress, pointed westward across the bush.

'Now we're getting somewhere,' said Ross with heavy sarcasm.

'Yes, baas.'

'Well, take us there for Christ sake!'

'Yes, baas.' John spoke almost inaudibly. He was pressed back against the door of the Land-Rover as if expecting a blow. He'd begun to use the word baas, Joe noticed, when he spoke to Ross.

The kraal was small, much smaller than Joe had expected, a collection of decrepit pole huts surrounded by a rough fence of cut thorn branches. Here and there thatch had slipped from the roofs and the holes had been patched with old sugar sacks bearing the Triangle imprint. There was a distinct smell of excrement. To the left and rear of the enclosure a twenty-gallon oil drum open at the top was sitting on a small fire. Wisps of steam played around it.

The man Joe took to be Elias was sitting on a low stool at the entrance to one of the huts. He was fifty, maybe older, dressed in a ripped shirt and over-large trousers. He appeared to be asleep. Ross paused for a moment, then hit the horn. The man jumped as though shot, and fell back out of sight into the hut. There was the sound of a woman's voice raised in anger.

Soon after, the owner of the voice appeared. She was a large female of indeterminate age, wearing a vivid orange dress made from a jira, a single length of cloth. She came to the entrance of the kraal and stood, hands on hips, as if daring them to come further. Ross told John to greet the woman and tell her they had come to discuss matters of importance with headman Elias.

John knew the woman. It was obvious from the way he approached her. Their conversation was brief. When he returned to the Land-Rover he said, 'She says she wants mealie meal, baas. She is starving.'

The fat woman in the gateway assumed a pitiable attitude.

'Who told her we had mealie meal? You?' Ross was furious.

'No, baas.'

'I don't believe you.'

The Shangaan retreated a pace or two.

'No mealie meal. Is that clear?'

'But, baas . . .' John glanced at the woman, worried.

'Tell her to fetch Elias. Tell her we may give her mealie meal if she fetches Elias.'

John returned reluctantly to the woman and gave her the message. She immediately began to shout at him, waving her arms, then she waddled swiftly back into the kraal. When she came back the Headman was with her.

He was very drunk. Twice the woman had to clutch at his arm to prevent him falling. As he got nearer Joe could see that his skin was dark, blotchy. There were sores on his cheeks and his shirt was stiff with what looked like dried vomit. Ross said, 'See those sores? He's been drinking kachasu. They make it from brown sugar and fertiliser with a little meths thrown in for good measure. It kills them after a while.'

It was clear that Elias was too drunk even to understand the questions that Ross put to him via John, let alone supply the answers. When Ross shouted at him in exasperation, he put his hands up to shield his face and sat down in the dust. The woman began to shout about mealie meal and point at the Land-Rover.

'I can't believe she's starving,' said Joe, conscious of the heat and the stench.

'She isn't. She wants it to brew beer. This place is a shebeen, an illegal drinking den.'

By now the woman was frothing at the mouth. She grabbed Ross's shirt, spraying him with flecks of spittle. He struggled with her, swaying as though engaged in an obscene dance. Then, with surprising swiftness, he drew back his arm and clubbed her in the face. She fell to the ground, moaning.

'For Christ's sake,' said Joe.

But Ross was already in the Land-Rover and the engine was running.

At Machuwete it took them two hours and a sack of meal before the aged headman finally got round to stating that he knew nothing of the kidnapping. At Chambuta and Machivukele the news that they were giving away mealie meal seemed to have preceded them and a crowd of women with buckets and sacks surrounded them as they drew up. At Hahlani, the headman, a cousin of John's, produced a small boy who said he had seen the bandits. The boy said there were two of them and they were white men. He was five years old, he told Ross proudly. His mother told them she was very poor and that her husband had died. They left two sacks of meal, one with the headman and one with John who said he was going to stay at the village because his wife was sick.

They were not sorry to leave him behind.

Joe took the wheel for the drive back to Chipinda. He drove deliberately fast, taking out his frustration on the vehicle, racing the engine not shifting into fourth on the occasional smooth sections of the track. Alarmed women carrying hoes and babies watched them as they passed. Hornbills scattered, squawking. Ross, who watched the performance in silence for a while, eventually said, 'You'll fuck up the engine.'

'So what?'

'So you'll fuck up the engine. It's your engine. You fuck it up if you want to.'

At a sudden corner Joe slewed the Land-Rover off the track into the long grass. There was a clunk as a rock or tree stump hit the sump guard. He wrenched at the wheel to gain control, then slowed. He felt suddenly hopeless, so weak he could hardly grip the steering wheel. 'I'm sorry,' he said quietly.

'Don't worry about it,' Ross said. 'It's been a bad day.'

And tomorrow would be worse. And the next day. And the next. More stinking tumble-down huts. More dead-faced shifty-eyed headmen. More drunks and geriatrics. Joe realised how much hope he'd pinned on finding the boy. Too much hope. In his optimistic moments he'd imagined him, his thin features, the two dogs still at his feet, standing respect-fully in the presence of his elders, telling all he knew. An overheard conversation maybe. The casually spoken name of a village. Something dropped by the men in their haste to get away . . .

It was pointless. Completely pointless. He began to wonder if he'd imagined the boy, if any of it was real. He should have taken Larry Wakeman's advice and gone home. He should have allowed the wounds to heal instead of coming down here on this wild goose chase with a man he hardly knew.

He glanced across at his companions: Enos sitting upright, staring ahead at the track; Ross, his eyes closed now, lolling against the door. What did it mean to them, all this? A pleasant excursion? An interesting interlude in the everyday humdrum of life in Harare with maybe a buck or two at the end of it? Or maybe, and the thought troubled him, maybe it meant the opportunity to hit fat women in the face, no ques-tions asked.

That day at Nyadzonya. . . . He could see them now, sitting tense and expectant in the cab of the Ferret as they drew up before the lines of singing, smiling people. The smell of sweat and sun-heated metal. The pressure of the finger on the firing button of the canon. And the noise, the stink of the smoke, the screams . . .

With an effort he pushed the vision from his mind and concentrated on the driving.

The sun was dipping quickly, hitting the screen at an angle, blinding him. He screwed up his eyes to see. They passed the track that led off to Machuwete and another flock of goats. Between the tall river trees the heat lay on the land like a golden fog.

Dust. It was dust. He could taste it now, sour and gritty on the palate where it drifted in through the open windows. It coated the screen in soft opalescent whirls. 'Where's this dust coming from?' he said to Enos.

'Herds. The boys are bringing the herds home. They've taken them to the river for water. Now they are bringing them home.'

They turned a sudden sharp bend. The first of the cattle were up ahead of them spread out across the track, brindled brown and white cows and calves, some with the humps and dewlaps of brahmans. In the centre of the herd stood a single black bull, its long horns curving slightly at the tips. Square cowbells, more like large tin boxes the bells, dangled from their collars, clunking dully. The cows were acutely thin, the points of their pelvic bones sharp enough, it seemed, to pierce their hides.

Joe brought the Land-Rover to a halt and switched off the engine. He felt a growing excitement. Maybe, just maybe . . .

For a moment or two the beasts halted, staring with damp brown eyes. Then, urged on by the press from behind they divided, passing the vehicle so that their stench and the small flies that swarmed around them invaded the cab. Above the cattle egrets danced and swooped, trailing long legs. Ross opened his eyes and slid his window shut. 'Fucking dust,' he muttered. Then, apparently went back to sleep.

There had to be a boy. Joe strained to see between the necks and bodies of the shambling beasts, but they were squeezed too close. He cursed softly, tapping impatiently on the hard plastic of the steering wheel. Then they were past, and the dust thinned.

He opened the door and looked back along the track. The cattle seemed to be finding their own way home. 'There are no boys,' he said, puzzled.

Enos shrugged. 'Maybe they're shooting birds.'

'Shooting birds?'

'They won't be far.'

Joe peered into the dense bush near the river, but could see nothing. If the boys were there they were staying well hidden. Disappointed, he restarted the engine.

Towards Chitsange they met the second herd. This time

there were more of them, perhaps fifty animals peeling up between the trees from the river, their legs still wet and muddy, their muzzles trailing spittle. And this time there was a boy.

He was about twelve, thin, wearing a grey shirt and khaki shorts. He had two scrawny kaffir dogs and a plastic bottle. He hung back in the trees watching, wide-eyed and suspicious.

Then Joe was certain. He shouted from the window in English: 'Hey, you! Boy!' Ignoring the cattle, he flicked the lever into four-wheel drive and swung the Land-Rover off the track, crashing through the tall grass and scrub.

Terrified, the boy turned to run, but Joe slid the vehicle to a halt and was out after him.

It was a short chase. The boy was agile, leaping branches, but Joe's legs were longer. He brought him down in a stand of elephant grass close to the river, crushing the boy's thin body with his bulk, twisting back his arm, waiting for the cry of pain. Surprisingly and disconcertingly there was none. The boy lay beneath him, breathing fast, offering no resistance.

Joe hauled him to his feet, pushed him back towards the Land-Rover.

'What in God's name do you think you're doing?' Ross was standing, hands on hips, waiting.

'The boy,' Joe said, gasping for breath, sweating, matted with dust. 'This is the boy.'

'You're sure that's the boy?' There was anger in Ross's voice.

'I'm sure.'

'So why did you have to go charging off into the bush, scaring the shit out of him? You've got a voice, haven't you? You could have told him to come here.'

'I thought he might escape.'

'Where to? He's got his cattle to bring home.'

Joe fell silent, his chest heaving.

'So what are we going to do now?' Ross said.

'Question him.'

'How? None of us can speak fucking Shangaan.'

Joe's brain raced. 'John. We could go back and fetch John . . .'

'Unoziva kutaura chiShona here?' Ross said. 'Do you know how to speak Shona?'

The boy remained motionless, staring at the ground.

Ross repeated the question. Again there was no response. He called to Enos who dropped to his haunches and began to speak softly to the boy. He spoke for a long time, sometimes indicating Joe. Eventually the boy muttered a few indistinct phrases. Enos said, 'He speaks Shona. He says he's never seen you before.'

'He's lying.'

The boy muttered again.

'He says he knows nothing. He says he was at school in Chikombedzi.'

'In August?'

'In August.'

Slowly the boy raised his head and his eyes met Joe's. There was a steady intelligence in his face that was disconcerting. 'I don't know you, baas,' the boy said slowly, unexpectedly in excellent English.

He held the gaze for what seemed like an eternity. Eventually, it was Joe who turned away. 'No,' he said quietly. 'You don't.'

Ross said nothing until they'd crossed the Lundi bridge then he said, 'You're a stupid bastard. I don't know why I fucking bother.'

'I'm sorry.'

'You're sorry. What difference do you think that makes?'

'It was a mistake.'

A mistake. Another mistake. All along there'd been mistakes, mistakes, mistakes. Ross said, 'I told you before we left Harare, don't do anything without asking me. And what do you do? You go straight in, feet forward and fuck the consequences. You know what you've done? You've ruined any chance we might have had of finding that boy.'

'I don't see why.'

'You think he's just going to take his cattle home and go to bed and not say a word about what's happened? It'll be all over Matibi by first light tomorrow. Then see how much we'll get out of them. They may even report it to the authorities, and we'll have the Army on our backs.'

162

Joe avoided Ross's eyes. 'I just thought . . . We were getting nowhere . . .'

'You thought! You do too much bloody thinking. Listen, when I said we'd had a bad day I wasn't too bothered. I didn't expect them to tell us anything today. It was a question of reassuring them, getting their trust. Now how much fucking trust are we going to get?'

Joe felt suddenly irked, petulant, like a small boy hauled before a school principal to explain a misdemeanour. 'If you were so keen on getting their trust, why did you hit that woman?'

'She was spitting at me.'

'So?'

'She was an old drunk. We wouldn't have got anybody's respect by giving in to her, giving her meal. That's the way it works.'

Enos nodded slowly. 'That's the way.'

Darkness had fallen swiftly. The lights from the Land-Rover laced the silent bush. Moths flittered like confetti in the twin beams. They reached the turn-off to Chipinda Pools. Joe slowed to take the corner. 'So what do we do now?' he asked quietly.

'I know what I ought to do. I ought to go back to Harare and leave you to stew in it.'

'But you won't?'

Ross's sudden smile was just visible in the glow from the instrument panel. 'I guess not. I don't know why. Maybe it's the thought of your wife and kids possibly still out there. No, we'll carry on for now. Check out those other villages Jack mentioned, and the squatters. Then head off down into Matibi. After that, well . . .' Ross paused. Then suddenly he said, 'Look.'

In the darkness of the bush ahead of them points of light danced and twitched. 'Impala,' he said. 'See their eyes?'

The animals leapt like acrobats between the twisted trunks of the mopanis.

Ross was right. The word had got around. The already sealed faces of the Shangaan closed tighter. Now, no-one asked them for mealie meal. Herd boys ran to hide when they saw the Land-Rover. In the kraals doors remained obstinately shut. For six days they tried, first the villages near the Lundi: Chipinda village itself, Chikwedziva, the squatters encampments on the west bank. Then they looped north, to the Chironga Irrigation scheme, and south again to Matihwa, Valemu and Masuamele. Gregory, a taciturn game scout lent to them by Jamie, interpreted for them and smoked large numbers of the cigarettes that he was convinced Joe had bought especially for his own exclusive use.

Beyond Masuamele they stopped asking about the herd boy and instead showed the pictures of Ellie and the children. As they moved further west their reception became more friendly. Children began to wave as they passed. At the dips, herd boys no longer scattered at the sight of their white faces. Women weeding the mealie fields gathered unprompted to shake their heads at the photographs. Three times they were stopped by the Army and questioned about their movements. Each time, mealie meal or such cigarettes as Joe could extract from Gregory's grasp had the desired effect. It got hotter and drier. Joe developed an irritating rash on the inside of his upper thighs and around his genitals. He felt a quiet despair, which at times even Ross seemed to share.

On Monday 9th they reached the Nuanetsi River and Chikombezi Mission. The Fathers were frank and friendly. They said that if a white woman and children had come through their area they would have heard about it for certain, and they hadn't.

It was pointless to go on.

That evening, as they drove back along the smooth well-graded road that skirted the northern boundary of the Gonare-Zhou, Joe took out the photographs once more. They were creased and dirty from the many hands that had held them. They'd become strangers, he realised, the three people he'd loved, still loved. Less substantial than ghosts.

Perhaps that was as it should be. It was more comfortable that way. And he needed comfort, God knows how he needed it. 'It's strange,' he said. 'I can't remember Ellie's voice now. I could remember it clearly until a few days ago, how it sounded, the little things she used to say. Now it's gone.'

Ross, who was driving, glanced at Joe and then back at the road. 'I'm sorry,' he said.

'Maybe that's the way it happens, things disappearing bit by bit. Memories, I mean.'

'Not all of them.'

'No, not all. I guess you remember the important things.'

Ross said, 'I remember more about my Dad now than when he first died, if that's any consolation.'

'I didn't know your father was dead.' It was the first time Ross had mentioned his family.

'It was a long time ago. I was ten. We lived in Gwelo at the time, and my father had gone to Bulawayo for the day. He was manager of a chemical distribution company. He had lunch with a friend, and when he was walking back to the car he died, just like that. On the pavement. It was some kind of stroke. He was forty. That's when I first started coming down to Chungwe for my holidays. I think Harry and Betty felt sorry for me. Yes, I remember quite a lot about him now.'

'But not his voice?'

'No, not his voice.'

They drove in silence for a while. Then Joe suggested, 'We could go to Matabeleland. Go to the villages there.'

Ross shook his head. 'That's not on, and you know it. Anyway, the Fifth Brigade are going back in. There's talk of a curfew. We'd be stopped immediately.'

'That wouldn't worry me.'

'Well, it would me. Forget Matabeleland, Joe. If we'd got hard evidence, if we knew exactly where we were going, then it would be worth the risk. Otherwise, no way.'

'So that's it, is it? That's the end?'

The end.

He should have prepared himself for this moment, he knew, but now it had come, it took him by surprise. He began to shake. He dropped the pictures and they scattered onto the floor beneath Ross's feet.

Ross brought the Land-Rover to a halt and retrieved them. As he handed them back to Joe he said, 'There's always Plan B.'

'Hey,' said Enos. 'Plan B. That sounds good. Plan B.'

'What's Plan B?' Joe asked quietly.

'You got a passport?'

Joe nodded.

'Fancy a little trip south of the border?'

'South Africa?'

'The very place. Good wine. Beautiful women. Sun-kissed beaches.'

'Soweto' said Enos.

'Soweto. It's got the lot.'

'I don't understand,' said Joe. 'You think they've been taken to South Africa?'

'Not a chance, but I've got mates down there.'

'Mates?'

'Mates.'

'From the war?'

Ross grinned, re-engaged first gear and they moved off. 'You're catching on fast,' he said.

Then Joe remembered. He'd only been half-paying attention at the time when Larry Wakeman had told him: 'They're down South, the Selous Scouts, working for the Boers. Down South.'

'You mean your mates might be behind all this?' he said.

'Don't be stupid.'

'But the cartridge case. You said it came from South Africa.'

'Correct.'

'And ZIPRA dissidents are being trained in the Transvaal?'

'Correct again.'

'So if your mates are training these guys, which you seem to be implying, they might well have organised it all.'

Ross looked at Enos. 'What are we going to do with this guy?' he said.

Enos grinned, took out his pipe and began to fill it.

'Listen,' said Ross, 'these mates of mine may not be exactly gentle people. They don't go around with flowers stuck in the ends of their FN's. But I can tell you this: they stop short of organising the shooting and kidnapping of respectable middle-class white people like you and your wife.'

'But they might know something about it?'

'Possibly, just possibly. Or they might be able to find out.'

Joe put the photographs away. 'You didn't mention anything about this before,' he said.

'I just wanted to make sure we'd finished down here first.'

'And we're finished?'

'We're finished.'

'There's Chenjerai. We haven't seen him.'

'Enos can catch up with him while we're away. A little bit of the old black solidarity will probably extract more information than we ever could. OK, Enos?'

'OK.' Enos didn't seem too thrilled at the prospect.

Ross noticed the reaction. 'Of course, you can always come down South with us,' he said.

'I'll stay here,' said Enos quickly.

Ross laughed and slapped his knee. 'I thought you'd see it like that,' he said.

The last night in Chipinda Emmy cooked impala steaks in red wine. The next morning they left early for Chungwe. Enos, sitting in the shade of a huge ebony tree, raised a hand in farewell as they passed.

At the ranch Ross went off immediately to telephone. He was gone for most of the morning. Joe passed the time chatting to Danny. The boy was agog to know whether there had been any shooting. When Joe told him there hadn't, he seemed disappointed. Betty came in and out, organising cups of tea, asking questions about Emmy McAllister. 'Such a shame they didn't have any children,' she said. 'They've been trying for years. It's too late now, I expect. I can't help wondering if it was him or her had the problem. She never would say.'

When Harry came back from the fields just before lunch, Ross was still in the office. After he'd washed he came in and drank a large glass of lemonade. He was about to pour himself a second glass when he stopped and said, 'I nearly forgot. There was a phone call came for you a couple of days ago.'

'For me?' said Joe, surprised. 'I didn't think anybody knew I was here.'

'Just a minute.'

Harry went out and returned soon after with a slip of paper. 'Yes. It was a bloke called Larry Wakeman. American, he sounded like. He wants you to call him urgently.'

'He's got news about Ellie?' Joe's heart was racing.

'He wouldn't say.'

'OK, thanks.' Joe took the paper. It had both Larry's numbers, home and office. It had to be urgent or he'd have just given the office number. He must have heard something, perhaps through his contacts in Zvarevashe's office or maybe some priest at one of the Matabeleland missions. 'Do you mind if I use the phone?'

'Go ahead. Ross should be finished any time. He'd just got connected when I went in to pick up that message. You think it might be good news?'

'It might.'

Harry gave a chuckle. 'That's the spirit. While there's life, hey? That's the way I work or I wouldn't be sitting here now.'

It was another fifteen minutes before Ross came in. He grinned and stuck up his thumb. 'We're on,' he said. 'I've arranged to meet him tomorrow night. We'll have to leave pretty sharpish after lunch. We'll stay over in Beitbridge.'

Joe said, 'Larry Wakeman called when we were down in Chipinda. He wants me to call him back urgently.'

The grin left Ross's face. 'He called here?' he said.

'Yes.'

'You told him we were coming here?'

'No. How could I have done? I didn't even know about this place. I thought *you* must have told him.'

'Like hell I did. That nosy bastard's into everything.'

'He might have some news about Ellie.'

'And pigs might fly.' Ross seemed very upset. It was because of Nyadzonya, Joe guessed. Because of Eva. Because of what happened in the river.

'Hey, come on, Ross,' Harry reasoned. 'There's no harm in Joe finding out what this bloke wants. Who is he, anyway?'

'A black American journalist. He's been on my back for the last three years.' Ross spun to face Joe. 'OK, you go ahead and call him. All I'll say is this: if we're not on the road by one-thirty, you can forget it. You can forget the whole thing.' He sat down heavily in one of the chairs.

'I'll go and phone,' said Joe quietly.

For nearly half an hour he tried. Eventually the man at the exchange said he might be able to get the call through to Harare sometime during the evening, but more likely the following morning. Should he book it? Joe told him to forget it and came through for lunch. He decided he'd try again when they got to Beitbridge. Maybe the line would be better from there. For once he was grateful for the Barton's custom of taking their meals in silence.

Part Four
The Transvaal

They made Beitbridge by six that evening. It was hotter than
Chungwe. Before they'd left they'd offloaded most of the
camping equipment and the rifles and stored them in a lockup shed near the house. They took only the backpacks filled
with enough clothes for their immediate needs, and a pair of
binoculars. On the drive south they spoke little. Ross refused
to say where they were going, or who they were going to meet
and Joe judged it wise not to mention Larry Wakeman. Ross
said that if asked he was to say they were going to visit the
Kruger Park to view game. On the roadside they saw
warthogs and, close to Beitbridge, carpets of yellow and
white flowers. When they stopped once to pee, the bush was
full of birdsong.

Beitbridge was tiny, dusty, a collection of banks and filling
stations. There was a white church, a police post with a watch
tower and tall radio masts, the customs buildings and not
much else. They checked into Peters Motel, a tatty pale green
collection of chalets grouped around a clouded swimming
pool. Red-coated waiters wearing black shoes and no socks
shuffled about with sullen expressions. White families
shouted to each other and splashed in the pool. The temperature at seven o'clock was ninety-six degrees farenheit. While
Ross was in the shower Joe slipped out to call Larry. Once
again he failed to get through.

They were at Departure Control when it opened at six-
thirty the following morning, lining up with the passengers
from the Harare/Johannesburg Express Motorways bus. The
single, harrassed immigration official stamped them through

without a second glance. The Limpopo River, glimpsed between the girders of the bridge, was surprisingly blue.

At South African Customs and Immigration they were the first to arrive and were forced to wait until white-uniformed officials came to open up the immigration hall. They filled in the blue forms, giving the name and address of Ross's mother in Durban as their South African contact. The official who dealt with them had three stripes for seniority on his shoulder tabs, and a brutal face. The clock in the hall, Joe noticed, was a gift from the Remington Arms Company, Syracuse, New York.

The official examined the passports closely, checking them with the forms. Then, without commenting, he took them into a small office at one side. Joe glanced at Ross but his face betrayed nothing. Perhaps this was routine. There would be a computer terminal next door, he guessed. The Johannesburg bus pulled up outside with a hiss of airbrakes and the hall filled with sweaty, jostling passengers. By the time the man returned a long queue had formed.

The official was clearly slightly suspicious. Maybe it was to do with the kidnapping, Joe thought, it must have received extensive publicity in South Africa. But the man made no mention of it. Instead he asked to see traveller's cheques, the papers for the Land-Rover. He asked whether Joe had a return ticket to Europe. Then he began to question them closely on their reasons for visiting South Africa and their destination there. Ross launched into a long explanation about how they were going to visit the Kruger Park because it was so much better managed than the Zimbabwe game reserves, which seemed finally to satisfy him.

'You've got a point there,' he said, 'A good point,' and stuck the white temporary residence permits into their passports and stamped them. Outside, the two black policemen raised the galvanised steel barrier and they were through.

In Messina, where they stopped to change traveller's cheques, green seed pods hung from the flamboyant trees and a dark brown army Land-Rover was drawn up outside the Barclays National Bank. Inside the bank Joe waited in line behind three pink-faced sweating soldiers, one of whom had two stars on his shoulder and a name tag reading 'Jansen'.

Through the window a tall radar tower bristling with aerials looked north across the Limpopo towards Zimbabwe. The distant spoil tips of the Messina Developments copper mines shimmered in the gathering heat.

They headed south on the N1, travelling at speed through dense mopani bush dotted here and there with baobabs and candelabrum trees. Suddenly Ross said, 'We were bloody good, you know that? Bloody good. The best counter-insurgency force there's been on the face of this earth.'

'The Selous Scouts?'

'Don't let anybody tell you otherwise.' Ross spoke with an urgency that puzzled Joe. 'We had Americans that came over, you know, ex-Green Berets, and they were amazed at the way we worked. Do you realise that we were credited, officially credited, with sixty-eight percent of all terrorists killed in Rhodesia during the war? Sixty-eight percent! And we lost less than forty men in the process. You know how we operated?'

Joe shook his head.

'We captured terrorists and turned them.'

'Turned them?'

'We gave them a choice. Either work for us and tell us all you know, or be killed. Most of them didn't take too much persuading. Once we'd turned those gooks we'd go into an area and pretend to be a new group of fighters just arrived from Mozambique or Zambia. Of course, we'd be mostly Africans, people like Enos, ex-Rhodesian African Rifles, and a handful of turned gooks. One or two Europeans, usually.'

'Weren't you a bit conspicuous?'

'We blacked our faces, but you couldn't fool the villagers close up. No, we stayed under cover mostly, directing operations, maintaining communications. Anyway, we'd arrive at a village and talk to the people. Once they were convinced we were genuine freedom fighters they'd send a mujiba – that's a contact man, usually a boy – to wherever the resident terrs were holed up, and arrange a meeting. Of course we'd got all the passwords and signs from the gooks we'd turned.'

'And then you shot them down?'

'Sometimes. Not if we could avoid it. Sometimes they got suspicious and we had to open fire but that meant our cover was blown. Usually we'd call in the Fireforce and make an excuse and leave.'

'And that worked, did it?'

'Like a dream, time and time again. Sometimes the poor sods got so confused they started shooting at each other.'

The road began to climb upwards between red sandstone boulders. There were farm stalls now, advertising lychees and mangoes for sale. After a while Ross said, 'Of course, eventually it stopped working. They got wise to us. And in the end there were so many of the bastards coming over that it didn't really make any difference what we did.'

'Which is when you moved against the camps?'

Ross glanced sharply at Joe. 'Who told you that?'

'I just picked it up.'

'Larry Wakeman told you?'

'He mentioned something about it. Nyadzonya.'

Ross pulled the Land-Rover out to overtake a huge articulated truck. 'He told you about his wife, did he?'

'Yes.'

'What else?'

'He said you went on that raid. He said you commanded one of the armoured cars.'

Ross fell silent. A tunnel loomed ahead. The sudden darkness shocked. Beyond it a sign read 'Hendrik Verwoerd Tonels Tunnels 1961'. They plunged almost immediately into darkness again. 'What are these mountains?' Joe asked.

'The Soutspansberg. It means Salt Pan Mountains. It's as far as the Boers got on their trek north.'

When they emerged finally into the sunlight, the smooth road, rimmed by white crash barriers, was still climbing upwards. Strands of combretum and mountain acacia had replaced the mopani. Small birds of prey soared on upcurrents. 'Listen,' said Ross quietly, 'there's something you ought to know about that camp, about all those camps. ZANLA deliberately put woman and children into them to get them granted refugee status by the United Nations. It was a trick they learned from the Palestinians. Then, if anything happened, they could scream massacre and show the world pictures of dead babies. Nyadzonya was the main ZANLA training camp at that time, and as such it was a legitimate target.'

172

'So that excuses what happened?'

Ross's reply was a long time coming. Eventually he said slowly, 'No, it doesn't excuse it. I'm not proud of what we did, though there are plenty of people who went on that raid who are. But it was war. You can't stop shooting at terrorists because there are women and children around. That way you'd never win. We aimed for the men but sometimes women got shot, sometimes kids. And don't believe the women were all innocent either. Many of them could handle a gun better than the men. Some of them were even involved in the training, Larry Wakeman's wife Eva for one. Of course there were some sadistic bastards in the Scouts, some people who just liked killing for the sake of it. There always are in any army. Some people got bush crazy, went literally a bit mad. They'd shoot anything that moved, especially if it had a black face.'

'How about you? Did you go bush crazy?'

Ross paused. 'A little,' he said. 'Maybe a little.' His knuckles were white where he gripped the steering wheel. Unaccountably Joe felt a pang of pity for the man, and the burden he had to carry.

As they wound higher the air became cooler and fresher. They passed a black woman carrying a long wooden bench on her head. Groups of children stared, not waving. A truck carrying a huge earthmover slowed them down to walking pace.

And then, quite suddenly, they were no longer climbing. Above them a sheer rock face soared skywards – Hangklip, Ross called it – and stretching away to the south was the great blue expanse of the Veld, with isolated kopjes rising from it like islands in a sea. Small thunderstorms trailing skirts of rain chased one another in the distance. Below lay the neat streets and white houses of Louis Trichardt. They stopped for a moment to look at the view, and then drove downwards towards it.

It was a quiet town off the main road: a few women carrying bags of shopping, solitary black men, a police station flying the South African flag, car dealers, an extraordinary triangular church. Ross went to the Hotel Louis to call ahead, confirming their arrival. Joe went into a drugstore to buy a

Coke. 'The Great North Kafee, Take Aways, Wegneem Etes' the board above the storefront said. At the counter a thin, acned white youth was serving a black man with a pie. He stopped the transaction when Joe entered, and uncapped the Coke. Joe paid for the drink and sat down on one of a line of black plastic chairs.

'You can't sit there,' the youth said suddenly. His accent was thick with his native Afrikaans.

'Why not?'

'Those chairs are dirty.'

Joe looked at the chairs. They seemed clean enough. Not comfortable, but clean. 'No, they're not dirty.'

'I'm telling you those chairs are dirty.' Dutty, the youth pronounced it.

Joe took a swig at the Coke. Looked again at the chairs.

'You can go into the steakhouse and drink your Coke.' The hostility, which had tinged the youth's voice from the start, increased. The black man, middle-aged and wearing work-man's overalls, looked on with a neutral expression.

Joe remained seated. 'I'm perfectly comfortable where I am.' He crossed his legs, understanding now. He'd been slow to catch on.

The youth tried another tack. 'You're embarrassing this man here.'

'I don't think so.'

But it was the black man who decided it. He said in a deep, slow voice, 'Go into the steakhouse, baas. Please.'

Joe stood up and put the half-drunk Coke onto the counter. He was trying to control his anger. 'OK,' he said, 'I'm going. But let me tell you something: it's not those chairs that are dirty.'

As he went out he glanced back. The white youth was shaking his head and saying something to the black man in Afrikaans.

Joe mentioned the incident when they were back on the road. To his surprise Ross, who was driving, became angry. He said, 'Don't you do that again. Don't you ever do that again while we're down here.'

'I don't see . . .'

'This isn't a bloody anti-apartheid crusade. If you want to

make yourself conspicuous that's the way to go about it. We're here to get what information we can and get out again fast. No fuss. No questions.'

'I just got irritated.'

'Well get un-irritated. Just use your brains, for Christ's sake.'

For a while neither man spoke. The road ran smooth and level across the wide Veld. Small farmsteads, little more than shacks, dotted the roadside. They passed a police post, white huts behind a security fence. At a sign marked 'R.36. Tzaneen' they turned left.

'That's where we're going, is it, Tzaneen?' Joe stumbled over the pronunciation.

'No.'

'Well, where?'

'You wouldn't know it.'

'Try me.'

Ross paused. 'Well, I suppose there's no harm in you knowing it now we're across the border. It's a place called Phalaborwa.'

'Near Letaba?'

Ross shot a glance at Joe. 'You know about Letaba?'

'Mtisi mentioned it. It was in the statement he read out. It was where the bandits he said attacked us were supposed to have been trained.'

'What else did he tell you?'

'That they came from some camp in Botswana – Dukwe.'

'He's probably right.'

'But they were the wrong men.'

'So you keep telling me. That doesn't stop the bandits we're looking for from having been trained there.'

Joe shrugged. 'And Letaba's near this place Phalaborwa, is it?'

'Not too far.'

Joe looked at the map they'd borrowed from Harry. He found Phalaborwa perched on the north-western edge of the Kruger Park. North of it was a river called Groot Letaba. The camp would be somewhere on that river, he guessed. It was in the Gazankulu Homeland. 'So what's Phalaborwa like?' he asked.

'A mining town.'

'Big, small, medium?'

'Medium, I guess.'

'And that's all is it? A medium-sized mining town?'

'That's about it.'

For the final hour, after leaving the banana and apricot plantations which surrounded Tzaneen, they travelled through flat, featureless mopani bush, broken only occasionally by small kopjes. Many of the dirt roads to the north, leading to the Lebowa or Gazankulu Homelands, were closed or marked 'Privaat'. Twice they saw Army helicopters in the distance, working low over the bush. As they approached Phalaborwa, strange lumpy columns of rock towered above the road.

The town was not what Joe had expected. He'd imagined some kind of dusty ramshackle pioneer place with crumbling clapboard buildings, but Philaborwa was sparkling new, like an English New Town or some respectable suburb of Los Angeles. Smooth, wide streets edged with black and white curbing. A shopping centre with pedestrian malls. OK Bazaar, CNA, Checkers, Sales House. Flowering shrubs in containers. Parking meters and white futuristic churches. New cars gleaming in showroom windows, neat single-storey houses in carefully landscaped lots. It crackled with wealth.

They checked in to the Impala Inn in Essenhout Straat, a wide, low building like so many others in the town, which was approached by a narrow horseshoe-shaped drive. In the lobby Joe became suddenly conscious of his dusty bush gear. The Impala had white, rough-plastered walls, a dark-beamed roof, a souvenir shop, signs to the grill room and the bar. It could have been a hotel anywhere in the world. In a corner an African Grey parrot screeched and whistled.

In the room they showered and changed. While he waited for Ross to finish, Joe flicked through a publicity brochure on the town, written mostly in Afrikaans. The place was set up, it said, in 1957, by the Phalaborwa Mining Company to exploit the huge reserves of copper, iron and phosphates discovered in the remains of a long-vanished volcano. It was now the biggest open-pit mining operation in Africa and the second biggest in the world.

176

He was still reading when Ross emerged from the bathroom, rubbing his hair with a towel. He picked up one of the beers that the waiter had brought in earlier and perched on the edge of one of the beds. 'Listen, I want to talk to you about what's going on down here.'

Joe put down the brochure. 'I was hoping you might,' he said.

'I perhaps should have filled you in before, but I wasn't quite sure about what kind of reception we'd get at the border, and I thought the less you knew the better.'

'You mean you were expecting trouble?'

'No, not really. But I didn't want to take chances.'

'You don't seem to have a lot of faith in me.'

Ross shrugged. 'I guess I don't have a lot of faith in anybody these days.' He drained his beer at a gulp, picked up a second and poured it. 'Right. What I know about the set-up here is not much. Just to the west of the town is the headquarters of the 7th South African Infantry Battalion. As far as I can gather they're involved in the recruitment and training of dissident forces for deployment in Zimbabwe and Mozambique. This training is being carried on at a number of camps and farms in the Gazankulu Homeland. There are at least five of these camps, including Letaba, probably more. The operation is being run by South African Military Intelligence, but the actual training is being carried out by regular army officers, including a significant number of ex-Selous Scouts.'

'Like your mate?'

'Like my mate. Also based near here is the 113th Shangaan Battalion, one of several tribal battalions set up in recent years. They're used for counter-insurgency work, particularly in Mozambique. Some of the black ex-Scouts are involved there. There's also a unit of the Reconnaissance Commandos here, "Recces" as they're called. They perform an S.A.S. role. Sabotage, counter-insurgency.'

'Also staffed by Selous Scouts?'

Ross nodded. 'And ex-Rhodesian S.A.S. blokes. You know what the saying is?'

'No?'

'Old Rhodesians never die, they just turn into South Africans.'

'But you didn't?'

'No,' said Ross. 'I didn't. Maybe I should have.' He took a sip at his beer. 'Now the thing you've got to understand about all this, is that officially none of it is actually happening. The South Africans deny any involvement with these dissident groups, so it's top secret. As a consequence everybody is very, very sensitive. Ask the wrong question of the wrong person and we could find ourselves in big trouble. And I mean *big* trouble.'

'OK,' said Joe slowly. 'I understand.'

'I hope you do. So no private enterprise. You stick to the story about visiting the Kruger Park unless I make it clear otherwise. You're an American who came to Zimbabwe to see game, and got unhappy with the conditions up there.'

'Like we told the guy at the border?'

'Right. Lay it on thick, if you like. Harrassment by troops, fuel shortages, bugs in the bed. . . . Use you imagination. They love hearing the place slanged off.'

Joe laughed. 'I'll give it a go,' he said.

'Mushi.'

Somebody, a waiter, was wheeling a trolley outside the door. Crockery rattled. Joe waited until the noise had ceased. 'If they're that sensitive, do you really think we'll get anywhere?'

'I don't know. Probably not. We've got one or two things in our favour, though.'

'Like what?'

'Like the fact that, strange as it might seem to you, these guys genuinely believe that they're holding the last frontier for white civilisation against the black Marxist hordes north of the Limpopo, and with my track record in the Selous Scouts as a known commie-basher they're likely to be less discreet with me than they would be otherwise. Secondly, of course, there's the fact that you and your family are white, which will gain your case a lot of sympathy. And thirdly, there's my mate.'

'You're pretty sure he'll help, are you?'

'I think so. He owes me one from the war.'

'You saved his life?'

Ross chuckled. 'You've been watching too many movies.

178

No, I just covered up for him. Lied a little when it counted.'

'What had he done?'

'One or two things he shouldn't have.'

'And that's all you're saying?'

'That's all.'

Ross finished his beer and began sorting out clothes to wear. Joe lay back on the bed watching, relaxing. Despite his apparent thinness Ross was well-muscled, compactly built. There was a thin white line on his back extending from his right shoulder blade almost to his waist. 'Where did you get the scar?' Joe asked.

'When I was a kid. I fell off a swing.'

'I thought you might have got it in the war.'

Ross chuckled again. 'No, I came through all that without a scratch, clean as a baby. Listen, this guy we're meeting is called Mitch Margiotta. His dad was an Eyetie. I may want to talk to him alone at some stage. If so, go for a walk or get an early night, OK?'

'OK.'

'You'll like him. He's a good guy. Stupid, but a good guy.'

After they had eaten they went to the bar. It was called the Dik Dik. The stools were covered with synthetic leopardskin. At eight-fifteen Mitch Margiotta arrived.

He was huge. Six foot three or four, blond-haired, with the red skin of somebody whose pigment soaks up too much punishment from the sun. He shook hands with Ross, acknowledged Joe's presence with a brief nod and refused the beer he was offered. He was clearly agitated by the presence of a group of men of military age drinking in the far corner of the room. He had the car outside, he said. It would be better to talk there.

The car was a metallic green BMW 323i. Ross took the passenger seat. They headed south out of town, past the mine complex where huge crushers and smelters winked with intense points of light, spewing smoke into the night sky. Piles of sulphur shone brilliant yellow as if they'd been treated with luminous paint. 'Mica 40km' a sign read.

'You've got a fucking cheek, man, coming down here,' Mitch said.

'I thought you'd be pleased to see me,' Ross said quietly, staring ahead.

Mitch snorted. A car passed them, its lights haloing his hair briefly with gold. 'This could get me into big trouble,' he said.

'You're used to trouble.'

'Not the kind of trouble they give you down here. You're wasting your time, you know that?'

'Maybe.'

Mitch half-turned to Joe, not taking his eyes from the road. 'Listen, I read about your case. It's tough, hey?'

'Yes.'

'You should have come down South if you wanted to see game, gone to the Kruger. That shit heap up there is no place to take a family.'

'I think he knows that now,' Ross said.

They drove in silence for a while. The road switchbacked. A motel. Farm entrances to the right. A steady trickle of oncoming traffic. Eventually Mitch said, 'So what makes you so sure it wasn't the Army?'

'What Army?' Ross's voice was terse.

'Mugabe's Army, the Fifth Brigade. That's what the guys were saying at the time down here.'

'It was ZIPRA.' Joe spoke softly. He was surprised at how certain he sounded.

'ZIPRA!' Mitch twisted momentarily to face him, then turned back to the road. 'ZIPRA, hey?' He laughed.

'We found a cartridge case.' Joe checked himself. He couldn't see Ross's face or gauge his reaction but he sensed he shouldn't have mentioned it.

'A cartridge case?'

'AK, Romanian,' said Ross. 'You want the headstamp numbers?'

Mitch shook his head. 'Jesus Christ,' he said. 'Why did you have to come down here?'

There was just bush now, and the smooth black road. Mitch pushed the speed up to beyond the one-forty mark. Hard-cased insects crackled against the windscreen. 'As a matter of interest, where are we going?' Ross asked.

'There's a party out beyond Mica. You remember Derry?'

'Derry Moss?'

'It's his girl's place. Most of the guys will be there: Piet Schoeman, Ricky Haslam, Jannie Strydom.' Mitch once more turned to Joe. 'Look, I'll try to help you but you keep your mouth shut, hey?'

'You heard what he said, Joe?' Ross didn't turn.

'I heard.'

He must have slept. He was wakened by the drumming of the tyres. They were on a dirt road now, deeply corrugated, brilliant white in the headlights. Mitch suddenly swung the car to the right. Ahead of them was a tubular steel farm gate. To the left was a black disc painted with white letters: 'J. Bouwer. Harmonic. 40.' Ross opened the gate.

The house was on a small kopje some five kilometres from the road, a low white building with a broad stoep. A wind pump and water tank stood to one side. There was a yard at the back, surrounded by neat outbuildings. Several cars and trucks were parked there. Some of them looked expensive: Jaguars, Mercedes, a red Porsche. Heavy rock music boomed through the mosquito screens on the open windows. 'Cecile's people are overseas,' Mitch said. 'She's got the place to herself.'

Mitch took a case of beer from the boot and they went to the door. They were met by a girl in a long white lace dress who looked to be in her mid-twenties. 'This is Cecile,' said Mitch. 'My great buddy Ross, and Joe.'

The girl greeted them formally. She was not pretty, fat-cheeked, with a thin gash for a mouth. Her movements seemed jerky, unco-ordinated. Then Joe saw why. She had an artificial leg which caused her to walk with a pronounced limp. 'Hey, man, it's Ross!'

A huge shout went up from inside the house, drowning the music. A confusion of bodies jammed into the narrow hallway. 'Hey, you didn't say you were down South, man!' 'The comrades kicked you out at last, you old bastard!'

Ross was grasping hands, reeling from backslaps. They were big men, most of them, bigger than Ross, many of them bearded. Ross attempted introductions. Joe smiled and nodded. The men were polite but not interested in him. They disappeared into the living-room, taking Ross with them. Mitch followed.

'Get yourself a beer,' Cecile said. She had a thick Afrikaans

181

accent like the youth in the drugstore in Louis Trichardt.

The place filled steadily, headlights searing the intense darkness of the bush as more cars arrived. The living-room was a large rectangle with a wooden roof and windows on to the stoep. Above the stone fireplace was a black and white photograph of P. W. Botha shaking hands with a pudgy-featured man. Cecile's father, Joe guessed. There were some books in Afrikaans. Glass ornaments. Joe sipped at his beer and sat in a leather armchair in a corner of the room, watching.

It was the women he looked at, as he did so often in crowds in unfamiliar circumstances. They were younger than the men, fussily dressed, showing sun-browned shoulders. They chatted together and drank drinks from small glasses at the edges of the room. One of the girls in particular caught his eye. She was young, twenty-two at the most, wearing tight candy-striped slacks and a pink tank top. Curled blonde hair fell to her shoulders. She was very pretty in a regular-featured way, like a woman in an American TV series. She was talking to a girl in a black dress, but Joe noticed that she was continually glancing at a tall dark-bearded man who was deep in conversation with Mitch, Ross and the other men in the centre of the room. She was being ignored, and didn't like it. Once, just once, the girl's glance strayed Joe's way and their eyes held for an instant before she turned back to her companion. Joe finished his beer and went to get another.

When he returned, Mitch's gigantic arm encircled his shoulders and pulled him to one side. He was sweating heavily, laughing. He'd already drunk a lot of beer. He said, 'You know what your friend Ross just asked Derry?'

'Which one's Derry?'

'The guy in the middle there. The one with the blue shirt.' Mitch indicated a thick-set man with a pockmarked face. 'You know what he asked him?'

'No,' said Joe. 'I don't.'

'He asked him if, when he went to bed with Cecile, she took her false leg off or left it on.' Mitch was shaking with laughter. There were tears in his eyes.

'And what did Derry say?' Joe asked, appalled.

'He said,' and Mitch paused as fresh laughter overwhelmed

him, 'he said, it depends on how he's feeling. Ek sê, man, that's so funny. It depends on how he's feeling. That's so funny.'

Joe looked across at the girl again. She was no longer angry, he saw, just bored. She was looking into a small mirror, poking at the corner of one of her eyes. For a moment he considered approaching her, starting a conversation. Maybe he could try out the Kruger Park story, refine the details a little. But he was a bad liar he knew, and he'd had too much beer. Best to keep quiet. All the same, she had a good body. Tight, firm-breasted, the curve of her legs accentuated by the stripes of her slacks. How long was it, he thought, since he'd sat at a party looking at a girl, wondering if he could pull her? Ten years? Fifteen? He felt a sudden sense of freedom, like he'd felt when he'd first arrived in London and taken that little room in the rabbi's house in Golder's Green.

There'd been parties then, endless parties in squalid rented flats in places like Canonbury and Tooting. There always seemed to be a Stones record on the player. 'I Can't Get No Satisfaction.' Occasionally he'd scored, creeping back into the darkened house in Hodford Road at two, three in the morning, clutching the limp, cool hand of some copy-typist or costing clerk, wondering if she'd notice he hadn't changed the sheets in weeks.

After that, of course, things had been different. There were the girls at St. Martin's who'd sat cross-legged in black jeans and talked of John Piper and David Hockney. And last of all there'd been Ellie. Then he hadn't wanted to pull girls any more. Not ever, not once. Not even when the opportunity presented itself like it had done in Paris, and again more recently in – where was it, Bradford? Bolton? Christ, he needed Ellie. He needed her. Needed her . . .

'Anti-social bastard, aren't you?' It was Ross on his way to the bathroom.

'I'm sorry.'

Ross belched loudly. 'Ach, forget it,' he said. 'Boring cunts the lot of them. Boring cunts.' He lurched through the doorway.

Somebody produced a rugby ball. It was Derry. It curved in a slow arc into the centre of the room, hitting the lampshade, swinging violent shadows onto the walls. The men rose to meet it, clutching at it, spilling beer, crashing into an untidy scrum on the floor, bellowing like bulls. A chair overturned, and a small table. Glass trinkets tinkled and flew.

For a moment the scrum heaved and groaned, and then Ross had the ball. Red-faced, his lithe body twisting, he slipped Mitch's grasp, wrenched open the windows and was out, across the stoep, onto the clipped grass beyond. The roaring men followed, sweating, laughing, colliding with doorposts, flattening shrubs, swallowed by the darkness.

Derry rushed in. 'I'll get the truck!' he was shouting. 'I'll get the fucking truck.' Cecile was screaming at him in Afrikaans, grabbing at his arm. He ignored her and was gone. There was a roar from the rear of the house, a grinding of gears, a crash of metal upon metal. Headlights slashed at the night sky. Cecile was still screaming, hoarsely now, tears in her eyes.

There was a second crash. Joe took his beer and went out onto the stoep. As he watched, a white pickup exploded through a frail trellis at the side of the house and squealed onto the lawn, trailing bougainvillaea. Its lights caught Ross still with the ball, dodging, laughing. Then somebody brought him down from behind and the others were on him, piling on, body on body.

'Derry!' Cecile was screaming in English now. 'Derry, stop it! For God's sake, stop it!' She hobbled out, blinded by the lights. A flying foot caught her, then a body. She fell awkwardly, her artificial leg twisted beneath her.

For a moment Joe thought she was going to be trampled, but Derry had seen her and was out of the truck, running towards her. He picked her up bodily and dumped her, still screaming, onto the stoep. 'Quit screaming,' Joe heard him say. 'Just quit screaming.' Then he was gone, back into the scrum, flinging himself horizontally like a diver entering the water, back into the heaving mass of bodies. Girls clustered round Cecile, comforting her, dabbing at her face with tissues. Joe sipped at his beer and then, suddenly nauseous, spat the mouthful onto the grass over the rail of the stoep. He felt lonely, acutely unhappy, a long way from home.

'They're animals,' the girl said. 'Animals.'

With the noise from the garden and Cecile's wails he hadn't

heard her approach. She had a gentle perfume which he recognised from Janey in the Studio: Miss Dior. Her fingernails, he noted, were painted pale pink to match the pink of the top she wore. 'Are they always like this?' he asked.

'When they're drinking. They're always drinking. You should know, they're friends of yours.'

'I've never seen them before, except Ross and Mitch. I came with them.'

'Who's Ross?'

'The thin guy. See him? With the bush shirt.'

The girl stared at the men, not interested. 'You're different. You're quiet. You're an American.'

'The Quiet American.'

'So what are you doing here?'

'Visiting the Kruger Park.'

'A tourist?'

'A tourist.'

Joe felt the girl's eyes on him, examining him, appraising him. 'You don't look like a tourist.'

'What do tourists look like?'

She laughed. 'Fat and old.'

'And I'm neither?'

'You're quite old,' she said. 'But not fat. I don't like fat men. Like your friend, Mitch. He makes my flesh creep. Ugh!' She shuddered.

The tall man, the one with the beard, the one she'd been looking at earlier, suddenly broke away from the scrum, his shirt torn, and ran close to the rails of the stoep. Whooping, the other men crashed after him.

'Bastard,' the girl said.

'Your boyfriend?'

She laughed bitterly. 'Some boyfriend.'

'What his name?'

'Piet. Piet Schoeman.'

'He's South African?'

'His father was – he's a Rhodesian. They're just scum, those Rhodesians. Animals. You want to walk?'

'Where?'

'Anywhere.'

Joe shrugged. 'OK,' he said.

'Just to get away from these pigs,' the girl said.

They didn't walk far. The night was too dark and they missed the track several times, colliding with fence posts, tripping on a cattle grid. The girl took his arm to steady herself. A car passed on the road below. At the house the shouting continued.

She told Joe her name was Kim and she worked for Foskar, one of the mining companies in Phalaborwa, in the Accounts Office. She was born in Ladysmith, she said, and her parents were English. She asked him what he thought about South Africa. Joe said he liked it. Which aspects in particular? Everything, Joe said, all of it. Most people, she said, most people who criticise us, if they came here and saw for themselves, they'd understand.

Joe told her he understood. He was conscious of the pressure of her hand on his arm, the touch of her skin. When they turned a bend in the track and the lights of the house were lost behind the trees he stopped and kissed her. She responded instantly, twining her legs around his, pressing her pelvis, her lips stopping his breath, tongue flicking. When they broke she said, 'I don't like it here. It's too dark.'

She took him to a guest hut, a small asbestos-walled building set apart from the main house in some trees. She felt above the door and found a key. There were twin beds and a shower. The place smelt of polish and stale air. She took her clothes off and lay on the bed. In the pale light from the window the dark triangle of hair between her legs was prominent.

Joe said, 'I should close the curtains.'

'Don't bother. Nobody comes here.'

'We did.'

'So?' There was a note almost of little girl petulance in her voice which repelled him. He felt his desire ebbing away.

'Well?' said the girl, after a while.

'Well what?'

'Is there something wrong with you?'

'No,' said Joe. 'No, there's nothing wrong.' He jerked at the buckle of his belt.

It was too quick. The girl climaxed immediately, writhing,

186

shouting, her nails rasping at the flesh on his back. Then she lay still. 'That was good,' she said. 'Was it good?'

'Yes,' said Joe, lying. He groaned and rolled off her.

'I like you. You're quiet. I like quiet men.'

'So you said.' He was thinking of Ellie now, thinking of the long, slow lovemaking she'd introduced him to when they'd first met. 'Oh, Christ,' he said.

'What's the matter?'

'Nothing. Nothing at all.' Everything.

She turned onto her side and looked at him. 'Those marks,' she said, indicating the wounds on his thigh and shoulder.

'Scars.'

'Bullet wounds. Piet's got bullet wounds. I recognise them. You were in the war?'

'Which war?' Joe's voice was terse. Her questioning was irritating him.

'The Rhodesian War.'

'No.'

'Piet was in the war. He was a Selous Scout.'

'I know.'

'These guys were all in the Selous Scouts. I hate them, the lot of them.'

'Then why do you go around with them?'

The girl fell silent. When she spoke again, her voice was bright. 'I'm going to take a shower. You want to join me?'

Joe shook his head. He wanted her gone. He was surprised at feeling no guilt, no disgust even, just growing irritation. She was looking at him keenly. 'You're funny,' she said. 'Maybe you're too quiet.'

'I'm tired, that's all.'

She got off the bed. 'You're sure you won't take a shower?' She was delaying things, Joe realised. Perhaps wanting to preserve the feeling of intimacy he did not share. She glanced down. 'Look at your things,' she said. 'All over the floor. You're an untidy boy, hey?' She laughed nervously, picked up his clothes and began to fold. 'I don't know what your mother would say.'

Joe turned to the wall. 'Just take your shower,' he said.

'Who's this?'

He swung back. The girl was holding the photographs of

187

Ellie and the children, flicking through them like they were dirty postcards. 'Where did you get those?'

'They'd fallen out of your pocket.'

'Give them to me!' He was shouting now.

The girl suddenly grinned. 'You'll have to catch me!'

Joe lunged at her and missed. She danced away, still laughing. 'Too slow!' She was taunting him.

He stopped, became conscious of his own heavy breathing, the trickle of sweat on his back. He said, very quietly, 'If you damage those pictures I'll kill you.'

'OK. OK.' There was uncertainty in the girl's voice. She handed him the photographs. 'I wasn't going to do anything with them, honestly.'

Joe stuffed the photographs into his slacks, his hands shaking. He had to get dressed, get out of there. The girl said, 'That's your wife and kids, isn't it?'

'Mind your own fucking business!'

'I'm right. I know I'm right. I recognised your name, Joe Lejeune. You're the one whose family got kidnapped. It was in the papers.'

'Well, you're bloody wrong!' Bitch! Fucking nosy prying bitch! He clawed at his shirt, wrenching his arms into it. A seam ripped.

The girl said, 'I know where they are.'

It was like he'd been hit hard somewhere in the guts. He stared at the girl, shaking his head, trying to clear it. When he spoke it was like his voice was somebody else's voice. Dislocated. Distant. 'What did you say?'

'I said I know where they are. They're in Mozambique.'

It was some kind of joke. It had to be. 'Mozambique?'

'I heard Piet talk about it with the other guys. He forgets I'm there sometimes.'

'What did you hear!' Joe was across the room, clutching at the girl's naked shoulders, shaking her. She squealed with pain. 'You're hurting me!'

He released her, his breath coming in short gasps. 'I'm sorry. Just tell me. Just tell me what you've heard.'

The girl backed off, fear in her face. 'They're in Mozambique, that's all I heard. They don't know what to do with them.'

'Who don't?'

'Piet and his mates. That's all I heard him say. He said, "I don't know what the fuck we're going to do about that bloody English woman and her kids."'

'You're sure he was talking about Ellie?'

'Ellie?'

'My wife.'

'I don't know. He didn't say her name.'

'Where in Mozambique? Did he say where?'

'No.'

Joe spun back, grabbing for his slacks. The girl became frantic, her face creased with terror. 'I shouldn't have told you this. I'm not supposed to know! Don't tell Piet. He'll kill me. Don't Joe, please!'

But he was free, and out, and running towards the house.

The men were in the living room, locked together, arm over shoulder, heads down, sweat-soaked, empty beer cans rolling and crushed by their stamping feet. They were singing:

> 'We're all Rhodesians
> And we'll fight through thick and thin,
> We'll keep our land a free land
> Stop the enemy coming in . . .'

Joe grabbed at Ross, shouting his name. The thin man half turned. 'Piss off,' he said.

'I've got to talk.'

'I said piss off!' Ross's head was down again, and he was singing.

> 'We'll keep them north of the Zambezi
> Till the river's running dry.
> And this mighty land shall prosper,
> For Rhodesians never die.'

Mitch spotted Joe. He lurched towards him. He was very drunk. There were tears in his eyes. 'They never die, man,' he was saying. 'Never. If you tell me they die, I tell you you're a fucking liar . . .'

'I want to speak to Ross.'

'What you want to speak to him for? What's so fucking important you wanna . . .'

'Where's Kim?'

Piet Schoeman had broken from the dancers and was scanning the room, heaving, sweating. 'Where's Kim? Cecile, you seen Kim?'

Cecile, who was sitting in one of the armchairs, pointed at Joe. 'Ask him,' she said. 'She went outside with him.'

Joe tried to say something, explain, but Schoeman was already moving towards him. He backed off, looked around for the door. The men had stopped singing now, and were staring at him. 'What have you done with her, hey?'

Somebody was trying to restrain the big bearded man, but he pushed the arm aside. 'Hey? I'm talking to you, man!'

'We went for a walk, that's . . .'

Joe didn't see the blow coming. It hit him beneath the ribcage, sent him sprawling back against the furniture, doubled up, fighting for breath. A second blow smacked against his teeth. Blood spurted. He was dimly aware of shouts, girls' screams . . .

There were men on Schoeman now, pulling him back, and Ross's voice: 'Get up, for fuck's sake!' Joe was being jerked to his feet, pulled towards the door. 'Give us your keys, Mitch,' Ross was shouting.

The yard. The car. Joe crouching beside Ross. Mitch face down on the back seat. 'Ek sê, man,' he was saying. 'I don't feel too good.'

'Shut it!'

Ross hammered the engine into life and they were away down the track, the suspension lurching like a boat at sea. Joe was dabbing at his mouth, swallowing blood. 'Mozambique,' he said.

'What the fuck are you talking about?'

'Ellie and the kids, that girl told me. They're in Mozambique.'

'Don't talk shit. He'd have killed you, you stupid bastard! What did you want to go and mess with his girl for?'

'I said they're in Mozambique.'

'Will you shut up about Mozambique.'

Ross was out, opening the gate, then they were onto the dirt road heading north. 'That's the lot, man,' he said bitterly. 'I've had it up to here with you. I think you're crazy. I think you've got a screw loose. Jesus Christ!'

The moon had risen, pale gold, silhouetting the fringes of the bush. Away to the right a helicopter moved slowly, searchlight trained downwards. When they reached the tar Ross put his foot down. There was a retching noise from the back and the stink of vomit. Ross wound his window down full. 'Thank Christ it's not my car,' he said, turning to face Joe. 'How's your face?'

'OK.'

It had been a sliding blow. Enough to cut, not hard enough to hurt badly. The bleeding had already stopped. 'Why won't you believe me? That girl was telling the truth.'

Ross snorted. 'From what I've heard she doesn't know what the word means. What did you do with her? You screw her?'

'I don't think that concerns you.'

Ross thumped his arm against the seat. 'Well, you're fucking wrong! It *does* concern me. Those guys are my mates. I've known Piet for seven years. Longer! And you go and screw his girl.'

'Well, next time you see your mate, you ask him where Ellie is – because he knows.'

There was a single loud belch from the back of the car. Snores. 'Did you hear what I said?'

'I heard,' Ross snapped.

Joe sucked at his split lip. It was like some sort of farce. No, not a farce, a nightmare. She hadn't lied. There'd been too much terror for that. 'They don't know what to do with them.'

'Who don't?'

'Piet and his mates. For God's sake, Ross, just listen to what I'm saying! You've got to go and see that guy and get the truth out of him.'

Ross reached forward and took a tape from the shelf. He slotted it into the player.

'Picture yourself in a boat on a river,' sang John Lennon.

'Ross!'

'You understand this,' said Ross, so quietly that Joe had to strain to hear, 'my mates don't kidnap white women. And if you don't shut up about it, I'm going to stop this fucking car and finish what Piet started.'

The storm which had been threatening all evening broke

191

about two-thirty. They'd felt the first heavy drops as they'd walked back to the hotel in silence after dropping Mitch at one of the sprawling white bungalows at the edge of the town. Now the rain was lashing the windows of their room with the ferocity of a fire hose, thunder cracking directly overhead.

Joe looked across at Ross, at the hunched shape of his back beneath the bedclothes. It was impossible to tell whether he slept. For a while he contemplated shaking him into consciousness, trying to pummel the truth into him, but he decided against it. Maybe in the morning he'd listen. There'd been too much beer. Too many old friends . . .

Proof, that was what he needed. The girl could get proof. There'd be some document somewhere. There had to be. Even a scrawled message on a phone pad would do. Where did she say she worked? The accounts office. He'd call her in the morning, meet her during her lunch break. She'd said it herself. She hated Schoeman and the Selous Scouts. Hated them. She'd co-operate. He'd be nice to her. Take her flowers, maybe, or perfume. Miss Dior. He was certain he was right about the perfume. He'd sleep with her again if he had to. She'd have an apartment somewhere in town. A good dinner. A few bottles. She'd do it, he was certain.

And then, when he had the proof? Christ! It was going to take so long, so bloody long . . .

He got out of bed and went to the window. The water of the swimming pool outside was just visible, steel-black, its surface jumping with the rain. At least one thing was clear. If the girl had been telling the truth, Ellie was alive. And the kids. Both of them. She'd used the plural, he was convinced of it. And Schoeman knew where they were . . .

Schoeman! Sod the girl. Sod the proof. He'd go for Schoeman. Get a gun. Force the truth out of the bastard. Shoot it out of him . . .

The shrill of the phone was like a physical assault. Joe spun towards it, but Ross already had the receiver in his hand. He'd been awake all the time, Joe realised, maybe even waiting for the call.

The conversation was brief. Ross spoke in monosyllables, grunting once or twice. He hung up quickly. 'OK, let's go,' he said.

'Go?'

'Home.' He was already across the room, pulling on his clothes.

'Zimbabwe?'

'Where the fuck else do you think I mean?'

Joe shook his head. He felt he was on some out-of-control roller coaster ride. 'It's the middle of the night, for Christ's sake.'

'Just get dressed!'

'You must be joking.'

Ross paused. When he spoke Joe could sense the fear in his voice, and the anger. He said, 'That was Derry. I don't know what you said to that girl, or what she said to you, but the shit's starting to fly. Piet Schoeman half-killed the cow then he went off to Military Intelligence Headquarters. If we're lucky we'll get across that border before they realise we've gone, but don't count on it.'

Not now. They couldn't just quit and run now! Joe felt himself beginning to shake. 'I'm not going until I've talked to Schoeman.'

Ross was bundling his clothes into his pack. There was something close to panic in the way he fumbled with the straps. 'OK, you stay. You stay as long as you want to. But I tell you this, man, it's not Schoeman you're going to be talking to.' He went to the door.

'Ross!'

He stopped. 'Yes?'

'Do you believe me now? Do you believe they're in Mozambique?'

Ross drew a deep breath. There was sadness in his eyes. 'I don't know what I believe, man. All I know is, serving twenty years for espionage in Pretoria Central Prison isn't going to do much to get your wife and kids back.'

They were clear of the room in three minutes. In reception Joe slapped two fifty rand notes into the hand of the bemused night porter. By the time they reached the Land-Rover the storm had plastered their hair flat to their heads. Then they were out, through the town, driving hard towards Gravelotte, sluicing the vast dark puddles that lay across the road.

They said little to each other as they drove. They'd make

the border by seven with luck, too early, maybe, for contact to have been made. Maybe. They were short on fuel. Near Duiwelskloof they had to stop and pour petrol from the jerrycans into the main tank. Ross thought there might be somewhere open on the N1 near Louis Trichardt. The rain eased a little. In the east one or two stars could be seen.

There was a police post at Soekmakaar, Joe remembered, and he tensed as the approached it. The floodlights were on in the compound, the rain-soaked Nissan trucks glittering. But there was no movement and they were past, curving down across the railway line through the dead, dark houses.

They hit the N1 as dawn broke, misty, barred with pink. The rain had stopped. They met a couple of empty African buses. At the police post close to the junction a black police-man in uniform was unlocking the gates in the security fence. His eyes followed them. They overtook a long truck hauling timber, and a battered yellow Toyota pickup. Black women, heads bent, wrapped in blankets, trudged in the direction of Louis Trichardt.

At the first turnoff they found a Mobil station and filled up with fuel. Joe checked his watch. Six a.m. He took over the wheel. Back on the road he pushed the speedometer up to 120 k.p.h. until Ross told him to slow down. There was no point in getting picked up for speeding. Ross seemed more relaxed now they had turned north.

Joe didn't see the police car until they were past it. It was concealed in the entrance to a track just past the sign to the Clouds End Motel. He'd already slowed, changing down to tackle the long climb up to the summit of the Soutspansberg, when he heard the siren, saw the blue light flashing.

'What do we do now?' he asked.

'Stop,' said Ross quietly. 'We don't have any alternative.'

As they pulled in, Ross said, 'Kruger Park. We've been to the Kruger Park.'

'The Kruger Park.'

His hands, Joe noticed, were shaking.

'Out!'

There were two policemen, white men in khaki uniforms. They had their hands close to their guns. It was the smaller of the two who did the talking. He had a thin face and a small scar above his mouth. A hare lip, Joe thought, or possibly a fight. The policeman repeated his command. Joe and Ross climbed slowly down onto the road.

'Hands out, legs apart.'

They spread themselves against the side of the Land-Rover while the bigger man searched them. It reminded Joe of American cop films he'd seen. For some reason he felt no fear. The man seemed disappointed at finding no concealed guns or knives. He handed their wallets and passports to his partner who began to examine them.

'Open the back.'

Joe took the keys from the ignition and went to the rear door. The bigger man followed him. He was blond-haired with a stupid face. A shaft of sunlight suddenly tipped above the rim of the Veld and the wet road shone.

Joe undid the backpacks, scattering the contents on to the floor of the Land-Rover. The policeman rummaged through them. 'That's all, is it? All you're carrying?' He picked up the Phalaborwa booklet, flicked through it and tossed it down.

'Yes.'

'It better be.'

Joe shut the door. The smaller man was asking Ross about the guns, holding the permits in his hand.

'We left them in Zimbabwe.'

'We'll find them, you know. We'll take this bloody thing apart.'

'Well, you're going to have to, because they're not here.'

'Don't be cheeky to me, man.'

'Listen,' said Joe, 'I don't know what this is all about. Will you tell me what this all about?'

The bigger man said, 'I thought I told you to bloody shut up.'

'In point of fact you didn't.'

'Well, I'm telling you now!'

For an instant Joe thought the policeman was going to hit him.

A small green truck passed slowly, chugging up the hill, belching smoke. The Africans in the back looked on with sullen, scared faces. The small man coughed as the black cloud from the exhaust hit him. 'Stinking kaffir truck,' he said.

There was a brief pause while the bigger policeman walked round the Land-Rover, examining it from every angle. The smaller man said something to him in Afrikaans. He shrugged, lay down on his back and examined the underneath of the vehicle. 'What's this?' Joe heard him say.

Ross bent to look. 'It's to protect the tank.'

'What you got in there? Dagga?'

'No,' said Ross wearily. 'There's nothing in there.'

'It'll have to come off.'

'That's your privilege.'

The policeman stood up. His back, Joe saw, was stained with wet and dirt from the road. 'Are you being funny?' he hissed.

'I welded it myself, that's all. I know how difficult it'll be to get off.'

'We'll get it off, don't you worry.'

'As I said, that's your privilege.'

The two policemen looked at each other. They seemed suddenly less sure of themselves. The small man went to the car and talked for a long time on the radio. Then he returned. 'OK,' he said. 'Let's go.'

'Where?' Joe asked.

'You'll find out where.'

The blond policeman rode with them in the Land-Rover, squashed between Ross and the door. He adjusted his gun, loosening the butt. The smaller man led the way in the police car, blue light flashing as if to emphasise the importance of the procession. To Joe's surprise they continued to head north. Messina? There'd be a Military Intelligence post there. Or maybe they'd turn off somewhere, an unmarked sideroad where the signs read 'Privaat'. And then what? Black men gathered at the roadsides watched them pass impassively.

It became increasingly difficult to concentrate on the driving. There was something unreal about the morning. It was like some kind of strange dream in which he was not personally involved, present only as an unseen observer. It was the effect of shock, he thought, or fatigue from driving for hours through the rain.

He began to think about what he'd say when they came to question him. They wouldn't believe the Kruger Park story, of course. There'd been no time to even visit the place. He'd try it, because Ross had asked him to try it. After that, he'd tell the truth. He could maybe reach an agreement with them. Sign some kind of statement absolving the South African government from blame in exchange for getting Ellie and the children back. After all, if the girl was to be believed it would be solving a problem for them . . .

But then, what if they didn't believe the truth when he told it, or if they didn't want to believe it? What if they kept on questioning him? He suddenly remembered a play he'd seen on TV about some detained political prisoner in South Africa. There was a big fat security policeman involved. Very unpleasant. What was his name, Swannepoel? It was too long ago to recall it clearly. This was the world of Steve Biko, Neil Agate, Nelson Mandela. He remembered reading about Biko's death; how he'd been chained to a grating, his head slammed repeatedly against a wall. He wondered how he'd face up to the violence if it came. He'd read too many of Ellie's Amnesty reports, that was the problem. They always seemed to be lying around in the kitchen and lavatory, with their carefully paragraphed, dispassionately described lists of the techniques they used in Chile, Russia, Argentina, South Africa, when people wouldn't talk. The wet sack over the head, the electrodes placed on toes, lips or genitals . . . Joe said, 'I want to see the British Consul.'

'The British Consul, hey?' The blond policeman smiled, shook his head slowly like it was a good joke he'd been told.

'What's so funny about that? I have a right . . .'

This time the policeman laughed out loud. 'You think you got rights, man?'

Joe caught Ross's eye. He could read nothing from the expression on the thin man's face.

There was going to be no interrogation. Joe only came to believe this fact when the hard-faced woman stamped his passport. 'We don't forget faces, you remember that,' she said. They'd swept through Messina, past the police compound, without reducing speed and reached the Beit-bridge border post just before seven-thirty. There'd been a delay while the woman checked and rechecked their depar-

197

ture forms, and while the small policeman had gone into an adjoining office, presumably to make a phone call. Then they were through.

Joe said, 'We can go?' He was trying hard to keep from showing the astonishment he felt.

'You can go.'

Ross took the wheel of the Land-Rover, seeming neither surprised nor pleased. The blond policeman kept his hand on his gun. As they turned the corner towards the bridge, Joe glanced back. The two policemen were standing, hands on hips, watching.

Part Five

The Lowveld

The food was swimming with grease, lukewarm, smelling faintly of decay. Joe prodded the sausage then put down his fork. They were at the Beitbridge Hotel, on the Zimbabwe side of the border. It was eight-thirty and, despite the shade under the bougainvillaea, hot.

'Just tell me,' he said.

Ross dipped a crust of bread into his egg. 'The ways of the white man are mysterious.'

Joe felt a sudden surge of anger. 'Not that bloody mysterious.'

Ross shrugged. He seemed depressed, defeated almost. He abandoned the egg-soaked bread and took a sip of his tea. 'I guess they just wanted us out.'

'The police?'

There was a suspicion of a smile at the corner of Ross's mouth. 'Military Intelligence – they're the guys who run South Africa these days, not the police, not parliament. What the military says goes.'

'But I still don't understand why they didn't question us.'

'Maybe they didn't have any questions to ask.'

'Do you believe that?'

Ross fell silent.

'Well?'

'I told you, I don't know what I believe.' Ross twisted his head, avoiding eye contact. 'You want more tea?'

'No.'

'Well, I do. Waiter! More tea!'

Joe said, 'Maybe they were scared of publicity.'

'What publicity?'

'If they arrested us, there'd be publicity. Maybe what they're doing would come out.'

'Maybe.' There was no interest in Ross's voice.

The waiter, a fat black man with a distinctive and unpleasant body odour came to take away the teapot. When he had gone, Joe said, 'As far as I'm concerned, it just proves that what that girl told me must be true.'

'And maybe you just screwed the wrong girl.'

'For God's sake!' Joe gripped at the edge of the table. It felt as if a tight band had been wound round his head, crushing his brain. A white family with two children a couple of tables away stopped eating to stare at him. He ignored them. 'I just want to know what you're going to do about it.'

'About what?'

'About getting Ellie back.'

This time Ross's eyes met and held his. 'Why should I do anything about it?'

'That's why you came down here, isn't it? To help me.'

Ross laughed but there was no mirth in it. 'Help you? Jesus!'

The waiter returned with the teapot and the bill on a saucer. He said, 'You finish soon, sir?'

'Soon,' said Ross.

The waiter didn't move.

'I said we'll finish soon!'

Muttering to himself, the man went away. Ross said, 'Maybe the Boers have got it right. Maybe there is something to be said for keeping the kaffirs in their place.' He began to pour the tea.

Joe closed his eyes against the glare of sunlight reflected from the surface of the nearby pool. His head was hurting now, the pulse of blood in his brain battering at his temples. 'I'm going back,' he said.

The pouring ceased. 'Back?'

'I'm going to get across that border somehow and find Schoeman. I'll get the truth out of him. If you're not going to help me, I'm going alone.'

'Across three miles of minefield and electrified fencing?'

'I'll get in through Swaziland.'

'Then I wish you luck.' Ross added milk to his half-filled cup, drained it and stood up. He put six dollars into the saucer. 'I'm going to call Harry, tell him to expect us.'

'I told you, I'm going back in.' The white family, Joe was now aware, were listening intently to their conversation. He didn't care.

'OK,' Ross said. 'You go back in. I'll call Harry.' He disappeared into the hotel.

'Bastard!'

Joe got up from the table. For a moment he considered following Ross, but gave up. It was pointless. His anger left him to be replaced by a growing feeling of self-disgust. If he'd had the guts to stay, maybe he'd have got to Schoeman somehow. But now? And Swaziland? Why the hell should it be easier to get back in through Swaziland?

He wandered out, blinking in the intense sunlight. In the pool a white butterfly was struggling with waterlogged wings amid the floating brown leaves. Without consciously intending to he knelt down and scooped it from the water with his hands, placing it on the sun-warmed tile surround. 'Bastard.' He said the word again, but more softly. It was over. He'd relied on Ross too much, and now it was over. He'd go back to Harare, to the High Commission, try to convince them of the truth of what the girl had said. They could bring pressure to bear . . .

And if they failed to believe him?

A black ant, he noticed, had found the stranded butterfly and was biting into its soft abdomen. Other ants were emerging from cracks in the tiles, scurrying towards it. He turned and walked quickly out to where they'd parked the Land-Rover. Ross could crawl to Chungwe for all he cared. It was over.

He wrenched at the door. It was locked. Ross had taken the keys.

The lobby was deserted, the public phone-booth empty. Puzzled, Joe pressed the bell on the desk.

Nobody came.

He hit the bell again harder. This time there was movement. A black man in a maroon jacket emerged. 'Yes, sah?'

201

'My friend. He came in here to telephone.'

'He is in Room 12, sah. On the first floor. He says his phone call is private.'

Joe took the stairs two at a time. What the hell could be so private about a phone call to Harry?

Through a large mahogany door to the right of the stairwell, Ross's voice just audible but incomprehensible. He seemed to be complaining about something. Joe hammered against the door with his fist. The conversation continued for a moment longer, then there was a click as the receiver was replaced. 'Yes?'

'I want the keys.'

The door opened slowly. Ross looked pale and unhappy. Joe repeated his demand. 'I want the keys to the Land-Rover.'

Ross stared at him for a moment, as if not comprehending. Then he said, 'They were seen.'

Joe lowered his outstretched hand. 'Seen?' He felt the hairs on the back of his neck prickle.

'Harry just told me. Apparently some Afs Jack Hammond was talking to yesterday saw a white woman and two kids being taken across the border back in August.'

'Ellie?'

'Who else?'

Joe clutched at the doorpost. 'Which border?'

'Mozambique.'

They were to go to Chungwe, Harry had said, and pick up the bush gear, then go down to the Flying Star. 'Why the bush gear?' Joe demanded as he spun the rear wheels of the Land-Rover on the loose dirt outside the hotel.

Ross shrugged. 'Maybe Jack fancies a camping trip.'

'Don't be stupid.'

Ross shrugged again and closed his eyes. For an instant Joe considered asking him about the other phone call, the one to Harare which the desk clerk had mentioned when he came to pay, but the elation took over. 'Mozambique!' he was shouting, over the noise of the engine. 'Now will you fucking believe me!'

They made Chungwe soon after one and found the fields

deserted, the house shuttered against the heat. Harry, who had been sleeping, was able to tell them little more than they already knew. He'd been in Chiredzi at a farmer's meeting when Jack had called the night before, and had only got the message second-hand. Danny helped them load the bush gear. By three-thirty they were at the Flying Star.

A houseboy in a fawn jacket led them into the living-room. Jack was drinking tea with a frail-looking elderly woman in a yellow sundress. He stood up when they entered, seeming surprised to see them. 'I thought you were down South,' he said.

'We were.' Ross spoke stiffly.

'Harry told you the news?'

'Yes.'

'You better come through.'

The old woman asked if they wanted tea. 'Later, Ma,' Jack said. 'We've got things to discuss.'

They followed him through the dining-room to what appeared to be a study. There were more books on Africa, kudu and sable heads. On one wall there were a series of 1:50,000 maps of the Lowveld joined together to form a massive spread. The chairs were leather-covered and voluminous. He motioned them to sit down. 'I don't know how much Harry told you,' he said.

'Only that they were seen crossing into Mozambique back in August.' Joe was trying hard to keep his excitement in check. 'You're sure there's no mistake?'

'As sure as I can be.'

'And they were OK, were they? Not hurt or ill or anything?'

'Apparently not.'

'Thank God for that.' Joe leaned back in his chair. Relief washed over him, comforting, like a warm bath. 'So who saw them?' he said.

'A kraalhead down in the Confluence.'

'The Confluence?'

Jack stood up and went to the map. He pointed to a narrow spur of land running down between the Sabi River and the Mozambique border which Joe, when he'd looked at maps of the area in the past, hadn't noticed. 'It's Chief Chingela's territory,' Jack said, sitting down again. 'I've known him for twenty-five years. I got a message from him asking me to go down there and deal with an elephant which has been terrorising the women when they go to fetch water from the river. When I got there there was a big meeting going on at his kraal. Apparently there'd been a raid.'

'A raid?'

'He said a band of about ten armed men came across from Mozambique the night before and attacked an isolated kraal at a place called Chimbi which is right on the border about ten miles north of Chingela's village. They'd beaten up the kraalhead, raped his youngest daughter and stolen fifteen dollars which is all the money he had. The kraalhead, also called Chimbi, was there when I arrived. He had a badly cut face and what looked like a broken arm. Apparently these raids have been going on for some time.'

'And there was one back in August?'

Jack nodded. 'Chingela said he hadn't heard about a kidnapping, but a white woman with two children had been seen crossing the border with a group of armed men about that time.'

'So why in God's name didn't he tell somebody about it?'

'Nobody asked him.'

'Nobody asked him?' There was astonishment in Joe's voice. 'But surely the Army . . .'

Jack laughed. 'They were obsessed with its having been a ZIPRA attack. When they'd finished at the kidnap site they spent their time working westwards through Matibi. I don't think any of them ever went near the Confluence, and even if they had done it's doubtful whether Chingela would have told them anything. They're very isolated down there, and suspicious of authority. The only reason Chingela told me is because he's known me for so long and trusts me.'

'And he's absolutely sure Ellie and the children were OK, is he?'

'Well, I don't suppose whoever saw them got too close.' Jack paused, and looked keenly at Joe. 'You realise, of course, that this is six months ago we're talking about?'

'They're still alive.'

'You seem very confident of that fact.'

Joe glanced at Ross. His expression was carefully neutral. 'I am,' he said. 'Do you have any idea who these bandits were?'

'Apparently the officers spoke Ndau, which is a Shona dialect, and the men, most of whom were young boys, spoke Shangaan.'

'MNR.' It was Ross who spoke, the first time he'd opened his mouth since they'd sat down.

Jack nodded. 'That's the conclusion I came to.'

Joe swung to face Ross. 'You're talking about those bandits Jamie McAllister mentioned that day up at the Planters? The ones being trained in the Transvaal?'

'The Mozambique National Resistance.'

'And are they being trained there?'

'As far as I know.'

'By Piet Schoeman?'

'Very possibly.'

'Very possibly!' Joe repeated the words with bitterness. 'You mean yes.'

'I mean very possibly.' Ross spoke quietly. He looked towards the door as if contemplating escape.

Jack interrupted. 'Listen, we can discuss all this later. Let me finish what I've got to say because it's important. This man Chimbi was obviously in pain so I said I'd take him up to the hospital at St. Peter's Mission, but he didn't want to go. He was worried about the men who'd attacked him coming back, and didn't want to leave his place unprotected. Apparently they're still here.'

'In Zimbabwe?'

Jack nodded again. 'They headed west, crossed the Sabi near the Chivirira Falls and disappeared into the Gona-re-Zhou. But Chimbi also said something else. He said that one of the bandits who'd attacked him had been in the group which had crossed the border with the white woman and children back in August.'

Joe stared at Jack. He could feel himself beginning to shake. 'You're sure of that?'

'Apparently the bandit bragged about it.'

Joe became conscious of his own breathing, the ticking of a clock somewhere in the distance. Ross, he noticed, had picked up a ceremonial axe from a stand near his chair and was balancing it on his outstretched palm. 'We've got to find this bastard,' Joe said.

Jack laughed softly. 'I thought you'd say that.'

'What did he look like, this guy?'

'Young. Chimbi said he had a tee-shirt with the word FANTA written on it.'

'And he didn't say anything about where they were being held?'

'No.'

Joe stood up, feeling suddenly close to panic. He went to the map. 'Where's the Chivirira Falls?'

'Hang on a minute,' Jack said. 'There's more.' He motioned Joe to sit down again.

'More?'

Jack nodded. 'My first thought was to get hold of you two and tell you what had happened, so after I'd dropped Chimbi at St. Peter's, I went straight to Chungwe. The place was bloody deserted so I went and found Emmanuel, Harry's cattle foreman, who told me you two had gone down South which was complete news to me. He seemed to have no idea when you'd be back. I didn't know what to do. You could have been away for weeks. I thought of going to the police at Chiredzi and trying to get some action from official sources, but then I thought, well, Christ, they're not going to do anything, are they? Especially since they've already told the world they've caught the people responsible. Then Emmanuel told me you'd left your man Enos down at Chipinda Pools.'

'So you went down there?'

'I couldn't think what else to do. Anyway, I found Enos and got together with him and Jamie and Chenjerai, who happened to be around at that point, and told them what I'd found out. And that's where we had a bit of luck. Chenjerai said one of his patrols had just come in and reported they'd spotted a band of armed men heading west, south of the Chihunja Hills. He was about to take a bigger group of his men and go after them. He was assuming they were armed poachers.'

'And they were this gang?'

'Pretty certainly. I didn't know what the hell to do. I was worried about Chenjerai going in. Anything could have happened, especially if there was a firefight. The man we're interested in might have got killed, or something might have gone wrong with the attack and they'd have scattered and we'd have lost him. I mentioned this to Chenjerai who agreed with me, amazingly enough. He said that anyway, it was strictly speaking the Army's problem.

'He sounds like a good guy,' Joe said.

'He is. I tell you something, if we'd had a few people like him on our side we might even have won the bloody war.' Joe noticed that Jack had given Ross a significant look as he had spoken. To his relief. Ross didn't rise to the bait.

'So what did you decide?'

'Well, at that point Enos took over. He announced that he was going in after them himself.'

'On his own?'

'That's what he said. Just to track them, find out where they were going.'

'And you agreed to that?'

'Jamie was dead against it. He pointed out, quite rightly, that this gang is obviously up to no good and it was his responsibility to report their presence to the Army. But Enos is a pig-headed bastard.'

'You can say that again.' There was a suspicion of a smile at the corners of Ross's mouth.

'So in the end we agreed that he should go. However, Jamie insisted that he should take a radio with him, and if it looked like the gang was about to mount a raid somewhere he should call in and we'd notify the Army. We also arranged for him to call in every night at six with a progress report. They sorted out a frequency which I can't remember. Jamie's got the details. It's a T48 he's taken. Remember the T48?'

Ross nodded.

'And I gave him my FN and forty rounds which I usually keep in the jeep. Jamie wasn't too happy about him taking a gun but Chenjerai didn't seem to mind. Enos seemed to know how to handle it.'

'He knows that all right.' Ross was grinning now. Joe saw that he had put down the axe.

'Anyway, to save time I offered to take him most of the way out to the Chihunjas in the jeep. There are a couple of tracks in that direction which are still passable. It was a bit tricky because it was dark by that stage and I didn't want to drive into the bastards. Before he got out I told him not to do anything stupid like trying to take the bloke single-handed. I hope he listened to what I said. I was just praying that you two would get back. Jamie thinks I'm crazy letting him go off like that on his own.'

'Maybe you are,' said Ross quietly.

'So what does that make you?' There was challenge in Jack's voice.

Ross smiled and spread his hands.

'I'll call up the Army if you want me to,' Jack said.

'No.' Ross's voice was suddenly hard.

'In that case get down there and find out what's happening. I'll call up Jamie and tell him you're coming.' Jack was already on his feet, heading through the door.

Joe stopped him. 'Why are you doing this for me?' he said.

Jack paused. Smiled. 'I guess I know what it's like to lose a family,' he said softly.

There was a voice from the living-room. 'Is that you, Jack?'

'Yes, Ma. I won't be a minute.'

'You didn't say much.'

'There wasn't much *to* say.'

'What do you mean by that?' Joe glanced sharply at Ross who was slumped in the passenger seat, braced against the parcel shelf, as the Land-Rover bucked and slewed over potholes and rocks. Joe was driving fast, too fast, but this time Ross hadn't mentioned it.

'I mean, you asked all the questions and Jack answered them. There wasn't any need for me to chip in.'

Joe snorted, and concentrated on the road. They were already past the dam, pitching between the piled-up basalt. 'Jack's a great guy. I don't understand why you don't like him.'

'Maybe I'm changing my opinion,' Ross said.

'Well, I hope so. Not many people would have done what he's done for me.'

208

'You're right there.' There was a hint of irony in Ross's voice.

There were cattle on the road, but Joe didn't slow down. The starving animals tottered sideways as if in disbelief, narrowly avoiding collision. Joe said, 'I don't understand you, I really don't. You come down here with me to find Ellie and the kids, and the moment we really get somewhere you seem to lose interest. What the hell did you come for if this is the way you're going to behave? Are you jealous of Jack or something?'

'Don't be stupid.'

'It's Schoeman isn't it?'

'Schoeman?' There was irritation in Ross's voice.

'You still won't believe he's the bastard responsible.'

He'd touched a nerve, he saw, from the sharpness of Ross's response. 'You give me one good reason why he should be.'

'You said yourself, he was training them.'

'I said it was possible.'

'It's more than possible, and you know it.'

Ross stared out of the window at the brown shrivelled bush. It was some time before he spoke again. When he did it was with something close to sadness. 'Have you ever been in a war?'

'You know I haven't.'

'You make good mates in a war. The best. You get to know them better than your wife, your mother. You get to rely on them.'

'That was then.'

'Do people change that much?' Ross swung fiercely to face Joe.

Joe shrugged. 'You tell me. Kim said she hated them.'

'Fucking whore!'

A dozen or so vultures clustered round the carcase of a dead cow rose slowly into the air, only mildly disturbed by their passing. 'At least she was telling the truth,' Joe said mildly.

Ross shook his head slowly. 'You don't understand,' he said quietly. 'You don't understand anything.'

'I understand enough.'

Ross laughed bitterly and turned his attention back to the bush.

209

They didn't talk again until they'd turned south and crossed the Mahande River bridge. Joe was forced to brake sharply to avoid a warthog. Glancing sideways, his eyes met Ross's. To his surprise the thin man grinned suddenly. 'You know something?' he said, 'I envy you.'

'Envy me?' Joe's surprise turned to astonishment.

'It's all so simple as far as you're concerned.'

'I wouldn't call it simple.'

'Maybe you wouldn't.' Ross seemed to reach some kind of decision. 'OK,' he said. 'You win. Let's go find this bastard and get him to tell us what he knows.'

'You mean that?'

'I mean it.'

Joe pushed his foot down hard on to the accelerator pedal. 'I just hope you do,' he said.

They made good time, better than even Joe had hoped for, and it was still not six when they approached Chipinda. During the drive Ross had become positive, almost eager. Joe sensed that whatever had been bugging him, and he was no longer sure it was to do with Schoeman, had been resolved at least for the moment. They'd discussed what would happen if the bandit gave them positive information. It would mean crossing the border into Mozambique. Ross had laughed and said, 'Just like old times.' They were still laughing as they arrived at the low bungalow above the Lundi where Jamie was waiting for them, the ridgeback crouched at his heels.

'Thank God you're back,' he said.

'Has Enos called?' Ross was out, Joe following.

Jamie shook his head. 'Emmy's listening for him. We'd best get in. Jack said you wouldn't be here till at least half-six. I was surprised when I heard your engine.'

'Joe drove,' said Ross.

The radio was set up on a table in a small room which doubled as a storeroom, off the kitchen. There were rows of jam pots on shelves, bags of flour on the floor. Emmy, who was sitting on the only chair, stood up when they came in.

'Nothing yet?' Jamie said.

'No.' She pushed a hand across her brow. Her hair seemed less tidy than usual and there were dark hollows around her eyes as though she'd slept badly. 'I don't like it,' she said. I just don't like it.'

'Then why did you agree if it was going to cause trouble?' Ross said reasonably.

'I didn't agree. He did.' She indicated her husband. 'He's afraid of Jack Hammond and that man Chenjerai, that's why. He lets them walk all over him. And where were you two? You should have been here.'

'Jack told you,' said Jamie quietly. 'They were down South.'

'Huh!' Emmy stalked out of the room and slammed the door.

Jamie sat down on the vacant chair. 'I'm sorry,' he said. 'She's a worrier. It all builds up inside. She doesn't mean what she says. She's as pleased as I am that there's some news. She's just concerned about what'll happen if this all gets out.'

'Well, it won't,' said Ross. 'Not unless we let it.'

'You tell her that,' said Jamie grimly.

'I will.' Ross smiled and perched himself on the table. He patted Jamie's shoulder. 'Come on, man, it's not that bad.'

'If they kill somebody and I could have prevented it, I'll never forgive myself.'

'Even a couple of munts?'

Jamie shrugged away Ross's hand. 'Yes,' he said coldly. 'Even a couple of munts. So what do you propose to do? Enos can't stay out there for ever.'

'I'll go and find him, then we'll lift the guy.'

'Just like that?'

'More or less, yes.'

'I'm coming with you,' Joe said quickly. 'You do know that?'

Ross twisted to face him. 'No, you're not.'

'You've just decided that, have you?'

'Yes.'

'I'm still coming.'

'And I say you're not. Is that clear?' There was a hard edge to Ross's voice.

Jamie interrupted. 'So what happens if something goes wrong? One of you gets killed or badly wounded? What am I going to tell the authorities?'

Ross switched his attention back to Jamie. 'You tell them we were visiting the park and met these guys by chance.'

'And you think they'll believe that?'

'You've given us a permit to be there. Say we're elephant experts or something.'

Jamie snorted.

'In any case,' Ross continued, 'we're not going to get killed. Not unless he insists on coming with us.' He indicated Joe.

'I do insist,' Joe said quietly.

Ross sighed and closed his eyes.

'And what happens when you've got this man, supposing you do get him?' Jamie said.

'We bring him back here.'

'And the rest of them? You just let them go scot free, do you?'

Ross shrugged. 'That's up to you. You can send in the bloody air force if you want to. It'll only take us a couple of days. Three at the most.'

Jamie was silent, looking as unhappy as Joe felt. There was a sudden crackle from the radio. Ross peered at the dials. 'What frequency?'

'Three megahertz. It's already set.'

'Call sign?'

'Zero Tango. Zero Charlie.'

Ross twisted at the knobs, grunting with concentration.

'He's already late,' Jamie said. 'It's twelve minutes past.'

'Give him time. You got a map handy?'

Jamie nodded. 'I'll get one.'

'And a beer?'

'I'll get one of those, too.'

As Jamie went out, Joe said, 'I'm serious, I'm coming with you. I couldn't stand sitting around here, not knowing what the hell was happening. Anyway, you need me to identify the right guy.'

Ross concentrated on the radio for a minute or two longer. 'I tell you this: if Enos doesn't call in tonight, there's a good chance none of us will be going anywhere.'

Jamie returned with three Castles on a tray. He had a

plastic-covered folder of maps beneath his arm. 'Still nothing?' he said.

'Not a squeak.'

Jamie put the beers on the table. Ross uncapped one and took a long swig from the bottle. 'That's good,' he said, wiping his lips. 'Now just show me where Chenjerai's patrol spotted these gooks.'

Jamie flicked open the folder of maps, scanned one of them for a moment and then pointed. 'Here,' he said.

Joe came to the table and peered over Ross's shoulder. Jamie was pointing at a spot near a thin tributary of the Lundi, marked the Muwawa River. It was some ten kilometres west of the Chivirira Falls on the Sabi where the tribesmen had said the bandits had crossed.

'Is there any water in that river?' Ross said.

Jamie shook his head. 'In a normal season, maybe. This year, no.'

'So they'll need water. Where's the nearest water?'

Jamie peered again at the map, but before he could answer the radio began to crackle again. Through the static an indistinct voice could be heard. Ross grabbed the handset. 'Zero Tango. Zero Charlie – do you read?' He paused for a moment, then repeated the question. 'Zero Tango. Zero Charlie – do you read?'

'It's him?'

Ross ignored Joe's excited query. 'Zero Tango. Zero Charlie – do you read?' He spoke in clipped, staccato tones, with mounting urgency.

Then, faint but unmistakable Enos's voice. 'Zero Tango – fives go ahead.'

'Zero Charlie are you OK?'

'Zero Tango – affirmative.'

'Zero Charlie – give your position, please.'

'Zero Tango – UN 976359. UN 976359.'

Jamie was flicking through the maps. 'Just east of the Lundi,' he said. 'Near Chibveve Pool.'

'Zero Charlie – roger. Do you have visual?'

'Zero Tango – affirmative. There are ten of them.'

'Zero Charlie – you have positive identification?'

'Zero Tango – affirmative.'

'Zero Charlie – stay there. Will rendezvous A.M. Do you read? A.M.'

'Zero Tango – roger. I read. How was Soweto?'

Ross grinned. 'Zero Charlie – see you tomorrow. Out.' There was a click and silence as Ross put down the handset and turned to Jamie. 'We've got 'em,' he said.

'I'll believe it when I see it.'

'You'll see it.' Ross picked up the map. 'You said it was near the Lundi?'

'Just here.' Jamie indicated the position. 'Chibveve Pool.'

There was a track, Joe noticed, a thin, red dotted line snaking down from Chipinda roughly following the eastern bank of the Lundi, passing a couple of kilometres to the east of Enos's position. Ross had spotted it too. 'Is this passable?' he said.

Jamie looked closely at the map. 'Just about. There's one or two bad patches. Deep dongas. If it rains, forget it.'

'You'll take us down there tomorrow morning.' It was a statement, not a question.

Jamie stiffened. 'You've got your own Land-Rover.'

'Which will stick out like a sore thumb. You were in the war, you know what I'm talking about. They won't look twice at a Parks vehicle.'

'Unless they decide to ambush it,' Jamie said.

'In which case, we'll be ready.'

'We?' said Joe urgently. 'You said we.'

'Did I?' Ross assumed a look of feigned surprise. He turned to Jamie. 'Tell us about Chibveve Pool.'

'It's just a pool midstream on the Lundi. There are usually half a dozen hippo.'

'Any reason why these gooks might have gone there?'

Jamie thought for a moment. 'Not that I can think of. They obviously need water, but the Lundi's perennial. They could get it anywhere from there. They're probably heading south to avoid Chipinda.'

Joe examined the map. 'That means they're heading for Matibi.' He was convinced now that Ross would take him.

'Your guess is as good as mine,' Jamie said.

'When they attacked us, they obviously went north. I wonder why they've gone south now?'

Jamie spread his hands.

Ross said, 'They probably haven't got a clue where they're going.'

'You mean, they're just going to wander about till they come across something worth attacking?'

'It has been known.'

There was a sudden clatter of pans from behind the closed door. 'Is Emmy cooking?' Joe said.

Jamie grinned and stood up. 'She believes in feeding her enemies as well as her friends. Let's go and drink our beers somewhere more comfortable.'

'You'll take us tomorrow?' Ross hadn't moved.

Jamie sighed. 'I guess so. Though, God knows, I need my head examined for saying yes.'

'And what about me?' Joe said to Ross.

'What about you?'

'I'm coming?'

Ross turned to Jamie. 'I think you're wrong,' he said. 'It's not you that wants your head examined. It's me.'

They ate outside on the concrete table, the air alive with the noise of frogs and cicadas. Emmy was more her old self, Joe noticed. She'd done her hair and put on a smear of lipstick. She even made a little conversation. When they had finished, Joe helped Ross to fetch packs, webbing, sleeping bags and various items of field equipment from the Land-Rover. They would take eight water bottles each. Emmy, who seemed resigned now to their going, made up ration packs to Ross's specifications. Pronutria mixed with powdered milk and sugar and sealed into meal-sized plastic bags, tea bags, more sugar, a handful of boiled sweets, rice, a tin or two of meat stew and chopped pork, and a couple of cans of orange segments. Jamie went into an outbuilding and returned with several strips of impala biltong. It seemed very little to feed them for three days, Emmy said, looking at the pile of food on her kitchen table. Ross said it would last them for a fortnight.

It took them a long time to check off the supplies and equipment, and to stow it into the packs and the various pouches on the webbing. They included extra supplies of sadza for Enos, and, at Jamie's insistence, a replacement Nicad battery for the radio. Joe slipped on one of the packs when it was full, and found it surprisingly light. Ross told him that by the time he'd got eight water bottles slung around him, and was taking his turn at carrying the radio which weighed twenty-five pounds, he might change his mind. Joe was relieved that the pressure of the strap on his shoulder wound didn't trouble him, and hoped fervently that any increase in weight wouldn't alter the situation.

It was past ten before Ross pronounced himself satisfied, straightened up from the kitchen table and accepted the cup of tea that Emmy had made him. Then, when he had drunk it, he turned his attention to the rifles and ammunition boxes that they had laid out earlier on the carpet in the lounge.

Jamie and Joe watched him as he began to strip and clean the guns. He was working on the 375 when Jamie suddenly said, 'Those are hunting rifles.'

Ross nodded, not pausing from his task.

Jamie said, 'They've got AKs, those bandits. Jack told me.'

'That's what they used on me,' Joe said.

Ross worked the cock action of the gun two or three times rapidly. 'So?'

Jamie hesitated. 'You ought to be taking an FN. Enos has got one.'

'If I had one, I'd take one,' Ross said quietly.

Jamie was silent for a moment, a worried look on his face, then he left the room. When he returned he was carrying a pair of canvas gun cases and a brown leather bag which Joe could see was filled with ammunition boxes and empty magazines. 'Here,' he said.

Ross looked up. 'What's that?'

'FNs. You said you wanted them.'

Ross smiled and put down the 375. 'Thanks.' He took one of the bags from Jamie and unzipped it.

The rifle was splashed with green and brown paint, and looked strangely unbalanced until Joe realised that there was no magazine fitted. It was immaculately clean and smelt of mineral oil. Ross quickly began to dismantle it.

'It's OK. It has been checked.'

'Thanks. I'll check it again.'

Joe watched him for a while, trying to understand the complexities of the mechanisms that were being laid out before him. 'Should I do mine?' he offered.

Ross didn't look up. 'You're not taking a gun.'

'Don't you think he needs one?' Jamie said.

'No. He's got no idea how to use one. He'll be safer without.'

'I thought you'd brought the .303 . . .' Joe began.

'No gun.'

'Then why did you bring one for me?' Joe was beginning to find Ross's dismissive tone irritating.

'I thought I'd have time to teach you to use it, but I haven't. OK?'

Joe glanced at Jamie who shrugged and went out carrying the second FN. 'So what happens if we get attacked?' Joe said when he was gone.

'You keep your head down and pray.'

Emmy, who had been clearing the kitchen in case the houseboys started asking questions, came in with a plate of cakes. 'Who's going to pray?' she asked.

When Ross had finished stripping, cleaning and reassembling the FN, they spent some time filling the squat magazines with cartridges, twenty per magazine, and fitting them into the pouches on the webbing. Between them they would carry four hundred rounds – ten full magazines, plus another ten boxes in their packs. While they worked, Jamie and Emmy sat together on the sofa, saying nothing. At one point, Joe noticed they were holding hands. It was almost midnight before Ross announced that he was ready for bed. He arranged with Jamie that they should be woken at five.

It was while he was undressing in the chintzy comfort of the guest hut that Joe raised the question of the gun once more. Ross, who was sluicing his face in the basin, towelled himself quickly dry and told Joe to sit down.

He sat. The feeling of unreality which had begun in South Africa and had continued ever since, seemed now to have taken him over completely. He was stripped to his underpants, sweating slightly. The wound in his leg had begun to throb.

'I want to talk to you,' Ross began. 'And I might as well do it now. We may not have too much opportunity tomorrow.'

'OK,' said Joe. 'I just think that . . .'

'I don't care what you think. Just listen.' Ross sat down on the rose-coloured easy chair that Emmy had thoughtfully placed beneath the window for the convenience of her guests. 'First of all, I don't know why the hell I've agreed that you should come tomorrow. I just want to get in there with Enos, do the job, and get out again with a minimum of fuss. But since you are coming – and I must be bloody stupid to have agreed to it – I want to tell you this. If you do anything, anything at all, except exactly what I tell you to do, I shall hit you so hard you won't get up again. Is that clear?'

Joe nodded numbly.

'Second, you're not going to take a gun because you're not competent to use one. Enos and I will have two FNs and four hundred and forty rounds between us, which is plenty. I'll show you how to operate my FN in case of real emergency, but with any luck we shan't have to fire a shot. We're out to lift this gook, not slot him.'

'Slot?'

'Kill, for Christ's sake!' Ross's irritation, Joe became aware, was masking his acute tension. 'I can't teach you bushcraft because I haven't got time and we need to get some sleep, but there are some things you need to know. The most important of which is that you don't know anything. So you stick with me at all times, unless I tell you otherwise. When I turn left, you turn left. When I sit down, you sit down. You walk immediately behind me, nowhere else. Do you understand?'

'I understand.'

'Well, make sure you do. Next, from the moment we leave that Land-Rover tomorrow, there's going to be total silence. That means you don't talk, you don't cough. If you get stung, or cut, you don't shout out – you grin and bear it. You watch where you walk at all times to avoid contact with dead wood, branches, loose rocks. You check your pack each morning to make sure nothing rattles. If you want to attract my attention, tap me on the arm and point at whatever it is. You'll see me using all sorts of signals to Enos, most of which you don't need to know the meaning of. The only ones you need to know is this one,' Ross raised his hand, 'which means halt, and this one,' he patted the air, 'which means lie down flat. The silence rule is to be maintained at all times, and that includes at night in camp. You don't even bloody snore.'

'I don't snore.'

'Well, keep it that way. And, lastly, if there should be a firefight, get down and get under cover, and stay there until you're told to get up. Don't, whatever you do, try to get a look at the field of fire because that's the quickest way to get yourself killed.' Ross stood up. 'Now I'm going to bed. It's been a bloody long day.'

That night Joe slept badly, waking frequently despite his fatigue. For the first time for many weeks the dreams of rape and pain and terror returned. And mixed with them were new dreams: of starvation and death, of swollen bellies and matchstick legs and skin stretched paper-thin over angular skulls. Twice he woke shouting and sweating. Once he heard the leopard cough as it padded on its nightly round.

Joe pulled himself upwards to consciousness. He seemed to have been asleep for no more than ten minutes. 'What's the time?' he forced himself to ask.

'Four forty-five. Get your clothes on.'

Ross was already dressed. They'd laid out the clothes the night before: long-sleeved shirts, shorts, bush overalls, veldschoens. They'd be hot, Ross had said, but it was preferable to getting ripped to bits in the thornbush. Outside the window it was still black.

Jamie, too, was awake. While dressing, Joe could hear him in the house, talking quietly to the dog. There was a clink of teacups, and soon afterwards a knock at the door. Joe paused from struggling with his overall straps to take the tea. Jamie said he'd back up the Land-Rover to the gate.

'Ten minutes,' Ross told him.

The tea tasted good, despite the powdered milk, scalding hot and strong. The sound of an engine lacerated the silence of the morning. They were about to leave when there was a second knock. This time it was Emmy in a flowered housecoat, curlers bunched in her hair. She was carrying two packets of sandwiches and a flask. 'Breakfast,' she said. 'Egg sandwiches. You like egg sandwiches?'

'I like anything,' Ross told her. 'Anything at all.' He took the food.

Joe smiled at her. 'Thanks,' he said. The smile was not returned. She stood for a moment watching them, her face betraying nothing. Then she said 'Good luck', and was gone.

Jamie kept the engine running while they stowed the packs, webbing, gun. Maybe that was why even Ross didn't hear the man approach. The voice, though soft, paralysed them momentarily into inaction. 'Mangwanani,' the voice said.

A small, compact black man was just visible in the faint light from the house. Joe was conscious of the whiteness of his teeth as he smiled. Ross returned the greeting cautiously. The man laughed. From the stoep, where it had been chained, the ridgeback growled and barked once.

'This is Chenjerai,' Jamie said in an irritated voice. He'd been trying to get them away without the man knowing, Joe guessed.

Chenjerai shook hands, looked at the packs and the gun case. 'Dawn patrol, hey?' he said, and laughed again.

'It'll be more than dawn if we don't get going,' Jamie snapped.

Chenjerai ignored the remark. 'Which one's Joe?' he said.

'Me.' Joe felt suddenly self-conscious under the man's gaze.

'Well, Mr. Joe, you get problems, you get trouble, you let me know. I'll be waiting.'

'Thanks.'

'There'll be no trouble.' This time it was Ross's turn to sound irritated.

Chenjerai pointedly made no response to the remark. 'I'll be waiting,' he said once more, and melted into the darkness.

There was a brief silence, perhaps to let him get out of ear-shot, then Ross said, 'Cocky little bastard, isn't he?'

'You're right about that,' Jamie agreed.

The thought struck Joe that five years earlier Ross and Chenjerai would have shot each other on sight.

They rode in the back at Ross's insistence. He arranged that when they reached the right place Jamie should bang on the partition and slow down, but he was not to stop. Jamie emphasised twice the importance of radioing in at six o'clock

220

each evening, same wavelength, same callsign. Ross grunted his assent.

At first the road was good, winding gently out past the office building and storesheds, following the east bank of the Lundi. Then suddenly they swung to the left and began to climb sharply upwards. Twice in the first few minutes Jamie had to halt to change down to a lower gear. As they climbed higher a bar of pale blue became visible in the east, throwing the distant jagged horizon into stark relief.

Joe and Ross ate the sandwiches that Emmy had provided and drank some of the tea from the flask. The bush closed in, invisible branches whipping and clattering at the roof as the Land-Rover pitched and lurched. Joe began to feel nauseous, shaky, aware of his stomach churning. When Ross produced a small tin from one of his pockets, he thought it was more food and refused it.

For some reason the refusal amused Ross who laughed loudly. 'You put it on your face, for Christ's sake,' he said. 'You don't eat it!' He laughed again, as though it was the best joke he'd ever heard.

Joe suppressed his anger and opened the tin. There was just sufficient light for him to make out what looked like a thick brown paste. 'I put this on my face?' he said.

'On your face, and hands, and neck.'

It was twenty minutes before Ross was satisfied with their appearance. By that time they were no longer climbing but bouncing across what seemed to be a sort of plateau. The light was increasing, intensifying by the minute. To the right, below them, the pools of the Lundi gleamed like discs of silver. Ross slipped the FN from its case and clicked home a magazine. They began to buckle on belts and webbing.

Joe fought at the nausea which had grown worse, threatening to overwhelm him. It was not the food which was causing it, he realised, nor the pitching of the Land-Rover but the most intense excitement he had ever felt. And somewhere deep inside him there was fear. He glanced across at Ross, wondering if he too felt the same, but his face was mask-like behind its brown covering, revealing nothing.

After five kilometres, maybe ten, it was difficult to judge, the track began to descend, quite gently at first, and then with increasing severity. They were forced to stop three times within a few yards to remove trees thrown across the road by elephants. The first shafts of sunlight smacked at the twisted trunks of acacias and combretums. Herons and storks squawked and yelled from the river.

They hit the dried up bed of a stream at speed, spewing sand skywards, and were up and out again, the dense vegetation that lined the river banks quickly thinning into scrub mopani. 'He'll break a halfshaft if he carries on like that,' Ross said, and grimaced.

'I'm going to throw up,' Joe said.

'No, you're not.'

He didn't.

With the sun came the heat. Joe felt the first prickings of discomfort as the sweat battled with the brown mess on his face. They'd been on the road for almost an hour and three quarters now. They had to be close. They eased their packs on to their backs and strapped them securely, pulled on bush hats. The Land-Rover yawed and skidded on the loose sand of the track.

It was while Joe was wondering whether Ross would have time to explain the workings of the FN as he'd promised that the double thump came from the front. He'd been expecting the signal, but the reality was a shock. 'Out!' said Ross tersely. 'Hit the grass, not the track.'

His heart racing, Joe wrenched at the handle. He felt like a man about to make his first parachute drop. He paused for a second, and jumped.

Ross followed, flicking the door closed as he did so. The Land-Rover picked up speed, showering dust, and was gone, bouncing out of sight behind the thick stand of trees.

Joe glanced at his watch. It was almost nine. They'd been squatting behind a huge fallen mopani for more than two hours now, not moving, not talking. Tiny flies flickered and irritated. Cicadas strummed. Doves cooed. A small group of impala, an impressively antlered male, two or three females and a single fawn, crossed the track close by, pausing to browse, apparently unaware of their presence. Ross raised a finger and sighted along it at the male, mimed a shot and grinned. He seemed unworried by the wait, more relaxed than Joe could remember having seen him, and yet at the same time alert to the slightest sound, the slightest movement. This was where he belonged, Joe realised. This was home.

Time passed: fifteen minutes, twenty. Joe had almost decided to break the rule of silence to ask the question which had been uppermost in his mind since they had left the Land-Rover – how they were going to make contact? – when Enos appeared. He was walking quite openly along the centre of the track, swinging his FN, singing softly to himself in Shona. Rifle apart, he could have been someone out for a pleasant Sunday stroll through a suburban park.

His face split into a wide grin as he saw them. He pumped their hands, patted Joe on the neck. His pack, which contained the heavy radio, might have weighed nothing. He said something in Shona to Ross who turned to Joe and said, 'It's OK, we can talk. They're across the Lundi out of earshot, he says. But keep your voice down.'

Joe nodded.

They found some shade off the road and crouched down while Enos explained the situation. He spoke English at Ross's insistence. It was safer than Shona should they be overheard.

He'd picked them up quite easily, he said. They seemed to be making no attempt at anti-tracking. There were ten of them, two Ndau-speaking officers wearing camouflage, and eight others, Shangaans in civilian dress, including the man in the FANTA tee shirt. They carried AKs. They'd made camp near the Lundi River. They were reasonably well-disciplined, posting sentries at three-hourly intervals, and seemed to know where they were going.

Joe asked if he'd heard any of their conversation, if he'd heard them mention Ellie or the children. Enos said he'd heard them speak, but nothing about Ellie. He'd gathered from what little he'd heard that the leader of the group was called Zamchiya, and that he was worried because they were making such slow progress. They'd broken camp at first light and crossed the river some way above the pool. They were now probably two hours ahead, maybe three. Ross asked if it was just AKs they were carrying, or anything heavier. Any

223

RPDs or RPG7s? They had a machine-gun, Enos told him. An RPD. Just one.

Ross nodded a couple of times and glanced towards the west, adjusting his FN in its sling. 'OK,' he said. 'Let's go. We've got time to make up.'

As they moved off, he once more warned Joe into silence.

It was easy to begin with, no problem at all. Scattered mopani, short scrub dotted here and there with taller trees. Small patches of grass greened by what little rain there must have been. Enos led the way, adopting a relaxed, loping stride that covered the ground surprisingly quickly. Ross followed and Joe, feeling fitter and fresher than he'd dared hope, brought up the rear.

For a while they followed a game track, a wide, beaten path heading due west, littered with enormous elephant droppings like deflated footballs. The track was joined by others, narrower, all converging on the river. The mopani gave way to long thorned acacias, what looked like teak or mahogany, and the occasional wild fig with families of baboons or dark-faced vervet monkeys displayed on its branches. Close to the river the sickly green bark of fever trees reflected the sunlight dully. There were doves everywhere, their constant cooing competing with the drilling of the cicadas.

The Lundi, when they reached it, was bordered by a sheer bank which rose maybe sixty feet above its wide sandy bed. Below and slightly to the left, a skein of thin meandering rivulets met in a broad pool from which the ears and nostrils of three or four hippos protruded like small lumpy rocks. There was the occasional grunt as one or other of them adjusted its position. Beyond the pool the river narrowed into a series of low rapids, and beyond that, far in the distance, vivid red cliffs rimmed the skyline. Joe remembered Jamie mentioning the cliffs. Chilojo, he'd called them.

They paused for a moment, while Ross and Enos conducted a short conversation in a virtually inaudible undertone, then they moved off again, following the river northwards to where a small gully bisected the bank. Without hesitating, Enos led them downwards, over tumbled rocks, across a short stretch of sand and into the first of the four narrow channels they were to cross.

The first of the channels was the deepest, reaching almost to their waists, the water surprisingly chill. Swallows darted at head height, dipping from time to time to skim the surface. Small flies buzzed and swarmed. Joe wondered, in midstream, about bilharzia and made a mental note to mention it to Ross next time conversation was allowed. He wondered, too, about crocodiles, and scanned the banks to left and right. He noticed that Ross had unslung his FN and was holding it ready.

Beyond the channels the bed was churned by a mass of game footprints: the dainty twin-toed imprints of antelope, the cow-like hoofmarks of buffalo, the huge circular pads of elephant. Ahead of them dense trees lined a low bank. They stopped to empty the water from their veldschoens then moved south, following the game tracks to where a small dried-up streambed joined the river.

At the mouth of the stream, Enos suddenly halted, dropped to his haunches and pointed down. Overlaid on the game tracks were the distinct outlines of human feet, some bare, some shod. They led upwards, along the course of the stream, skirting boulders to be lost in the dense shade of the overhanging trees.

It was a gentle climb up and away from the Lundi, the shade giving welcome relief from the increasing heat. As they climbed, Joe felt the first twinge of pain from his shoulder, and adjusted the straps on his pack. He drank a little water from one of his bottles.

The tracks, easy to follow at first in the soft sand, became more sporadic. Their pace slowed. They no longer walked single file but, still keeping to the rear of Enos, Ross began to zigzag to the left and right of the main line. Joe, as he had been instructed, followed dutifully. Luminous lizards, sunning themselves on exposed rock surfaces, scuttled into cracks at their approach.

Some three hundred yards up the streambed, Enos stopped once again, and cast around in a broad circle. Then, apparently satisfied, he moved up the bank and into the thin curtain of thorn scrub that rimmed the channel.

They emerged into what at first sight looked like an English meadow, dotted with white flowers. It was not grass, but a

225

tiny, creeping, thin-leaved plant coating the bare soil. Small hooked thorns detached themselves and dug deep into the soles of the veldschoens. The tracks of the bandits, Joe noticed, carefully skirted the area, leading out beyond a stand of massive baobabs, their soft trunks shredded by the tusks and teeth of elephants.

They stopped for a short while beneath the biggest of the trees to drink water. Ross distributed boiled sweets from the supply in one of his pouches, their barley sugar taste reminding Joe of childhood. Far away, on the low horizon, small clouds clustered in swarms in a milky blue sky.

After a while they picked up a road, no more than a narrow track, its flat red surface strangely smooth, unmarked by the passage of animals or man. The bandits had rested near the road, it was obvious from a concentration of prints beneath a small, broad-leaved tree. Enos spent some time examining the marks, glancing occasionally at Ross. He was trying to estimate how much time the men had spent there, Joe guessed. When they moved off, it was with more caution.

For perhaps ten kilometres they followed the road, never touching its surface but staying a few yards from it in the bush. The tracks were fainter now, and several times Enos was forced to stop and cast about him until he picked them up again. The sun rose higher in the sky, shimmering from the mopani leaves, leaching the colour from the landscape. To the south, a strange, steep-sided, flat-topped plateau towered above the surrounding bush like a beached ocean liner.

The tension that Joe had felt when he'd left the Land-Rover lessened by degrees as fatigue began to take over. As they worked westwards, not even the excitement of the hunt could sustain him. It became a matter of putting one foot in front of the other, concentrating always on the bobbing pack on Ross's back. Small flies, the mopani flies of which Ross had spoken, surrounded him in black dancing swarms, crawling into his ears and nose, drinking at his sweat. He became careless, colliding with fallen branches, once tripping and clutching at Ross's pack to save himself. The look of cold anger that Ross gave him revived him for a while, but not for long. The pressure of the strap on his shoulder became agonising, making him want to cry out. Ross was right, he thought. Dead right. He shouldn't have come. It was stupid. Crazy . . .

At an outcrop of red rocks the road swung suddenly northwards. They followed its course for some time before Enos raised his hand to call a halt. He'd lost the tracks, and despite casting round, he didn't pick them up again. The urge to find some shade and collapse into it became almost overwhelming to Joe. He gestured to Ross, pointing at a nearby acacia. Ross ignored him and instead, walking abreast of Enos, perhaps fifteen feet to the left of him, led Joe back in the direction they had come.

It was close to the red rocks that a sign from Enos indicated that he was once more on to the spoor, and without pausing they continued, now towards the north-west, along narrow game tracks and from time to time through the unmarked bush itself. Joe began to drop further and further behind, and twice Ross had to pause to allow him to catch up.

They were maybe four kilometres from the red rocks when Enos once more raised his hand. Ross stopped suddenly, so suddenly that Joe collided with him, but this time there was no anger, just a finger raised to his lips to indicate total silence.

Joe fought to control his heaving breath, wiped away the wetness from his forehead and tried to listen.

Eventually he heard it. From somewhere in front of them, how far away he couldn't tell, came the distinct sound of a human voice.

Enos slipped his pack from his back and, clutching his FN, edged forward through the bush towards the noise. When he returned he nodded, and signalled to Ross, a clenched fist with his thumb pointing towards the ground. Joe tried to work out the meaning of the signal, but failed. He realised, with a start, that Ross was trying to catch his attention, pointing to a small pool of shade beneath a thicker than usual mopani, and indicating that he was to sit down. Gratefully, Joe did so. In complete silence, Ross and Enos joined him.

They remained beneath the tree for three hours. From time to time they drank water and chewed at the strips of salty biltong that Jamie had given them. Despite the heat, the rest refreshed him and Joe began to take a greater interest in his

227

surroundings. The bandits were obviously very close by, no doubt sheltering from the worst of the sun just as they themselves were. Their voices were quite distinct now. Mostly it was conversation conducted in an undertone, but occasionally there were sharper, louder remarks and once a short cry of what could have been pain.

Towards the end of their wait, Ross picked up his FN and slipped silently out in the direction of the voices. Joe wondered whether he'd decided to attack but when he returned sometime later he repeated the clenched fist signal that Enos had given, and sat down again. The sun slid slowly round the sky.

It was after four when at last they heard the men leave. There was a clatter of what sounded like steel on stone, a couple of sharp commands. Joe made to follow, but a touch from Ross cautioned him to stillness. He pointed to his watch, indicating that they would wait another half hour. Seemingly unconcerned, he drank some more water and unwrapped a sweet.

When they did move off it was more slowly, and with the cooling of the day, Joe found it easier to maintain his pace. The pain in his shoulder had numbed to a dull ache, and his leg, which had hurt earlier, now felt fine. How close they had been to the bandits Joe only realised when Enos dropped to his haunches to examine a patch of ground beneath a spreading broad-leaved tree hung with sausage-like fruits. It was next to a dry river bed, maybe a hundred yards from where they had sat. Enos searched the site thoroughly, but found nothing. Then, pausing only to exchange signals with Ross, he walked purposefully across the stream and into the bush beyond.

For an hour they maintained a steady pace, Enos only losing the tracks once. Still they headed north-west. The level bush became broken into numerous sharp-edged gullies which forced them to slow even more. Thornbush began to replace the mopani. Once, in the far distance, Joe saw a solitary bull elephant, its bulk towering above the low scrub through which it ambled.

At around five-thirty they arrived unexpectedly at a high seven-stranded game fence. Ross took the maps that Enos had been carrying, flicked through them until he found the one he was looking for, and pointed. Peering over his shoulder Joe could see that they were at the very edge of the Gona-re-Zhou. Beyond the fence the Matibi tribal area began, with numerous kraals indicated by the now-familiar hump symbol.

To Joe's surprise, the bandits hadn't crossed. Instead, they had followed the fence towards the north-east, keeping within sight of it but a little way into the bush. Maybe Ross had been right. Maybe they were just wandering randomly, looking for something to attack. But if that was the case, surely there were plenty of targets in Matibi? There were so many questions he wanted to ask.

He wasn't given the opportunity. They were moving very slowly indeed along the line of the fence, stopping every few yards for Enos to listen. At six o'clock Joe motioned to Ross, tapped his watch, and pointed at the radio, the top of which was protruding from Enos's pack. It was time to call Chipinda. Ross shook his head and pointed to his lips. Joe understood.

It was almost immediately afterwards that Enos called a halt. He indicated that they should wait, and crept forward alone. When he came back he made an inverted V with his fingertips. Ross nodded, turned, and looked back the way they had come. Immediately to the east, maybe half a kilometre from where they stood, the bush thickened slightly. He pointed out the area to Enos, who nodded in turn. The V sign had meant the bandits were making camp for the night, Joe guessed, and that was what Ross intended to do.

They approached the spot cautiously, in a broad dog-leg movement, Enos how bringing up the rear and stopping from time to time to obliterate their tracks with a broken branch. When they arrived, Joe realised with surprise that they had turned through a hundred and eighty degrees and were facing due west into the setting sun.

It was a strange place to camp, he thought, too exposed, but Ross and Enos seemed happy enough with it. There were a few flat, reasonably clear patches between the twisted stems of the trees, and they selected one of them each, maybe twenty feet apart, and dumped their gear. Their positions formed the points of a roughly equilateral triangle. Ross indicated that Joe should take off his pack, clear his area of stones, twigs and other debris and spread out the thin foam mattress and sleeping bag. While Joe was doing this, Ross dug out a hole with his bush knife, into which he put the small Camping Gaz cooker he had brought. He began to heat water in a mess tin. The flame, Joe noticed, was kept low, presumably to minimise noise and glare. The second cooker, which Joe had been carrying, was given to Enos, who did likewise. While the water was heating, Ross stripped and cleaned his FN, and reassembled it carefully. Then, when he had finished, Enos took his own FN and did the same. It was a ritual, Joe guessed, that the two had been through many times before.

They drank tea, and ate meat stew and rice, Enos joining them for the meal. By the time darkness fell, plates, cups and cookers were clean and replaced in the pack. Only the sleeping bags and rifles remained out.

The night asserted itself, the silence split by the whine of cicadas which seemed to increase in volume as time went on. The sky was an intense black, pierced by stars more vivid than Joe could remember having seen before. Slightly puzzled as to what to do next, he sat on his sleeping bag and waited. Ross and Enos, presumably doing the same, sat completely silent and invisible in the darkness. Something, a large insect maybe, scuttled through the fallen leaves near his feet. He wished he had a torch to see what it was and drew his legs into his chest.

The rustling increased. There were two insects now, or perhaps it was a snake. He wondered what he would do if it was a snake.

And then he felt the touch of a hand on his shoulder. It was like an electric shock, the touch, and Joe almost cried out. It was Ross.

He sat down on the sleeping bag, put his lips close to Joe's ear and began to speak in a whisper so slight that Joe had to strain to catch each word.

'You've done well, bloody well. I got a bit worried about you in the middle of the day, but we had to push on to make up the time difference. Normally we'd rest up during the heat. What's happening now is this: we're going to get some shut-eye, Enos and I, then later we're going to go see what we can do.'

'You're going to try and take him tonight?'

'If we can. If not, there's always tomorrow. Now listen to me, this is important. When we're gone, I want you to stay here. Don't move, don't make a sound, and for God's sake don't try to follow us! If there's a firefight, the same thing applies. Just stay here. You'll be perfectly safe. If for any reason we don't come back, don't panic. Give it thirty-six hours. You've got plenty of food and water. Then, at first light the day after tomorrow, head due west. Cross the game fence into Matibi. Find someone to take you to the road, then hitch, beg or buy your way to Chipinda. Jamie will know what to do. You clear on that?'

'Yes.'

'The map reference of where those gooks are camped, by the way, is UM 807381. UM 807381. You got that?'

Joe repeated the figures. 'I think so.'

'Good. Now, just so you know it's us when we come back, I'll make this noise as we approach.' Ross cleared his throat softly and emitted a low, eerie hooting noise. 'Go go go-go-go,' it sounded like.

'What the hell's that?' whispered Joe.

'The giant eagle owl. There are a few around here, so if you hear one it's either the genuine article or us.'

'You want me to stay awake while you're gone?'

'No. Get a good night's sleep. You need one.'

'But what if somebody comes?'

'They won't. And even if they do, they won't walk right through here. Just keep quiet and they won't have a clue you're anywhere around. OK? I'm going to get my head down. I suggest you do the same.'

Ross made to rise, but Joe restrained him. 'The FN,' he whispered. 'You said you were going to show me how to use the FN.'

Ross was silent for a moment. 'Tomorrow,' he said. 'When there's a bit of light.'

'I'd just feel safer if I had a gun with me while you're gone.'

'No guns, I told you.'

'But, Ross . . .'

231

'Get some sleep, hey?' and he was gone.

Joe tried to sleep, but it wouldn't come. It was too hot in the sleeping bag. He tried lying on top of it, but felt exposed. The insects – and there were insects, it wasn't just his imagination – rustled constantly at the dried leaves all around. Sometime later the moon rose in the east, at first bright red and flickering so that for one crazy moment he thought the bush was on fire. Then fading as it rose, through orange to bright yellow.

It was like some sort of signal. With its light the night noises of the bush began, half-familiar from forgotten wildlife films: the deep booming of lions, the whoops and yelps of what Joe assumed were hyena. He felt a prickle of fear. They sounded so close. Too close. Twice there was a loud crack as something, an elephant probably, broke branches from a tree. Unknown birds squawked and shrieked.

He was still not asleep when Ross and Enos left. They conferred for a short while in low whispers, heads together, dimly visible in the moonlight. Enos, he could just see, was uncoiling something. It looked like thick wire. He saw Ross nod. They strapped on their webbing, picked up their rifles, and were swallowed instantly by the darkness.

He must have dozed, because it was the lions that woke him. They were closer, he was convinced of it, maybe moving in for the kill. He could hear the sharp intake of breath before each roar. Something, a small animal, scuttled through the camp at speed, as if terrified for its life. They were frightened of fire, lions, he knew. If only he could light a fire . . .

Something touched his bare ankle and he leapt to his feet, sweating and shaking. The moon was brighter now, directly overhead. It was a large insect, a spider it looked like, maybe three inches across. He lashed at it with a stick, but it was too fast. Then, suddenly conscious of the noise he'd made, he sat down again. Christ Almighty, it was only a spider. Only a bloody spider. . . .

Time passed, how long he had no means of telling. The lions, he was relieved to find, came no closer. The moon moved sedately round the sky. He uncapped one of his water bottles and drank deeply of the contents. The water was warm and tasted of plastic, giving no refreshment. He tried to think,

232

to sort the jumble of hopes, fears and impressions into some kind of order, put a perspective onto what was happening. He failed. Gradually, the acuteness of his fear left him.

Ross and Enos returned sometime before dawn, as silently as they had left, the gentle owl hoot heralding their arrival. Seeing that he was awake, Ross approached Joe. 'No dice,' he whispered. Then he removed his webbing, climbed into his bag and apparently fell instantly asleep. Enos followed suit.

Joe remained awake for a while longer. Then he too, ignoring the spider, lay down and slept.

They were up soon after first light, eating pronutria and drinking water. Four of the eight water bottles he'd been carrying were already empty, Joe noticed. It was Tuesday, Daraprim day, and this time he remembered. Ross nodded his approval as the pills were dished out. While they were eating, Ross filled Joe in on the events of the night before, speaking in the same almost inaudible whisper. They'd got up pretty close, he said, established the pattern of sentry placement, which he guessed was standard, but because of the layout of the place they'd been unable to take the man without a firefight, and that was too risky. They'd try again tonight.

Joe asked about the wire he'd seen Enos uncoiling. Ross smiled and drew a line across his throat. Joe felt strangely relieved that nothing had happened.

When they had rolled and stowed their bedding and utensils, Joe picked up Ross's FN. Ross sighed and took it from him. Swiftly, he demonstrated the pre-firing sequence, how to fit the magazine, operate the cocking handle to compress the return springs, how to slip the catch from safe to automatic. 'It pulls a little to the left when you fire,' he said, still using the same whisper. 'But I don't suppose that'll bother you.'

'Why not?'

'Because you won't be using it. OK, let's get blacked up and get going.'

It was better than the day before. The empty water bottles relieved the weight, and the stiffness Joe felt as they set off soon went. Enos set a slow pace, pausing frequently. They picked up the tracks with little difficulty, and after checking out the place where the bandits had camped, followed them, still heading north-east, still close to the game fence.

About four kilometres up, Enos halted and pointed at the fence. The third and fourth of the seven strands of wire were buckled slightly, as if they had been prised apart, Ross nodded and they squeezed through. They were in Matibi.

It seemed no different, the bush beyond the fence. A little barer, perhaps. There were signs here and there of trees having been hacked with axes, presumably for firewood. They could see no huts and no signs of cultivation.

The tracks of the bandits bent westwards, and Enos dropped the pace still further. Glancing at his watch, Joe saw it was still not yet nine o'clock. After about a kilometre, they crossed the broad, dried-up bed of a stream. There were other prints now, human and cattle. Numerous paths snaked between the trees. Beyond the stream they stopped for a short while for Ross to consult the map. Looking at it, Joe saw that the bandits were deliberately avoiding areas of settlement, heading for the road, the Chikombedzi road that they'd driven along so often during those fruitless days they'd spent searching for the herd boy.

They were close to it now, very close. They heard the sounds of an engine, a small truck probably, the silencer blown. And voices. Twice in the next few minutes they were forced to take cover, once to avoid an old man, the second time to conceal themselves from two girls carrying hoes. Judging by the relaxed attitude of the girls, chatting and laughing as they walked, the bandits, too, had chosen not to show themselves.

Perhaps a hundred metres from the road Enos suddenly signalled and dropped to his stomach. Ross and Joe followed suit. They waited while he eased himself forward. This time it was only a matter of minutes before he returned. He once more made the clenched fist sign, thumb downwards, pointing first in the direction he had been, and then at a small kopje to their left, indicating that they should climb it. It was low, more a mound than a kopje, topped with dense thorn scrub. A narrow path led towards its summit. Still prone, Enos edged himself upwards. Ross beckoned to Joe and they began to follow.

It seemed a long way, an infinitely long way. Inch-long

thorns dug at Joe's knees, drawing blood despite the protection of his overalls. Sweat blinded him. At the top he collapsed, chest heaving, amidst a clutter of rocks and broken branches.

It was some minutes before he had recovered sufficiently to take notice of his surroundings. The thornbush was thinner than it had seemed at ground level, but still gave good cover. Ross and Enos had wriggled forward a few feet and were peering downwards, Ross using the pair of small field glasses he carried in one of the pouches on his pack. Slowly and painfully, Joe pushed himself to join them.

They were perhaps fifty feet above ground level, but because of the flatness of the surrounding bush the road was visible for a considerable distance in either direction, twisting like a smooth white snake between the low acacia and mopani. To the left of them, maybe a kilometre away, the bush had been hacked back to create mealie fields in which the bright clothing of women and children was visible as they bent to weed between the waist-high plants. Beyond the mealie fields was more bush, and in the far distance, the conical roofs of numerous huts. Here and there plumes of smoke floated into the already paling blue sky.

At first Joe thought the bandits must have crossed the road and were now hidden from view in the denser thornbush to the west. But then he saw them.

They were immediately below, slightly to the right, concealed in what looked like a deep ditch but was probably a hole dug out to provide material for the building of the road. Enos was right, there were ten of them. Two of them wore camouflage fatigues, the rest a ragged assortment of civilian clothes. And one of them, crouching to the rear of the group with his back to the kopje, was wearing what had once been a yellow tee shirt.

Joe strained to see what they were doing. The two men in camouflage, presumably the Ndau officers, were concentrating on something at their feet. The others seemed to be checking the weapons they carried. The curved magazines of their AKs were clearly visible. They made no sound.

They were resting maybe, carrying out a little routine maintenance on their guns before going on . . .

And then one of the officers moved slightly. Laid out before him, with its muzzle pointing towards the road, and supported on a bipod, was a machine gun. The two men were fitting what looked like a circular drum to a catch immediately in front of the trigger, concentrating intently on their task.

Joe was suddenly apprehensive. For a simple robbery surely AKs would have been enough? He glanced at Ross. If he shared the feeling of apprehension, he didn't show it. He seemed relaxed, untroubled by what was going on beneath. It was almost as if he had been expecting it. Maybe it was a precaution, the machine gun, some kind of back-up in case of attack by the Army. Maybe . . .

Joe eased himself sideways to catch what little shade was available. Above, a pair of black eagles circled lazily. From somewhere far away came the shouts of children playing, and once the sound of a bell.

Ten minutes passed, then fifteen. From the direction of the huts a small boy on a large bicycle, with an even smaller boy perched on the carrier, wobbled towards them. The bandits, obviously invisible from the road, froze.

The boys passed and were gone, their passing marked only by the clanking of a loose chain guard. The silence returned.

Joe closed his eyes. Maybe Ross's mood was catching, but there seemed to be a dreamlike quality about the morning as if some slow, intricate ballet was being played out before him in which he had no part, and over which he had no control. For a short while, he almost dozed.

And then, despite himself, he began to think about Ellie. This was her world now, the bush, the heat, guns. And the kids, it was their world too. He felt a sudden surge of love for them that took him by surprise. They'd be thin and tough and no doubt talking Ndau or Shangaan like a native. And they'd be waiting for him, still waiting . . .

It was so long ago, that day he'd lost them, it seemed like a different lifetime. It must have been just the same then: the men crouched by the road, the check on the weapons, the silence, the long, long wait. With a shock, Joe realised that somewhere, maybe miles away, a car was probably even now moving towards them. Perhaps a rancher and his wife on their way to Chiredzi for the month's shopping. Maybe even a family of tourists, as adventurous and naive as he and Ellie had been . . .

There had to be some way of stopping all this. There had to be! He should have insisted they called Jamie last night. They could have gone far enough back into the bush for it to have been safe. The Army could have been alerted.

And then what?

He opened his eyes and looked down again. The bandit in the yellow tee shirt had finished checking his gun and was lying back, hands behind his head. The word FANTA was now clearly visible. He was young, no more than seventeen – Joe had been right about his age – thin, regular-featured, his hair cropped close to his head. One of his companions, a youth of about the same age in a torn blue shirt, said something to him. He smiled, teeth gleaming. There was an air of excitement about him, about both of them, of anticipation.

Joe reached across and took the field glasses which Ross had put down, focussing them on the youth. He remembered him clearly now, not just the tee shirt but the face. There was a slight cast in his left eye, and what looked like dried spittle adhering to his chin beneath his mouth. It was the face he'd seen when he'd shouted at the kids, and the man gripping their wrists had stopped, turned . . .

Joe knew suddenly that without any hesitation he could put a gun against that face and pull the trigger. A single shot – no, two. He'd hurt him first, make him talk. Make him scream. Sod Jamie! Sod the Army! This was his affair. His and nobody else's.

A slight movement from Enos caught his attention. He was pointing to the north. Joe swung the glasses in the direction indicated. In the far distance a column of dust was approaching. Whatever it was was moving fast. The faint sound of an engine penetrated the silence, getting louder by the second.

The bandits had heard it, too. One of them, a young boy in a ragged fawn shirt, was crawling forward under cover of tall grass, presumably to check out what was coming. He stood up cautiously, gazing intently along the road.

For perhaps thirty seconds he remained totally motionless, looking, listening. Then suddenly, as if in extreme panic, he ran back to where his companions lay and threw himself headlong amongst them. Joe caught the excited chatter of their voices.

Peering northwards again, he saw the reason why. An armoured troop carrier, dull brown, headlights blazing and filled with soldiers, was bearing down on them at high speed.

For an instant, Joe thought the bandits were going to attack but instead they flung themselves flat into the base of their hole. Their fear was almost tangible.

Ross had tensed, too, Joe saw as he handed back the glasses. Both he and Enos silently worked the cocking levers on their guns, easing themselves forward into better positions.

The troops *had* to see the bandits. They had to. They were high enough to see them, perched maybe fifteen feet from the ground in the back of their vehicle. There were at least twenty of them, FNs held skywards . . .

But they didn't. They weren't even looking outwards, most of them, and those that were were staring straight ahead along the line of the road. Engine screaming, the truck was past and gone, leaving dust and the faint stink of diesel.

Ross caught Joe's eye and shrugged, turned his attention back to the men below. Enos took a sip from his water bottle.

It was almost noon when they saw the bus, the bright yellow one that Joe remembered seeing once or twice when they'd been travelling through Matibi. It was moving slowly south, its roof stacked high with boxes, suitcases, bags of meal.

At the sound of the engine, the lookout boy once more crept forward. This time there was no alarm as he returned to his companions. Instead, picking up their guns, they walked slowly into the centre of the road. Only the two officers, one of them now prone behind the machine gun, remained concealed.

'They're gonna take that fucking bus,' Joe heard Ross whisper.

Enos nodded. Both men checked their FNs yet again. Joe felt his guts churning. A black ant was crawling across his hand and he brushed at it violently.

The bus was a long time coming, trailing its cloud of dust and diesel smoke. As it neared, Joe could see that it was full, people pressed three to a seat, some standing. There were what looked like live ducks in a crate on the roof. One of the bandits, the youth in the blue shirt, stepped forward and held up his hand.

At first Joe thought it was going to stop. It slowed, the driver's apprehensive face clearly visible through the dust-flecked windscreen. Then, suddenly, it accelerated.

The bandits scattered as the vehicle thrashed towards them, its engine howling. For a moment it looked like it was going to get through.

Then the machine gun sounded.

It was a long burst, stunning in its intensity. The bus lurched as one of the back tyres blew, steel meeting stone in a stream of sparks. Small holes sowed themselves across the yellow panelling. A window splintered, then another, suddenly opaque with blood. The vehicle slewed, the driver fighting the wheel. There was an audible bang, this time from a front tyre. For a short distance the bus skated sideways under its own momentum. Then slowly, very slowly it seemed, it toppled on to its side, door downwards, and its engine cut.

For a second there was silence. Then the screaming began. It was like no screaming that Joe had ever heard before, low-pitched, like the howling of wolves. The AKs were firing now, pumping round after round into the body of the bus. Something – blood? diesel? – began to trickle across the surface of the road. A couple of ducks, freed by the impact, stood for a moment by the stream, then fled, squawking, into the bush.

There was the sound of glass breaking. A man's head emerged from the interior of the bus, then a pair of arms as he levered himself upwards. He was shouting something, his black face pale with terror. For a moment he hung there, then his face was gone, red blood spattering the yellow paintwork.

Somebody stove in the rear window. People began to fall into the road, bleeding, screaming. The firing became intermittent as the bandits began to pick their targets. A woman in a blue dress with a baby. Two young men in light suits. The driver, his arm mangled, spreadeagled across the side window of his cab, twitching as the bullets slammed into him.

The people in the bus were coming out quickly now, faster

than the bandits could fire, scattering, running. A young boy of maybe fourteen almost made it before he twisted backwards, screaming, into the tall grass. A girl of twelve or so, bleeding from the wrist, threw herself headlong into the hole where the two officers lay. One of them caught at her, but she evaded him. The other picked up the machine gun, turned with it, and fired a burst at her retreating back. She fell, rolling over and over, and was still.

Still the people were coming. Some of the bandits had stopped firing and were fitting new magazines. Others, including the youth in the FANTA shirt, were tearing at the clothing on the still-twitching bodies, pocketing watches and small sums of money.

Taking advantage of the lull, a tall man in blue overalls, his face smeared with blood, broke free. At first it seemed that he too was making for the hole in which the two officers lay concealed, but at the last moment he veered to the right, and to Joe's horror began to climb the kopje, scrambling upwards over rocks, through thornbush, the harsh gasps of his breath clearly audible. A couple of shots, badly aimed, smacked into the red soil to his left, a third ricochetting away with a whine.

With a scarcely suppressed expletive, Ross rolled over twice, his FN at ready, and then the man was upon them, his feet catching at an exposed root, crashing forward. He was up immediately, his wild eyes meeting theirs, taking in the FNs, the webbing. Then he was gone, half-running, half-sliding, downwards into the bush.

There was smoke now, coming from the bus, and a single soft explosion. Flames began to flicker. The screams, which had died for a moment, began again, this time thinner, higher. An old woman, her clothes on fire, fell into the road and was immediately stilled by a single shot. Hands were visible, arms waving and curling from the broken windows. There was what sounded like a baby crying.

Then the fire took the bus, flames shooting skywards, black smoke pumping, and the screams were gone.

For a moment, even the bandits seemed stunned, pausing from their looting, falling back as the heat hit them. They were still watching, AKs cradled, when a shrill whistle made them turn.

The two officers, upright now, were gesticulating violently. The bandits hesitated then slowly, reluctantly, it seemed, drew back across the road, some of them coughing as a slight breeze blew smoke from the bus into their faces.

Where they went after that, Joe didn't see. He had his eyes closed and was retching up the contents of his stomach onto the red rocks at his side.

He couldn't see the smoke any more, but maybe he was looking in the wrong place. It had been there for a long time, hanging above the edge of the bush like a low-lying storm cloud. He wanted to ask Ross about the smoke, but he was walking too fast, and the sun was too hot.

He'd lost his bush hat someway back. He hadn't noticed it going and at first it hadn't bothered him, but now it felt like his head was going to explode. He groped at his pack for the spare, but couldn't find it. If they weren't walking so fast he could stop and look for it, but he'd tried stopping once already and Ross had got furious and jerked him onward. His thighs hurt where the rough material of his overalls rubbed them. He must have peed himself back there on the kopje without realising it. That was the only thing that would account for the wetness he felt. He tried walking splay-legged like a kid in a nappy, but it was too slow.

It was bad, and getting worse. Low scrub with a lot of fallen trees. Sometimes he could see Enos a long way away, sometimes the silver leaves hid him completely. Sometimes he lost Ross too. Each footstep was a conscious effort, an act of will that blocked all thought, all sensation except for pain. The pain was constant, unchanging. He was aware of mopani flies clustering at his mouth and eyes, but they no longer bothered him.

At the edge of a steep gully he tripped, falling awkwardly backwards onto his pack, and it was only when Ross forced water between his lips from a bottle that he realised he was crying. A spasm of pain, fresh pain, shot brainwards from his thigh, transfixing him like a lance thrust. 'Please,' he heard himself saying out loud, 'please, I've got to stop.'

'No way do you stop.' Ross's whisper seemed to come from a long distance away, like a dimly-heard voice from another room. There was a bush hat being pushed on to his head, hard hands beneath his armpits hauling him upwards. 'Now, walk,' the voice said.

He walked.

It was sometime later, a long time, that he heard the helicopters. There were two of them, sweeping the bush to the west. It was Ross stopping and pointing that made him realise they were there. It was cooler now, the sun reddening and expanding as it dropped, throwing the bubble shapes of the machines into silhouette. The helicopters were there for perhaps five minutes, no more, then they were gone, the beat of their engines lost in the shrill of the cicadas.

The sight of them seemed to cheer Ross. He made an obscene single-finger gesture in their direction, and flashed a grin. Joe responded weakly, uncomprehendingly, glad only of the rest.

They were close to a river as darkness fell, the Lundi it had to be. The bush thickened, tall trees drooping tangled lianas. Unseen birds squawked and yelled.

Ross's touch on his arm halted Joe suddenly. Enos, he could just see, was still moving, slowly now, merging into the gathering gloom. He returned soon afterwards as silently as he had gone, and sat down at the base of a thick-trunked tree. They sat down with him.

They sat there for a long time, drinking water, chewing biltong, sucking sweets. The darkness was intense, pierced by few stars. Enos and Ross conducted a conversation in a whisper so slight that it was a while before Joe realised it was happening. Something, geese probably, croaked softly in the middle distance.

Slowly Joe felt his strength returning. The intense headache that had battered at him during the last section of the march began to fade. If it really was the Lundi they were close to, they had come a long way he realised, a very long way. He swallowed a salt tablet that Ross gave him, and drank more water.

It was then that the noise began, soft at first, a muffled swish of what sounded like great feet, the occasional low rumble. Elephants. There seemed like hundreds of them. Straining his eyes he could just see their rounded shapes, like

242

mobile mountains, filing in procession towards the river.

For maybe fifteen minutes Joe watched them pass, the gentle sounds suddenly drowned by roars, belches, screams, as the lead animals hit the water, and reinforced instantly by other sharper noises. Buffalo he suspected. There was a sudden strong odour that reminded him of wet afternoons at the zoo.

He was glad of the stink and the noise. It stopped him thinking. The moon rose dimly, flickered and filled. He became aware that Enos had taken the loop of thick wire from his pack and was gently uncoiling it, and that Ross was checking and cleaning his gun.

He must have dozed, because he was only vaguely aware of them leaving; a whispered remark close to his ear, then the rustle of dead leaves. The sense of his own solitude intruded slowly. The bellowing from the river had quietened now, and was mingled with the sounds of lion and hyena. The moon had shifted and was hanging in the blackness of the sky almost overhead. He moved slightly to ease the growing stiffness in his shoulder, and unwrapped another sweet. For the first time for many years he wished he smoked.

It was difficult not to think. So difficult. It was the old woman who kept returning to trouble him. The flames leaping from her clothes, her face, toothless, lips stretched. It was the youth in the FANTA tee shirt who'd shot her, he now realised. His action of turning with the gun, aiming, pulling the trigger, replayed itself slowly in Joe's mind, occasionally splintering into fixed images like the frames on a strip of film. And the screams were there, too, mingling with the noises of the bush but harsher, more insistent.

He flipped the leather cover from his watch and tried to read the time. It was two something, it looked like, or maybe three. It seemed a long time already that they'd been gone. Something grunted and muttered from a tree close by, baboons or maybe a leopard. He felt curiously unafraid.

He rested his head on his arms and tried to sleep.

Shots. Those had to be shots. He jerked his head upwards, peering in the direction of the sound. There was a brief scream. Then silence.

He was thinking that maybe, just maybe, they'd been part of his dream, the shots, when he heard them again. A single crack then a cluster of three or four. There was a man's shout, an African voice using a language he didn't understand. And a crash of movement in the bush. He pressed himself closer to the tree, hoping that the shadow it cast would lend him invisibility.

Then he saw them. They were moving quickly, two figures caught momentarily in the moonlight, one of them carrying a dark bundle on his shoulders. There was a sharp comment in Shona. It was Ross's voice. He heard Enos grunt in reply. He waited for the owl hoot as they approached, but this time it didn't come.

Gasping with the effort, Enos threw the bundle he was carrying onto the carpet of leaves beyond the shadow of the tree. It was the youth in the FANTA tee shirt.

Joe was on his feet immediately, peering down at the face. 'He's dead,' he said out loud.

'He will be if you don't get out the fucking way! Just get a fucking bedroll, quick!' Ross's voice was tense, urgent.

With shaking fingers Joe unstrapped the roll from his pack, handed it to Ross who stuck it under the youth's neck, throwing his head back. Clearly visible around his throat was a single, vivid dark line, blurred here and there by what looked like trickles of blood.

Dropping to his knees, Ross took a deep breath, pinched the youth's nostrils tight with his thumb and forefinger, and applied his lips to the gaping mouth. Joe saw the youth's chest rise, falter, fall. Again Ross blew. Again the chest rose and fell.

Twice more he blew. Then he stopped, his fingers at the youth's neck, feeling for the carotid artery. 'Shit!' He spat the expletive at the face before him, clenched his fist and slammed it down hard into the centre of the youth's chest.

The noise of the blow was clearly audible. There was a sudden gasp, a gurgle. The youth's protruding ribcage quivered and expanded. Yet again Ross applied his lips, then swiftly whipped away the bedroll and swung him onto his side, left knee bent. The youth groaned loudly, and what looked like vomit or saliva trickled from his mouth. 'Jesus Christ,' said Ross quietly. And again. 'Jesus fucking Christ.' He knelt for a moment, head bowed, hands on knees.

The youth lay there for a long time. He vomited again. Breathed loudly, deeply. Enos, Joe noticed, had picked up an FN and was holding it aimed at the back of the youth's head. Ross stood up, wiped his mouth, pulled on his pack. He was obviously anxious to be going, yet concerned that the youth should have time to recover. Eventually, as if coming to a sudden decision, he swung to face Joe. 'Put your pack on. Help me get him up.' There was a harshness to his voice despite the whisper.

Joe did as he was told and, joining Ross, he hauled the boy to his feet. He stank of vomit, his head lolling, but he was breathing. Joe could feel the shudder as each draught of air entered his lungs.

Ross glanced at the sky, as if to check the stars, and they began to walk, supporting the limp body beneath the armpits, Enos following, one FN slung, the other held pointed at the space between the youth's shoulder blades.

At first the youth's legs dragged, but gradually they began to move, taking some of the weight. After maybe fifty yards he began to struggle, shouting once. Enos moved up close and hissed something in Shona, jabbing forward with the muzzle of his gun.

Immediately the struggles ceased. Joe could see the whites of the boy's eyes, feel the fear. Enos said something else, but it was obvious that the youth didn't understand him.

For two hours they walked. It was slow. On several occasions they stopped to give the boy water, which he drank with difficulty, grimacing with pain at each swallow. After a while he was able to walk unaided, though he was obviously still weak. Joe tried to ask Ross about the shooting but was cautioned to silence.

After moonset they stopped, resting against the smooth trunk of a fallen baobab tree, drinking more water. Ross dozed, his head slumped onto his chest. Enos stayed awake, his FN trained on the youth.

Dawn came in slowly, pale green fading to washed yellow. Still Ross slept. The boy, too, Joe noticed, had also fallen asleep, curled into a foetal position at Enos's feet.

Judging by the vegetation they were still close to the river. Vervet monkeys swung and chattered. Glossy long-tailed starlings looped from tree to tree. Joe checked his watch. It was five-thirty. Feeling suddenly hungry he took a strip of biltong from his pack and chewed at it. Enos, his FN resting across his legs, did the same. The black man caught Joe's eye and grinned, pointing down at the sleeping youth.

The veil of fatigue that had masked Joe's brain for the last two days suddenly lifted as the realisation sank in. They'd done it! They'd fucking done it. He glanced down again at the boy. He'd expected some sign of recognition from him, but so far there'd been none. He seemed so young, vulnerable in his exhaustion. He'd talk, Joe knew. There'd be no problem there. The urge to kick him awake, begin shouting questions at him became almost overwhelming. Christ, he missed them – Ellie, Cassie, Ben – more so now this boy had brought them closer. In two weeks, three weeks maybe, they'd be together again. He jerked a lump of biltong from the strip and chewed it violently. Looking up he saw that Enos was laughing at him gently, sharing his pleasure and anticipation. It was as if the events of the day before – the terror, the exhaustion, the killing – had never happened.

It was past six before Ross woke, angry at being allowed to sleep for so long. Ignoring Joe he immediately took the dull green radio from Enos's pack, screwed in the new Nicad from his own, and plugged in a flexible gooseneck aerial. Pausing only to check the maps, he picked up the handset and pressed the transmit bar. 'Zero Charlie. Zero Tango. Do you read?' With increasing urgency he repeated the call, his voice sounding unnaturally loud in the silence of the morning.

To Joe's surprise somebody, Jamie obviously, answered immediately.

The conversation was brief, clipped, hostile, Ross giving map references, answering questions in staccato monosyllables. He signed off, dismantled the set and replaced the components in the various packs. 'We've got two hours to cross this bloody river and pick up the track,' he said out loud, the hostility still in his voice. 'So let's quit pissing about. The sooner we're out of here the better. And I want silence from now on, is that clear?'

Joe nodded. The youth, who had woken at the sound of Ross's voice, sat up and looked round in terror. Enos jerked him violently to his feet.

They reached the track at seven-thirty, close to the deep gully that Joe remembered Jamie hitting at speed as they'd come down from the plateau. The tyremarks of two days before were still clearly visible. Ross indicated that they should sit down beneath a large, podded combretum, concealed from the road by a patch of dense thornbush.

Joe wondered if it was safe now to break silence but a glance at Ross decided him against it. He had picked up his FN and was beginning to clean it, working slowly and meticulously, stripping it down to its component parts, laying them out in order on his bush jacket, paying particular attention to the inside of the barrel, the chamber, and the gas mechanism. Joe watched, hypnotised almost by the firm, measured movement of cleaning rod and cloth. For half an hour Ross worked the gun in total silence before reassembling it. Doves, gathering in huge numbers in the trees round about, filled the air with their cooing. White butterflies flitted.

When he had finished, Ross fitted a new magazine and took over guard on the boy. Enos laid down, and seemingly went immediately to sleep. Lulled by the gathering heat, Joe too closed his eyes.

A sudden shout woke him. It was the youth, cowering back against the tree, blood gushing from his mouth. Ross stood over him, the butt of his rifle raised as if for a second blow. It didn't come. Slowly he lowered the gun, said something sharply in Shona, and sat down again. Enos, who had opened one eye to take in the scene, closed it. The boy whimpered slightly and dabbed at his mouth. Ross brushed a fly from his cheek, looked at Joe and shrugged.

The silence closed in once more.

It was maybe half an hour later that they heard the Land-Rover, revving high as it descended from the plateau, the dust from it clearly visible above the trees. They shouldered their packs and, hauling the boy to his feet, moved swiftly towards the road.

247

Jamie was travelling so fast that at first it looked like he hadn't seen their frantic signals as they emerged from the bush but then he slid to a halt fifty yards or so beyond them, reversed, turned, and drove slowly back. He ignored Joe's greeting, looked long and hard at the still-bleeding figure of the youth, and told them to get in. Enos propelled the boy into the back with the muzzle of his FN and closed the door. Ross and Joe joined Jamie in the cab.

For a while he said nothing, wrestling with the gears as the Land-Rover ground upwards away from the river. 'Why didn't you call in when you said?' he finally challenged them. 'Twice you missed. Twice! Once I could have understood, but twice, no.'

'It was too risky.' The sound of his own voice, after having been silent for so long, made Joe suddenly self-conscious.

'More risky than not calling in?'

'I don't understand . . .'

'Too right you don't. He does, though. He understands.' Jamie indicated Ross with a jerk of his thumb.

Ross made no acknowledgement of the gesture, staring straight ahead at the track. There was a screech as a protruding branch scraped along the side of the cab. Glancing sideways, Joe saw that Jamie was shaking with what looked like anger. 'Well?' the warden demanded.

'Well, what?' There was a hint of weariness in Ross's voice.

'Why didn't you call in?'

'Joe told you. It was too risky.'

Not taking his eyes from the road, Jamie said, 'You make me sick, you know that? You and people like you. I thought we'd got rid of you bastards when the war was over, but I was wrong. Bloody wrong. You ought to be stood up against a wall and shot. You know what's happened?'

'We've got some idea.'

'Twenty-seven people are dead, and God knows how many maimed for life. Twenty-seven! Including Simon, one of our houseboys. Emmy drove him to the road to catch that bus. He was going home to Chisumbanje to see his wife and children. You know about that bus?'

'Yes,' said Ross bluntly. 'We know about that bus.'

'Twenty-seven people.' Jamie's voice choked. 'Twenty-seven people. Women and little children. Christ Almighty, I'll never forgive myself for letting you bastards do what you did. Never.'

'There was nothing we could have done.' Ross's voice was neutral.

'Nothing! What do you mean, nothing? We sat by that wireless, me and Emmy, in shifts the whole time you were gone. You could have called in any time. Any time. But you didn't. Oh no. It was too risky. You might have had to stop what you were doing and let the Army do the job they're paid for.'

'We thought they were just going to rob the bus,' Joe said quietly. 'We had no idea they were going to . . .'

'With a bloody machine gun? You need a machine gun to rob a bus full of unarmed people?' Jamie broke off, forced to concentrate while the Land-Rover pitched and rose through a series of shallow gullies. They were near the top of the plateau now, the gradient easing. A group of black and white crows, pulling at something at the side of the road, rose into the air.

He turned, about to say more, but it was Ross who spoke. His voice was harder now. 'In the back of this Land-Rover is the one person in the whole of Zimbabwe who can lead us to Joe's wife and kids. That's why we went into the bush in the first place, to get that gook. And we got him, OK?'

'And sod the consequences. It doesn't matter to you that twenty-seven people are dead, just so long as you get the man you wanted. But then it wouldn't, would it? They're only blacks. Ignorant munts. They're of no importance. How much chance do you think there is of his wife and kids still being alive over the border? You tell me.' Jamie was almost in tears now.

'There's a good chance.'

'Enough chance to sacrifice the lives of twenty-seven people? And where the hell are the rest of those murdering bastards now? On their way home, congratulating themselves on a job well done?'

'No.'

'What do you mean no?'

'I mean no.'

A look of alarm spread quickly across Jamie's face. 'You

249

mean they're holed up somewhere waiting to do it again?'

'I mean they're dead.'

'You killed them?' Jamie's alarm turned to astonishment.

'Six of them. Maybe seven. They're just south of that big watercourse that joins the river near Chibveve Pool. The other two are somewhere in the bush. They've got no weapons and no water. We smashed up all the hardware they had. I guess Chenjerai can take care of them, or the Army. As you say, they need to do something to earn their money.'

There was a long silence. To the left, a curve of the Lundi became visible, sown with rapids, the sun glinting from the water. Joe glanced at Ross. It seemed impossible that so many of them could be dead. It had been over so quickly. There were so few shots. He felt a surge of admiration, tempered with slight fear. And Ross was right. There was no way they could have stopped that attack on the bus, no way. And even if there had been, he now knew he didn't care. They'd got the guy that mattered. It was simple, like Ross had said. Bloody simple.

'Ross is right, you know. There's nothing we could have done,' he said.

To his surprise, Jamie pulled the Land-Rover to a halt. He spoke quietly. 'Listen to me: I don't care what you could or could not have done. It doesn't alter what's happened. And the fact that you've killed those bastards doesn't alter it either. What am I going to tell Simon's wife when I see her? That I knew about those bandits? That I did nothing to stop them? You turn up. You eat our food, sleep in our beds, and then you do this to repay us. I don't want to see either of you again, is that clear?'

'That's pretty clear.' Ross seemed totally untroubled by Jamie's words.

'I should just kick you out here and now, but I don't trust you not to make more trouble. If you showed some remorse for what you've done, I'd maybe feel different. But you don't. As it is you can't come back to Chipinda – not that I'd allow you to even if it was possible. The place is crawling, and not just with Army. There's a bloody great police detachment camped outside my security fence right now. They were the ones who told me about the attack, about Simon. They've

250

even been asking bloody awkward questions about whose Land-Rover I've got parked there, stuffed with bush gear.'

'So what do you propose?' There was a note of contempt in Ross's voice.

'It's not what I *propose*, it's what I'm going to do. After you finally deigned to call in this morning, I got on to Jack Hammond. He's going to meet us to the north of here, where his land joins on to the park. What he does with you after that is his business.'

'That sounds fine to me,' Ross said.

'It all sounds fine to you. You don't give a shit, either of you. He's as bad as you are.' Jamie indicated Joe. 'Just don't try coming back, that's all.' He started the engine again. 'You know what the police and Army think? They think it's ZIPRA attacked that bus. They're probably into Matibi already, putting the boot into those poor sods yet again. And what happens when somebody tells them about you two cruising around there a couple of weeks ago asking questions? I suppose you told every Tom, Dick and Harry you met you were based at Chipinda with good old Jamie McAllister.'

'We told nobody.' There was threat, now, in Ross's words.

'But they'll know. What do I say when the Army turns up and starts asking who the hell you are?'

'You'll think of something.'

'Like what?'

'Like getting Chenjerai to go down to Chibveve and pick up those floppies, and calling up whoever's in command around here and presenting them to him on a plate. You never know, they might even give you a bloody medal.'

Jamie gave Ross a look of intense hatred, and jerked the Land-Rover into motion.

There'd been a track once, a long time ago, peeling out from the crook of the main track where it dipped down towards Chipinda. Glancing to his left as they entered it, Joe could see, far below, the khaki-clad figures of armed policemen milling around near the office complex. Two, possibly three, Puma ATCs drawn up in a line.

It was slow, very slow. Half-grown mopani and thorn saplings grew up from the centre of the track. Numerous fallen trees had to be sawn and shifted. A couple of times they had to winch the Land-Rover out of the deeper gullies. It was mid-afternoon before they reached the game fence that marked the northern boundary of the park and the beginning of the Flying Star.

There was another track, better maintained, on the other side of the fence, but no sign of Jack. Jamie swung the Land-Rover to a halt, 'Out,' he said, 'And don't break down the bloody fence when you get through it.' They were the first words, apart from comments on the state of the track, that he'd spoke in the past three hours. As he drove off, bouncing from sight between the low mopani, Joe realised that he'd failed to ask for the return of the radio or the FN.

Beyond the fence they established themselves beneath a broad acacia and waited. Ross got out a stove and brewed tea which the boy refused. They mixed and ate a bowl of pronutria each, and finished the last of the biltong. The boy ate the food he was given with a speed and ferocity that shocked Joe, gulping it down in huge mouthfuls despite the obvious pain from his throat.

For a short time after they'd eaten, Ross tried to question the boy in Shona, but it seemed that apart from a few simple commands, he understood nothing. They'd need a Shangaan speaker for the interrogation, it was obvious. Joe hoped that Jack would be able to come up with somebody.

It was pleasant under the tree, doubly pleasant because they were able to talk again. Enos lit a pipe and puffed cheerfully. Ross lay back, his head against his pack, bush hat tilted over his face. The youth, too, seemed to sense the mood, his eyes travelling between the three of them constantly, giving him something of the air of a trained sheepdog, ready to respond to the slightest command.

Only Joe found it difficult to relax. Despite the sense of exhilaration he felt at the boy's presence, Jamie's remarks about the Army going into Matibi worried him. He mentioned his worries to Ross who laughed. 'He's not stupid. The moment he gets back to Chipinda he'll get together with Chenjerai and they'll work out something between them. He'll move heaven and earth to avoid trouble. Chenjerai will be keen enough to claim the glory for slotting those gooks, and he'll no doubt round up the two who escaped. Why the hell should the army bother about us, even if somebody in Matibi does volunteer the information, which I very much doubt? They'll be quite happy to get back to barracks and let Zvarevashe tell the world about the latest inhuman ZIPRA atrocity, and how the Army moved in to restore law and order. It's all power to their elbow.'

'You seem very sure of that.'

Ross laughed again. 'This is Zimbabwe, man, not England. Nobody gives a shit about the truth unless it suits them.'

'And it won't suit them this time?'

'When does it ever?'

Joe noticed that Enos, too, was laughing.

Jack arrived at four-thirty, alone in the jeep. He greeted them tersely, told them to get in, turned and drove at speed back in the direction from which he had come. Joe and Ross sat on the canvas seats beside him. Enos and the boy stood in the back, clutching the roll bar.

They followed the game fence for a short distance, then swung north. The track was rough but passable, edged with low thorn and mopani scrub. Shouting to make himself heard above the noise of the engine, Ross said, 'It's good of you to come, Jack.'

He shrugged. 'Jamie didn't leave me too much alternative. He reckons I'm as responsible as you are for what happened, and I think I agree with him. Was there no way you could have stopped it, for Christ's sake?'

'No way.'

'I wish I could believe you.'

'They're dead,' Joe said.

'Who's dead?'

'The bandits who did it.'

Jack turned to Ross. 'You?'

Ross nodded slowly. 'Six, probably seven. A couple got away. I told Jamie to tell Chenjerai to go after them.'

Jack was silent for a while. 'That's something, anyway,' he said. He indicated the boy in the back. 'And that little runt's the one you were after, is he?'

'Yes.'

'Shangaan?'

253

'I reckon so. He understands a bit of Shona, not much.'

'So you haven't got anything out of him yet?'

'Nothing.'

Jack shook his head. 'I couldn't believe it when I heard what had happened. It wasn't a robbery, it was a bloody massacre. I don't understand it. Why the hell did they trek all that way just to kill a load of innocent people? What were they trying to achieve, for Christ's sake? Apparently they hardly stole anything.'

'A few things,' said Joe. 'They stole a few things.'

'You saw it?' Jack's face creased with disbelief. 'You actually saw it happen?'

'We were on a kopje near the road.'

'And you still did nothing to stop it?'

Ross's voice hardened. 'We had two FNs between us. They had a bloody RPD as well as God knows how many AKs. What do you suggest we did? We tried to take them the night before, but it just wasn't on.'

'So you just watched it happen?'

'It wasn't very pleasant,' Joe said.

'No,' said Jack with heavy irony. 'I don't suppose it was.'

They drove on in silence through level, featureless bush. A small herd of impala, disturbed by their passing, bounded away, leaping like grasshoppers. After a while, Jack glanced at Ross and said, 'So what do I do with you now, hey?'

'We'll go back to Harry Barton's place.'

'You must be joking. There's half the bloody Zimbabwe Army rampaging up and down the Chiredzi road. In a day or two I could get you there, maybe, but tonight, no way. No, I've been thinking about this one. You need to keep your heads down for a while until this lot blows over, for my sake as well as yours, and you need somewhere to work on that little bastard you've got in the back there. I'd take you to the house, but it's too risky. The Army are bound to show at some point, and even if they don't somebody's going to start asking questions. So I thought what I'd do is take you up to a place I've got on the Mulovelo River. I built it sometime back for the Yank hunters so its pretty comfortable. Nobody'll disturb you there, I guarantee that. Suit you?'

'It'll suit us,' Ross said.

Jack cleared his throat, spat out over the side of the jeep. 'I thought it might,' he said.

It was dark when they reached the Mulovelo River, and Joe was surprised to see lights burning. There was what looked like a largish square hut surrounded by a tall security fence. Behind it, still within the compound, were three or four thatched rondavels, their white walls reflecting the dazzle of the headlights. Jack swung the jeep through a pair of high gates onto a patch of beaten earth in front of the main hut, pulled to a halt and switched off the engine. A tiny black man in baggy khaki shorts and a white singlet came out to greet them. He had bare feet. 'This is Thomas,' Jack said as they got out. 'He's from Malawai and legally he ought to be there still. Soul of discretion, Thomas.'

Thomas grinned broadly. 'You want to eat, baas?' he said in good English.

Jack nodded. 'We want to eat.' To Joe he said, 'I dropped off some supplies on my way down so there's plenty to keep you going. He's not a bad cook, Thomas. I got him to clear that lockup shed round the back there. We'll stick our friend in there for the time being and talk to him later, after we've had a shower and some scoff.'

'A shower?' Joe was astonished.

Jack laughed. 'You look like you could use one. The amounts those Yanks pay to come here, they expect it. There's water purification, a Meadows generator to give us a little light, pink toilet paper. . . . You name it, just like home. This is where we eat and do anything else we feel like doing.' He walked swiftly into the main hut.

It was open-fronted, furnished with a long trestle table and camp chairs. A couple of bare bulbs hung from the rafters. To the rear of the hut was an open door, beyond it the three rondavels, an ablution block, and behind that, a few yards to the right, a low breeze-block shed roofed with tin. The whole compound was shaded by a couple of huge acacias, hung with the inevitable weaver bird nests.

Jack said something to the boy in what Joe took to be Shangaan, and they led him through towards the shed. As they approached it, the youth's eyes widened with fear. Jack spoke to him again, this time in a sharp voice, and Enos propelled him inside with the muzzle of his FN. The door was shut, bolted, padlocked. Enos prepared to take up position at the door, but Jack stopped him. 'You go and wash up,' he said. 'Our friend won't be going anywhere.'

The rondavels were neat, small-windowed, with smooth concrete floors. Joe and Ross were to share the centre one, Jack said. Enos could sleep in the one on the right. Inside the centre hut were a pair of camp beds, a couple of hard chairs and an oil lamp. There was a clean bush shirt laid out on each of the pillows. Jack was right. It was just like home. Better. Joe groaned, threw himself face down on to the grey blankets of the nearest bed, kicked off his shoes. 'You clean up first,' he said to Ross.

Ross had to wake him for his shower, and it was perfect, the most perfect he could remember. The water, heated outside in a tank by a mopani wood fire then piped into the compact shower room, was lukewarm and caressing. He let it play on him for a while, not moving, and then, shocked by the sight of his face in the mirror, spent a long time scrubbing at the sweat-streaked blacking that stained his skin. There was pink, scented soap, and on a rail a collection of neatly folded green towels. Afterwards, dressed in the clean shirt, he joined Ross, Jack and Enos at the long table, and they ate steak and sadza served by the cheerful Thomas, and drank a couple of Castles each, miraculously chilled, while moths and beetles twisted and darted at the electric bulbs.

They talked while they ate but it was as if temporary censorship had been imposed. Joe found himself, like the others, for some reason avoiding any mention of the bus, or the boy waiting to be questioned. Instead, Jack spoke of a trip he'd made before Christmas up to a mission to the west of the Mwenezi River, and the starvation he had found there. The nuns were getting a hundred and fifty cases of malnourished children a month at the mission clinic, and many deaths, he said. The women were gathering at the mining posts and stores and offering themselves as prostitutes to get money to feed themselves and their children. And even then, when they had money, there was often no food to buy. The truck drivers would bring beer down into the tribal lands, he said, because they could charge a premium on it. But not mealie meal.

They spoke a little, too, of London, and the IRA bomb that had exploded outside Harrods in December, and the coup in Nigeria. Enos, who seemed to be remarkably well-informed, joined in with the occasional quiet comment and puffed at his pipe. The moon rose.

It was almost nine before Jack got up from the table and went with Enos to fetch the boy, pausing to close and lock the gates of the security fence. Hyenas were beginning to call in the distance.

They stood the boy beneath one of the bulbs at the end of the table and waited while Thomas brought him a plate of food, a mound of sadza sprinkled with chopped meat and a few beans. The boy again ate ravenously, using his hands, gulping water from a plastic jug between mouthfuls, glancing apprehensively at the gathered circle of faces, at the FN on Enos's lap as he did so. His lip, where Ross had hit it, had swollen, giving his face a lopsided appearance. The mark of the wire was still vivid on his neck.

Watching him eat, Joe felt the excitement, the anticipation, lulled by the comfort of the shower, the beer and the meal, begin to return. He examined the boy's face closely, searching for signs of recognition in him but seeing none. He ate like a frightened animal in whom starvation has temporarily overcome fear.

When he had finished, Thomas was called to fetch the empty plate and there was the sound of running water from the cook hut at the side. Ross leaned back on his chair, put his feet on the table, turned to Jack and said, 'Tell him we're going to ask him some questions. And tell him that if he doesn't tell the truth we shall kill him like we killed his comrades.' His voice was neutral, disinterested almost, like a continuation of the conversation they'd been having.

Jack raised an eyebrow and took a sip of his beer. 'I take it you've appointed yourself question master,' he said.

'Take it how you like.'

Jack shook his head slowly then shifted to face the boy. He spoke in Shangaan.

At first it seemed like the boy had not heard. He stood

motionless, quivering slightly, staring down at the floor. Jack repeated his words more loudly, and this time the boy replied. His voice was hesitant, almost inaudible, distorted with fear. Jack said, 'It's going to be difficult. It's a different dialect, hard to understand, but he says he'll answer the questions.'

Ross nodded slowly, glanced at Enos and grinned. 'I thought he might say that. Ask him his name. Where he comes from.'

Jack put the question to the boy. Again the reply was a long time coming. 'He says his name is Jonas Ndima. He says he comes from Muzamane in Gaza province.'

'And how old is he?'

'He says he is eighteen.'

'Ask him how long he's been a member of the MNR.'

This time the boy appeared genuinely not to understand. He glanced quickly at Ross, then at Jack. Joe could sense his terror increasing. Ross suddenly swung his feet from the table and thumped on it with his fist. Beer bottles rattled. One fell and rolled slowly in a semicircle. The boy jumped as if shot. He began to talk quickly, then stopped. 'Well?' said Ross.

There was irritation in Jack's voice. 'He says he was kidnapped two years ago and forced to work for the blangueti.'

'Blangueti? What the fuck's the blangueti? Tell him we don't understand this word blangueti. Sounds like bloody Italian food.' Ross laughed briefly.

'I'll try him with Renamo. Maybe he'll understand that.' Jack put the word to the boy who nodded vigorously and without prompting launched into a long, rapid speech. When he had finished he stood, panting slightly, looking at Jack.

Jack shrugged. 'I understood about half of that. I think what he said is that he was out looking after his father's cattle when he was captured by some men with guns. Blangueti seems to be a nickname for them. He was then taken to a camp near Machaze in Manica province and told that if he tried to escape he would be killed. He was given a gun . . .' Here Jack broke off and addressed another question to the boy who replied equally volubly. Jack nodded and resumed. 'He says he had two weeks' training and then was told to go out and get food.'

'He can't have been too good at it, by the look of him,' said Ross, and grinned.

'He says he attacked lorries and stores to get food.'

'All on his own?'

'There were eight of them, he says.'

It was going to take a long time, Joe sensed. A very long time. His anticipation was giving way to impatience. 'What about Ellie?' he said to Ross. 'I want to know about Ellie.'

'We'll get to that.'

'When?'

'When I'm ready.' Ross spoke curtly, almost brutally. To Jack he said, 'Ask him how long he stayed at this place, at Machaze.'

'He says a year.'

'And then?'

It was Jack's turn to get impatient. He said. 'Do we have to go through all this, for God's sake? Let's just ask him what the hell happened back in August.'

Ross was quiet for a moment then he said, very slowly. 'If you think you can do this better than I can, just say the word and I'll piss off.'

Jack spread his hands wide. 'OK, you know best. You always did.'

'What's that supposed to mean?'

'You know.'

There was a long, awkward silence. Enos tapped out his pipe loudly into an ashtray. Unable to stand it any longer, Joe said, 'Please, Ross, just get on with it.'

'In my own way?'

'Any bloody way.' He was like a child, Joe thought. A bloody spoilt, stupid child.

Jack spoke again to the boy. There was a lengthy reply. 'I've just asked him what he did after he left Machaze. Happy now?' He looked at Ross.

'I'll be happier when you've told me what he said.'

'He says he was taken to a big camp in Inhambane province and given more training.'

'What was the name of this camp?'

'Tomé.'

'Ask him if he saw any white people there.'

'You mean Ellie?' said Joe quickly.

'I mean white people.'

Jack put the question. The boy hesitated then replied cautiously. 'He says there were six white men there.'

'Portuguese?'

'English. He says they spoke English. They came by helicopter. He says there was plenty of food at Tomé.'

'Did they train him, these white men?'

The boy shook his head at the question, muttered his reply. 'He says they didn't train him, but they were there. He was taught to use and RPG7 and an RPD.'

'And then?'

'He went back to Manica province to a new camp near a place called Macobere. He says they were told to attack buses and health posts. He says there was no more food.'

'So they decided to come across to Zimbabwe to look for food?'

'He says yes.'

'Who decided this?'

'His unit leader.'

'Name?'

'He says he was called Tomate.'

'And this was in August last year?'

'Yes. He says that Tomate had been to Zimbabwe before and knew where to get food. He says Tomate knew a way through the minefield.'

'What minefield?' said Joe.

Not looking at him, Ross said. 'There's a minefield three kilometres wide along the border. It was laid during the war. The Army are supposed to have cleared it, but that's a matter of opinion.' To Jack he said, 'Ask him what happened then.'

Jack relayed the question. 'He says they didn't find any food so they went towards the west. After three days they came to a road. Tomate told them to wait. After a long time they saw a car. There was a white man and a woman and two children in the car.'

Joe leaned forward and rested his arms on the table. He was uncomfortably aware of the pressure of his heart pounding against his ribs. He took a sip of his beer. It tasted warm and sour. 'This guy Tomate,' he said, 'did he have a beard? Some kind of skin complaint?'

Joe watched the boy closely as Jack translated. Surely the boy had to recognise him now. But there was nothing. His face remained blank, registering only quiet fear. His reply came back in the same monotone. Jack said, 'He confirms that. Tomate had a beard, bad skin. It was him who pulled the trigger, I presume?'

Joe nodded.

'Not the kind of face you forget in a hurry, hey?' Jack smiled sympathetically. The boy began speaking again. He spoke for a long time. After a while Jack interrupted him. 'He's going too fast for me to keep up, so I've had to stop him. What he's saying is basically this: they stopped the car and took food and money and went into the bush. They took the people from the car with them. When they got a short way from the road, the white man tried to escape, so Tomate shot him.'

'He's lying.' A surge of anger smacked at Joe's guts like a kick from a horse.

'I'm just telling you what he says.' Jack spoke mildly.

'And I say he's fucking lying! I was trying to get to Cassie. She'd cut her leg. It was bleeding. I was trying to get to her. That's what I was trying to do. Make him tell you. Just make him fucking tell you!'

'Take it easy, hey?' Joe felt Ross's hand on his shoulder.

He wrenched it free. He was shouting now, screaming. 'You won't make him tell you? OK, well I will! I'll make him tell you!' He launched himself across the table towards the boy. Beer bottles flew. 'You tell them the truth, you little bastard, or I'll kill you! I'll fucking kill you!'

There was an arm round his neck, throttling the breath from his body, forcing him back into his chair. Ross's voice shouting something at him. He fought the encircling arm, but the grip was too strong . . .

For a moment longer he struggled, and then the anger left him as suddenly as it had come. He felt weak and close to tears. Ross released him and he slumped forward onto the table, head on hands. 'I'm sorry,' he was saying. 'I'm sorry.'

He remained for a while, eyes closed, conscious only of Cassie's face, her voice calling him. Then, slowly, he became aware of Jack saying something to him, telling him to relax, saying that he believed him, telling him to have another beer.

He looked up, not at Jack but at the boy. There was a change in him, Joe could see instantly. There was more than terror in his eyes now, almost a kind of awe.

Ross, too, was aware of it. He gave a rumble of laughter. 'I think the penny's dropped, man. I think he finally knows who you are. I reckon he thinks you're a ghost.'

The boy backed away slightly, glancing out towards the bush. He went a couple of steps until a shout from Ross stopped him. Enos had the FN levelled.

The boy swayed slightly, seeming close to collapse. Jack pulled a chair forward motioned him to sit down. There was a sudden strong stench.

'He's shat himself,' Ross said, laughing again. 'The little bastard's shat himself. Hey, Jack, how about you telling him that Joe here's an ngozi. See what he says to that.'

'Don't be stupid.'

'Just tell him, hey? Say that if he tells us a single lie again we'll hand him over to Joe.'

Jack gave Ross a slow look of disgust.

'OK,' said Ross, still laughing. 'I'll tell him. Hey, you, Jonas! Ngozi, hey?' He pointed at Joe.

The effect was immediate. The boy buckled into the chair, his eyes rolling high into their sockets, the muscles of his face taut and twisted. There was a froth of spittle on his lips.

'You bastard,' said Jack slowly. 'You utter bastard.'

'Will somebody tell me what's going on, for God's sake?' Joe was watching the boy with increasing alarm. He was in spasm now, jerking like a puppet.

Ross's laughter intensified. There were tears in his eyes he was laughing so much. 'Just look at him, man!' he was saying. 'Just look at him. Have you ever seen anybody so fucking terrified, hey? Give the little bastard a taste of his own medicine, right?'

Jack stood up suddenly. 'I'm going to bed. I can't take any more of this. You make me sick.' He threw a bunch of keys on to the table, and walked quickly out of the rear door.

Joe was on his feet immediately, following him. He caught up with him near the ablution block. 'Jack, for God's sake! He still hasn't told us about Ellie. You can't just walk away.'

'I can do whatever I like.'

'Please, I need your help.'

'You know what he's just done, your friend Ross?'

'No.'

'He's probably frightened the poor little bastard to death. I mean it. I'm not joking. You know what an ngozi is?'

Joe shook his head.

'It's an avenging spirit, the worst kind. It might be hard for you to believe, maybe, but that boy believes it. They're killers, these spirits. They come to avenge a death. People literally die of fright, or they go mad when they think there's an ngozi after them. He's a bloody sadist, that man Tobin. A bloody sadist. I was beginning to think he'd changed since the war, but he hasn't. He never bloody will.'

'But I've got to find out about Ellie.' Joe was beseeching now. 'Please.'

Jack softened suddenly. 'Tomorrow morning, hey? There'll be time enough then, if that poor sod makes it through the night.'

He turned and disappeared into the ablution block.

Joe didn't go back to the main hut. Instead, he went to the rondavel and lay down on the bed, overwhelmed by exhaustion and despair. He heard the slamming of a door, the shuffle of feet. Ross and Enos passed close by, talking in undertones, presumably taking the boy back to the shed. There was a sudden silence as the low hum from the generator cut, then darkness. He decided to stay awake until Ross came in. There were things to say, questions he wanted to ask. But exhaustion claimed him, and still fully dressed, still with his veldschoens on his feet, he fell into a profound sleep.

The sun woke him, slanting through the window above his bed, hitting him full in the face. For a moment he stared blankly at the tight pattern of thatch in the rafters above his head, not knowing where he was. Then he remembered the boy. He sat up suddenly, his whole body aching, and looked across at Ross's bed. It was empty though there were signs that it had been slept in. The boy, for Christ's sake! He went out at a run.

It was late, gone eight o'clock, the sun already above the barbed wire rim of the security fence. Thomas, carrying a yellow plastic bucket of water, grinned and said: 'Morning baas.' Joe nodded, uncertain. There were voices from the main hut: Ross and Jack.

They were at the table, sitting in the same places as the night before. A large enamel teapot and a sprinkling of mugs had replaced the beerbottles. 'The boy . . .' Joe said.

Jack smiled. 'He's fine. Enos and Thomas are seeing to him. Cleaning him up a bit.'

'But you said . . .'

'We went to see him last night, Ross and me, after you were asleep. We had a word with him. He's still not too certain about you, but he's OK. When Enos and Thomas have done we'll get him over here and carry on where we left off. Have some tea.'

Jack pushed the teapot across the table. With unsteady hands Joe poured himself a cup. He looked at Ross. He seemed different this morning, quieter, chastened almost. 'Sleep well?' The thin man said.

Joe nodded.

'I meant to talk to you last night, but you were out cold.' Ross seemed unsure of himself. 'Listen, I'm sorry about what happened. I don't know what came over me. I could have fucked things up really badly. It was only thanks to Jack that I didn't.'

The rancher shrugged. 'We had a long talk, Ross and I, sorted a few things out. We'll get somewhere this morning, I promise you. We've decided that I'll ask the questions. It'll be quicker apart from anything. That doesn't mean you have to keep quiet, of course, but I think it'll be better if I do most of the talking.'

Maybe it was the fatigue that was still with him despite the sleep, but Joe felt confused, unsteady. He looked at both men in turn, trying to understand. 'He really thought I was one of those ngonis, did he?'

'Ngozis.' Jack nodded. 'Oh, yes. It runs bloody deep, especially across the border where they don't get too much education.'

'And you're sure he'll be OK now?'

'You can't be sure of anything, but I reckon so.'

Joe sipped at his tea. It was over-brewed and bitter. There

264

was an awkward silence. Ross stood up suddenly. 'I'll go check how they're getting on,' he said, seeming glad of the excuse to go.

There was another longer silence. Joe became aware of the cooing of doves. Glancing out between the poles that supported the roof he saw that the lodge had been built on a low rise overlooking a dried up river. To the left was the earth wall of a small dam, and beyond it the reflected blue of a pool. The bush stretched out featureless to a range of blue hills on the horizon. 'What was it you and Ross sorted out, then?' he said.

'A few things.'

'Things from the war?'

Jack nodded. 'Misunderstandings. I told him my side of the story. He told me his.'

'What happened? It must have been pretty bad.'

Jack paused. 'It's over,' he said. 'It's a long time ago. Maybe I'll tell you sometime but not now.' He glanced round. 'You want something to eat? Some bread or something? I'll call Thomas.'

Joe said he wasn't hungry.

There was still fear in the boy's eyes, but he seemed calmer now. Somehow Jack seemed to have won his confidence. He was no longer wearing the FANTA tee shirt but a voluminous bush shirt and shorts, the size of the garments emphasising his acute thinness. Jack steered him to the chair at the end of the table. There were no guns visible.

When the boy had sat down, Jack spoke to him for a while softly in Shangaan, once or twice emphasising points with movements of his hands. The boy made no response, his eyes straying from Jack from time to time to rest upon Ross or Enos but avoiding Joe. When Jack had finished, the boy remained silent for a long time. Then suddenly he began to talk. Eventually he stopped. Jack translated.

'He's talking about what happened after you were shot, Joe. He says Tomate was worried about the Army, so they took the woman and children further into the bush. Then, when they had got a long way from the road, they stopped. Tomate was going to kill the woman and children with an axe but then the woman said something to him in his own language, Shona presumably, and he decided not to kill them.'

Joe could feel the tension mounting in him again. An axe! Christ, it could have been worse, so much worse than he'd even imagined in all those bad dreams. 'What in God's name did she say to him?' he asked quickly.

'He says he doesn't know. I didn't realise your wife could speak Shona.'

'Oh, she can speak it all right. She's a good linguist. Bloody good. I wonder what the hell she said?' Joe found himself suddenly close to tears. 'She's bloody amazing, you know. A bloody amazing woman. Christ. . . .'

Jack reached out, squeezed his arm. 'In that case, we'd better get on and find her, hey?' He smiled and turned back to the boy.

There was another lengthy exchange in Shangaan. Eventually, seemingly satisfied, Jack said, 'Apparently, after that, they travelled back to the place where they had crossed the border, presumably down there in Chief Chingela's territory. It took them four days, he says.'

'And the kids? What's he say about the kids?'

'He says they got very tired and they had to carry them. He says the woman didn't get tired. He says that when they got back into Mozambique they went to the place he told us about yesterday where he had been sent to train: Tomé. It took them ten days to get there.'

'And Ellie and the kids were still OK, were they?'

'He says yes, they were still all right. He says he was pleased to go to Tomé because he knew there was always food there.'

'So what happened then?'

Jack broke off for more conversation with the boy. Then he said, 'The Commander-in-Chief at Tomé, who's name was apparently Maianga or something similar, got very angry and beat Tomate with a kwekwere, that's a rubber whip.'

'There's some justice in the world, hey?' Ross gave Joe a wink. It was his first comment of the morning.

Jack continued, 'He says that the white woman and children were put in a separate place.'

'What sort of place?' Joe asked,

'He doesn't know. There were other people there who had been captured. Maybe they were put with them.'

266

'And what about these white men he mentioned yesterday? How did they react to what had happened?' Ross asked.

'He says he doesn't know.'

Joe said, 'And they're still there, are they? Ellie and the kids. At this Tomé place?'

'No. Apparently a few days after they arrived at Tomé it was attacked by the FPLM – the Mozambican Army. It was a very big attack, he says. Many shells.'

'Christ.'

'He says that when the attack began he managed to escape, and went north with his comrades to Manica province.'

'And they took Ellie and the kids with them?'

'No.'

Joe's alarm intensified. 'Then what the hell's happened to them? Did the Army. . . ?'

'He says he doesn't know what happened to them during the attack, but he has heard something about them. He says he's heard that they were taken to a place called Nhamasi.'

'By the Army?'

'No, not by the Army. He says this place Nhamasi is in the mountains.'

'Which mountains?'

'He says he doesn't know what they're called. He says they are in Manica province.'

'There's a lot of fucking mountains in Manica province,' said Ross slowly. 'Can't he be a bit more specific?'

'I don't think so.'

'But they're still there are they?' Joe was frantic now. 'They're still OK? They weren't hurt or anything. I . . .'

'He says he thinks they're still there. He doesn't know if they were hurt or not.'

'Oh, Jesus.'

Jack paused, looked at Joe sympathetically. 'I don't think he knows anything else, Joe. I'm sorry.'

There was a brief silence. Joe breathed deeply, fighting to gain control of his racing heart. Then Ross said, 'Did you ask him if he's been to this Nhamasi place?'

Jack shook his head, turned to the boy and put the question. 'He says yes, he has been to Nhamasi on several occasions, but not since the white woman and children were taken there.'

'So he knows how to get there?'

'He says yes. He says it is four days to the north of the Save River.'

Ross glanced out at the bush for a moment, calculating. 'That's a hundred k. at the most. Somewhere round about Espungabera, I guess.' He looked at Joe. 'I reckon this little gook had better take us there, don't you, Joe? Then we can find out for ourselves how Ellie and the kids are doing. What do you say?'

'What do you think?' he said quietly.

They spoke to the boy for a while longer, but it was obvious that he knew nothing more about Ellie. After he had escaped from Tomé, he said, he'd joined up with a group of comrades and they'd set up a new base at a place called Mossurize, close to the Zimbabwe border. They'd made several raids across into Zimbabwe, looking for food, always crossing the border at the same place. Several times they'd killed elephants and forced the local peasants to transport the meat for them. Sometimes planes had dropped ammunition for them by parachute. They'd been attacked by a Mozambican Army unit in November and in the resulting firefight several of them had been killed, including Tomate. Then they'd been given a new leader called Zamchiya. He had come from Chinhica Camp. There were white men there. Two weeks ago, one of the white men had come to Mossurize and had told Zamchiya to go into Zimbabwe and kill many people. He didn't know why. Ross asked him quickly if he knew the white man's name. He said he didn't.

'So what now?' Jack asked.

They'd put the boy back into the shed and were eating bread and cheese and drinking more tea. It was noon, and it was getting hotter.

'We go over and find them and bring them back. What the hell else do you expect us to do?' Ross chewed at a piece of cheese and swallowed audibly.

'Joe could go to Harare and see the British High Commissioner. Now we know where they are and who's got them, they could put pressure on.'

'Don't be stupid. What's he going to tell them when they

ask him how he's found out about all this? They won't believe him, and if they do we'll find ourselves up to our necks in shit. In any case, who's to say they're still at this Nhamasi place?'

'The boy thinks they are.'

'We'll see about that.'

'They're useless,' Joe said. 'Bloody useless.' The tension of the interrogation had faded, and he was surprised to find himself feeling calm and decisive.

'Who are?' Jack asked.

'The British High Commission. I've met them. I know what they're like. They'll do fuck all, and anything they do will take months – years, probably. And what about the Zimbabwe government? Do you think they're going to admit they lied about it being ZIPRA? That they tortured that poor bastard to get a confession out of him? Ross is right. We've got to go in there ourselves.'

Jack sighed deeply. 'I suppose you're right,' he said. 'But it'll be bloody risky.'

'So?'

'I mean, if you go over, if you find out where they are, how do you propose to get them out? Go up to whoever's in charge and ask politely? There'll be three of you – four if you take the boy, which I presume you will. You're going to take on a whole camp full of trained insurgents, are you? The four of you?'

'If we have to.' Ross spoke quietly.

'You're crazy.' Jack shook his head. 'You're bloody crazy. You want to commit suicide, do you?'

Joe saw the muscles in Ross's jaw tighten and waited for the explosion. To his surprise, none came. Instead, Ross picked up a second piece of cheese, folded it into a slice of bread and resumed eating.

'And what about weapons, hey?' Jack continued. 'I've got one more FN, but I've got hardly any ammo. Jamie's got plenty down at Chipinda, but he's hardly likely to hand it over in the circumstances.'

Ross glanced at Enos who was once more smoking his pipe. 'Don't worry about weapons,' he said.

Jack switched his gaze quickly from Ross to Enos then back

again. 'I was right,' he said with sudden vehemence. 'I was bloody right! I knew you bastards had put down a cache somewhere around here. They were in those trucks you brought in. When was it, round about Christmas '79? Am I right?'

Ross shrugged.

'I'm right. Christ, there must be enough for an entire bloody army there. How many loads did you bring in? Four? Five?'

Ross took another bite. Enos puffed at his pipe.

Jack swung to face Joe. 'You know what these bastards thought? They thought there was going to be bloody civil war after Lancaster House, and they thought the poor bloody munts would call them in to sort the whole mess out. They had the whole thing sussed, so they thought. They were going to seize the key buildings, surround the ZANLA assembly points – Operation Quartz, they called it. And just in case things went a little wrong, they stuck a few arms caches around the place, like right here on this ranch. They couldn't believe it when Mugabe won; still can't, after four years. Oh, yes, you'll be OK for weapons. Houtie slayers, that's what they used to call them. And if you find out where they are, just let me know, hey? I could do with them off my property.'

He drained his tea and stood up. 'Listen, I've got to go back to the house. I've got things to see to. I'll be back in the morning. Make yourself comfortable. Thomas'll look after you. Anything you want me to get?'

'You got any maps?' Ross said.

'Of Mozambique? You must be joking. Are there any? I've got a couple of one in two hundred and fifty thousand sheets of Chiredzi and Chipinga. They stretch over the border a bit, but there's not a lot of detail.'

'Bring them.'

Jack saluted ironically. 'Yes, sir. Anything else you require?'

'A couple of old tyres and as much fencing wire as you can spare.'

'Tyres?'

'Tyres.'

Jack raised an eyebrow. 'Your wish is my command.' He

opened the security gates, threw his keys at Ross, got into the jeep and was gone.

When the noise of the engine had died, and the dust had melted into the yellow haze that hung over the bush. Ross got up and went out of the rear door. He returned soon afterwards with one of the FNs and a cleaning kit. He laid them on the table in front of Joe. 'OK,' he said. 'It's time for afternoon school. Strip it. Clean it. Stick it together again. By the time we're finished I want you to be able to do it with your eyes closed.'

Joe looked at Ross, picked up the gun and held it uncertainly. There was a lot he wanted to talk about, and it hadn't included dismantling an FN. 'We ought to discuss things.'

'Later, when you've done the gun.'

'About the boy . . .'

'Strip it.'

Joe lowered the rifle gently on to the table. Enos, he could see, had settled back in his chair with a grin on his face, obviously contemplating an afternoon's entertainment. Ross said, 'You watched me do it enough times back there in the bush.'

'Yes, but . . .'

'Try removing the magazine, hey?'

Joe picked up the gun again and pulled at the magazine. It failed to budge. Enos burst into peals of laughter then threw up his hands in mock terror. The muzzle of the FN, Joe realised, was pointing straight at his chest. He swung the gun away, wrenched again at the magazine. 'It's stuck!' he said, between gritted teeth.

Enos's laughter intensified. 'It's stuck!' he mimicked. 'It's stuck, Ross!'

Despite himself, Joe too began to laugh. 'Bastards,' he said.

Ross removed the gun gently from his hands. 'OK,' he said. 'You watch. Number one, put the weapon at safe. I'd taken the precaution of doing that already, luckily for Enos. Number two, hold the gun in your right hand by the pistol grip, hold the magazine in your left, and with your left thumb press down the magazine catch. Pull the magazine down and forward. Well, what do you know, it isn't stuck at all.'

Ross grinned, put the magazine on to the table. 'Number three, pull the cocking handle back and release to clear the chamber. As he did so, a single cartridge clattered out, rolled towards Enos and fell towards the floor. Enos caught it and returned it to the table still laughing. 'You got that?' Ross said.

Joe nodded.

'OK, I'll reload and you do it, I can see this is going to be a long afternoon.'

It was. By the time Thomas brought them tea at three-thirty, the gun was stripped. Joe had cleaned the barrel and chamber, the slide, the breech block and firing pin. He'd finally, after much sarcasm from Ross and laughter from Enos, understood the workings of the gas mechanism, stripped and cleaned it, and had learned which parts to oil, and when. And he'd learned to lay out the various components in the correct order for re-assembly. By five, when Enos, who'd wandered off for a while into the bush humming a song to himself, had returned, Joe had stripped and reassembled the gun three times, and there was no more cause for laughter.

'OK,' said Ross at last. 'That'll do.'

Joe put down the gun carefully. He no longer saw it as a gun, but as a collection of black oily pieces temporarily gathered together into a single, rather pointless object, a sort of high velocity construction toy. His hands were filthy and stank of machine oil. 'I'm going to get a wash,' he said. 'Then we'll talk.'

'That's what you think, do you?' Ross said.

Joe stood up. 'That's what I think.'

Ross looked at his watch. 'Let's see,' he said. 'We've got two hours' daylight left, maybe less. You can clean up later. Go get our packs. Empty them. Bring them back here. Then go and get four breeze-blocks. There's a stack of them round the back.'

Joe hesitated, puzzled. 'Move it!' Ross suddenly shouted.

'You better do what he says,' Enos said. And grinned again.

Joe looked at them both for a moment or two, conscious of a rising anger. Then he went to fetch the packs and the blocks.

They were heavy, the blocks, and he could manage only two at a time. By the time he had fetched all four he saw that Ross had put the first two into his own pack. He told Joe to do the same.

'Put it on,' he said.

Joe put the pack on.

'Strap it tight.'

Joe strapped it tight. The weight of the blocks wrenched at his shoulder. Ross was already moving towards the gates, his own pack in position. Outside the compound he paused and winked. 'I read in *Time* magazine how keen you Yanks are on jogging. What's that place in New York – Central Park? OK, here we are in Central Park. Let's go. Ten k's before it gets dark.' He broke into a trot. A little way up the track he turned and glanced back. 'What the fuck are you waiting for?'

Joe began to run.

They ate with the boy, that second night, chopped meat and sadza, seemingly Thomas's only speciality. Perhaps it was to compensate for the night before, perhaps merely to win his confidence for the future, but during the meal Ross and Enos seemed to be making a conscious effort to be pleasant to the boy, conducting stilted conversation in Shona. He made little response but seemed more relaxed, perhaps sensing that his story had been accepted as the truth. Only Joe still seemed to have the capacity to inspire fear in him, and he strenuously avoided eye contact.

Towards the end of the meal, Ross switched his attention from the boy to Joe. 'How you feeling?' he said.

'OK.' It was true. He did feel OK. For a while after the run he had wanted to die, but he'd recovered remarkably quickly. He was getting fitter. The realisation cheered him.

Ross nodded his approval. 'You'll get there,' he said. 'I reckon we can give it ten days to get you into shape, give you a bit of practice with the FN and ram a little bushcraft into your skull. I think we can manage that between us. What do you think, Enos?'

Enos paused from lighting his pipe. 'Back to school, hey?' he said, and once more burst into peals of laughter.

'And then we go across?' Joe said.

'I guess so.' Ross paused. 'When we're ready. There's a hell of a lot to do in the meantime: talk to Jonas here in a bit more detail about this Nhamasi place, make ourselves some maps if we can't get hold of any, get the right hardware and enough of it.'

'You think he was telling the truth?' Joe indicated the boy.

'He was scared enough.'

'And you think Ellie and the kids are still at this camp?'

'Maybe, maybe not. If not we're going to have to find out where they are, and go and fetch them from there.'

'You make it sound so bloody simple.'

Ross paused again. 'Do I?' He looked at Enos. 'What do you think, Enos? Is it simple?'

Enos nodded, still laughing.

'There sits a confident man,' said Ross. He looked at his watch. 'I reckon we should get some kip, hey? I want to get off at first light tomorrow. We've got a way to go.'

'Where the hell are we going?' said Joe, puzzled.

'Shopping.'

Despite his fatigue, Joe found it hard to sleep. Glancing across, he realised that Ross, too, was still awake. 'What are you thinking about?' he said.

'This and that.'

'Like what?'

'Like where do we go from here.'

'I thought you'd worked all that out.'

'There's details. There's a lot to think about.'

Ross was lying, Joe sensed, and shifted onto his side to see him better. The moon gleamed palely through the window, emphasising the hollows in his cheeks and around his eyes. He looked more like a corpse than a man. 'Why are you doing this, Ross? You've never told me.'

'Doing what?'

'Doing all this. Risking your life.'

'It's better than fixing cars.'

'That's not the reason.'

'It's a lot of the reason.'

'And the rest?'

'The rest is my business.'

'You don't want to talk about it?'

'No,' said Ross curtly. 'I don't.'

Joe eased himself once more onto his back and stared up at the blackness of the roof. He said, 'I'll never be able to repay you for what you're doing, you know that?'

'Who said anything about payment?' Ross laughed with sudden derision. 'What do you think I am, a fucking mercenary? You've been reading too many of those bloody paperback books.'

'All the same . . .'

'Listen, maybe I like risking my life, hey?' He spoke vehemently. 'Maybe it's all I've got to risk. Now will you shut up about it?'

'If you say so.'

'I do say so.'

Silence fell. Outside the night noises gathered and swelled. Nhamasi. Joe repeated the name several times under his breath. Nhamasi. Nhamasi. Somewhere in the mountains. It would be cooler in the mountains. There'd be good water, maybe. Green grass. Maybe Ben had learned to swim by now, if the river was deep enough, no longer needing the reassuring grip of Ellie's hands at his waist as he kicked and splashed. Christ, they'd have a story to tell their school friends! He could see the heading in Cassie's exercise book in her big, uncertain writing: 'What I did in the holidays'. It would have done them good, all this. Made them tough, self-reliant. Tougher than he'd ever been.

And Ellie?

He had a sudden vision of her standing naked in front of the long Victorian mirror in the bedroom of the flat, lifting her breasts with her hands, examining herself before turning towards him with a smile on her face. 'Not bad for a middle-aged woman,' she was saying. 'Not bad at all.'

It was her one vanity, her body, and the memory of it made him laugh softly.

'What's so funny?' Ross said.

'Nothing. I was just thinking about Ellie.'

'What about her?'

'I was thinking about her standing in front of a mirror with

275

no clothes on, if you must know.'

Ross snorted. 'I thought I heard a bit of heavy breathing.'

'It wasn't like that,' said Joe, irritated.

Ross laughed again. 'No, of course not. Just don't do too much of it, though. It'll send you blind.'

'Bastard.'

There was another silence then Joe said, 'I wonder what she said to that guy?'

'God knows. You'd better ask her when you see her.'

'I just thank God she could speak Shona.'

'All the best people speak Shona.'

'She'd been practising it, you know. Everywhere we went. Mangwanani this. Mangwanani that. I got annoyed with her at times. I told her she was showing off. But thank God she did.'

'She's a survivor,' said Ross quietly.

'You think so?'

'I think so.'

Outside a hyena howled. Ross shifted in his bed. 'Get some sleep, hey?' he said.

'Yes.'

Joe slept.

They left before dawn, taking the boy with them, moving southwards easily through the sparse bush. It was fifteen, maybe twenty kilometres before Ross called a halt near a group of jumbled rocks, handed Joe the FN and told him to watch the boy. Then he and Enos went on alone. They made three trips in all. Twice they returned with flat unmarked wooden boxes, rope-handled. The third time they were gone longer, and emerged with what looked like a machine gun and a couple of AKs splashed with camouflage paint and stinking of grease. They paused for a short time to drink water and chew at the hunks of dry bread that Thomas had given them, then started back.

It took them a long time, the return journey. Ross and the boy took one of the boxes. Joe, the rifle slung across his back, sharing the other with Enos. It was heavy, very heavy, and Joe found the strain it put on his shoulder agonising. The rope handle cut deep grooves into his palms. By the time they reached the camp the sun was already setting in the west.

Jack was back, his jeep drawn up in the compound. He came out of the main hut to meet them, beer bottle in hand. 'Been for a walk, I see,' he said with mild sarcasm.

'A bit of a walk,' said Ross curtly.

'Anywhere I'd recognise?'

'Nowhere you'd recognise. Anywhere we can put this stuff?'

'Try the hut you're sleeping in.'

'Why didn't I think of that myself?' Ross said.

Jack had brought more beer, a couple of crates of it. When they'd stacked the boxes and guns in the rondavel they returned, uncapped a bottle each and one for the boy.

'I've got the stuff you wanted,' Jack said.

'And the maps?' Ross said.

'And the maps. I also brought you yesterday's *Herald*. I thought you might fancy a little light reading. He took the paper, which had been tucked into one of the beer crates, and handed it to Ross.

Ross glanced at the front page briefly. 'You want to see this?' he said to Joe.

'Why not?' Joe spread the paper on the table. There was a single, dominating headline: '27 dead in Matibi Bus Massacre'. He scanned the report beneath. It was terse, factual, fundamentally accurate, relying heavily on the eyewitness account of one of the survivors, a Comrade Canaan Mukume, and mentioning that the attack had taken place close to where 'a family of British tourists had been ambushed in August last year'.

Beneath it there was a picture of Samuel Zvarevashe and the report of a press conference he had held in Harare following the release of the news. It was headed 'ZIPRA Blamed for Atrocity', and quoted the Minister as saying that the attack 'bore all the hallmarks of the work of ZIPRA dissidents trained in South Africa', and that 'it marked a significant escalation in the dissident's determination to intimidate the local population'.

Joe looked up at Ross. 'You were right,' he said. 'They're blaming ZIPRA.'

'Well, what d'you know.' Ross sucked a mouthful of beer

277

from his bottle, ignoring the paper.

'You think that was what was intended?'

'By whom?'

'By whoever sent those bandits over. Schoeman, maybe?'

Ross wiped his lips. 'It's possible,' he said finally.

Jack said, 'They've been to the house.'

'Who has?'

'The Army. They came yesterday afternoon when I was there.'

'And?'

'I told them I knew nothing and they went away again.'

Joe looked at the paper again. 'There's no mention of those gooks you killed, Ross.'

'Should there be?'

'Maybe Jamie hasn't told anybody about them.'

Ross laughed ironically. 'Oh, I reckon he's told them. What do you think, Jack?'

'God knows,' said Jack.

'And you don't care?'

'That's about it.' He paused, looked hard at Ross. 'I tell you one thing I do know,' he said slowly, 'I want you out of here as soon as possible.'

Ross raised an eyebrow. 'You've changed your tune suddenly.'

'They're going to be asking questions.'

'I thought you just said they'd already asked them.'

'Not just the Army, everybody – the boys, the house servants. They're going to want to know where I keep disappearing to.'

'Tell them you're visiting a sick relative.'

'In the middle of the bush?'

Ross glanced at the boy, at Joe, turned back to Jack. 'Ten days,' he said quietly. 'I need ten days. I need time to work on Jonas here. I want to make sure that if he comes with us he stays with us. And Joe doesn't know one end of an FN from the other. I can't do that overnight.'

Jack rested his forehead in his palm. 'Christ knows why I got myself into this,' he said. 'Christ knows.'

The boy ate with them again that night. At Ross's insistence they stopped referring to him as the boy and began

278

to call him Jonas. Jack talked to him in Shangaan as they ate, and Jonas became almost chatty in reply. Jack explained that the boy was telling him about the village he grew up in, and how many cattle his father had. When they had finished, and Thomas had cleared away the plates, Jack fetched the maps he'd brought from the jeep and spread them on the table.

They were better than Joe had expected, overlapping the border by maybe fifty kilometres, the river systems, hills and main settlements clearly marked, though there was no indication of villages or areas of cultivation. They showed Jonas the maps and Jack asked him to point to Nhamasi. He looked confused, and put his finger down somewhere to the north of Chiredzi. It was obvious that he couldn't read, and possibly had never seen a map before.

Ross found it. Not the place, but the river. The Nhamasi was marked as a small tributary of the Buzi River, twenty kilometres or so to the south-east of Espungabera, and no more than thirty kilometres from the Zimbabwean border, on the eastern edge of the mountain range that stretched down from Inyanga, through the Chimanimanis and south. 'Nhamasi,' Ross said, calling Jonas over, pointing to the river. The boy nodded, but seemed none the wiser.

'It's bloody close to the border,' Joe said excitedly. 'Bloody close. It'll take us a day, no more . . .'

'You must be joking,' said Ross.

'But look. If we drive to Mount Selinda then slip across somewhere, we'll be there.'

Ross paused. 'Did you ever get to Mount Selinda on your travels?'

'No.'

'Well you should have done. It's a very beautiful place. There's just one problem.'

'What's that?'

'The Fourth Brigade. They're practically shoulder to shoulder along the border there, and we don't have a Mozambican visa.'

'Does that matter?'

'What do you think?'

Jack said, 'He's right, Joe. I was up there a couple of weeks ago at the Mission. The place is swarming, and not just with

279

Army. There's Mozambican refugees all along the road, most of them starving, and cholera checkpoints . . . It's impossible.'

'So what do we do?' Joe felt suddenly hopeless.

'We get Jonas to take us out the way he came in.' Ross turned to Jack. 'You think we ought to let Chingela know what's happening?'

Jack nodded. 'I've got to go down there in any case to see about this elephant. I reckon if I tell him you're after the people who've been coming across and attacking his kraals he'll be only too pleased to help. And I tell you this, he knows the Army patrol movements better than the bloody Army itself does.'

Joe said, 'You sure it's wise telling him?'

'The moment we set foot on his land he'll know, whether we tell him or not.'

'And what happens when we get over the border?'

'We go and find your wife.' Ross spoke bluntly.

'It's a hell of a way.'

Ross grinned. 'You wait, man,' he said. 'By the time I've finished with you it'll seem like a stroll in the country.'

It was late before they went to bed. They spent the remainder of the evening talking to Jonas. He appeared happy, almost enthusiastic, when he learned that he was to guide them to Nhamasi. He was to be given a gun, Ross explained to him, and they were going to trust him. If he did as he was told, and proved worthy of their trust, he would be well rewarded and would be allowed to stay in Zimbabwe when they returned, and work for Jack on his ranch. Jack raised an eyebrow at this last comment, but nevertheless translated it. Jonas became even more enthusiastic.

They spent some time questioning him about the camp. It was quite small, he said. Maybe two hundred people but perhaps it was bigger by now. It was in a valley near a river. Jack fetched a piece of paper and asked him to draw a plan of the camp. Once more the boy look confused and produced a series of meaningless squiggles.

He seemed little wiser when Ross switched the questioning to MNR and Mozambican troop positions. There was a large Mozambican Army garrison at Espungabera, he said, with many guns, but he was unable to say how many men. And the two or three other places which he said had Army units were either not marked on the map or were situated beyond its edge.

Ross seemed strangely unworried by the lack of hard information they'd managed to obtain. When Joe mentioned his own concern, as they made their way back to the rondavel in the soft darkness, he dismissed it. 'There's time,' he said.

'Breathe in. Fire. Breathe out.'

Joe glanced up at Ross for a moment, seeking confirmation that he was positioned correctly, then settled back onto his stomach. They'd rigged up the firing range against the mound of red soil thrown up during the building of the dam. It wasn't satisfactory, Ross had said, but it would have to do. A rough human figure, crudely drawn with white paint on a sheet of hardboard, was set up against the earth bank.

With an effort of concentration, Joe breathed in, aligned the foresight peg in the centre of the rearsight aperture and squeezed the trigger. The gun bucked hard against his shoulder and the barrel swung skywards. The target was unmarked. 'Again,' said Ross. 'And relax.'

Ten rounds later, Joe clipped the top edge of the square of hardboard. Fifteen rounds later he hit the painted figure above its left knee. By the end of the morning he'd blown a gaping hole where the body used to be. Walking up to examine the target, temporarily deafened and crunching cartridge cases underfoot, he felt a sudden surge of pleasure and smiled broadly at Ross's nod of approval. The overheated gun in his hand was like a new found friend.

The first day set the pattern for the half dozen days that followed. The mornings spent shooting, always shooting. Prone. Kneeling. Standing. Single shot. Quick fire. Two-eyed. The gun got hot then cooled. Countless new magazines were filled, clicked into place, emptied. They ran out of hardboard and paint for the targets and Jack went back to the ranch to fetch more. Enos and Ross constructed what they called a jungle lane, a path through a particularly dense patch of thornbush with yet more painted targets springing up unexpectedly at the jerk of a length of fencing wire, or tyres

281

swinging Tarzan-like from the taller trees across the field of vision.

Slowly Joe's response and accuracy improved. By the Wednesday he was practising drake shooting – analysing likely concealment spots for a potential enemy at the bases of large trees, rocks or thickets, and firing into them at ground level, two shots each, before moving on quickly at a crouching run. Enos set up small concealed targets which, increasingly, Joe found himself able to hit without even catching sight of them.

Jonas, too, spent his mornings shooting. He'd been given one of the AKs and followed Joe onto the firing range or through the jungle lane. He seemed to be trying hard to please, and the accuracy of his shooting was impressive. Sometimes Ross and Enos would take their turn, using whatever weapon was to hand – AK, FN, and more and more often, the RPD machine-gun with its now familiar circular drum.

They took a brief rest at noon, and then, ignoring the heat of the day, spent the afternoons setting up mock ambushes, establishing signals, arcs of fire, filtering silently through the bush to take up pre-determined positions. Or else skirmishing, moving forward under fire towards a chosen target, alternately running, then dropping flat and squirming on their stomachs, Joe trying desperately to ignore the fatigue and the scream of the bullets over his head.

They broke off around five, usually. Pausing only to drink water and clean the weapons, they loaded their packs with breeze-blocks, three each now, and ran ten, sometimes fifteen, kilometres until darkness fell.

And even then it wasn't always over. Three times, unexpectedly, Ross announced after they'd eaten that they were going out into the bush again. During those nights they walked long distances, concentrating on establishing and maintaining contact with each other, moving silently without lights, using compasses and, less successfully in Joe's case, the stars to determine direction. On each of these nights they ended up at the range, using the moonlight and sometimes night sights to pump yet more rounds into the crumbling hardboard figures dimly visible against the dark mound before them.

Joe didn't think of much during those days, concentrating only on fighting the constant fatigue he felt, trying to understand and carry out the instructions that Ross and Enos gave him. But his confidence grew. The FN became like an extension of his body, and he began to glory in the sensation of power it gave him. He found himself adopting the slang that Ross used, talking of 'slotting gooks', of 'floppies', 'sitreps' and 'sticks'. He was a good shot, he realised, an instinctive shot. Ross confirmed it. And each day brought him closer to Ellie.

Jonas, too, was changing. He was able to meet Joe's eye without fear now, and once, just once, when they'd finished a particularly arduous skirmish, he ventured a smile. He'd put on weight despite the exercise, eating double, sometimes treble the amount of sadza and meat that Joe could manage. He was no longer locked into the storage shed at night, but shared the left hand rondavel with Enos.

Maybe it was Enos coaching him, maybe he knew more than he'd originally admitted, but his Shona improved rapidly and by the end of the week he was able to understand quite complex commands, and even, once or twice, to venture opinions of his own.

On the two evenings they spent round the table drinking beer, and during rest periods in the bush, Ross again questioned him closely about the Nhamasi camp, about patterns of sentry placement and patrol frequency. Gradually details were revealed. The camp, it seemed, was set into the flat area created by a curve of the river. There was sometimes water in the river, sometimes not. On the western side of the river there was a steep bank covered with thick vegetation. There was one track into the camp, guarded by sentries. There was a parade ground, and a football field. The Commander lived in a large hut near the parade ground. Jonas wasn't sure about sentries and patrols, he said, but at Mossurize they sometimes sent out patrols at night and at first light, sometimes not. Sentries were changed two-hourly, and were posted along the track into the camp and sometimes on high ground in the bush. Twice Joe tried to ask him whereabouts in the camp he thought Ellie and the children might be being held, but he seemed to have no opinion on the matter.

Jack came and went, sometimes joining them for the evening meal, sometimes staying overnight. He brought supplies: diesel for the generator, beer, a crate of fresh oranges. He made the occasional laconic comment about the amount of ammunition they were wasting, and how it was his taxes that had paid for it, and on the Tuesday he mentioned that the Army had been to the house again, this time a different patrol who apparently knew nothing of the previous visit. Twice during the week, on Monday and Wednesday, helicopters flew low over the bush to the west.

On Thursday Joe went with Enos to pick up more ammunition from the cache. They ran there through the cool of the early morning, Joe revelling in his new sense of fitness. Then, carrying the heavy box between them and stopping frequently, they retraced their outward tracks back to the camp, Enos pointing out the evidence of their earlier passage – crushed leaves, broken twigs, even ripped cobwebs and squashed ants. He compared the long strides that they'd made earlier, running, with the short, deep footsteps they were making now as they carried the box homewards. And they listened for the giveaway bush danger signs, the loud 'g-way' call of the grey loerie or the 'vic-tor vic-tor' of the honeyguide bird.

It was during this homeward walk that Enos, for the first time, began to talk about himself. He'd joined the Rhodesian African Rifles at eighteen, he said, following in his father's footsteps, and from then, until the end of the war, the Army had been his life. He'd been selected for transfer to the Selous Scouts in 1974, and had joined up with Ross to form a two-man reconnaissance team in 1976. He had a wife at home in Gokwe who looked after the cattle and cultivated his fields. He had five children. When Joe asked him about the woman in Chitungwiza he shook his head. No, she was not his wife, but her two children were his. He'd enjoyed being a soldier. The pay was good, and during the war the Army had looked after his wife and children. He didn't want his children to be soldiers. He wanted them to be doctors, lawyers, schoolteachers. When Joe asked him why he hadn't deserted from the army to join up with ZANLA to fight for Independence, he shook his head again and laughed. That was politics, he said. He didn't know about politics.

And as they walked, to his surprise, Joe found himself talking about his own hopes and fears in a way he'd never been able to with Ross.

It was after dark when they reached Mulovelo, and there was something wrong, Joe sensed it the moment they entered the compound. Jack, who'd been back to the house that day to fetch mealie meal and yet more hardboard, was seated at the table with Ross. Jonas was nowhere to be seen. At first Joe thought the boy must have escaped, but he appeared moments later, chewing a green mealie cob.

'What's up?' Joe said.

'That's what's up?' Ross slid a copy of the *Herald* across the table.

Joe glanced at the front page then, horrified, sat down and began to read the lead report.

EX-SELOUS SCOUT SOUGHT
AFTER MATIBI BUS MASSACRE
Herald Reporter

A massive manhunt is underway in the Gona-re-Zhou and surrounding area following the revelation by one of the survivors of last week's bus massacre in the Matibi 2 Communal Land that the band of ZIPRA dissidents responsible were being commanded by two white officers.

'The news was given by Cde Samuel Zvarevashe, Minister of State (Security) in the Prime Minister's Office, at a hastily-called press conference in Harare yesterday evening, when he revealed that a survivor of the massacre, Cde Tichafa Sibanda, had reported seeing two armed white men concealed on a kopje overlooking the ambush site.

'Subsequent enquiries have revealed that the two men were almost certainly members of South African Military Intelligence who have been living in Zimbabwe, posing as ordinary citizens. One of them has been named as Ross Tobin, an ex-member of the Selous Scouts who was living until recently at Nyabira.

'Cde Zvarevashe said that Tobin and his companion, who was not named, had visited South Africa recently, crossing the border at Beitbridge on January 10th, and returning on January 11th, two days before the attack. While in South Africa they are believed to have made contact with officials from South African Military Intelligence.

'On their return to Zimbabwe they are believed to have gone into the Gona-re-Zhou on foot, after having convinced National Parks officers at Chipinda Pools that they were on a camping holiday. There, Cde Zvarevashe alleged, they had a pre-arranged meeting with a band of newly-arrived ZIPRA dissidents who carried out the massacre under their command.

'It is probable that the pair have already left Zimbabwe, presumably lifted out by air from somewhere in the Gona-re-Zhou, but until this is confirmed, the hunt for the two men will continue at a high level,' Cde Zvarevashe said.

'It was also revealed at the same press conference that the Security Forces have killed seven of the bandits responsible for the massacre, having successfully tracked them down to a hideout close to the Lundi River. Three other members of the gang are believed to have escaped, and are currently sought by troops and police.

'Commenting on the news, Cde Mtisi said that South Africa's involvement in what he called "this barbarous act of terrorism" marked a new escalation in their pernicious policy of destabilisation in the southern half of the country, and he called for international recognition and condemnation of their action. "The deaths of those twenty-seven innocent people will not go unavenged," the Minister vowed.'

Joe put down the paper slowly. He felt dazed, unsteady. 'Jamie?' he said.

Ross shrugged. 'Maybe.'

'Bastard!'

'I said maybe.'

'Then who?'

Ross shrugged again. There was an untouched beer on the table in front of him, Joe noticed. Joe had expected anger, but curiously there was none. Ross seemed calm, too calm.

'That guy on the kopje,' Joe said slowly.

'What about him?'

'We should have stopped him.'

'How do you suggest we could have done that?'

286

He was silent. They both knew there was only one way they could have stopped that man.

Jack broke in. 'You want to call this whole charade off before you get yourselves even deeper into the shit? Because I do, I'm telling you that.'

'No.' Ross spoke so softly he was almost inaudible.

'How do you mean, no?' There was mounting fury in Jack's voice. He indicated the paper with a jerk of his thumb. 'If you believe that thing, and I do, there's half the bloody Army out looking for you. How long do you think it'll be before they cotton onto the fact that you bastards are up here playing at soldiers and using my property as your barracks? I'm surprised nobody's reported hearing gunfire as it is.'

'There'll be no more gunfire.'

'Too right there won't! And there'll be no more bloody gunmen either.' Jack stood up.

'Where are you going?' said Joe alarmed.

'Back to the house.'

'For God's sake . . .'

'Don't "For God's sake" me! When they come for you I intend to be a long way away from here. I'm going to deny any knowledge of you, you know that?'

'We know that,' said Ross.

Jack pointed at the ammunition box on which Enos was sitting. 'I suggest you dig a bloody great hole and bury that lot and all the other hardware you've got, and just gap it out of here.'

'No.' Ross's voice remained soft.

'You're good at saying that, aren't you? What are you going to do when they get here – stage Rourke's Drift part two?'

'We'll be gone.'

'Across the border?'

'Yes.'

Jack shook his head and gestured towards Joe. 'It's him I feel sorry for: not just losing his wife and kids, but getting involved with you.'

'Don't.' Joe felt a cold anger building inside him.

'Don't what?'

'Don't feel sorry for me. I don't need you or anybody feeling sorry for me.'

Jack stood silent, breathing heavily, looking Joe up and down. Eventually he said, 'You've changed. What's that bastard been doing to you?'

Joe met his gaze and held it. 'We're going over,' he said slowly. 'We know where they are. We're going to get them. There's no way you or the Army are going to stop us.'

'No,' Jack said. 'I don't suppose there is.'

He walked over to the jeep and got into the driving seat. Glancing at Joe, he seemed to reach a conclusion. 'Listen, I still think that underneath it all you're a nice bloke, and I want you to get your wife and kids back so I'll go down to the Confluence first thing in the morning and see the Chief. I'll clear it for you to go through there tomorrow night. Don't tell me that doesn't give you enough time, because that's all you're getting?'

'That's fine by us,' Joe said quietly.

'If the Army comes in the meantime, though, that's your business.' Jack looked over towards the cookhut. 'Thomas!' he yelled.

'Yes, baas!'

'Get your stuff and get in here.' To Ross he said, 'I hope one of you bastards knows how to cook.'

Thomas came running out, clutching a small cloth bundle, and jumped into the back of the jeep. The engine roared into life, headlights slashed at the bush, and Jack was gone.

'Thanks,' Joe said.

'For what?' Ross threw back his head, tilted his bottle and drank.

'For staying with it.'

Ross drained the beer. Put the bottle down onto the table with a click. 'Are we going to eat or what?' he said. He glanced towards the cookhut door.

'I mean it. If you want to quit just say so. I'll go over with Jonas . . .'

'Can you cook?'

'A bit, but . . .'

'Go and cook, then.'

Joe made no move. 'Listen, Ross, we've got to talk about this. The Army . . .'

'Fuck the Army.'

'Yes, but what happens if they come?'

'They won't come.'

'You seem pretty damned sure of that.'

'I am.'

Joe felt concern giving way to exasperation. 'OK,' he said, 'even if they don't come now, what the hell happens when we get back?'

'You ring the British Consul, get on a plane, go home.'

'And what about you? What are you going to do? The minute you show yourself back in Harare they'll . . .'

'I'm getting kind of hungry. How about you, Enos?'

'Sod the food.'

Ross ignored Joe, speaking in Shona to Enos who got up from the ammunition box and shambled over to the table. He sat down next to Ross who began to talk to him at length, still in Shona. A couple of times Enos picked up the paper and looked at the report. Once he shook his head. Jonas, who seemed oblivious to everything that had been happening, finished his mealie cob and threw it into the yard. He immediately produced a second from his pocket and began to chew that.

As Ross's monologue continued, Joe's irritation increased. Eventually he said, 'Look, will you answer me, for Christ's sake? What the hell are you going to do?'

'I'm talking to Enos.'

'And I'm talking to you! Anyway, what's so bloody secret that it can't be said in English?'

'Nothing.'

'So tell me.'

Not looking up, Ross said, 'I'm telling Enos that you're prepared to sign a blank cheque payable on your Harare bank account, which you will give to him tomorrow before we go, with your authority to draw out the entire amount contained in it.'

Joe met Enos's steady gaze. 'OK,' he said.

Ross pulled a second bottle of beer towards him and uncapped it. He stared at it for a moment. 'I thought you'd say that,' he said. He raised the bottle to his lips and drank.

'And what else were you saying?'

'This and that.'

'Like what?'

'Like what happens to my house and dog.'

'What is going to happen to them?'

Ross eyed Joe coldly. 'I think that's my business, don't you?'

Joe felt a sudden chill. He got the strange impression that he was talking to a ghost, a dead man. 'Of course it's your business,' he said, and walked into the cookhut.

It didn't take him too long to get the food. Thomas had already done most of the work, and the kitchen was surprisingly well equipped. He added a bit of chilli to the meat, and some okra he found which improved things. He felt nervous and on edge. He tried to fathom Ross's behaviour but Jonas, drifting in and out, watching the food with hungry eyes and begging for scraps, prevented him. No more than fifteen minutes had passed before he emerged with the plates.

Ross and Enos were still sitting together but their mood had changed. Ross seemed expansive and cheerful. Maybe it was the beer. There were more empty bottles on the table. Joe put down the food.

Ross examined it with exaggerated caution. 'What's this then?' he said. 'Chef's Speciality?' He put a forkfull into his mouth. 'Christ, it's hot! What the hell did you dose this with?'

'I put a few chillis in it.'

'A few! Christ, man, shoot another beer over here quick. My bloody mouth's on fire!'

Joe handed him another beer from the crate. Ross drank half, and forked in more of the meat. 'Why don't you trust me?' Joe pressed him. 'You've never trusted me.'

Ross burst into fresh laughter. 'You serve food like this and you expect me to trust you?'

'I'm serious.'

'He's serious!' Ross swung to face Enos. 'Hey, Enos, he's serious. You realise that? This man's serious.'

Enos made no response but carried on sedately eating his food.

290

Ross said, 'Hey, Joe, you want to hear a true story? I swear to God it's true.'

'No.'

'Well, I'll tell you anyway. It was a couple of years ago. This white family coming up from Beitbridge, been down South on holiday. They get stopped at a roadblock near Rutenga. A kaffir policeman orders them out. "Take your shoes off," he says. They look puzzled. He tells them again: "Take your shoes off." So they take their shoes off. He looks inside them carefully, poking about under the lining, in the toes. Then he asks them if they've got any other shoes. They say yes. "Get them out," he says. So they open their cases, get them all out: tackies, sandals, best brogues, the lot. He looks at them for half an hour, can't find a thing inside them. Eventually he says, "OK, you can put them back and go." So they go. They can't make out what the hell he was looking for. When they get back to Harare they mention what happened to a friend of theirs who's a Superintendent in the police. And do you know what he says to them?'

Joe shook his head.

'He says . . .' Ross broke off, laughter once more engulfing him. 'He says, "We ordered them to check out people's boots." You know, *car* boots. They thought he meant . . .'

'Boots,' said Joe quietly.

'You've got it. That's true, I swear it.' Ross resumed eating, still chuckling.

Joe stirred the mound on his plate then put down his fork with a clatter, intensely angry. 'Do you have to tell jokes like that in front of Enos?'

'Enos doesn't mind. Do you, Enos?' Ross glanced sideways.

Again, Enos made no response.

'See,' said Ross. 'He doesn't mind. He likes a joke, Enos.'

'Well, I didn't notice him laughing.'

'Oh, he was laughing. He was definitely laughing. You've got to laugh, hey?' Ross swigged at his beer and chuckled again, pointing at Jonas who had abandoned his fork and was shovelling huge lumps of sadza and meat into his mouth with both hands. 'Just look at that boy eat. Have you ever seen anybody eat like that? You know what he thinks this is? He

291

thinks it's the last supper. That's a good one. The Last Supper. Which one's Judas, hey?' He paused and looked around. 'Christ knows.' He burst into fresh laughter. 'That's a good one, hey? Christ knows who Judas is! If Christ doesn't know, who the fuck does? That's bloody good. Bloody good. Look, put those beers on the table. Don't just fucking sit there.'

Enos and the boy went off early to bed. Joe stayed around a while, drinking a bit, still trying to get Ross to talk, but failing. Around ten he too went to bed. As he lay there he could hear Ross singing: 'We're all Rhodesians. And we'll fight through thick and thin. We'll keep our land a free land . . .'

It didn't matter, Joe decided, before he went to sleep. Nothing mattered. They were going over. That was all he needed to know.

There was a crash from the direction of the main hut, and the sound of breaking glass.

Joe opened his eyes and looked across at Ross's bed. It hadn't been slept in. He swung himself to his feet, pulled on his shorts, his by now stinking bush shirt, and went outside.

The sun was well up, its heat smacking at his neck. He went through into the main hut. It was empty. Beer bottles littered the table, some toppled. The floor was strewn with broken glass. Ants heaved and scurried over the remnants of food on the plates. The security gates hung open.

'Ross!' His voice sounded unnaturally loud in the silence of the morning. He walked swiftly towards the ablution block.

'Mangwanani.'

Joe spun on his heels. Jonas had apparently materialised out of thin air a few feet behind him, smiling hesitantly. Joe returned the greeting curtly. 'Ross? Enos?' he said.

The boy shook his head slowly as if not comprehending.

'Oh, for God's sake,' Joe said out loud. Why the hell didn't the little bastard speak English? He tried again, more slowly. Jonas raised an arm and pointed uncertainly towards the south.

'They've gone to get more ammunition? Bang! Bang!' Joe imitated the firing of a gun.

Jonas nodded enthusiastically.

'Well, I hope to God that's what you mean.' The anxiety that Joe was feeling switched to irritation. They might have had the courtesy to wake him or at least leave him a note. In any case, he and Enos had already got ammunition, a bloody great box full. What the hell else could they need?

He glanced southwards as if expecting them to still be visible between the twisted tree trunks then turned back to the boy. 'What in God's name are you staring at?' he snapped. Jonas retreated a step or two.

Sod Ross! Sod him! Making out it was all a joke, telling him nothing, treating him like he was some sort of irresponsible kid. Well, it was going to stop. There was going to be no more of it. No more.

The boy followed him everywhere that morning, like a stray dog anxious to endear itself to a new master. He stood outside the door while Joe took a shower; followed him into the kitchen when Joe went to make tea, and ate most of the remainder of the dry bread. He stood silently watching as Joe collected the empty bottles from the table and stacked them in the crates.

A couple of times Joe shouted at him, but it seemed to have no effect. Finally, Joe thrust a broom into his hands and indicated that he should sweep up the broken glass from the floor.

Joe sat down on one of the chairs. So what was he supposed to do to fill the morning? Sit around in the sun like some senior citizen? He contemplated taking the FN and firing off a few rounds on the range. That would make him feel better. So what if some wandering bloody herd boy did hear the noise? He glanced into the cookhut. They'd need rations. OK, they'd get rations. Shouting at Jonas to hurry up with the sweeping, he got up, went into the hut and began to bring out everything edible he could find.

There seemed very little, and there'd be Ellie and the kids to feed on the return journey, too. There were two or three tins: meat, fruit, beans. A few things left over from their earlier trip into the Gona-re-Zhou, rice mostly. And mealie meal. At least there was plenty of that, just over half a sackful. Maybe they could shoot game or trap things. Otherwise it was going to be sadza all the way.

It took him a long time to divide up the meal. He found plastic bags in the cookhut which Jonas, gladly abandoning his sweeping, held open as he scooped in the coarse flour. The bags were too big, smaller ones would have been better, but there was no alternative. The mound on the table grew.

Gradually, as the rhythm of the task took over, Joe's irritation faded. A squat brown kingfisher-like bird with a red beak and an irridescent blue flash on its wings perched itself on a trailing branch of one of the acacias and clicked a monotonous call. A small antelope, a bushbuck or maybe a duiker, was momentarily visible between the trees by the river. There was a single loud splash from the direction of the dam.

How long would it take them? Six days, maybe. Somehow they'd do it, he was sure of that now. There was a tin of peaches on the table, produce of South Africa. Joe smiled. They were Ben's favourite, tinned peaches. He'd save them for him, slip the tin down into the bottom of his pack somewhere and forget it was there. Then, when they were clear of the camp somewhere safe, he'd say, 'Hey Ben, I've got something here for you.' He could see his son's excited face, like Christmas morning. 'You've got a present? What is it, Daddy?' Then he'd get the peaches out, open them slowly and divide them equally, absolutely equally, one for Ben, one for Cassie. One for Ben, one for Cassie. And then, when they were finished, he'd put his arms round them both and kiss their foreheads just below the hairline, and Ellie would say, 'You always did spoil those kids, Joe,' and give him one of here smiles, her soft lips parted. Christ they were so close. So close . . .

The roar of an engine. Joe glanced up, suddenly apprehensive. The noise was coming from the west. He could see a smudge of dust in the far distance. He looked at his watch. Nine forty-five. Jack? It was too soon for Jack.

He left the table at a run, racing for the rondavel and the FN standing against the bed. He grabbed it, fumbled for a magazine, clicked it home, cocked it. He screamed at Jonas: 'Get your gun, for Christ's sake! Bang! Bang!'

The boy stood still, as if cemented to the floor. Joe pushed past him.

294

The bush. He had to get into the bush. It was a death trap, the security fence, a cage. His heart pounding, he raced for the gate, streaked through it and into the thick grass edging the river. 'Jonas!' he was screaming. 'Jonas! For Christ's sake!'

Jonas didn't make it. He was still standing uncertainly in the gateway, looking in Joe's direction, when the vehicle arrived. It was a new white Toyota Land Cruiser, its chrome-work gleaming despite the coating of dust. It swung in towards the compound and slid to a halt inches from the boy.

Joe raised his gun, sighted it. It pulls to the left, he was telling himself. It pulls up. Compensate. Aim . . .

The driver's door opened and Larry Wakeman got out.

Joe almost fired. He felt his finger tighten on the trigger as the shock hit him. In God's name, what was Larry Wakeman doing here? He was wearing an immaculately laundered bush shirt and shorts and new green veldschoens. A gold watch gleamed against the copper brown of his wrist. He said something to Jonas in Shona. The boy made no response. Larry walked past him a few yards into the compound, turned and said something else in a different language, one that Joe recognised but couldn't understand. It sounded like Spanish, or more likely Portuguese.

Jonas muttered something, Larry nodded and looked around him, taking in the table, the piles of food and the ammunition box. Then he said, quite distinctly in English, 'It must be kind of uncomfortable lying out there by the river, Joe. Why don't you come on out and make me a cup of tea?'

Joe glanced down the track, scanning the bush to either side. It could be a trap, a set-up. An Army stick could be moving up on foot, silently taking up position even as he lay there. He strained his ears listening for something, anything, that would betray their presence.

Larry Wakeman spoke again. 'I don't have too much time, Joe.'

For perhaps another minute, he remained motionless. There were no sounds from the bush save for the warbling of doves and cicadas. If he stayed where he was, he was thinking, maybe Larry would give up, go away.

And then where would he go? To the nearest telephone?

To one of the Army units on the Chipinda road?

Slowly, and with his FN levelled, Joe got to his feet. 'What do you want?'

Larry turned towards him, a smile on his face. 'Well, if it isn't Lazarus risen from the dead. How you doing?'

Joe pushed the gun forward in what he hoped was a gesture of menace. 'I said, what do you want?'

'A cup of tea. Isn't that the thing to offer a guest on a social call? Where's your friend Mr. Tobin?'

'Around the place.'

Larry looked round. 'I don't see him. I rather think if he had been about he'd have made himself known by now. Where's he gone? To get more of the same?' He indicated the ammunition box.

'You still haven't told me what you want.'

'To talk.'

'What about?'

'About the kind of trouble you're in. I also want to stay alive so if you'd kindly slip that lever round to the letter S and point the barrel in another direction, I'd feel a whole lot safer.'

Joe ignored the request. 'You're on your own?'

'Just me and my shadow.'

'Who told you we were here?'

'A little bird.'

'Who!' Joe closed his finger over the trigger.

Larry laughed. 'You've got kinda touchy since we last met. Correction, you were always touchy. If you must know, it was a friend of mine.'

'Jack Hammond?'

'The owner of this spread? No way. No, I bumped into somebody I used to do a little bushwalking with back in seventy-eight, seventy-nine, up in the Nehanda Sector around Mount Darwin. He used to be called Comrade Jinx in those days, his Chimurenga name. You probably know him better as Chenjerai.'

'Chenjerai? But Chenjerai doesn't . . .'

Larry laughed again. 'What Chenjerai doesn't know isn't worth knowing. I'm surprised you haven't cottoned onto that fact already.'

'And he just told you, did he, just like that?'

'With a little bit of persuasion. I had to convince him I had your own best interests at heart.'

'My best interests!'

'And a damned good story.'

'So you struck some kind of deal, did you?'

'With whom?'

'With the Army. You get your story, then they come in and pick me up.'

'If you believe that, then I guess I'll go. You don't have a clue what you've gotten yourself into, do you? OK, you go ahead. Get yourself killed. I won't try and stop you.' He walked to the Land Cruiser and got inside.

Joe hesitated then lowered his gun. 'You wanted a cup of tea?' he said.

Larry nodded.

'OK. I'll make you one.'

Larry sipped at his tea. He held the cup delicately, rather as a woman might hold it. 'You didn't call me,' he said.

'I tried two or three times.'

'And then?'

'I stopped trying. There seemed no point.'

'Mr. Tobin wasn't too gone on the idea, I'd guess.'

'We got information.'

'So I gather.' Larry turned to Jonas. 'Who's your friend here?'

'Jonas.'

'Just Jonas?'

'Jonas Ndima.'

Larry said something to the boy in Portuguese and held out his hand. Jonas shook it uncertainly. To Joe, Larry said, 'I presume Jonas here lists his pastimes as "Bus Massacres" and "Kidnapping". Am I right?'

Smug bastard, Joe was thinking. So bloody smug. Yet there was something about Larry that he couldn't help liking, a kind of honesty. 'Why did you come down here?' he said.

Larry laughed. 'You know how it is. When you get fed lies and half-truths for too long you get kind of frustrated. So I decided to break the sacred rule of Zimbabwean journalism, and the recent extension to the Emergency Powers Act, and come on down to the Lowveld and find out what was going on for myself.'

'Why should I tell you anything?'

'Help me win the Pulitzer Prize, maybe.'

Joe suppressed his irritation. 'I nearly shot you,' he said.

'I was aware of that fact.'

'Don't think I still won't.' Joe looked down at the FN he was cradling.

Larry spoke swiftly and persuasively: 'Listen, you give me an exclusive on this, tell me all you know, and in return I'll not only tell you what I know, but I'll try and get you out of this in one piece.'

'There's nothing you can tell me that I need to know.'

'You're sure of that?' He smiled.

'I'm sure.'

Larry sipped at his tea. 'OK,' he said, 'forget the exclusive. Who needs fame? Who needs a plum job on the *Washington Post*? I'll tell you anyway.'

'Ross will be back soon. He's not going to be too happy finding you here, you know that?'

'I kind of worked that out for myself. Let me see, where can I begin this saga? I know, with a name: Ronnie Mulholland. Ring any bells?'

'Why should it?'

'I didn't think it would, somehow. Perhaps I should explain. Ronnie Mulholland is, or was, one of the numerous Deputy Directors of the C.I.O., and a white man to boot. Anyway, one day Ronnie has this idea and he goes along to see his boss, a certain Comrade Samuel Zvarevashe. He pulls up a fireside chair. "Samuel," he says, somewhat hesitantly, always bearing in mind that Comrade Samuel is an ex-member of the infamous Crocodile Gang and has a reputation for biting off people's heads. "Samuel," he says, "about this Lejeune character: I think I know how we can fix him".'

'Fix me?' Joe was listening with mounting horror.

'Well, you see, they'd been having a bit of trouble with this guy. They'd found a perfectly good ZIPRA bandit, persuaded him to confess to the killing of this man's wife and kids, amongst other unsolved crimes, and there was a trial coming up which they couldn't afford to lose. It should all have been perfectly straightforward – except this guy Lejeune, despite signing a statement, was refusing to acknowlege that they'd got the right man. Not only that, he was behaving somewhat strangely, associating with known criminals, trying to purchase firearms.'

'How the hell . . .?' Joe stopped.

'How do you think?'

'The white Datsun!'

Larry smiled. 'They never were renowned for their subtlety, the C.I.O. OK, we'll add that to the mix. They also realised that you'd gotten to know you were being tailed. Of course they could have always stuck you into protective custody until the trial began, and certain C.I.O. operatives who shall remain nameless were all for that. But it wasn't on. The international press would have had a field day. Can't you just see the headlines: "Kidnap Survivor Arrested"? And Mugabe, as you no doubt realise, is a wee bit sensitive to world opinion. No, what Mugabe wanted, and Zvarevashe, was a straightforward trial proving South Africa's involvement with ZIPRA beyond doubt, in the full blaze of western publicity. That way, when they moved into Matabeleland, as I have good reason to believe they're about to do again, everyone that mattered would know the reason why and not ask too many awkward questions. Somehow they had to make you play ball. It was a real problem.'

'So?'

'So Ronnie tells Samuel about this guy he knows from the war, living up at Nyabira.'

There was a long silence. Joe looked down into his teacup then slowly up again at Larry. Eventually he said, 'I don't believe any of this.'

'I think you do.'

'Bullshit. I know what you think of Ross, you've made that perfectly plain. Why don't you just piss off and leave us alone?'

'My sources . . .'

'Fuck your sources!'

Larry sipped at his tea again. 'You seem to have developed

a certain allergy to the truth, Joe, if I might say so.'

'The truth?'

'The truth.'

Joe fell silent again, acutely depressed and close to tears. It had all seemed so simple, so bloody simple. Why the hell did Larry have to come down here and say all this? 'What you're telling me doesn't make any difference,' he said. 'We know where Ellie is and we're going to get her.'

'Just hear me out.'

'Why should I? So you can get a story?'

'So you know what you've really let yourself in for.'

'I know perfectly well what I've let myself in for.'

Larry shrugged. 'Please yourself,' he said quietly.

A single ant, a survivor, maybe, from the swarm that had besieged the dirty plates earlier, scurried across the surface of the table and disappeared over the edge. Joe followed its progress. It was ironic. All along he'd wanted the truth but now that it was being presented to him on a plate, a dirty plate, he didn't want it. He looked up at Larry. 'OK,' he said eventually. 'Just tell me. But cut out the shit, hey?'

Larry raised an eyebrow. 'As you wish. Where was I?' He paused. 'Oh, yes, this guy from Nyabira . . .'

'Ross. Just try calling him Ross.'

'OK. Ross would be ideal to keep an eye on Lejeune, Ronnie said, because despite his war record he was really committed to the new Socialist Zimbabwe, and truly repented his former evil ways. In fact, he was willing to do anything to prove his new commitment. He could maybe even take Lejeune down the Chiredzi and come up with "independent" evidence to convince him that the story he'd been fed was true. I gather you found a cartridge case?'

'Yes.'

'You found it yourself?'

Joe's depression intensified. He'd forgotten about the case. Once or twice he'd meant to ask Ross about it, but it had slipped his mind. Maybe, subconsciously, he'd meant to forget about it. He said, 'Ross found it.'

'And Ross checked it out?'

'Yes.'

Larry smiled gently. 'I'm glad you're with me,' he said.

300

'Anyway, to cut a long story short, Zvarevashe was naturally none too keen on Ronnie's proposal. There aren't exactly too many ex-Selous Scouts on Mugabe's payroll. But Ronnie's a cool operator. He learned his tricks under Ken Flower during the war. There'd be no security risk, he said. And even if the whole thing blew, who the hell would believe this Lejeune guy? A Selous Scout planting evidence to implicate the South Africans? It would cast doubt on everything else he claimed. Plus, of course, the whole deal would save money. Tobin would no doubt do it for expenses alone.'

'So Zvarevashe agreed?' said Joe quietly.

'Eventually. What swung it in the end, so far as I can gather, was Mulholland's suggestion that Lejeune's obsession with finding his wife and kids could provide ideal cover for a fact-finding trip down South where Tobin had ex-colleagues from the Scouts who were currently with ZIPRA in the Transvaal training camps.'

Joe thumped the table. 'How do I know you're not working for these bastards yourself? You seem to know all the answers.'

'Not all of them.'

'You could have fooled me!'

'Listen,' Larry said, 'that day you came to see me at the office, after you'd come from Mtisi, I was convinced you were deluding yourself. The whole thing checked out: the names, Twoboy Khumalo's Shangaan mother, everything. I just felt sorry for you. I didn't want to see yourself get into more trouble, but apart from that it was the end of the matter as far as I was concerned. Then, when I heard you'd been seen in town with Ross Tobin just after Christmas, it seemed to me more trouble was just what you'd found.'

'So you called me?'

'I called you.'

It was the heat, maybe, but Joe became aware of an increasing tightness in his chest, a feeling of breathlessness. 'What made you change your mind?'

'About your story? I got a visit four, five days after I'd called you. This Catholic priest I vaguely knew from one of the Matabeleland missions came to see me at the office. He was worried about the husband of one of his communicants

301

and wondered if I could do anything to help. This guy, an ex-ZIPRA combatant, had been picked up by the Security Forces back in October, and had apparently confessed to the kidnap of your wife and children.'

'Ndhlovu?'

Larry nodded. 'According to the priest, and I had no reason to disbelieve him, Ndhlovu had a perfect alibi. He was actually sitting outside the mission church drinking beer at the time the attack happened.'

'So why did it take the priest so long to get to you?'

'It was his last resort. He'd been trying to get to see Ushe-wokunze, who was then Minister of Home Affairs, for the past two months with no success. Finally he came to me. He thought maybe publicity would help.'

'And you said you'd help?'

'There was a guy's life at stake. Of course I said I'd help. So when he'd gone, I arranged a meeting with my contact at the C.I.O. It took a fair few of the US dollars I keep for the purpose, plus a couple of bottles of imported Johnny Walker, but in the end he confirmed what you'd suspected. The whole damned thing was a set-up. That was when I learned what Mulholland and Tobin were up to.'

'And that was when you tried to contact me at Harry Barton's place?'

'I thought you ought to know. Also I thought we could plan some strategy for that poor bastard's defence before the trial came up. There's still time. They haven't fixed a date for it yet. I'm not even sure they've officially charged him.' Larry looked steadily at Joe. 'You must have suspected Ross was up to something?'

Joe was silent for a long time. Eventually he said, 'To be honest, just so long as we found Ellie I didn't care. I still don't.'

Larry smiled. 'Maybe you're right. At least you seem to have succeeded.'

'Yes.'

'You want to tell me where she is?'

Joe hesitated. 'I'm not . . .' He broke off.

Larry poured himself some more tea. It was cold and stewed. He examined the cup with distaste for a second or two, then pushed it from him. 'You still think I'm going to gap it out of here and head for the nearest Army patrol?'

'No . . . but . . .'

'Then tell me. I'm on your side, man. I was hoping you'd have realised that by now.'

Joe drew a deep breath. 'They're at a place called Nhamasi. It's an MNR camp in Manica Province, near the Buzi River.'

'In the mountains, hey?'

'You know the place?' Joe felt a sudden surge of hope.

'Not the camp but the area, yes. I came through it two or three times in '79. There's a lot of trees there, one hell of a lot of trees.'

'Trees?'

'Wattles. Gums. Vast plantations of the damned things. It's one of the main MNR strongholds, southern Manica. I reckon they must be in control of fifty or sixty percent of the entire province, Listen, before we get too heavily into geography, just clear something up for me, will you? How did your friend Tobin react when Jack Hammond told you your wife and kids had been taken into Mozambique?'

'He wasn't too pleased. I couldn't work out why.'

'Maybe you know now.'

Joe looked up, unable any longer to disguise the distress he felt. 'So you're saying that the whole time, the whole time we've been down here, Ross has just been stringing me along?'

'Something like that.' Larry lay back in his chair, raising a hand to shade his eyes from the sun which was slanting beneath the thatch. 'But that's not the end of it. It hasn't been officially released yet, but two days ago they arrested Ronnie Mulholland. If my information is correct, they're going to charge him with being a member of South African Military Intelligence.'

'So?'

'I'm still trying to work out all the implications but one of them's already clear: they've decided to tar Mr. Tobin with the same brush.' Larry pointed to the *Herald* which was still lying slung across the back of one of the chairs. 'I see you've been catching up on the news. Fascinating lead article, I thought.'

'You might call it fascinating.'

'It made your friend a wee bit mad, I'd guess.'

'He was upset, yes.' Joe met the black man's gaze. 'Are you now trying to tell me that Ross is working for the South Africans?'

Larry paused. 'I'd kinda hoped you'd be able to tell me that.'

'How the hell should I know?'

'You went down South with him, or has the *Herald* got it wrong? You must know what happened down there.'

'We went to a party.'

'A party?'

Joe closed his eyes. None of it made sense, none of it. And even if it did make sense, what the hell did it matter? 'At Phalaborwa. We went with a mate of Ross's.'

'An ex-Selous Scout?'

'Yes.'

'And there were other Selous Scouts there?'

'Yes.'

'And?'

'We got some information.'

'Who got the information? You or Ross?'

'I did.'

'You want to tell me what this information was?'

Joe broke eye contact. 'I met a girl.'

'A girl?'

'The girlfriend of one of the guys. She said she'd heard them talking about an English woman and two children being held in Mozambique, and how they didn't know what to do with them.'

'Who didn't?'

'Her boyfriend. People he was working with.'

'Name?'

'Piet Schoeman.'

Larry nodded. 'Ah, Mr. Schoeman.'

'You know him?'

'Of him. And what did Ross say when you told him what the girl had said?'

'He didn't believe it. He said she was lying.'

'And then?'

'They kicked us out.'

A look of surprise spread across Larry's face. 'They kicked you out? Who kicked you out?'

'The police. Military Intelligence. I don't know.'

'You weren't interrogated?'

'No.'

Larry was silent for a long time. Jonas, Joe noticed, had picked a hole in one of the mealie bags and was removing small quantities of flour with a wet finger and transferring it to his mouth. Seeing Joe watching him he stopped guiltily, like a small boy caught out. Eventually Larry said, 'I think I may have misjudged your friend.'

'Misjudged him?' There was bitterness in Joe's voice. 'I thought you said you knew all the answers.'

'I said I knew some of them. With what you've told me, I now know more.'

'So tell me.'

Larry stood up and stretched. He stared out over the bush for a moment, then, to Joe's astonishment, squatted down and began to do a series of press-ups, counting loudly as he did so. At fifty he stopped and stood up again, sweat glistening on his forehead. He returned to his chair, nodding jovially in response to Jonas's uncomprehending stare. The gesture irritated Joe. 'Well?'

Larry took out an immaculately laundered white handkerchief and patted his brow. 'OK,' he said. 'Fact: Tobin has been working for the C.I.O. He planted evidence to convince you that you had been attacked by ZIPRA dissidents.

'Fact: when you weren't totally convinced by the evidence, he suggested a trip down South.' Larry was counting off the points on his fingers.

'Fact: he made contact with ex-Selous Scouts involved in ZIPRA training. Presumably he intended to stay down there for as long as possible, using your quest as cover.

'Fact: what he hadn't counted on was that some of the same guys involved with ZIPRA were also involved with the MNR, and that quite independently you would come up with evidence that your wife and kids were not only alive but being held in Mozambique. Result? Total fucking disaster. I assume you wanted him to go see this Schoeman guy and get some hard information from him?'

Joe nodded.

'And he refused?'

'I told you. He wouldn't believe that what the girl had told me was true. He said that none of his mates would get involved in the kidnapping of a white family.'

Larry smiled. 'Touching.'

'He seemed pretty convinced about that.'

'I'm not surprised. Now, here's where things get a bit more complicated. Let's stay with your wife and kids for a minute. Here I'm going to speculate, but I think I'm on pretty firm ground. It seems clear to me that the kidnapping was a total mistake. OK, so this patrol was meant to go into Zimbabwe, maybe even ordered to by Schoeman, who I'd guess is Military Intelligence Liaison Officer for that particular sector of the MNR Command. But what it wasn't meant to do was take hostages, especially not white hostages, and take them back over the border. In fact, I'm surprised they didn't kill the lot of you on the spot. Jonas have anything to say about that?'

'He said they were going to kill Ellie and the children with axes.' Joe spoke quietly.

'So why didn't they?'

'She said something to their leader.'

'Like what?'

'I don't know. Ellie spoke in Shona. Jonas said he didn't understand.'

'Maybe she told him she was Mrs. Thatcher's daughter.' Larry laughed loudly. 'Anyway, whatever it was it obviously convinced this guy that if he took them back alive he'd earn a few merit points. Did Jonas let on what happened when they got back to Nhamasi?'

'They went to Tomé. He said the commander there whipped the guy.'

Larry nodded. 'I can't say I'm surprised. In his place I'd have done the same.' He paused. 'It's my guess that you've got Schoeman to thank for Ellie and the children being alive, assuming they still are.'

'Schoeman?'

'Maybe it was like Tobin told you. Maybe he couldn't bring himself to order the cold-blooded murder of a white woman and children. Or maybe, and more likely, he reckoned they could come in useful at some later date: perhaps in negotiations, or perhaps to discredit Mugabe internationally. They could be waiting for Ndhlovu's trial to blow the fact to the press that they're alive. Who knows? What was not intended by Schoeman was that his damn stupid girlfriend would, one, overhear him discussing the matter with his buddies, and two, then go make you a free gift of the information. I assume you had to fuck her to get it?'

Joe shrugged.

Larry spread his hands, grinned. 'So who cares? Now, another guess. I reckon the military brass who pay Schoeman's wages have got no idea the MNR are holding your wife and kids, or that Schoeman is protecting them, and for reasons best know to himself he wants to keep it that way. So after his girl confesses what she's gone and done, he's got problems. Obviously, the longer you hang around, the more likely you are to get picked up and tell what you've heard. So he arranges to warn you, presumably through some third party, that the authorities are gunning for you and you'd better get the hell out. Tobin doesn't argue. He's shit scared of being detained and interrogated in case his C.I.O. connection is blown, and Schoeman counts on him having enough influence over you to make sure you go too. And that's what happens. A free run to the border, plus Schoeman probably made an unofficial call to the local police to get them to persuade you not to change your minds. You still with me?'

'Yes.'

'Make any sense?'

Joe took a couple of deep breaths. 'I suppose it does,' he said.

'Good.' Larry brushed at a fly which was bothering him and eased his position in the chair. 'So where does that leave your friend Tobin?'

'I don't know.' Joe spoke harshly, resentment beginning to replace the despair he felt. Larry seemed impervious to his mood.

'I tell you where it leaves him – nowhere. He's not only failed to convince you that Ndhlovu and his crew were responsible, but he's allowed you to come up with information which, if blown, would seriously damage the credibility of the Zimbabwe government. Added to that, the moment you get back north of the border you get independent corroboration of the story. He's in a fix. Tell me, did he contact anybody when you got back?'

'Harry Barton. That's when he found out about Jack's news.'

'Nobody else?'

Then Joe remembered. 'Harare,' he said quietly. 'He called Harare.'

'Any idea who?'

Joe was silent for a while. 'Ronnie Mulholland?'

Larry grinned. 'You're catching on. He trusts Mulholland, so he contacts him and tells him everything. He probably reasons that Ronnie, having set up the whole thing, will be as anxious as he is to shovel the shit under the carpet. My guess is Ronnie told him to ditch you and disappear.'

'Disappear?'

'Go to Botswana. I don't know.'

'But he didn't, did he?' Joe's resentment was turning rapidly into anger. 'He came up here and risked his life to get hold of that bastard.' He jerked a thumb at Jonas.

Larry raised an eyebrow. 'God knows why.'

'How about he just wanted to help me get Ellie and the children back? Or is that explanation too simple for you?'

A smile played about the black man's face. 'You believe that, do you?'

'Yes.'

'Then what more can I say?' Larry glanced around almost as if he expected to see Ross coming through the gate, gun levelled. But the yard was empty save for a few dancing flies. He turned back to Joe. 'OK,' he said, whatever his reasons, he comes on down to Chipinda with you, and in you go. And what do you know? Within forty-eight hours the pair of you get yourself spotted taking a grandstand view of a massacre. Back in town, Comrade Zvarevashe can't believe his luck. It's all the evidence he needs to nail Mulholland, who, I know for a fact, he's been after for some time. So he arrests him, and just to set the scene, he announces to the *Herald* and anyone else who's interested that ex-Selous Scout Ross Tobin, plus a conveniently unnamed companion, had led the dissidents responsible. He also announces that the pair of you have been airlifted out of the country. And you know why he's done that?'

'No.'

'I'll tell you why he's done that. Because you're still being set up.'

'Set up?' Joe looked at Larry incredulously.

The black man shook his head slowly. 'Come on, man,' he said. 'You must have wondered why the Army have stood back and let you play soldiers up here for so long.'

'They don't know we're here, for Christ's sake!'

Larry laughed. 'You must be joking. There's a unit of One Brigade commandos up at Chisumbanje. What do you think they're doing with their days? Going for nature walks? Of course they fucking know you're here. It's exactly where you're intended to be. Zvarevashe wants you to go over. He wants you and Tobin out of his hair once and for all. And I've no doubt that as soon as you cross the border, the Mozambican Army will be provided with map co-ordinates of your position and an open invitation for a little firing practice. A couple of dead white South African mercenaries will look pretty good at their propaganda parades. And even if something does go wrong, like your being taken alive, well, Tobin's track record speaks for itself, and you're just a demented psychopath unhinged by grief who's gone along with him for the ride.'

'Bullshit!' Joe's hands were hurting where he gripped the arm of the chair.

'It's not bullshit,' said Larry quietly. 'And what's more, I believe your friend Ross knows perfectly well what's happening.'

'Are you crazy?' Joe stared in disbelief.

Larry shrugged. 'Tell me something: has he posted sentries since you got here?'

'No.'

'Doesn't that strike you as a bit strange, given the Army are likely to show at any time? Look, I'd guess that somehow they've got to him, maybe via your good friend Jack Hammond, or possibly on one of his bush walks, and convinced him that if he pulls off this rescue mission he'll be back in favour. He's stupid enough to believe them. And in any case he doesn't have a whole load of options to choose from. But I tell you this: the moment you cross that border you're dead.'

Joe was silent for a long time. He was thinking about the night before. Ross had seemed certain, too certain, that the Army wouldn't come. And if Larry was right? A surge of anger hammered at him. The bastard knew far too much. He must be part of it somehow. Joe couldn't work out how, but it didn't matter. None of it mattered. 'We're going over,' he said.

Larry shook his head slowly, disbelievingly.

'Ross reckons we can do it.'

'The four of you? This isn't a bloody Clint Eastwood movie.'

'I trust him.'

Larry laughed with bitter irony. 'You trust him? After all I've just told you?'

'Yes.'

Larry picked up a teaspoon and began to fiddle with it. 'Look,' he said, 'even if you make it to Nhamasi, what then? You think you're just going to be able to go in and take the place? How much do you know about the MNR?'

'Enough.'

'How much is enough?'

'I know they're fucking murdering bastards, and that's enough for me.'

Larry nodded slowly. 'Oh, they're that all right. Only, did you know that the whole damned thing was originally set up by the Rhodesians, and that the first units were trained up at Bindura by the Selous Scouts, including your friend Ross?'

'So?'

'So anything he can do, they can do. And there's a whole lot more of them than there are of you.'

'We'll find a way.'

'Christ, man!' Larry brought his fist down onto the table with a sudden bang, making Jonas, who was still picking at the mealie meal, jump as if shot. 'Will you listen to me? Short of a fucking pre-emptive nuclear strike, there's no way you're going to succeed. It's suicide, man. And Zvarevashe wants you to commit it.'

'That's what Jack Hammond called it,' said Joe quietly.

'Well, he's right. Which is why I'm telling you to do it my way.'

'Your way?' There was contempt in Joe's voice.

'Come back to Harare with me. Go see Martin Ewans at the British High Commission. Tell him everything you've found out. I'll corroborate the story. Believe it or not, Britain still has some clout in this part of the world. They can put heavy pressure on the South Africans, and no doubt they've got unofficial ways of getting to the MNR High Command in Lisbon. I wouldn't put it past Tiny Rowlands to have a contact or two in that department. Believe me, if your wife and kids are still alive, you've got a damned good chance of succeeding.'

'And how long is that going to take? A year? Two?'

'Weeks, maybe.'

'Don't talk shit.'

'It's not shit,' said Larry mildly.

Joe picked up the FN which he had rested against the chair, moving his hands slowly over its cool surface. 'We're going over,' he said. 'And you're not stopping us.'

Larry shook his head sadly. 'You're crazy, you know that? He's got to you, that guy. Really got to you.' He stood up. 'I guess there's nothing more I can say to you in that case.'

'Nothing.'

Larry walked over to the Land Cruiser and opened the door. 'It's been nice talking to you,' he said. 'It's not too often I get the chance to drink tea with a dead man.'

It was then, and only then, that Joe realised he couldn't let Larry go. It just wasn't possible. He raised the FN, pointing it at the centre of the journalist's chest. He was aware of a dryness in his mouth, a slight headache developing. 'Stop,' he said.

Larry paused. 'Stop what?'

'Come away from that vehicle.'

Larry didn't move. There was a hint, just a hint, of fear in his eyes. 'Is this absolutely necessary?' he said.

'I said, come away from that vehicle.'

Larry still didn't move. 'You're crazier than I thought,' he said. 'You think I really care enough about what happens to

311

you to turn you in, even supposing they want me to? I'm not even supposed to be down here in the Lowveld in the first place. Christ, man, I just want to get out of here, and fast, before your unpleasant friends return.'

'Move!'

'You're not going to shoot me, so why don't you put that gun down?'

Joe squeezed the trigger.

At the last instant something, pity maybe, or fear, made him swing the gun hard away to the left. Bullets slammed into the white bodywork of the vehicle. A tyre blew. The Land Cruiser lurched sideways. Larry was on his stomach, crawling. 'OK,' he was shouting. 'I get the message. I'm going nowhere.'

Click. Click. Click . . .

The noise was beginning to irritate him. That, and the fact that Ross still hadn't shown. It was two-thirty, and hot. 'Can't you get a move on, for Christ's sake?' said Joe.

Larry glanced up from the RPD feed belt into which he was slotting cartridges. The clicks were coming from the tiny nibs on the belt as they engaged with the extraction groove at the rear of each brass case. 'You want this done right?'

'I want it done right.'

'Then don't hassle me.'

Joe fell silent again and shifted the FN to take the weight off his legs. For almost an hour he'd sat there, watching, saying nothing, as Larry and Jonas had filled every spare magazine in the place, lining them up in rows like something for sale in a supermarket. The ripped aluminium inner skin of the now almost empty ammunition box on the table gleamed dully in the sunlight. Soon there'd be nothing left to do except wait.

Christ Almighty, where were they? It would be dark in what, four hours? Jack could turn up any time. And then, if they still weren't back . . .?

For a moment he was afraid that they'd been picked up by the army and would never come. A couple of rounds each. Unmarked graves somewhere only the hyenas would be watching. It would be so quick, so simple . . . Maybe Larry knew this all along, and had waited until they were separated

312

before he moved in. 'Get Lejeune's confidence,' he could imagine Zvarevashe saying. 'You're an American, you speak the same language. He trusts you. We'll do the rest . . .'

With an effort Joe pushed the doubt from his mind. He tried to think about Ellie, about making love to her slowly, softly, on a lace bedspread in some cool, clean room. But the vision wouldn't come.

Click.

Click.

Bastard! He should have killed him. He should have emptied a magazine into that tight black body, put a few stains on that oh so perfect bush shirt. So fucking smug. There was a smile on his face even now.

'Quit grinning,' Joe said.

Larry didn't look up. He paused for a moment, then continued clicking the cartridges into position. 'I'm not grinning,' he said quietly.

'It breaks your heart to see something like that, hey?'

Ross's voice!

Joe spun on his chair as if knocked sideways by a sniper shot. He grabbed at his FN to stop it falling, shock making his voice harsh. 'Where the hell have you been?'

'Getting a few goodies. I told Jonas to tell you.'

'He can't speak English, in case you've forgotten.' The relief that Joe was feeling came out as anger.

Ross shrugged. He was standing with Enos in the gateway, his bush shirt dark with sweat. They must have been there for some time, Joe realised, watching and waiting. Enos caught his eye and nodded. They had full packs and slung AKs. 'Jesus, I hate to see something like that. How long d'you have to wait to get that thing, Larry?' Ross was indicating the Land Cruiser, Joe saw.

'A couple of years.' Larry sounded surprisingly calm.

'A couple of years? Then some trigger-happy bastard lets rip with an FN and fills it full of holes. Makes you want to weep, hey?' Ross walked up to the vehicle, examined the holes in the bodywork closely and shook his head. 'Criminal,' he said. 'Fucking criminal.' Still shaking his head he came over to the table, Enos following. Both men eased their packs gently to the ground.

'He was leaving,' Joe said. 'I couldn't just let him go.'

Ross ignored the remark. Slumped into a chair and surveyed the table. 'Been busy, hey? Is there any tea on the go?'

'I'll make some.' Joe stood up, puzzled and irritated. 'Just make sure he . . .'

Ross grinned at Larry. 'You're not going anywhere, are you, Larry? Not for a while, anyway.'

'If you say so.' Larry continued to fill the belt.

Ross looked up at Joe. 'You see. No problem.'

Joe held the gaze for a moment or two before turning towards the cookhut. He'd been prepared for anger – violence even – but this? The condescension in Ross's manner was infuriating. He lit the gas and put the kettle on to boil. When he came out, he saw that Enos had sat down next to Jonas. Larry had finished the belt and was curling it carefully, from the left, into the open drum.

Ross slapped his thigh. He seemed almost cheerful. 'Well,' he said, 'quite a tea-party, hey?'

Joe said, 'Chenjerai told him we were here. I didn't know what to do. I . . .' He stopped.

Ross shook his head again. 'The bloodhounds of the international press, hey? Bloody hard to shake them off. I just wish you could have aimed that houtie slayer somewhere else except at the piece of mobile real estate over there.'

'At me, you mean?' Larry spoke quietly.

Ross grinned. 'Well, you've got to admit there's more fucking journalists than there are brand new Land Cruisers knocking about the place. So what have you two been talking about? Baseball? The Empire State Building?'

'He told me,' Joe said softly, his anger gone.

'Told you what?'

'About you and Ronnie Mulholland.'

Joe watched Ross closely. Apart from a slight intake of breath there was no reaction. The grin remained on his face. 'My favourite subject,' he said.

'Why didn't you tell me?' Joe said, unnerved. 'I'd have understood.'

Ross suddenly burst into loud laughter. 'You'd have understood? Christ, Yank humour really gets me, you know that?' He turned to Larry. 'So you thought you'd just come along and tie up a few loose ends, hey?'

'And try to stop this guy getting himself killed.'

'And what did he say to that?'

'He shot up the Land Cruiser.'

Ross tutted. 'Inconsiderate bastard.'

Larry eyed him in silence for a while, as if trying to anticipate the possible reaction, then he said deliberately: 'They want you dead, Ross, you know that?'

'Me?' Ross pointed to his chest. 'Me? You're talking to me?' He laughed again.

'That doesn't bother you?'

'Should it?'

Larry shrugged. 'It'd sure bother me.'

'That's your problem.'

Larry held his gaze for a long time, seeming totally unafraid. Finally he said, 'Do you know something? I feel sorry for you. Really sorry for you.'

Ross breathed deeply and looked out into the bush. 'You've got a strange way of showing it,' he said very quietly. When he swung round to face Joe, the smile was back in place. 'Hey, what about that tea, man? My tongue feels like its spent all day inside a kudu's arsehole.'

Ross drank three cups of tea quickly, before the others had finished their first. 'Cosy,' he kept saying between gulps, looking round him. 'This is really cosy.' He belched loudly after he'd emptied the last cup. Larry, Joe saw, was watching Ross closely with the attitude of a man trying to forge an intimate relationship with an unexploded bomb. Despite himself, Joe felt an unexpected surge of compassion for the journalist. 'What are we going to do with him, Ross?' he said.

Ross belched again, and stretched. 'What do you suggest?'

'We could disable the Land Cruiser. Keep him here till we're gone.'

Ross turned to Larry and winked. 'He's really got the down on your Land Cruiser, this guy. What's it ever done to him to deserve this, hey?'

'I want an answer,' Joe said.

'You want an answer? That's all you ever fucking want is answers.' Ross spoke with sudden vehemence. 'We've wasted enough time on fucking answers. We've got things to do.' He

315

stood up and went to the packs that he and Enos had brought, and took out a dull green club-shaped object about fourteen inches long. 'You know what this is?' He held it up to Joe.

He shook his head.

'A 32Z rifle grenade. Belgian. Effective range one hundred metres direct, five hundred metres indirect. We got four of these.' Ross began to lay out the contents of the packs on the table next to the magazines, listing the items as he produced them, like a woman her purchases after a shopping spree. 'Four 36M hand grenades. Half a dozen 80's. That's white phosphorous. One Claymore mine. One detonator for same. One length of Cordex. Four M962 fragmentation grenades . . . Everything we need except a new battery for the Claymore, night vision equipment and tactical air support.' He turned suddenly to Larry. 'You making a note of all this?'

'Should I be?'

'You call yourself a journalist, that's what you should be doing – taking notes. You could make yourself a fortune.'

'You flatter yourself.'

Ross laughed, too loudly. 'Don't give me shit like that,' he said. 'You need this story. You wouldn't have risked coming here if you didn't. You need it badly.' He jerked a thumb in Joe's direction. 'You don't give a monkey's tit about his wife and children, just so long as you get your story.'

'That's not true.'

'It's true, man. It's fucking true and you know it. I can guess what they're saying in New York and London or wherever you send your lies. They're saying, "What's with this black bastard? Has he lost touch? And anyway, who the hell wants to know about Zimbabwe? Who the fuck is interested in that tin-pot third world dictatorship?"'

'It's a democracy,' said Larry. He was still calm, but it was obvious that Ross's word had hit home. Joe watched the pair of them closely.

Ross laughed again. 'Some fucking democracy.'

'You flatter yourself if you think people are going to be interested in this pathetic little farce.'

'In that case, why don't you get off my fucking back?' Ross walked quickly round the table and placed himself squarely in front of Larry. He was sweating heavily, Joe noticed. 'Hey?' His voice rose to a shout. 'You've been on my back for the last four years. I can't even have a crap without you knowing about it before I do. Well, I tell you this, you black bastard, this is the last time, the last fucking time!'

He swung round, picked up one of the rifle grenades from the table and thrust it at Larry's face. 'I ought to stick this in that bloody FN, ram it up your arse and pull the trigger. It's that bitch of a wife of yours, isn't it? Isn't it!'

He thrust the grenade at Larry again, harder this time. The journalist twisted back desperately, trying to avoid the impact. There was a sudden crash as his chair toppled, and then the two men were rolling on the ground. The grenade spun away. 'It's that bitch of yours!' Ross was shouting. 'It's that fucking bitch of yours!' His fist rose and fell twice. There was a spray of blood.

'Ross, for God's sake!' Joe launched himself beneath the table, grasping for the grenade. He clutched it and pulled back. Ross's flailing feet smacked at his jaw . . .

'Dekara, dzikama adzore mwoyo, usazvinetse!'

Enos moved faster than Joe would have believed possible. His arm was round Ross's neck, pulling him away from the journalist. Ross broke free. For a moment Joe thought he was going to turn on Enos but suddenly it was as if his strength had left him. He stood, holding on to Enos's arm, seeming confused and unsteady.

'Sit down,' Enos said in English. Ross collapsed into a chair, leaned forward and rested his head on his hands.

'You OK?' Enos said to Larry.

The journalist nodded and got to his feet. His nose was bleeding violently, wetting his chin and staining his shirt. He groped for his handkerchief, pressed it to his face. 'Thanks,' he said.

Enos shrugged and returned to his seat.

Joe carefully replaced the grenade on the table. 'Should I make some tea?' he said.

Nobody answered. The kingfisher had returned to its perch on the acacia and was clicking its song. Eventually Joe sat down. Only Larry remained standing, holding on to one of the rough mopani poles which supported the roof.

317

For minutes, it seemed, the silence held, broken only by the kingfisher and Larry's sniffs as he attended to his nose. Joe wondered whether he should talk to Ross, comfort him, maybe.

When Ross began to talk, it was to no one in particular. 'Do you know what it's like, being treated like you've got leprosy? Do you? Any of you? Because that's the way I've been treated. A couple of times I was offered jobs. A guy I knew wanted me to manage his farm out near Beatrice. Another time I got a job with Denwood Motors, selling Peugeots. Good jobs. Not bad pay. And what happens? Suddenly they change their minds, offer the jobs to some semi-educated black. "I'm sorry," they say. "Nothing personal. It's just that the powers-that-be want more blacks in positions of responsibility, and your war record's against you."

'So I start mending cars. I make a bit, a little bit, and then what do you know? I get the tax inspector on my back. "Have you kept proper records? Have you declared all your income?" I can't move.

'And why do you think all that was happening, hey? I must have been stupid. I could have gapped it down South to where my mates were. I could have been training ZIPRA to come back in to Zimbabwe and kill and maim. I could have been earning a good screw. I could have been driving a BMW.

'But, no, I chose to stay on. You know why? Because I thought, the war's over. Because this is my country, and I wanted to help it grow and become a decent place, and not go the way of Uganda or Nigeria or any of those other black cesspits. I believed in this country. Believed in it! You understand what I'm saying?'

'Yes,' said Joe quietly.

Ross pointed at Larry. 'Well, he doesn't. Him and his wife. They're still fighting the war. It doesn't matter to them that Nyadzonya was – how long? – seven or eight years ago. And that I was a lot younger in those days, and a lot more stupid, and believed what Smith and his cronies told me. They don't give a shit about that. All they want is vengeance. They won't come along to my house and put a bullet in my head. No, that would be too simple. Instead, every move I make, they're there. "He's a Selous Scout," they're saying. "One of the butchers of Nyadzonya. Don't have anything to do with him."

'OK, so I killed. I've killed a lot of people. Does that make me different from half those bastards who're now Government Ministers, tell me that? It was war. People kill. People get killed.' Ross broke off.

'I'm sorry,' said Joe softly.

'You're sorry? What the hell good does that do?' He pointed again at Larry. '*He* says he's sorry for me. Him. Zvarevashe's little pet. Yes sir. No sir. He says he's sorry for me.'

Larry shook his head slowly. Maybe it was to stop the bleeding, Joe couldn't tell. Ross wiped at the sweat that was trickling into his eyes.

'So you really were working for Ronnie Mulholland?' Joe said.

'I had no choice. That black bastard over there gave me no choice. Him and his wife. I didn't like doing it, but I did it. Ronnie said they might leave me alone if I did it. Christ, I must need my brains tested.'

'So why are you still helping me?'

Ross shrugged. 'You know how it is,' he said.

'No,' said Joe. 'I don't.'

Ross was silent for a long time. Then he said, 'When you get to know someone . . . Those pictures you showed me . . . those kids' faces . . .' He stopped, embarrassed.

Joe put his hand gently on to Ross's arm, feeling close to tears. 'Hey, man,' was all he managed to say.

They began to pack, quietly and efficiently, dividing up the ammunition, the grenades and the food. Joe placed the can of peaches carefully beneath his spare bush shirt. Larry remained where he was, standing near the roof support, saying nothing. It was as if there was nothing left to say. Water was going to be a problem. There was no water where they were going, Ross said. Not until they reached the mountains. Enos questioned Jonas about water. 'Mvura,' he called it, using the Shona. Jonas, who had not stirred from his seat at the head of the table all afternoon, seemed vague about where they might find it. They found eight spare water bottles in the cookhut, which, added to the ones they already posessed, made thirty-two. Ross cut four six-foot square sections of plastic sheeting from a roll they discovered behind the storage hut and quietly explained the mechanics of constructing a survival still to Joe. By five-thirty the packing was complete.

They ate sadza and one of the cans of beans as darkness gathered and the frogs began to call from the reedy edges of the dam. Larry joined them for the meal, still saying little except in response to direct questions from Joe. He neither confirmed nor denied Ross's accusations. After they had eaten, Joe wrote out a blank cheque and drafted a letter authorising the transfer of his Harare funds to Enos. They blacked their faces. A hyena howled somewhere a long way away. A second animal answered, closer.

Shortly after eight, a tired-looking Jack arrived. He seemed only mildly disturbed by Larry's presence. They left immediately, heading south along a rough track, before turning east towards the rising moon. Larry stood quietly watching them go. He made no gesture of farewell.

Part Six

Mozambique

Jack drove fast despite the track, rear wheels thrashing at the soft sand. From time to time he veered into virgin bush to avoid obstacles. Joe sat in the front next to him, his FN upright between his knees, Ross on his left. Enos and Jonas sprawled in the back. Nobody spoke. They dog-legged east, then south, then east again. After an hour they came to a high game fence with a padlocked gate which Jack opened, using one of the keys from the bunch which had rattled and danced on the metal shelf next to the steering wheel. Moths tumbled drunkenly in the headlight beams.

There was a range of hump-backed hills to the south, silhouetted in the moonlight. The Chihunjas, Jack called them. To the north was the game fence, and beyond that the sporadic twinkling of firelight from huts in the Sangwe Communal Land. The track broadened and swung south once more, climbing up over a low pass in the hills then descending steeply. Every few minutes they lurched into deep, dry gullies, always at speed, the impetus carrying them clear. The bush levelled, low scrub wrecked here and there by elephants. Small herds of impalas leapt and scattered, their eyes flashing points of fire.

How far south they drove, Joe had no means of telling. It seemed a long way. He was conscious only of the lurching of the jeep, and the increasing ache in his legs as he braced them against each fresh impact. From time to time Ross shifted beside him. Once he took out a handkerchief and blew his nose.

Then, unexpectedly, Jack slowed, and turned east again on

to what looked like little more than a game track. The bush thickened rapidly, augmented by tall riverine trees strung with lianas and the occasional giant baobab. After a kilometre or two he pulled the jeep to a halt close to a deeper than usual streambed. 'This is it?' Joe asked, conscious of a sudden rise in tension.

'This is it.' Jack held his wrist close to the illuminated dashboard to read his watch. 'Twelve thirty-six. They're sending someone to pick you up here. If you make reasonable time you'll be across the border before first light, no problem.'

He switched off the engine and killed the lights. Joe could hear Enos muttering something in Shona to Jonas in the back. The engine clicked as it cooled. Somewhere close by there was a gentle sound of running water.

'Kaziwai.'

They didn't see the boy, or hear him, until he spoke. Jack switched on a small torch and aimed it in the direction of the voice. The boy was small, no more than twelve years old, wearing oversized shorts and shirt. He had bare feet. Jack spoke to him softly in Shangaan and the boy replied. 'His name is Henry. He's one of Chingela's nephews. He can speak a bit of Shona.'

Ross was already out, helping Enos and Jonas to unload the packs and weapons. By torchlight they strapped on webbing, and slung waterbottles. Joe eased on his pack, bracing himself against the weight.

'OK?' Ross said quietly.

'OK.'

Jack said, 'The best of luck, hey?'

'Thanks.' Joe knew he should say more, but for some reason he couldn't find the words.

'I think I'll go and have a word with that journalist on the way back. If he's still there.'

'You do that,' said Ross.

Jack climbed into the jeep, revved it hard, swung it in a semicircle through a patch of thornbush and was gone.

It was the Sabi they could hear, a few yards away, deep in its gorge. They paused on its bank, waiting for their eyes to adjust to night vision, staring down into its black, fast-flowing waters. Then, following the boy, they moved south along a narrow but obviously well-used path. At a point some five hundred metres from where Jack had left them, the high banks suddenly fell away and the river broadened. The boy stopped. 'Hokoyoi! Makarwe,' he said.

'He says watch out for the crocs.' It was Enos who translated.

The boy stepped hesitantly into the water, the ripples around his legs gleaming dully in the hazy light from the half moon. Joe sucked in a deep breath and followed.

If the crocs were there, they didn't show themselves. The water was quite warm, no more than knee deep. It was an easy crossing. Beyond the river was a sandy beach churned by the hooves of cattle, and beyond that a mealie patch fenced with thorn, the plants surprisingly high, tasselling already. And there were huts, a group of them, the black cones of their roofs sharply outlined against the paler sky to the east. A dog barked, and another, then both were suddenly silent. No lights showed.

The boy was moving quickly eastwards along a broad, cattle-beaten path. There were more huts, some of them set close to the track, others half-hidden in the trees. As they walked, Joe formed the uncanny impression that in each hut there were people lying awake, listening to them pass, knowing who they were, expecting them.

Then there were no more huts, just the bush – spare, over-browsed, the bare soil littered with small broken rocks that clattered underfoot. They crossed a dirt road marked with deep tyre tracks, and a narrow dried-up streambed. Nightbirds shrieked in the distance.

It became uncomfortably hotter. Joe was conscious of the sweat trickling down his chest beneath his bush shirt. A haze of cloud drew itself across the moon, darkening the landscape. Rain, maybe? He turned to ask Ross.

'Maybe.'

They didn't break pace.

It was two hours, perhaps longer, before the boy stopped. The moon was only dimly visible now, the bush an intense black. The boy whispered something in Shona to Ross who said, 'We're approaching the border. He says don't leave the path because of the minefield. Stay in touch contact. And silence, OK?' He repeated the instructions in Shona to Jonas, and to Enos who was bringing up the rear.

It was impossible to see the path. Joe put his hand on the boy's shoulder, felt the touch of Ross's on his own. They shuffled forwards, moving down a shallow incline, the bush, Joe sensed, thickening with each step they took. He expected some sort of security fence but if one was there, he didn't see it. Instead, the path dipped more steeply, strands of vegetation whipping at face height. and then there was the river.

It was narrow, a few yards of sluggish black water, a sharp eastern bank. Joe remembered the map. This would be the Rupembi, the twisting stream that marked this section of the border before disappearing into the marshes to the south. They were in Mozambique.

Mozambique.

Like a stroll in the country, Ross had said. Joe smiled at the thought, breathing deeply to control the tension that was building within him. He glanced round, half-expecting a shout, a challenge, a burst of automatic fire. There was no sound, save for the whine of the cicadas. The darkness was intense, suffocating, blanket-like. Too dark even for night-glasses to penetrate.

He had expected the boy to turn back at the river, but to his surprise Henry didn't. He walked on, faster now, presumably more confident of the path. He'd obviously been briefed to take them beyond the border zone. It would be Jack who'd insisted on that. Joe experienced a sudden pang of affection for the lonely rancher. If they succeeded, it would be Jack's doing every bit as much as Ross's. He'd repay him somehow, think of something.

After a while, they crossed a rough track, a border patrol track, probably. The ground began to rise, gently at first, then more steeply, split by sharp gullies. Maybe three kilometres from the border, Joe felt the boy hesitate, turn. There was a whispered comment, a brush of bare flesh against his arm, and then he was gone, as silently as he had come. To the south lightning flickered softly, illuminating broad sections of the sky. There was no thunder. No rain.

How far they walked that first night, it was impossible to tell. They hit the ridgetop as dawn broke, and set up camp in a clump of scrubby trees just beyond, dog-legging into it in the now familiar way. They cooked and ate sadza, spread out bedrolls. While they ate, Ross organised sentries on two-hourly duties, positioned close to the ridge with a clear view of the path. Enos, who as usual seemed completely impervious to fatigue, was allocated the first duty, followed by Jonas, then Ross, with Joe taking the last. As Enos moved into position, Joe lay down on his bedroll, arranged his FN so it would be instantly available, and pulled his bush hat over his eyes. He'd been awake, he realised in the split second before he lost consciousness, for almost twenty-four hours.

Helicopters.

Joe was awake at once, grabbing for his rifle, screwing up his eyes against the searing light. God in Heaven, it sounded like there were hundreds of them.

There was a low whistle. Ross was sliding down towards him, gesticulating urgently. He was pointing to a patch of scrubby thornbush in a wedge of the red rocks, maybe fifty yards from the camp. Joe understood. Clutching his bedroll and pack he threw himself onto his stomach and squirmed towards it.

It seemed so far. There was too much sky. Enos, he was dimly aware, was taking up position to the right, in a rock-strewn gully, setting up the RPD on its bipod. He couldn't see Jonas.

He flung himself between the twisted stems, gasping with pain as the long thorns slashed at him. He thought only about what Ross had told him in training: stay silent; safety catch forward for instant fire; get comfortable. A sharp stone smashed at his ribcage, driving the breath from his body. But he was on, past it, pitching himself further and further into the deep shadow thrown by the spreading leaves.

It was then, and only then, that he saw the machines. Through a cleft in the rock he saw them – four of them; no, five – camouflage-marked, machine-guns mounted on external rigs, quartering the bush at tree-height in a shallow valley to the south-east. Two of them were small Alouettes, he guessed

– the other three much larger.

And there were troops.

How many of them, it was difficult to say. They were moving slowly, perhaps a hundred yards between each man, already beginning to climb the ridge. Win the firefight, Ross had said. Go to ground and win the firefight. He hadn't said what to do if there was a whole fucking army about to walk all over you . . .

Bastards! Now the shock had gone, it was anger Joe felt, a deep, clean anger like a knife-cut. It was so stupid to die. So bloody stupid. There was no fear and that surprised him. Just anger. Jesus Christ, Ellie, he was saying to himself. You've got a jerk for a husband. A real jerk. To go and die on you like this. So close. So goddam close after all this time. Ellie Ellie Ellie. I'm gonna die, Ellie. Cassie. Ben . . .

OK. OK. He could take two of those bastards. Maybe three. Enos could take a dozen of them with the RPD, maybe even one of the choppers. Christ, that would be good. That would be so good. Wait for my move, Ross had said, then win the firefight. Win. Win. Win. He fumbled in his chest pouches for the spare magazines and laid them out on the flat red rock before him. He checked the change lever on the FN yet again. OK, he was ready, He'd never be so ready ever again . . .

One of the helicopters had broken from the valley, its elongated shadow snaking across the stripped red earth. It was moving fast suddenly, like it knew where it was going. He could see the pilot clearly, his white helmet, and the machine gunner hung out on the rig. Joe raised his gun. He'd hit the pilot, he decided, in a long burst. It was in range now. It had to be in range: the sun flashing from its screen, its rotors battering the air, filling the whole world, it seemed, with its noise. He should hit it now. NOW. He twisted frantically, straining to hear the first shots from Ross that would be his cue.

What in God's name?

A trail of brilliant white led from the campsite to where he lay. It was moving, tumbling, dissolving as the wind from the rotors hit it. It was like it had been put there on purpose. It was like . . .

He glanced down and only then did he understand. Somehow, crossing those rocks he'd ripped into his bedroll and it had spewed out its contents. White cotton, kapok, terylene . . . Christ, what the hell did it matter what it was? Those gooks in the chopper had seen it. He knew now they'd seen it.

Bastards! He shouted the word out loud into the roar of the engine, swung the FN skywards again. The dull green belly of the machine blocked out the sun. He tried to sight but the whole world was being smashed flat around him, sticks, leaves, thorns, leaping like living things. His eyes and mouth filled with the dust. He tried to roll clear, but the branches and rocks gripped him.

For a minute, maybe more, the helicopter hung above him, jigging from side to side like it was doing some kind of crazy dance. Then it swung away to the north. A shrill whistle, loud enough even to pierce the battering of the blades, made him turn. The men were coming in quickly now, ten or twenty of them, ducking from boulder to boulder as they tackled the slope. The helicopter, Joe became aware, had stopped, and was turning towards him, its pointed nose dipping as it began its run . . .

And then, quite suddenly, it was no longer there.

He didn't see where the rocket came from, nor did he hear the explosion as it hit, but he saw the streak of flame from its tail as it drove into the machine just beneath and to the rear of the main rotor column. The helicopter twisted twice and dropped vertically behind a patch of lichen-covered rocks. A ball of fire shot skywards, swallowed instantly by a column of pumping black smoke.

A rocket.

Joe stared at the smoke uncomprehendingly. The moment had frozen in his brain. Neither Ross nor Enos had rockets, he was certain. So who. . . ? For the first time he began to feel fear.

His eyes swept the valley, the ridge. The men, he saw, had stopped climbing towards him, and they too were staring at the smoke. There was a staccato shout of command. Two shrill whistle-blasts.

Then the machine-guns began, two or three of them, interspersed with the rattle of semi-automatic fire. The firing was coming from away to the left, beyond where the helicopter burned, the bullets lacing the twisted thorns and whining from the rocks.

'Commandante!' one of the men on the ridge was screaming. 'Commandante!' He was a large man, his shirt black with sweat. He'd been hit in the neck. Joe could see the red blood clearly as it oozed between his clutching fingers. A couple of his companions paused momentarily to return fire then they were away, following the rest of the men as they raced downwards to where the helicopters were gathering, circling like vultures.

For a short while the machines continued to circle, spitting flame from their guns, covering each other as they dropped down into the valley bed, hauling the fleeing figures aboard. Then they were gone, climbing fast, heading south into the sun.

'Commandante!'

Only the wounded man's screams broke the heavy silence that followed. 'Commandante!' Sometimes the screams were cut short by chokes, coughs. For minutes at a time they ceased altogether, only to begin again, louder and more insistent.

Sometimes Joe could see the man. Sometimes he was hidden behind rocks or thornbushes. He was crawling, head down, not going anywhere, his arms wet with red blood which glistened in the sunlight.

It was during one of the periods of silence that Joe saw the first of the attackers. He emerged from the bush close to where the column of smoke still pumped from the wrecked helicopter. He was dressed in camouflage fatigues and was carrying a bazooka tube slung across his shoulder. He paused cautiously at the valley lip, then began to descend. There were other men following, maybe thirty of them. They wore forage caps on their heads and were carrying AKs and RPDs, fanning out, moving from rock to rock in a series of fast, jinking runs.

'Commandante!' The wounded man's screams increased in intensity suddenly. He'd moved up closer to where Joe lay, maybe thirty feet below him. He too had seen the men coming, and was levering himself upwards on a rock. 'Commandante!' There were tears streaking his face above where the necklace of blood began. He began to walk unsteadily towards the nearest of the approaching figures, holding out his arms. He was welcoming them, Joe realised with mounting horror. He believed they were his own comrades come to take him home.

The attacker, a boy younger even than Jonas, stopped. He waited until the wounded man was almost within touching distance. Then he raised his AK and fired a short burst into the man's stomach. He fell silently, face downwards, and was still.

There was more firing now, from way down in the valley close to where the helicopters had taken off. There'd been men left behind, Joe guessed, and they were holed up, fighting for their lives.

The firing went on for some time, maybe half an hour, then there were two sharp explosions in quick succession. And silence.

This time there were no screams, just the gathering sounds of the superheated bush. Cicadas. Doves. The attackers were out of sight behind a fringe of low riverine trees, and it was only much later that Joe saw them again. They were moving north in a single long column, loaded down with weapons, two or three to a man.

They stayed visible for perhaps a mile, winding between the stunted mopanis, before they were swallowed by the contours of the land.

Fucking insects. They gathered beneath the flattened thornbush like they were attending some sort of insect convention, twisting, humming, biting. As the heat increased, they clustered at the corners of his mouth and eyes, drowned in his sweat. At first he tried to brush them away, but it cost too much energy and he became concerned that the movement might attract attention. Instead, he tried to concentrate on a column of black ants which had emerged from the shade of one of the rocks and was passing close to his face, foraging for small particles of dead leaf. He drank some water and chewed at a small strip of biltong which he discovered in one of the pockets of his pack. There was no sound or signal from Ross, Jonas or Enos.

For a long time, as he lay there watching the ants or staring out over the great blue plain of Mozambique, he tried to make sense of what had happened. It was an MNR patrol, he supposed, which had spotted the helicopters and moved in, a small-scale skirmish in a small-scale war, of no interest to anybody. As the hours passed, the whole thing seemed to take on the quality of a bad movie, a piece of fiction played out for his benefit. If it hadn't been for the dead man, gently swelling in the sun beneath him, he might even have come to believe that it had never happened.

It was late in the day before Ross came. There was a low whistle, the single crack of a twig, the sudden pressure of a thin body next to his. 'You OK?' Ross spoke in a low whisper.

Joe nodded.

'Lucky, hey?'

'I guess so.'

Joe waited for Ross to say more, but he remained silent. He seemed gentler than usual, vulnerable even, in need of company. After a while he took out a map, orientated it, and began to trace across it with his finger. The dry valley beneath them was the Honde, Joe saw, and they were to cross it and head east, presumably after dark, until they reached the Cahora Bassa powerlines. They would follow them northeast to the mountains. There'd be some sort of cutline through the bush, he supposed, beneath the pylons. They'd make better time that way, especially if they continued to move at night. Joe remembered Ross mentioning the powerlines earlier when they'd examined the map back at Mulovelo. They ran the length of the western border of Mozambique from the Cahora Bassa dam south to the Transvaal, crossing the Buzi River close to Nhamasi. The MNR had blown the line back in 1981, he recalled Ross saying, which had blacked out large areas of northern South Africa. He borrowed the binoculars and tried to spot the lines beyond the far ridge, but failed. They were close, though. They'd maybe reach them tonight if things went well.

As he handed the glasses back he said, 'You still think we can do it?'

'Yes.'

'Larry thinks we're crazy.'

'So we're crazy.'

Ross's confidence cheered him, and his physical presence. He shifted to ease the growing cramp in his legs. 'I thought we were going to die this morning."

Ross smiled. 'That makes two of us. I reckon that must have been the entire bloody Mozambican Airforce.'

'So why did you come, if you knew they were going to be waiting for us?'

Ross paused. 'You think I knew that? You really think I knew that?'

'But Larry said . . .'

'He talks shit.'

'But he was right.'

Ross took a deep breath and ran his finger along the magazine of his AK, tracing its curve. 'Maybe,' he said softly. 'Maybe.' He switched his gaze out into the gathering dusk. The darkened hollows of his cheeks made his face seem like a skull, bare of flesh.

Suddenly Joe realised that it was no longer pity, or fear, but something close to love he felt for this strange man. 'Look, if we get out of this, come back to London with us,' he said.

Ross smiled again. 'I don't think that's my scene, somehow.'

'But you can't go back to Zimbabwe, for God's sake.'

Ross fell silent. Eventually he said, 'No, I can't go back there.'

'So where are you going to go?'

'Who knows?' Ross stared intently for a moment at the bush beneath them, then raised the binoculars to his eyes. 'We've got visitors.'

'Visitors?'

He gave the glasses to Joe and pointed. A hunched black shape was just visible, moving between the rocks, easing itself cautiously, silently, towards the place where the dead man lay. A hyena.

It was then, and only then, as he watched the animal close in, that Joe understood.

They left, soon after seven, moving slowly at first, picking their way downwards through the rocks, conscious of the

331

hyenas which had scattered from their feast. As the moon rose it became easier, Enos padding softly in the lead, clearly visible in the pale light. By midnight they were beyond the second ridge, making good time through a strange, wrecked, leafless landscape that reminded Joe of pictures he'd seen of napalmed areas in Vietnam. They made a detour south to avoid a small fire they saw burning in the distance, and once, around four a.m. they heard a helicopter flying fast and low towards the north. It had no navigation lights.

They reached the powerlines as the moon set and made camp soon afterwards, maybe a kilometre from the closest of the stark black gantries.

As they moved north it was the days that were the worst, the inactivity and heat making them seem endless. It became difficult to remain alert during the two-hour watches, impossible to find sufficient shade to sleep comfortably in between. By the third day the water was running low, and when they ate, Joe had to force himself to swallow the unappetising sadza.

The nights, though, were easier. They made good progress through the dessicated mopani, their senses tuned to the pale moonlight, the moving shadows. Joe had been right, there was a cut-line beneath the cables, a track half-obscured by scrubby regrowth, presumably intended for maintenance crews. They didn't use it. It was too exposed, Ross explained, and might be mined. Instead, they stayed out to the west of it, keeping it always in sight, waiting for the mountains.

On the third night they crossed a dirt road, little more than twin wheelruts in the deep sand; the Espungabera-Massangena road, Joe deduced later from the map. The following night they crossed another, this time better graded and obviously more frequently used, winding east towards Machaze. Twice more, they heard helicopters, both times heading south, and once, north of the Machaze road, they spotted a group of armed men, maybe fifty of them, moving quite openly along the cut-line. It was an MNR patrol from Alguendo Camp, Jonas said, he recognised two of the men. He thought they were going to Machaze to look for food.

It was that same morning, during his watch, that Joe saw the mountains. What he had at first taken to be a blue cloud mass to the north resolved itself, as the heat of the day built, into a series of round-shouldered humps rising from the flat sandveld. They seemed disappointingly small. Somehow he'd expected jagged peaks like he'd seen in Inyanga, not these piffling mounds. But they were the mountains. They had to be.

He fetched the map and, using his fingers as dividers, estimated the distance. Thirty kilometres at the most. A couple of night's trek. A bit of a climb. Then . . .

By the time he came to wake Enos, it was like he'd lived with the shape of those mountains all his life.

The carcass of a cow long since gutted by hyenas was inadequate cover, but it was all there was. Ahead of them lay a jumble of bleached poles. Beyond, a single hut, missing its thatch, leant at a crazy angle.

For fifteen minutes they had lain there, stomachs pressed to the still-warm floor of the empty kraal. There was no sound. No movement. Nothing. Joe hoped to God Jonas was right and there was water at the village. There was a well, he'd said. Good water. Clean. It was a risk, but they'd had to take it. They were down to half a bottle of water each. They couldn't wait for the mountains. A few yards to the left of the cow, propped against a rock, there was a sign. 'O POVO É A FORÇA PRINCIPA E DECISIVA NA REVOLUÇÃO' it read, its letters dimly visible in the moonlight. It was made from what looked like a section cut from an old oil drum, and riddled with bullet holes.

Joe was beginning to think it wasn't a village at all, but a single abandoned hut, when a signal came from Ross and Enos was up and running. He moved forward at a low crouch, the RPD at ready, easing himself flat to the hut wall, edging round it, his dark shape scarcely visible against the gapped poles.

Joe tensed and slipped the change lever on the FN to automatic. If it was going to happen, it was going to happen now.

It didn't. For a long time, an infinitely long time, it seemed,

Enos remained motionless as if nailed to the rough timbers. Then, with a quick firm gesture, he indicated that they should break cover and join him.

It was not until he reached the hut that Joe understood the reason for Enos's confidence. There was no village any more.

It must have been big once, very big, judging by the extent of the kraals. Now only a couple of huts still stood, if anything more delapidated than the one which gave them shelter. Where the other huts had been were dark circles, a few charred timbers. Broken pots, stools, cooking stones, occasional scraps of clothing littered the area in between. To the right, maybe fifty yards from where they waited, there was a section of wall, the remains of what looked to have been a rectangular mudbrick building. And next to it, its circular concrete rim still apparently intact, was the well.

'OK?'

Enos nodded in response to Ross's hissed question, checked his gun, then moved out quickly towards it. Joe made to follow but a touch from Ross restrained him. He just caught the single word breathed into his ear. 'Mines.'

About five metres from the well Enos stopped suddenly, knelt down and began to inch himself forward with extreme caution, examining the soil minutely, occasionally brushing at it with his hands. Joe held his breath.

Nothing. Enos reached the rim, pulled himself upwards into standing position and peered inside. He shook his head a couple of times and indicated that they should come forward to join him.

It was as they approached that Joe first noticed the smell. It was a peculiar smell, damp, fusty, like old rotting blankets. It was not pleasant, not unpleasant. Despite the heat of the night, Joe felt himself shiver.

It got worse, the smell, the closer they got. It was coming from the shaft, so strong now he almost gagged. Ross reached into his pack and produced a small torch that Joe hadn't seen before. He put his arm into the well and switched it on.

They looked like old sacks. That was his first impression. Old sacks, tied and dumped into the water, dozens of them, not floating, but jammed against the rough walls . . .

Then Joe saw the face.

It was looking straight up at him, its eye sockets gaping, teeth bared. There was a second face to the left of it, and a third. There was the stump of an arm, the flesh peeled back onion-like from the exposed bones. And resting against the arm, where the neck would have been if there'd been a neck, was the almost clean skeleton of a baby.

They found water eventually, late the following afternoon. Enos had slipped off into the bush, taking Jonas with him, and they'd found buffalo tracks leading to a small stagnant pool in the crook of a dried river. They collected the water at dusk, straining it into bottles using the foot of a pair of nylon tights which Ross produced, then adding a couple of Halazone tablets to each. Joe drank deeply. The water tasted, but it *was* water and it was safe. They must have swung north-east the night before, because when they left the pool they picked up the powerlines surprisingly quickly. By dawn they were close to the mountains, camped in a growth of thick acacia scrub.

Joe spent most of his watch looking at the mountains. They rose abruptly from the bush maybe five kilometres from where he sat, a series of humped ridges, climbing upwards to the north-west, split in a couple of places by what looked like deep river valleys. The power lines didn't deviate but rose die-straight over the closest of the ridges like the supports for some kind of alpine ski-lift. Larry had been wrong about the vegetation, he decided, examining the slopes with the binoculars. There were no wattle and gum plantations, at least not within sight, just thick bush climbing to perhaps a thousand feet, then thinning, becoming patched with what looked like pale olive green grass and outcrops of red rock.

Later, while the sadza was boiling, he studied the map with Ross and Enos. It looked easy. A few kilometres of bush, the first horseshoe-shaped ridge, then the steep Buzi valley. To the west there was a strange star-shaped area of low ground where three rivers – the Nhamasi was one of them – joined the Buzi. There'd be settlements there, Ross thought, if the map was accurate, so they'd stay out to the east. Then, beyond the Buzi, there was a second, higher ridge marked with a couple of peaks rising to about 2500 feet, and what looked to be a

335

small plateau. They'd use the high ground, circle round to the east, and hit the Nhamasi a few kilometres from the confluence close to where Ross had circled the probable position of the camp. It wasn't far. Taking the scale as accurate, it was fifteen kilometres at the most. Unless there were problems, they could do it in the night.

Joe felt the first shivers of excitement. Tonight. A couple of ridges, a river valley, and they'd be there. It seemed impossible that they were so close.

Darkness seemed a long time coming.

It was Jonas who led them out, crossing the cut-line once more before turning north. During a long, slow conversation in simple Shona he'd told Enos about a path he knew, a route the MNR had checked out in case of attack. It avoided the villages. Privately, Joe felt doubtful about the existence of the path or, if it did exist, the boy's ability to find it. But at least they were going in the right direction. Ahead of them the black bulk of the mountains loomed ever larger, blocking out the stars. They crossed a couple of tracks and what might once have been a properly graded road. To the west the occasional flicker of firelight betrayed the presence of a village. By ten they were climbing.

Joe was right. There was no path. The vegetation was thinner than it had seemed from a distance, and there were more rocks. They levered themselves upwards between the stunted trees, gasping with the effort. Spiky aloes, their dried flower-heads like rusty candelabra, ripped at their exposed limbs. Something, baboons it had to be, crashed off to the left with a sudden explosion of sound. It grew cooler, the leaves slippery with dew. Where the trees fell back and the grass took over, the press of their feet released the sweet smell of herbs.

It took them three hours to reach the top, and they rested in the deep shadow of a huge egg-shaped wind-smoothed boulder. The moon was well up now, reaching its zenith, less than half-full but still surprisingly bright. Below them the thin silver strip of the Buzi wound through its V-shaped gorge. To the west a few dim points of light confirmed what Ross had predicted, the presence of a settlement at the confluence. The powerlines, which crossed the ridge a few hundred metres from where they sat, straddled the valley like dark metallic six-armed giants, undeviating in their march northwards. The scene had a bleak beauty to which Joe, despite his growing excitement, was able to respond.

It was like a pain, the excitement, like something that had colonised his body, occupying it entirely, intensifying with each minute that passed. Despite the fatigue of the climb he was impatient during the rest, drinking too much water, a couple of times getting to his feet and straining his eyes northwards to where Nhamasi lay. When the time came he was the first to shoulder his pack, and it took a quiet word from Ross to prevent him taking the lead.

Jonas found the path, at least that was what he said it was. To Joe it seemed more like a rainwater gully. It descended rapidly towards the river in a series of sharp zig-zags, skirting the larger boulders, occasionally dropping vertically, stepped with flat slabs of dark rock. Close to the river the bush thickened. Tall trees, msasas Joe guessed, blocked out the moon. A night-ape screamed.

The water was black, loud, fast-flowing. They paused to refill their bottles, Ross doling out the requisite Halazone tablets like a parent distributing sweets. They crossed close to the rocky lip of a small waterfall, their feet braced against the current.

It was easier beyond the river, the slope gentler, the path more established. By dawn they had turned westwards into a spoon-shaped basin of rock, its naked surface stained pink by a new light from the east. Ahead of them another low ridge, a jumble of boulders, a few stunted shrubs.

They made camp among the boulders as the first rays of sunlight hit the distant rockfaces to the west. It was while they were drinking tea, spreadeagled on their stained bedrolls, that Ross pointed to the ridge and gave a thumbs-up sign.

Joe understood.

Sleep. Ross had insisted on it. Joe had wanted to carry on, take a look at the camp, try to spot Ellie or one of the kids. But no, he had to sleep first.

He closed his eyes, opened them again. How was he supposed to sleep when they were so close? Count bloody sheep? If he shouted loud enough they'd probably hear him, they were that close. He contemplated trying it for a moment, then turned over, searching for some comfort on the rocky ground.

He glanced at his watch. Eight-twenty. They'd be up by now, no doubt, Ellie and the kids, facing another day, preparing to do whatever they did to pass the time, still waiting for him as they'd waited for him for so many days, so many months now. Still waiting.

They'd be different. Changed. He'd have to get used to that fact. Tougher. Thinner. Like strangers. He'd have to make allowances. He'd have to try to understand what they'd been through. He'd have to . . .

The thought struck him like a hammer blow. They probably weren't waiting for him at all. Why the hell should they be? They'd seen him shot. They'd seen him fall. Unless they'd seen a newspaper, unless Schoeman had told them, they'd think he was dead. Jonas had thought he was dead. Nobody had told *him*. And all the time he'd been constructing these visions, these pointless bloody dreams! An ngozi. He was still an ngozi . . .

He shifted again onto his back. Ross, he saw, was also still awake, staring upwards into the washed blue of the morning sky. Thinking of what? And Enos, sitting motionless among the rocks, the RPD across his knees, what was going on in his mind? They were still strangers, he realised, still total strangers despite what they'd been through together. Only Jonas slept.

For a while he watched a hawk, black against the brightness of the sky, buffeted by upcurrents, sometimes beating its wings rapidly. He envied that hawk, Christ how he envied it. In his mind he became the hawk, plummeting down towards the place where Ellie was, and Ben, and Cassie. 'I'm not dead,' the hawk was shouting to them. 'I'm not dead. I'm coming. I'm coming . . .'

A fist in his ribs, a hand across his mouth. He shot up to consciousness like he was in some kind of crazy high-speed elevator. Ross was gesticulating silently, pointing to the south, the way they had come. Joe grabbed his FN and, still shaking with the suddenness of waking, squirmed towards the skirt of boulders that surrounded their sleeping place. Enos? Jonas? Jonas's bedroll was empty, Enos gone from his sentry position. There was a cry, a soft uncertain cry, like a baby crying. What in God's name. . . ?

A boy walked slowly across the rock bowl towards them. He could have been no more than seven, pot-bellied with malnutrition and with sticks for legs. He was dressed in a few tatters of undyed cotton and clutching what looked like a small bark whip. In front of him, thinner almost than he was, were three black and brown goats. It was the goats that had been crying.

Joe flicked the change lever to automatic and sighted. The boy would spot them any minute now . . .

There was a touch on his arm. Ross was shaking his head, pointing at the gun. Joe understood. Crazy. He must be crazy. There could be no shooting. It was too close. Far too close. Ross, he saw, had taken his bush knife from its sheath . . .

The first of the goats was at the rocks, squeezing between them. Joe could smell its stink. Small flies danced. The animal stopped, its yellow eyes walling with fright. It backed off . . .

A single cry, that was all. Enos had risen from a small depression screened by a clump of aloes a few feet from the boy and was onto him, crushing him to the ground, blocking his mouth, twisting his arms behind him. There was a short struggle, then stillness. Jonas, concealed to the left, got to his feet and walked across to where the pair lay.

For a moment, Joe thought the boy was dead; that somehow, using some technique he hadn't heard of, Enos had broken his neck, stopped his heart. But then he heard the sound of Shona being spoken.

Enos spoke for a long time, still not moving, the boy spreadeagled beneath him. After a while, Joe saw, he removed his hand from the boy's mouth, and there was some kind of faint reply, tremulous with terror. Enos exchanged glances with Jonas, then stood up.

The boy lay prone for a second or two, as if unable to believe that he was free, then scrambled to his feet and ran off down the hillside with surprising speed. The three goats followed, chasing frantically like eager dogs.

Enos watched them go, his head slightly to one side as if memorizing the direction they took, then turned and came quickly across to where Joe and Ross lay, Jonas padding softly at his heels. 'We go,' he said in English. For the first time since Joe had known him, he seemed jumpy, apprehensive.

Ross nodded. They swiftly rolled their bedding and secured their packs. Enos checked out the campsite carefully, eliminating all traces of their presence. While he did so he was talking rapidly and quietly in English. He'd told the boy they were a patrol from the camp, he said, and that they were looking for Government mujibas – spies. He'd told him that if he mentioned meeting them when he got back to his village they would know he was a mujiba, and they would come to his kraal and cut his throat and the throats of his entire family. The boy had believed him, he thought, but they couldn't stay where they were. There was a risk.

'You should have killed him,' Joe said, angry.

Enos looked at him for a moment or two, then shook his head. 'No,' he said slowly. 'That would not have been appropriate.'

They followed the ridge, Enos leading. The daylight made Joe feel strangely exposed. The bare rock disappeared and the bush thickened, tangled growths obviously greened by recent rain, speckled here and there with fragrant yellow and white flowers. After half an hour they stopped. Enos retreated a short way to eliminate their tracks, then they rested, drinking water.

It was a good place to rest, close to the ridgeline, the vegetation giving excellent cover. The ground sloped gently, then increasingly sharply towards the west, fringed with tallish trees. Small birds whistled and darted among the branches.

It was when he had finished drinking, and was watching a tiny yellow and brown lizard which had moved out of the undergrowth to sun itself near his left foot, that Joe smelt the woodsmoke. It was an unmistakable smell, reminding him of autumn in England. It was coming from the valley below. He

340

glanced at the others. They too had smelt it. He felt himself beginning to shake. Woodsmoke. Where there was woodsmoke . . .

Before he could ask the question which was forming on his lips, Jonas had answered it for him. He'd wriggled swiftly forward to the screen of trees, eased himself between them, and peered down. He returned immediately with a look of excitement, almost triumph on his face. 'Nhamasi,' he whispered urgently. 'Nhamasi!'

Joe parted the fringe of grass gently, like parting the hair of a woman to whom he was going to make love. He levered himself an inch or two closer to the rim of the valley. Ellie. It was Ellie's hair he was parting. He looked down.

Beneath him lay what at first sight looked like a ramshackle, impoverished African village: groups of rough pole and dagga huts tucked into a loop of the river, a few patches of mealies, a couple of empty kraals. There was washing drying on low bushes, a number of fires burning. There appeared to be no perimeter fence, no fortifications of any kind. Apart from three emaciated women sitting motionless beneath a tree, a small black toddler white with dust at their feet, there was no sign of life.

Joe glanced up quickly at Ross who was lying prone beside him. This was the wrong place, he was suddenly convinced of it. A real camp would be neat, ordered, efficient, not like this. That little bastard had been lying to them to save his own skin. There was no Nhamasi Camp. There never had been. This was just some bloody village he'd brought them to. A distinct smell of human excrement mingled with the woodsmoke.

He must have made a noise because Ross had his index finger to his lips and was shaking his head slowly. Jesus Christ, surely . . .

He was pointing to something: a square, tin-roofed building set to the rear of an extensive patch of bare beaten earth. Joe hadn't noticed the building. It had a narrow stoep, was partly shaded by a low acacia. It looked like a beat-up African store, missing the signboard. It too seemed deserted.

He was wondering why Ross had indicated it when something caught his eye, a movement. There were people on the stoep, it was so difficult to see with the black shadow it cast.

And there was an aerial, it had to be an aerial attached to the side of the building, waving gently in the light breeze. A radio, in an African store? As he watched, a man stepped down from the stoep, crossed to the acacia and began to urinate. He wore camouflage fatigues, and had an AK slung.

Joe turned to get binoculars but Ross had them clamped to his eyes. He had a small pad of buff-coloured paper spread out before him, and a stump of pencil.

Ellie. Ellie. Ellie.

Was she in one of those huts? There was a row of them immediately below, square not round like the others, and one bigger hut, open front and rear like the one at Mulovelo. No, not like the one at Mulovelo. There were pumpkins in the mealie patches that bordered the river. He could see the pale flowers.

Ross was drawing a plan. He'd marked the line of square huts, sketched in the loop of the river. Near the square huts he'd written the word 'Barracks' and put a question mark.

Any one of the huts was large enough to hold all three of them. It was a definite possibility. And if not there, where? In some sweltering back room of that shack where the soldiers were? The one Ross had marked 'Command Post'?

Or maybe not there at all. Maybe nowhere. Jonas hadn't been certain. He'd said they'd been taken to Nhamasi, but he didn't know if they were still there. They could be hundreds of miles away. Up North. Dead.

No, not dead.

He must concentrate. Be patient, systematic. Jesus, the binoculars! He should have got himself a pair. Jack would have had some to lend if he'd only thought to ask. He was crazy even thinking of crossing the border without binoculars.

OK, he'd use Ross's eyes. Follow the map as it grew. What was it he used to say to Ben? Take it steady. Finish the job you're doing before you start on the next. Good advice. The best. He'd work right to left like Ross was doing, starting down there where the valley wall met the river.

There was a largish group of huts there, maybe twenty of them, crumbling pole and dagga, circular, squeezed up close. 'Povo' Ross had written against those huts. Povo. People. There was no question mark this time. There was a flash of blue, a woman coming up from the river carrying a galvanised water can on her head. She was heading towards the huts.

That was what had confused him, he suddenly realised, the fact that there were women and children here. He should have expected it. There'd been women and children at Nyadzonya after all. Maybe these ones were here for the same reason. There were a few scrubby trees. Some of the huts had smoke filtering through the thatch. Cooking huts. In a small clearing were some large oil drums covered with flat metal sheeting. Kachasu? Beer? He remembered the drum in that village in Matibi, the drunken woman. Sex and beer. That would be the reason those women were here. Sex. Beer.

There was a small square building to the left of the povo huts, close to the Command Post. It was built of brick or mud, more likely mud, tin-roofed with a wooden door. 'Armoury' Ross was writing next to it, again with a question mark. Beside it was a tiny open rondavel, more like a shelter than a hut. It was some kind of guard post, no doubt. Behind that was a strip of cultivated garden, the white logs of a kraal.

Slowly the plan developed on the buff paper. A row of three or four more square huts behind the Command Post. There was a water tank; what might have been the football pitch that Jonas had mentioned. There was a second brick-built shed – and next to that, slightly to the rear, a larger, rectangular mud-walled building roofed with what looked like cracked asbestos sheeting. It had a small window blocked with wire netting, or maybe reed matting. The door, facing inwards, stood open.

Joe glanced up again at Ross. He was examining the building closely, taking his time. Could this be it? There was something about the place that made it seem right. Joe squinted at the black rectangle of the doorway. Christ, if she'd just show herself, or one of the kids. Just a glimpse. That was all they'd need.

For a while longer Ross concentrated on the building then, as if satisfied, he drew it into his plan and continued.

Another kraal. A couple more guard posts. Another cluster of pole and dagga shacks. What were probably latrines behind a long screen of woven grass fencing. A kitchen area immediately beneath where they lay, deserted though fires

343

were burning. And on the valley side, maybe fifty feet below them, a narrow path which Ross indicated as being probably for the use of foot patrols.

That was it. Nothing more. Jonas had said the place was small. He was right. That should make it easier when they went in, if Ellie and the kids were there.

Joe glanced along the main track to where it wound in from the south, following the river before swinging up towards the Command Post and what was obviously the parade ground. Its entrance to the camp was obscured by a spur of rock jutting from the valley side. Maybe there were more huts way back there which they couldn't see. Maybe this was not the main camp at all but some kind of annex.

Where in God's name were they? Once more he searched the buildings beneath him. Surely they weren't locked in permanently in one of those closed huts, with no light, no exercise. That building Ross had marked down as the armoury, it could just as well be a prison. For some reason he found himself thinking of 'Bridge on the River Kwai', the movie, where the Japs had put Alec Guinness in that tin shed. What was it called, the Sweat Box? His memory was vague. He must have been a kid when he saw it last. No, not like that. It wouldn't be like that at all. They were at a different camp perhaps, somewhere better run. Not this place. He must have been crazy to think it was just an African village. It was evil, sinister. He could smell the evil, the stink of it, like something dead, rotting in the sun. Christ, he wished he had some binoculars.

There was movement from Ross. He was backing cautiously away from the edge. Joe continued to stare down at the scene below for a moment or two before reluctantly following. They joined Enos who had set up a sentry point close to the ridgeline, Jonas beside him. Ross exchanged a few whispered words with him in Shona, then turned to Joe and beckoned. He was going south to find a new vantage point.

They found it, a couple of hundred metres from where Enos sat, more exposed this time, lacking tree cover, the rock made slippery by a spreading growth of succulent. Once more they eased themselves slowly forward on their elbows.

No, it was certainly no village. Beneath them, close to the

valley wall, where the povo huts ended, there was a guard post and a rough wooden boom slung across the track. Two youths, in civilian clothes this time, but with AKs leaning against the wall of their crude shelter, were playing what looked like a game of draughts on a faded red and white board. And on the far side of the track, mounted on a trailer, was a large unmanned twin-barrelled machine gun.

Joe glanced at Ross who appeared not to share his concern at the sight of the gun. He was rapidly sketching in the positions of the guard hut, the boom. The machine gun was indicated by a firmly marked X, next to which he wrote '14.5mm × 2'. 'Russian,' he whispered, in response to Joe's query. 'Anti-aircraft. Probably captured from the Mozambican Army.'

From this new position more huts were visible. The Command Post was bigger than it had seemed, the size of a small bungalow, and there was a lean-to shelter tacked on to the rear of the open-doored mud and asbestos hut. But still no Ellie.

'You got any idea where she might be?' Joe put the question as calmly as he was able.

Ross shook his head slowly. He paused, then swept the camp again with the glasses. 'Come to that,' he said, 'where the fuck is everybody else?'

Enos too, was worried. When they had returned he went off alone to make his own survey of the camp, concentrating on the area of the povo huts at the northern edge of the river bend. He reported back mid-afternoon, shaking his head. He'd seen no sign of Ellie and the children, though when pressed by Joe he agreed that the asbestos-roofed hut could well be where they were being or had been held. There were at least two hundred men based at the camp, he thought, though at the moment there seemed to be no more than twenty-five present, and there were too few women. It occurred to Joe that maybe they'd had warning of an attack, and had dispersed into the bush, possibly taking Ellie and the kids with them. But judging by the relaxed attitudes of the men in the Command Post, and the sentries at the boom, that seemed unlikely.

If not that, what? Enos questioned Jonas for some time

about likely reasons for the men's absence, but he seemed as puzzled as they were. It was obviously possible that there was a major MNR assault underway somewhere, maybe to the north against Espungabera or Chimoio, but if that was the case, why take the women? The one certain thing he had established, Enos said, was that there was a big beer drink being planned. They were brewing a lot of beer, the women who had stayed behind. A lot. He'd seen them sieving it which meant it was almost ready. The men were obviously expected back soon.

And Ellie? Was she expected back, too?

Ellie Ellie Ellie. Joe repeated the name over and over to himself beneath his breath, like a chant, like a mantra. She seemed further away from him now than she'd ever been. He took out the photographs, smoothed the creases, once more he tried to fix in his mind the shape of her face, jawline, nose . . . He failed. And the children? Cassie? Ben? Six months was a long time. Too long.

Depression came in at him, so acute that it seemed to suck the strength from his body. He buried his head in his hands.

Ross cooked sadza, but Joe wasn't hungry. He ate a mouthful or two of the tasteless pap, then rejected it. Jonas cleared the tin without being bid. When the meal was finished, the three of them, Ross, Enos and Jonas, drew close together and began a lengthy whispered conversation in Shona, occasionally referring to Ross's diagram of the camp. A couple of times Joe tried to get them to talk in English, but they ignored his requests. His depression deepened. At last, unable to stand any more, he asked Ross for the binoculars. They were handed over without a word. He went to the position he and Ross had occupied during the morning, amongst the trees and long grass, and lay down.

It helped to have the binoculars, and for a time it was almost pleasant lying there. It was late afternoon now, gone four, the stifling heat of the low bush dispersed by the altitude and the gentle easterly breeze. He settled down to make another systematic survey of the camp.

There were a few more people around: one or two men with AKs; several women, some with babies strapped to their backs, working in the kitchen area or attending to the beer drums. A rhythmic thumping came from the povo huts to the north. Mealies being pounded, Joe guessed. From the Command Post, bizarrely, was the sound of rock music playing.

At four-thirty, two men, AKs slung, left the Command Post and walked out along the main track beyond the spur of rock. Soon afterwards the two youths Joe had seen earlier playing draughts returned. A sentry changeover, obviously. One of the youths went into the latrines, squatted briefly, then joined his companion who was talking to the women in the kitchen area. There were some loud shouts from the Command Post, a burst of laughter, more rock music.

Joe spent a long time examining the asbestos-roofed hut. It was primitive but in pretty good repair, certainly adequate for a woman and two children. The crude shelter they'd seen at the back could well be accommodation for a guard. The slanting sun had lighted the open doorway slightly, and something – a bed, was it? – was just visible inside. The thought that it was a bed cheered him. Africans slept on straw mats not beds. It would be just like Ellie to insist on having a bed. He could hear her asking for it quietly, not raising her voice, getting her own way.

He was still smiling at the thought when something to the south, where the track curved round the outcrop of rock, attracted his attention.

It was a goat.

It was brown and black, bony-legged, bleating loudly. It paused, looked back the way it had come, then trotted forward again. It was followed immediately by a second goat, then a third. And a boy.

The boy!

Joe twisted back, signalling frantically. They were still talking, the three of them, Enos emphasising some point with a raised finger, and it was a second or two before they saw him. They slid silently in beside him on their bellies. Joe pointed. Ross grabbed the binoculars. 'Little bastard,' he hissed.

'The same boy?'

Ross handed the glasses to Enos who squinted down them. 'The same boy,' he said.

It was like a farce, a crazy bloody evil farce. His headache, vaguely present all afternoon, intensified, pounding at Joe's temples. It felt like his head was going to burst. 'You should have killed him, Enos. Why in God's name didn't . . .'

'Shhh.' Ross had his finger to his lips cautioning him to silence. He didn't take his eyes from the boy.

The boy approached the Command Post and hesitated. He seemed uncertain. There was movement from the stoep and the sound of an adult male voice, surprisingly clear considering the distance. There was a burst of laughter. 'What the hell's going on?' Joe's eyes sought Enos, questioning.

'One of the men is saying he fancies goat meat for supper.'

The boy was scared, that much was apparent even without the glasses. He backed away as if expecting some kind of blow. Whether he said anything it was impossible to tell. He turned and drove the goats rapidly towards the group of povo huts to the north, disappearing between them. There was the sound of a woman's voice, a few more bleats from the goats, then silence.

Joe glanced at Ross, but he didn't respond. He was staring fixedly at the narrow path the boy had taken between the huts. He reached over, took the binoculars from Enos, but instead of using them himself pressed them into Joe's hand. 'Take a look,' he whispered.

Joe focussed the glasses.

Walking slowly out between the huts was a white woman, and following behind her, in single file, were two children. White children. One boy. One girl.

Ellie. And Cassie. And Ben.

Joe wasn't sure what happened next. He only knew he was trying to get to his feet. Maybe he was going to call out to them. It was as if a timed explosion had gone off in his body. Ross was on him, holding him down, whispering something he didn't understand.

It was Ellie! Dear God, it was Ellie! He had to go to them. He had to . . . It was so hard to steady the glasses, so bloody hard. He fought with his shaking limbs.

Ellie.

She looked so thin, and the kids were spindle-legged, knock-kneed like the boy with the goats. Ellie had lost her hair, the soft brown curls that had always framed her face. Now it was cropped close to her head, like an African woman, like those Jewish women in the Holocaust documentaries. Jesus, they were so thin!

And silent.

They walked one behind the other silently, like cowed schoolkids following an over-strict teacher. There was a large raw patch on Ellie's left cheekbone. Some kind of ulcer, it looked like. And there was something wrong with Cassie's skin, too. It was scaly, flaky . . .

Bastards! They were fat enough, those bastards on that stoep, listening to Duran Duran or whoever it was. They had food. They had mealie meal. And what were they doing with it – making bloody beer while Ellie and the kids starved. . . .

They'd use the grenades, hit that fucking shack from all sides at once, silence bloody Duran Duran and those murdering motherfuckers for good. Twenty-five men, Enos had said. They could take twenty-five with no problem, no bother . . .

Jesus, they were alive! ALIVE! They must go get to them now.

'Cool it, man,' Ross whispered, gently touching his arm.

Joe wrenched himself free. A pebble, dislodged by the movement, clattered a short way down the valley side then stopped. 'I'm sorry,' he said, finding himself suddenly close to tears.

He loved them, that was all he knew. Loved them. Just loved them.

They were opposite the Command Post now, Ellie slowing, reaching back, taking the children's hands. A man in camouflage fatigues, the same man who moments earlier had shouted to the boy, watched them pass. This time he said nothing. Ellie neither looked at him, nor acknowledged his presence. She bent to say something to Ben as they walked. He, apparently, made no reply. They went towards the asbestos-roofed hut.

They were alive.

Joe lowered the glasses and wiped his eyes. A sudden, unexpected feeling of peace washed over him like the warm water of a comforting bath. They were alive. He exchanged glances with Ross, who, as if sensing his change of mood, winked. Alive. Alive. Now all they had to do was get them out. Think. Plan. Make sure nothing went wrong. Nothing.

Ellie didn't go into the asbestos-roofed hut. Instead, to Joe's surprise, she led the children down a narrow beaten path beside it, and disappeared to the rear. He scanned the area beyond the hut, but they didn't reappear.

Surely not that tiny lean-to shelter? Surely they weren't living in that place they'd seen round the back earlier? Part of the roof had been missing, he remembered, there'd been bare poles, rotting thatch. He glanced at Ross again, seeking reassurance. He shrugged, indicated that they should go to the southern vantage point, the one overlooking the camp entrance. They could see from there.

They went, leaving Jonas on guard. Enos led, moving swiftly because of the gathering dusk. The vegetation was already damp with dew. There was a sudden chill which made Joe shiver. Once more he pressed the glasses to his eyes. 'They're there,' he said.

They were a long way away, maybe five hundred metres, and it was difficult to see, but they were there. Ellie was seated in the doorway of the shelter, her batik skirt, the same one she'd put on that morning in Mutare so long ago, slung between her legs. The children were on either side of her. They seemed to be eating something with their hands from what looked like calabashes or maybe rough earthen pots. A large galvanised water can stood beside them.

There could be no doubt now. None. In his worst dreams there had always been some sort of reasonable hut, something that would at least keep out the rain. But this?

They were eating quickly, with a jerky eagerness that reminded him of Jonas, scooping the food into their mouths. Ben finished first, then got up and went into the shelter. He came out soon afterwards with what seemed to be a small wire model of an aeroplane. He showed it to Cassie who nodded. Ellie washed the bowls using some water from the can, then all three of them went inside.

Joe turned away, shaking his head to try to clear it. The headache had returned. There was the fresh taste of blood in his mouth. He must have bitten into his lip without realising it. At that moment he hated those bastards with their guns and their rock music; he hated Africa, with an intensity that stopped his breath.

They should go in now, not hesitate, not even think about it. They could make it to the Command Post, use the grenades, get Ellie and the kids out and be across that river in a matter of minutes. There was nothing to stop them. Nothing. It was dark. The moon not yet up. The place wide open.

Yet still they waited.

They'd been lying there, Ross and Enos, in the same positions for what seemed like an eternity. They'd surveyed the shelter, the narrow path that led from it down to the river between the wrecked kraals. They'd made notes, conducted brief discussions in whispered Shona, spent more time looking at the big machine gun near the entrance boom. Now it was too dark to see. What more could they want? More information? Surely to God they had enough information?

Joe pulled at Ross's arm to attract his attention. 'What the fuck are we waiting for?' he whispered urgently.

Ross didn't reply. There was no need. Joe became suddenly aware of the faint sound of singing. It was coming from behind them, from way down in the valley to the south. Gradually the sound swelled, intensified. It was more a chant than a song, a single voice shouting the phrase, then many voices, male, female, picking it up, amplifying it. He peered into the darkness trying to indentify the source of the sound, but it was impossible to see.

A light flicked on the camp, then a second. They were mounted on the trees, one of them in the acacia above the Command Post. Joe hadn't noticed the lights before. There must be some sort of power source available. No doubt it also powered the radio. Men were coming out of the Command Post, gathering on the stoep, spilling down into the lighted circle immediately in front of it. Other figures, women mostly, were running, shouting, ululating.

The column was visible now, a single dark undulating shadow snaking in past the raised boom. It was impossible to tell how many people it contained; perhaps a hundred, perhaps more. They were mostly men but some women and a few boys. It seemed to be some sort of baggage train.

As it reached the first of the povo huts the singing stopped and the column lost its coherence. There was more shouting. Joe could see what they were carrying now, as the light from the trees hit them. It was arms.

Guns, bundles of AKs and RPDs tied with tape. Ammunition boxes. Rocket launchers. Mortars. What looked like some sort of missile launcher, a Sam 7 maybe. Dismantled sections of a number of larger guns slung on poles – antiaircraft guns he supposed. And on the heads of the women, boxes of what could have been mines or rockets.

'Let's go.' A hiss from Ross, a sudden movement. Enos was already away, invisible in the blackness. Confused, worried by the mass of people below and the weapons, Joe followed. It was very dark with no moon yet and several times he collided painfully with rocks or thorn bushes. He was thinking about Ellie. It was impossible that she could be sleeping through all this. She would be watching, somewhere out of sight, puzzled and as frightened as he was. There were so many guns down there. Too many guns. Enough for an entire bloody army.

They found Jonas where they had left him, still watching the camp, half-hidden in the fringe of trees directly above the latrines. He pointed downwards and began to chatter excitedly in what Joe took to be a mixture of Shona and Shangaan. He was silenced instantly. Despite the noise from below, the hoarse shouts, the trills of the women, and now the thump of a drum somewhere to the left, Ross was obviously taking no chances.

Ross had been right about the brick hut, Joe saw. It was the armoury. Its door hung open as the arms and ammunition were fed inside rapidly, supervised by dark figures in camouflage fatigues. The hut seemed too small to contain all that weaponry, a fact which puzzled Joe until Ross explained that a lot of it was no doubt being stored below ground. A second drum began to sound, deeper in tone, away to the right.

Relieved of their burdens, the men and women from the column were dispersing rapidly, some to the barracks, others to the clusters of povo huts. The drumbeats intensified. Women scurried back and forth carrying large pots and galvanised cans, sadza, no doubt, and beer. One hell of a lot of beer. 'Looks like they're going to have a party,' Joe whispered, putting all the lightness into his voice he could muster.

Nobody laughed. Ross said, 'It's time we talked.'

They'd worked it all out earlier, he realised, no doubt during those long irritating conversations in Shona. It irked him that as usual he was the last to know. They were sitting where they'd left the packs in the thick bush close to the ridgeline. The moon was up by now, gleaming palely, the noise from the camp comfortingly distant.

Ross spoke quietly. The plan, he said, was deliberately simple. They'd wait two or three hours to give the beer time to take effect then, when everybody was three-quarters drunk, Jonas and Enos would go into the camp through the main gate, saying they'd come from Alguendo and giving the relevant passwords if necessary. They'd join in the beer drink. Then, at the right moment, Enos would leave the party, saying he needed to pee. He'd go to Ellie's hut, take out any guard there might be, though it didn't look like there was one, and lead Ellie and the children down the path between the kraals to the river. Joe would be waiting at the river. He'd help them across and head due west as fast as possible. Enos would then return to the beer drink and carry on as though nothing had happened. With any luck it would be morning before anybody at the camp even realised they'd gone. That way there'd be plenty of time for Joe to get them well clear of the camp by first light. And most important of all, there'd be no shooting.

There was a long silence after Ross had finished talking. Was it really credible that Enos could pass himself off as a visiting MNR fighter, even to a load of drunks? Joe glanced at the black man. He was nodding slowly, obviously well satisfied with the proposal. They spoke Shona, of course, the Ndau officers who ran the place, so there'd be no language problem. And Jonas was no doubt known to many of the Shangaans. It occurred to Joe that despite Ross's authoritative tone the essence of the plan had probably originated with Enos. The thought was strangely comforting. And there'd be no shooting. He was glad of that. He was suddenly painfully aware of the softness of the children's bodies. 'And what happens when we've got them out?' he asked.

Ross cleared his throat softly. 'You just keep going due west. Use your compass. It's twenty-five, thirty kilometres at the most to the border. Travel at night. Stick to the high ground, avoid the roads, and don't get caught. When you get to the border, find a recent game path, one the elephants use if you can, or keep an eye out for parties of refugees and follow them. That way you'll get across the minefield OK. Then head for the nearest white face and shout for help. I'd go for the American Mission at Mount Selinda.'

Joe hesitated, puzzled. 'You mean, I'm going to be taking them out alone?'

'Yes.'

'But we could arrange some sort of rendezvous. I don't understand . . .'

'No rendezvous. Just get them back across that border as fast as you can. You've surely done enough bush walking by now not to need your hand held. Or am I wrong?'

Joe glanced at Enos, seeking reassurance that what Ross was saying could possibly be right. There was no response. He turned back to Ross. 'If I have to,' he said. 'I can do it if I have to. It just seems . . .'

'So you'd prefer we play hide and seek with each other while those gooks down there come out looking for us?'

'No.'

'Then cut the crap.'

'I'm sorry.' Joe fell silent, still not totally convinced.

Ross checked. 'You're clear on what you've got to do?'

'Yes.'

'Mushi.' He bent and began to unstrap his pack. 'Let's get this bloody hardware sorted.'

Joe made no move. 'There's one thing you haven't told me.'

'What's that?'

'What you're going to be doing while this is all going on.'

Ross looked up slowly. 'You're a nosy bastard, aren't you?' There was an edge to his voice.

'I just want to know.'

There was another silence. Enos, Joe saw, was watching

Ross closely. For a long time it seemed like Ross was not going to reply then, suddenly, he said, 'I'm the insurance man.'

'Insurance?'

'Just leave it at that, OK?'

'I don't see why . . .'

Ross wrenched at his pack viciously. 'I said, leave it!'

Joe was about to say more, but he felt a touch on his arm. It was Enos. 'Leave it,' he said. 'Please.' There was something close to sadness in his eyes.

It happened quickly after that, too quickly. Joe felt like he was on some out-of-control switchback ride. Ross, once more decisive and in command, supervised the division of the contents of the packs. Enos and Jonas took the AKs and a couple of magazines each, Ross the grenades, the Claymore and the RPD. Joe was given the FN, most of the remainder of the food, the map and the binoculars. Also, at Ross's insistence, the medical kit. The spare webbing, packs and ammunition were buried beneath a flat rock, and the surrounding area checked out throughly by Enos to ensure that no clue remained as to their whereabouts. Around ten Enos and Jonas left, slipping away to join the main track into the camp some two or three kilometres to the south.

It was a strangely unemotional parting: a swift double handshake from both men, which Joe as usual fumbled, a whispered 'Good luck' from Enos. As they left, Enos said something in Shona to Ross, who nodded but made no reply. The darkness swallowed them instantly. Joe stood for a moment, feeling suddenly vulnerable, staring in the direction they had taken. Then, at a signal from Ross, he turned, eased on his pack and cradled the FN. 'OK,' he said.

At first they followed a narrow overgrown path that Enos had checked out earlier. Once or twice, where the valley lip fell away, the camp became visible beneath them. The main lights were out now but there were numerous fires which threw the huts into sharp relief, illuminating small knots of dancers, mostly women. Other women were walking swiftly between the povo huts and the barracks, pots of beer on their heads, or serving the men who sat round the fires in wide circles. There were shouts, bursts of clapping, snatches of incoherent song. The drums hammered. It was looking good, very good. Without breaking stride, Ross turned and raised a thumb in approval.

To the north of the camp, beyond the last of the huts, the valley narrowed, its sides steepening into a sharp V. It became difficult to walk, the bush thickening, trees tangled with creeper. A couple of times Ross halted, checking for outlying sentry positions. There seemed to be none. They were either totally stupid or totally confident, the gooks who ran the place, Joe thought. He suspected the latter. It didn't say too much for the firepower of the Mozambican Army.

They crossed the Nhamasi a kilometre or so upstream where a small gushing tributary joined it. The water was surprisingly cool and clear, and they both paused to drink. Beyond, the valley side was laced with paths, littered with jagged stumps where wood had been taken, no doubt for fuel or for the building of the camp itself. Some fifty feet above the water they turned southwards. Shortly after midnight they reached the steep, gouged western bank of the river immediately to the rear of Ellie's hut.

For a minute or two, it seemed longer, they crouched in silence, looking out at the camp. There was not much to see, the fires, the dancers, the drinkers hidden for the most part by the black shapes of the huts. Only the river was clearly visible immediately beneath them, silvered in the moonlight, and the beginnings of the path where it wound up between what looked like a vegetable patch and the poles of the empty kraals. Joe strained his eyes to see Ellie's shelter, but it was lost in the darkness to the rear of the asbestos-roofed hut. Maybe he should cross the water, hide somewhere in one of the kraals. Yes, perhaps that's what he'd do when Ross was gone. He'd be closer. He'd be able to see better. To his amazement he felt no fear, just intense exhilaration. It was like the best moments of sex. No, better. It was like . . . Dear God in Heaven, it was like nothing else he'd ever felt!

There was movement from Ross. He was unstrapping something, removing his waterbottles. He pushed them towards Joe. 'You'll need these,' he said.

Joe looked at them, surprised. 'But you'll . . .'

'Take them. There's gonna be four of you.' It wasn't a request, it was an order.

Joe glanced up at the thin man beside him, and their eyes met. It was too dark to read his expression clearly. 'Thanks,' he said softly.

'Don't mention it.'

There was a short silence. Joe formed the impression that there was more Ross wanted to say. Instead, he stood up. 'I'll see you then,' he said.

'Yes.'

He turned away. Paused. 'Just don't fuck this up, man,' he said, and was gone.

It was the river that was the problem, and the short strip of beach beyond. Anybody standing near the barrack huts to the rear of the Command Post would see him clear as day. They were deserted, Joe was convinced, yet it was difficult to be absolutely sure. Speed would be the best policy, he decided. It would take him, what, thirty seconds or less. Then he'd be into cover amongst those vegetable plants. If only there was cloud to hide the moon. And yet he needed the light. Fifteen minutes. He'd give Enos fifteen more minutes . . .

He shifted to ease the stiffness in his legs and back. He'd been sitting, resting against his pack, his feet wedged beneath a skewed root for more than two hours now, just waiting. It was the one thing they hadn't covered during their briefing, how long he was supposed to wait. He cursed himself for not thinking to ask. It was already two-thirty. Surely they could have given him some sort of deadline. Say three a.m. Yes, three would have been reasonable. And then . . ?

He picked up the glasses, squinted again in the direction of the asbestos-roofed hut. Jesus, it was so dark, so bloody dark. He couldn't even see the sodding shelter, let alone suss out what was going on up there. Half an hour earlier he'd been almost convinced that Enos had gone in. He'd seen a shadow, he thought, some sort of movement to the right of the hut, and had tensed, adjusting his FN, preparing to slip down to the river. But nothing had happened. He must control himself, not let his imagination play tricks . . .

It was that bloody drumming. It made it so difficult to think clearly. It had got louder if anything as time had gone on, less co-ordinated, punctuated monotonously by the shrill blasts of a whistle. Jesus, didn't they ever get tired, those drummers? Small green lights were flickering close to the margins of the river. Fireflies. It was almost like they were strobing to the sound of the drums . . .

There was another sound from closer by, a woman's high-pitched laugh. Ellie? Surely it wasn't Ellie? He swung the glasses away to the left. Two figures, a man and a woman it looked like, were silhouetted momentarily in a strip of fire-light close to the Command Post. They were heading for the barrack huts. There was more laughter, a sudden sharp metallic sound he couldn't identify . . .

In God's name where was Enos? It would be light in two or three hours. They'd need to be well away from the camp by then. There was something wrong, he became convinced of it. They'd been picked up entering the camp. They were even now being interrogated. Jonas had betrayed them. Or something hadn't checked out, the password maybe. Enos must have been crazy to think he could just walk into the place like that. Just plain fucking crazy.

OK. Three a.m. Forget the fifteen minutes. He'd set his own deadline. Three a.m., then he'd go. That gook should be finished in the barrack huts by then, whatever it was he was doing. If not, well, he'd just have to take the risk. Sod Ross, Sod him. What the fuck did he mean by insurance? Always a bloody mystery. It always had to be a bloody mystery. If he'd stayed put the two of them could have been in and out by now. Easy. No problem.

And if Enos was being interrogated, or Jonas? How long would they hold out? A gun in the guts. A knife, maybe, inserted into the muscle, twisted slowly . . .

Joe shook his head to clear it, unscrewed the cap of the waterbottle. He took a couple of mouthfuls of the tainted, foul-tasting water and spat. 'Don't fuck it up,' Ross had said. 'Don't fuck it up.' So who the hell was fucking it up now?

The couple were still in the barrack huts when Joe crossed the river. Five past three. He'd given it an extra five minutes. He left his pack and waterbottles concealed behind the tree root. He'd pick them up on their way out. He took only the can of peaches. For some reason it seemed important to take the peaches.

It took him longer to cross than he'd intended. The river was not deep, but its bed was wedged with slippery rocks. He made a lot of noise crossing. There were beans growing in the vegetable patch. He slid between the matted plants waiting for the shouts, the shots that would prove he'd been seen.

But there were none. The drums and whistles continued unchecked. Nothing moved except the moon. In half an hour it would be out of sight behind the mountains to the west. Surely he could see the shelter now? He pushed at the clinging tendrils . . .

Just. The outline of its sagging roof was visible, the sharper edge of its corners. It was fifty metres from where he lay, no more. He pulled the binoculars from the pouch. They didn't help. They merely seemed to make the darkness more intense. He'd have to get closer, a lot closer. He checked the FN, worked a little more blacking into his face. There was a heap of what looked like firewood just to the left of the shack. That would give him cover. Now. He said the word to himself out loud. NOW! He twisted forwards into the flat moonlit rectangle of the nearest kraal.

It seemed like a mile, a hundred miles, the longest journey he'd ever made. The moon pinned him to the hard-packed earth. Small flint-like stones flayed at his knees and elbows. A litter of poles forced him to his feet and he ran the last few metres leaping the obstructions like some sort of demented hurdler, plunging into the dense shadow of the woodstack.

He clutched at the logs, fighting for breath, deafened by the thumping of the drums. He was bleeding somewhere. His knees. He could feel the wetness. No matter. He was close. Close enough. Just a few feet now. He could almost reach out and touch the place. He swung the FN in a slow arc, checking out the shadows. It was OK. It looked OK . . .

And then he saw Ellie.

She was suddenly there, to the right of the large hut, caught in the moonlight. She was walking slowly towards the shelter, not looking to the left or right. He could see her face clearly in the pale light, white, expressionless, hopeless . . .

So that was why Enos hadn't moved. He must have checked out the hut earlier, found she wasn't there, decided to wait. She'd been at the beer drink, no doubt. Or maybe at the povo huts. Maybe there was a sick child she was tending. Or a birth . . .

He was forming her name on his lips, about to break cover, go to her, when he noticed she was being followed. It was a small man, thin. Too small to be Enos. Jonas?

No, not Jonas. He was wearing camouflage, the man. No gun. He swayed slightly, shouted something loudly in Shona.

Ellie stopped. She didn't turn. The expression on her face didn't change. The man shouted again. He was drunk. He put out a hand towards the hut as if groping for support. Still Ellie did not turn.

The man lurched towards her. Gripped her by the shoulders. She tried to resist, but he pushed her back towards the wall of the hut, held her there, pressing himself against her . . .

Then Joe knew he was going to have to kill him.

There was no anger involved in the decision. He felt surprisingly calm. He raised the gun, levelled it, steadied the barrel. He curled his finger onto the trigger.

'Hey you!' Joe was forced to shout twice before the man heard him. The African muttered something, turned from Ellie, took a few unsteady steps towards the woodpile.

It was easy. A couple of seconds pressure on the trigger, a string of dull explosions, no louder it seemed than the pounding of the drums. The man crumpled, pitched forward . . .

And then, suddenly, there was no time left. Joe was hurling himself towards Ellie, clutching at her, screaming. 'Ellie it's me! It's Joe!'

She didn't recognise him. She didn't seem to know him. There was terror in her face. She tried to pull away, but he held her, thrusting her towards the shelter. There was no time. No time. 'The kids. Get the kids for Christ's sake!'

It was dark inside, so bloody dark, but he found them. They were pressed against the far wall, the kids clasped together, wailing. He twisted the FN over his shoulder and grabbed at them. They fought with him but he found their wrists, gripped them, jerked them to their feet. 'It's Daddy,' he was trying to tell them. 'It's OK. It's Daddy . . .'

They were out. Ellie was so slow, hardly moving. 'Go!' he yelled at her. 'Just go! The river!' Not releasing the kids he rammed into her. She stumbled and half fell. 'Go!'

They were down the path now, Ellie in front, the kids' feet skidding in the dust. The drums had stopped. There were shouts. Joe became aware of a figure clutching a large gun moving swiftly towards them from the left. It came in at a low crouch, dropping from sight behind the jumbled poles. Christ, there was no cover. None. Joe threw the kids forward, anticipating the shots.

None came.

'Quick, man! Go quick!'

Enos's voice.

But the kids stayed down.

Joe wrenched at them. Cassie was screaming, rigid, her feet dragging. She bit at his hand. He smacked her once, sharply.

And then there was another man.

This time up ahead. He was blocking the path. He seemed to be shouting something, gesturing, beckoning. The curved magazine of the AK was clearly visible as he turned in the moonlight.

Not stopping, Joe fired from the hip. The man fell, screaming, writhing. He was still holding the AK. Joe fired again, and again. The body bucked as the bullets slammed into it. The flashes from the muzzle of the FN lit up the man's face.

It was Jonas.

Jonas. Joe tried to understand that it was Jonas, this man with the AK, this man who was still twisting, twitching, refusing to die. But he failed.

They were past. Ellie had Ben now, he had Cassie. At last Ellie seemed to understand. The river. The stones. Cassie slipping, disappearing beneath the water for an instant. Coughing, gasping . . .

A shot. Joe glanced back. There were a lot of men now, one hell of a lot of men. They were streaming out between the huts. He turned, still in the river, jerked at the trigger.

The men hesitated, one of them fell. Then they came again. There was a smack, a sudden cry from Ellie. She'd stopped and was looking down at her left hand. It hung from her wrist, limp, dripping, like a squashed fruit. She'd been hit. Dear God, she'd been hit. Joe screamed at her. 'Go!' he was screaming. 'Go go go!' He swung round. He could take one or two of them, he was thinking. One or two.

But the men were no longer coming. There was a sudden long burst of automatic fire from where Enos lay hidden, and they were colliding with each other, throwing their arms into the air, tumbling into untidy heaps.

And there was an explosion.

The first explosion was so muffled that Joe scarcely noticed it. He was hauling the kids up between the trees when it happened, urging Ellie onwards.

But he heard the second explosion clearly, and the third. Then there was a whole chain of them, each one louder than the last. He glanced back. The whole northern end of the camp seemed to be drowning in a great lake of fire.

Someone had hit the armoury. He stared at the flames for a moment before he understood. It was the Insurance.

At the top of the ridge Joe stopped, ripped the sleeve from his shirt and bound Ellie's hand. He'd forgotten his pack, the medical kit, the waterbottles, he realised. But he had the peaches.

While he worked he told the children about the peaches. Then, when he had finished, he drew their dirty, emaciated, tear-streaked faces close to his and showed them the can. The label was wet from the river, torn. 'I've been saving these for you,' he said.

But they didn't seem to understand what he was saying.

Epilogue

On Thursday February 9th 1984, Joe Lejeune, his wife Ellie and their two children were apprehended by a Mozambican Army patrol as they attempted to cross the Espungabera – Machaze road close to the Zimbabwean border. A number of shots were fired. They were taken to Party Headquarters at Espungabera, and subsequently to Manica Provincial Military Command Headquarters at Chimoio.

On February 11th they were flown south by military Dakota to the Mozambican capital Maputo where, after ten days of questioning and medical treatment during which Ellie had two fingers of her left hand amputated, they were handed over to British Embassy officials. They were flown home to London on February 24th.

Following an unofficial agreement between Zimbabwean, Mozambican and British governments, little publicity was given to the case on the grounds that it 'might jeopardise the sensitive negotiations' then underway between South Africa and Mozambique. However, the semi-official Maputo newspaper *Noticias* later claimed that the Mozambican Army had 'attacked and destroyed a bandit camp at Nhamasi in Southern Manica' in early February.

On March 16th, on a specially-levelled section of the dry bed of the Nkomati River on the Mozambique–South African border, President Samora Machel of Mozambique and Prime Minister P.W. Botha of South Africa signed a non-aggression pact in which both sides undertook 'not to resort individually or collectively to the use of force against the sovereignty, territorial integrity and political independence of each other'.

MNR representatives were not present at the signing.

Despite the agreement, massacres and kidnappings in Mozambique continue. It has been revealed that prior to, and immediately after, the signing there was a massive increase in the supply of South African arms to MNR camps in central Mozambique. At the time of writing the capital, Maputo, is all but cut off from the rest of the country due to constant MNR attacks on road and rail communications.

Larry Wakeman was declared a prohibited immigrant and expelled from Zimbabwe in late April following a series of articles revealing massacres by the Korean-trained Fifth Brigade of the Zimbabwean Army in Southern Matabeleland. He is currently in New York, working on a book about post-independence Zimbabwe. His wife Eva is still in Harare where she is an active member of the ZANU Woman's League.

Jack Hammond continues to run the Flying Star Ranch on the borders of the Gona-re-Zhou.

Following enquiries by Barclays International, it was established that the sum of $Z6,384, the entire contents of Joe's account at their First Street, Harare, branch was withdrawn on March 7th by Enos Kupfuma, on production of a letter of authorisation. The account was closed.

At Joe's request, Penny and David Sweetman drove out to Ross Tobin's house at Nyabira in early April. They reported that the house was being occupied by squatters. Enquiries made locally gave no indication of the whereabouts of the owner.

More gripping Fiction from Headline:

WEB OF DRAGONS

A POWER-PACKED THRILLER OF DRUGS, GOLD AND TREACHERY

MICHAEL HARTMANN

THE SCARS OF BETRAYAL ARE ETCHED AS DEEPLY IN HIS MIND AS THE LIVID WOUNDS UPON HIS FACE.

For seventeen long years Don Stanton has waited for revenge: he has founded a vast and powerful opium empire upon his desire for vengeance. And now the time has come – a massive cache of gold will be the bait to entangle his betrayer.

From the hellish cauldron of the Vietnam war to the exotic bustle of Hong Kong; from the snow-capped peaks of Switzerland to the notorious Golden Triangle, and from the corridors of power in Washington to a bloody show-down in the Far East, the innocent and guilty alike are entrapped in the murderous web.

FICTION/THRILLER   0 7472 3006 4   £2.95

The ultimate courtroom drama

THE
JUDGEMENT

HOWARD E. GOLDFLUSS

Christmas Eve. Beautiful millionairess Andrea Blanchard
lies dead in her apartment – brutally strangled. The police
move fast to arrest the obvious suspect: her toy-boy lover
has a key to the apartment and is found right outside the
luxury skyscraper.

A twist of fate brings Jorgensen to trial before the
distinguished judge Allen Sturdivant – ironically the very
man who should himself be in the dock. . .

So begins a superb courtroom drama of unrelenting tension
and suspense. By its nail-biting conclusion, the scales of
justice are brought shockingly back into balance.

FICTION/THRILLER   0 7472 3095 1   £2.95

Headline books are available at your book-shop or newsagent, or can be ordered from the following address:

Headline Book Publishing PLC
Cash Sales Department
PO Box 11
Falmouth
Cornwall
TR10 9EN
England

UK customers please send cheque or postal order (no currency), allowing 60p for postage and packing for the first book, plus 25p for the second book and 15p for each additional book ordered up to a maximum charge of £1.90 in UK.

BFPO customers please allow 60p for postage and packing for the first book, plus 25p for the second book and 15p per copy for the next seven books, thereafter 9p per book.

Overseas and Eire customers please allow £1.25 for postage and packing for the first book, plus 75p for the second book and 28p for each subsequent book.